LAZY DRAGON

Chinese Stories from the Ming Dynasty

明代短篇小說選
楊憲益、戴乃迭選譯
白杰明編

Chinese Stories from the Ming Dynasty

LAZY DRAGON

Translated by Yang Xianyi and Gladys Yang

Edited by Geremie Barmé

Joint Publishing Co. (HK)

Published by
Joint Publishing Co. (HK)
9 Queen Victoria Street, Hongkong

First published October 1981
Second impression May 1987

Printed in Hong Kong by
C & C Joint Printing Co., (H.K.) Ltd.
75 Pau Chung Street,
Kowloon, Hongkong

Paperback ISBN 962·04·0136·0

Contents

List of Illustrations

Preface

The ambitious young official who drowns his wife because he resents her humble origins as the daughter of the chief of the beggars in the capital and wants to marry into a distinguished family; the pedlar who through endless kindness and devotion wins the heart of the most elegant and expensive call-girl in town so that she rejects her aristocratic patrons and admirers to marry him; the constables who try to murder prisoners they are escorting; the trader captured by Japanese pirates who is forced to join them until recaptured by Chinese troops twenty years later; the burglar of genius who can walk up walls and imitate the accents of thirteen provinces; the man who sets out on a trading voyage with nothing but a basket of tangerines and returns with a fortune; the judges who with few exceptions are stupid if not venal and regularly condemn innocent men and women; the husband who comes home with fifteen strings of borrowed cash and sets off a train of disaster by telling his wife as a joke that he has raised the money by pawning her to a stranger — the range of characters and situations even in this selection of only ten of the hundreds of stories that have come down to us from late mediaeval China is extraordinary.

Stories such as these, which are taken from seventeenth-century collections, were written versions or imitations of the ones told in city market-places for hundreds of years before that. These spoken tales had to appeal to the tastes, sympathies and prejudices of the paying public, which included many small traders, prostitutes, and others who made their livings in commerce and the service and manufacturing industries of the capital cities. The stories had to be interesting throughout as dull passages could lose an audience, and the need to hold a potentially fickle public taught the story-tellers a mixture of skills that the writers of contemporary popular television scripts would recognise: quick characterization to enable the audience to place the characters; heroes and heroines with whom they could identify, and villains reminiscent of their enemies; fast-moving story-lines with plenty of action, but not so complicated that the audience gets lost; the mixture of tension and comic relief, and climaxes built up to then tantalizingly delayed; lively and colourful dialogue.

When such stories were put into written form — whether they were transcriptions of spoken originals, or imitations in the story-teller's manner — the writer tried hard to keep the style of the popular entertainer, and the publishers who printed them evidently believed that this was what the public wanted. The stories are none the worse for preserving the show-business flavour of the spoken tale, and for showing us what urban society looked like to the common man and woman between the thirteenth century, from which the earliest may date, to the seventeenth. Outside of stories and dramas such as these, we generally see pre-modern China through the eyes of officials and their class, who wrote nearly all the surviving records. Although the collections from which the ten stories that follow are drawn were written down by members of the élite, they preserve much of the flavour of the market-place, and show a sceptical, even hostile, attitude towards the pretentions of scholars, magistrates, and the well-born.

These versions are by the *doyen* and *doyenne* of the translation of Chinese literature into English, Yang Xianyi and Gladys Yang. Eight of them first appeared in a larger collection, *The Courtesan's Jewel Box* (Beijing: Foreign Languages Press, 1957), that has long been out of print and eagerly sought after; the other two have not previously been published. This volume has been ably edited by the highly talented young Australian scholar Geremie Barmé, whose many accomplishments include the rare one for a Westerner of writing a regular column in Chinese for a big Hong Kong paper.

These stories are a marvellous read in themselves that also enable the modern reader to imagine what it was like to live in the great cities of mediaeval China, whose size, wealth and splendour so dazzled Marco Polo that he talked about them for the rest of his life to an incredulous Italy. Their nearest visual equivalent is the infinitely detailed and lifelike scroll painting by Zhang Zeduan, *Qingming shang he tu* (Easter on the river), that shows the bustling streets, bridges, waterways and suburbs of the eleventh-century Northern Song capital Bianliang (Kaifeng). The reader who wants to find out more about the later Song capital Lin'an (Hangzhou) will learn much from Jacques Gernet's *Everyday Life in China on the Eve of the Mongol Invasion*. Meanwhile here is a ten-course banquet to be savoured and enjoyed.

W. J. F. Jenner

21 July 1980

Introduction

A great variety of traditional Chinese writing has become available to the western reader during the last few decades, yet the view of feudal Chinese society is still sadly limited. The more sensational exploits of 'emperors, kings, generals and ministers' as well as the ethereal pleasures of 'scholars and beauties' as represented in translations of poetry, essays, drama and novels have prevented greater attention being given to the more everyday and prosaic activities of the less privileged members of the society. This selection of vernacular Chinese short stories has been made with the aim of introducing the reader to some of these other facets of the rich and varied world of traditional China.

Early Chinese fiction deals almost exclusively with tales of the supernatural. So common were themes from traditional myths and miraculous happenings that the fiction produced from the third to the ninth centuries AD was called 'transmissions of the strange' (*chuanqi* 傳奇). Early collections of such tales were usually short and contained only the bare outline of stories. It was during the Tang Dynasty (618-907AD) with its unprecedented economic and political stability that these previously laconic records of the miraculous became the basis for longer and more detailed works of literature. Men of letters, their literary perceptions enriched by the flourishing of poetry and prose writing during the Tang and living amid the rich variety of urban life, began to write stories of literary quality. One of the primary functions of these stories during the height of the Tang was to provide a means through which aspiring scholars could impress the imperial examiners prior to the official examinations. This 'familiarization with (a writer's) works' (*wenjuan* 温卷), as it was called, made story writing both a legitimate and even essential activity for the literati desirous of recognition.[1]

These early short stories dealt mainly with the supernatural, love and chivalry. Their style was inspired by the clarity and directness of the 'ancient literature' movement (*guwen yundong* 古文運動) that developed in Tong times as a reaction to the flowery and precious literature that had been fashionable since the Han Dynasty. It was in these Tang short stories that artisans, merchants, beggars, courtesans and priests — the people of the cities — first moved into the centre of the stage of Chinese literature. However, as the stories were written by scholars for their friends and superiors, the language used was that of the classics. This limited readership of the new literature to those who had mastered the difficult and terse written language. Even with a restricted audience, the Tang short stories, through their detailed plots, characterisation and liveliness of language, remained popular with later generations of readers and formed a basis for the story-teller scripts, plays and vernacular short stories of later dynasties. There was also vernacular story-telling in Tang times, but no trace of this was known until some fragments of stories written in colloquial language were found in the remote monastic library at Dunhuang during this century.

The Song Dynasty (960-1127AD) saw a further development of both the rural and urban economies. The major

---

1. Liu Kairong, *Researches on the Tang Short Stories* (*Tangdai xiaoshuo yanjiu*) (Beijing: Shangwu yinshuguan, 1950), pp. 13-17.

cities, Bianliang (the capital of the Northern Song, present-day Kaifeng in Henan Province) and Lin'an (the capital of the Southern Song, present-day Hangzhou in Zhejiang Province), became centres of trade and craft with large urban populations. It was in the market places of the large towns and cities of the Song that the story-tellers with their repertoire of tales and poetry became one of the main sources of popular entertainment. Vying with puppeteers, acrobats, musicians and diversions of all kinds in the area set aside for amusements in each market-place (the *washe* 瓦社 or *wazi* 瓦子), the story-teller came to occupy a privileged position. Members of this new profession often had backgrounds as varied as the characters in the stories they told. The descendants of merchants, impoverished city dwellers, monks, nuns and even a number of scholars who had failed the official examinations came to join the ranks of the new entertainers. The number of story-tellers quickly grew and they established a guild, the Society of Masterful Talkers (*Xiongbianshe* 雄辯社), both to protect themselves and ensure the transmission and development of their art. The profession became so popular and socially acceptable that noted story-tellers were often invited to perform at the banquets and gatherings of the rich and sometimes at those of the imperial house itself.

The stories told in the market-place were primarily based on traditional or historical tales. It is recorded that of the various types of story-tellers, those whose specialities were stories about people in the cities, miraculous happenings and tales of romance attracted the largest audiences. A good story-teller was as much of a craftsman as any artisan in the market-place. A writer of the period commented that they could "tell tales of either the present or the past, the words flowing out like a stream."[2] Though surrounded by the performers and other distractions of the market, members

2. Beijing daxue zhongwenxi, *The History of the Chinese Novel* (*Zhongguo xiaoshuoshi*) (Beijing: Renmin wenxue chubanshe, 1978), p. 67.

of the Society of Masterful Talkers could "conjure up a scene as though it was before the listener's very eyes. People would listen with all of their attention forgetting their fatigue, fearful lest they miss what was being said."[3] Story-telling remains popular in China today, and historical tales are still told to eager audiences with a talent and humour that could rival the best of the Masterful Talkers.

Through constant retelling and revision the story-tellers' tales developed a more consistent and literary form. The story-tellers had often required some form of prompt book, for the lengthy and often complex tales could not all be transmitted orally or remembered without some sort of written aid. These prompt books or 'scripts' (*huaben* 話本 or *xiaoshuo* 小說) contained the basic structure of a story as well as providing set pieces of poetry or songs that could be used by a story-teller during a performance. The scripts of some of the more popular stories were, it is thought, reworked by writers into the form of short stories. These writings, no longer the skeletal prompt books of story-tellers, were the first examples of a new popular literature — the vernacular short story.

In keeping with their derivation from spoken tales, the Song scripts retained various oral devices. Many of the Song and Yuan stories that are extant today have a prologue consisting of a short tale with a theme similar to that of the story that follows. Such a prologue was used by the story-teller to allow the audience to gather and quieten down without missing any of the main story. The stories also contain pauses and rhetorical questions, while there is a lavish use of poetry for descriptive purposes. The reader of such stories will often find himself being addressed directly as though by some invisible narrator. The action of the plot develops quickly, rarely lingering on descriptions of characters. To make sure that the reader has not missed the message of the

3. Ibid.

tale, the narrator often concludes with a pointed moral.

The earlier preference of story-tellers for material based on traditional myths and tales broadened during the Song to include love stories, accounts of the daily life and tribulations of the common people as well as realistic descriptions of the ruling classes, detective stories and chronicles of contemporary events. Through the popular literature dating from the Song Dynasty, a picture of city life in traditional China can be pieced together. For all of the volume and detail of the official histories, Confucian historians and writers did not regard writing about the doings of the urban population as either a useful or necessary occupation.

The years of the Mongol-Yuan Dynasty (1279-1368AD) though resulting in few classical masterpieces, did allow the consolidation of Song script writing as a literary form. The Ming Dynasty (1368-1644AD) re-established a stable economic order and peace. Rural prosperity and expansion of trade led to a renaissance of economic and cultural life throughout China. The Song and Yuan scripts became increasingly popular and collections of stories were made by men of letters who saw in this new form of writing an effective vehicle for the propagation of Confucian morality among urban dwellers. Apart from the reappearance of older stories, new stories that imitated the Song script format were also written. These 'imitation scripts' (*nihuaben* 擬話本), though very similar to the Song stories, were written solely for a reading public. The development of inexpensive printing techniques gave city-dwellers access to the printed word for the first time. Nevertheless, such was the influence of tradition and accepted conventions that even these 'imitation scripts' retained the peculiarities of the story-tellers' tales. Even the lengthy historical novels that were written during the Ming Dynasty read as though they were recorded by a member of a story-teller's audience. No doubt their writers hoped thereby to enable readers to imagine the liveliness with which a good performer animated the events and the people of a tale as he told it.

Stylistically the Ming stories were an improvement on the Song and Yuan scripts. This was largely due to the fact that professional men of letters were more constantly involved in the writing of short stories in the Ming. The contents of the stories had also changed. Although the overtly moralistic and fatalistic themes of the Song stories remained, the Ming writers reduced the importance of the supernatural and concentrated more on the realistic representation of everyday life. Yet the writers and compilers of the Ming stories did not experience philosophical and religious developments comparable to those that led to such dramatic changes in European writing in the sixteenth and seventeenth centuries. The authors of Ming 'imitation scripts' still saw the world in terms of the Confucian, Buddhist and Taoist philosophies. Thematic variety was thus limited by the fairly static social and philosophical conventions of the day. Although the involvement of the literati in the writing of the short stories had led to the development of a new form of literature, divorced from its origins as a living folk art, the vernacular story became increasingly stereotyped and rigid. Few changes were seen in Chinese fiction until the beginning of this century, more than three hundred years after the appearance of vernacular short stories in print.

Widespread popular interest in colloquial stories during the Ming encouraged book merchants and printers to make collections of stories and supply the ever growing market. As a result, Ming scholar-officials were commissioned to collect, edit and publish old stories. New stories by the editors or their friends written in imitation of the Song stories were also included. The largest and most significant collection of this type was undertaken by the Ming scholar, dramatist and popular literature expert, Feng Menglong (馮夢龍 , 1574-1646AD).

Feng was born into a well-known Confucian family in Suzhou, an important cultural and trading centre. Being born into a family at the top of the social scale Feng was given a thorough grounding in the Confucian classics in his youth. Yet failure to pass the official exams led him to develop the less moralistic side of his character. Much of his early life was spent in frequenting wine houses and brothels. This afforded him an insight into the lives and nature of people who had been previously outside the range of his social experience. In middle age an unhappy love affair with a courtesan led Feng to give up his libertine ways. He spent the rest of his life collecting popular literature, writing, and engaging in political activity.

Feng Menglong's works include volumes of ballads, collections of satirical writings, plays and short stories, edited and sometimes written by himself. The most lasting and influential of Feng's numerous works is his collection of one hundred and twenty vernacular short stories. The stories are divided into three volumes of forty stories each, popularly known as *The Three Tales* (*Sanyan,* 三言). They are *Tales to Illuminate the World* (*Yushi mingyan,* 喻世明言), *Tales to Warn the World* (*Jingshi tongyan,* 警世通言) and *Tales to Awaken the World* (*Xingshi hengyan,* 醒世恆言).

Although all of the stories in *The Three Tales* were Song-Yuan scripts or later imitation scripts written originally for the purpose of entertainment, in Feng Menglong's view the didactic function of these popular stories was of paramount importance. Even though he made this selection of stories at the request of a book dealer, Feng was careful to explain the purity of his intentions. In the introduction to the collection Feng, taking the pen-name of Master of the Villa of Azure Skies, expresses the hope that the stories he had chosen would 'bring courage to the faint of heart, purity to the depraved, depth to the shallow and repentance to the obstinate.' He believed that 'though one may recite the *Classic of Filial Piety* (*Xiaojing,* 孝經) and Confucius' *Analects* (*Lunyu,* 論語) in one's youth, these works may indeed not touch men's hearts as do these stories.' Like the authors of the morality literature of medieval Europe, Feng Menglong was faithful to the prevailing philisophy of the time. His writings too aim to edify as well as entertain.

The stories in *The Three Tales* include works based on scripts from the Song and the Yuan dynasties, while there are also pieces written during the Ming, a few of which are 'imitation scripts' written by Feng Menglong himself or his associates. Feng also rewrote and polished a number of the older stories giving them a new emphasis. He renamed a number of the stories in accordance with the thematic changes he made, at the same time corrected dating and any other obvious errors. *The Three Tales* is today the most important collection of popular Chinese short stories made during the imperial age. At the time it inspired a number of other collections of stories and some of Feng's works were made into plays. Though widely reprinted and read during the seventeenth century, Feng's collection was proscribed by the puritanical Qing emperor Kangxi (1662-1722) no less than six times as being 'licentious writings.' In his sixth edict banning Feng's *The Three Tales* and other collections of popular literature, the Kangxi Emperor made it an offence punishable by one hundred strokes to be in possession of Feng's works. Thus, although *The Three Tales* had been very popular, the Qing imperial prohibitions proved so effective that at the end of the 19th century no complete set of the collection could be found in China. The standard modern edition of *The Three Tales* is based on photographic copies of the original edition preserved in Japan.

Following the publication and widespread success of Feng Menglong's *The Three Tales*, numerous other collections of vernacular short stories were commissioned by Ming Dynasty publishers. The most outstanding of these later works was the two volume *Astonishing and Miraculous Tales* (*Pai'an jingqi*, 拍案驚奇) written by the dramatist and scholar-official Ling Mengchu (凌濛初 , 1580-1644). Born and raised in an office-holding family in the prosperous

Jiangzhe area in the lower reaches of the Yangzi River, Ling had a long official and literary career. In his later years Ling, like Feng Menglong, was commissioned to produce a collection of short stories by a book merchant. The result was two volumes of stories written by Ling Mengchu himself and entitled *Astonishing and Miraculous Tales I & II* (*Chuke pai'an jingqi*, 初刻拍案驚奇 and *Erke pai'an jingqi*, 二刻拍案驚奇). Ling had based his stories on popular and well-known incidents of the day. Yet ethics rather than entertainment were obviously foremost in his mind when he wrote his stories. Ling nevertheless states in his introduction, "Although there are tales herein that are of dreams and ghosts, some true while others fabricated, my aim in writing them has been solely for the edification of my audience." In fact, Ling's stories are more obviously orthodox and didactic than Feng Menglong's works. However, the salacious aspects of a number of Ling's tales suggest that the author allowed himself considerable liberty in delivering his message.

Despite the differences in quality, Feng Menglong and Ling Mengchu's works are often mentioned together as *The Three Tales* and *The Two Tales* (*Sanyan erpai*, 三言二拍). So popular were these two collections that during the Qing Dynasty a number of stories were taken from each work and made into a new volume of forty stories entitled *Strange Stories of the Past and Present* (*Jingu qiguan*, 今古奇觀). Because of the important position of Ling's stories in the development of Chinese vernacular literature, two tales from *Astonishing and Miraculous Tales* have been included in this selection.

The present volume contains ten stories. Each story has been selected for its readability and literary merit. Although the subject matter covered by Feng and Ling in their stories is broad, the tales contained here are representative of the most popular themes. The ten stories presented here were all written in their present form during the Ming Dynasty. In content they cover the period from the tenth to the seventeenth centuries —— from the height of the 'script' literature to the time of its revival. Of these stories, 'Fifteen Strings of Cash,' 'The Ghost Came Thrice,' 'The Oil Vendor and the Courtesan,' 'The Old Gardener' and 'The Beggar Chief's Daughter' are set in the Song Dynasty. 'The Strange Adventures of Yang Balao' is set in the Yuan Dynasty, while the remaining four stories describe events, real or imagined, of the Ming Dynasty.

In the original all the stories retain the characteristics of story-tellers' tales. Lengthy prologues, rhetorical questions and the use of long passages of descriptive poetry are common. As these devices tend to bore the modern western reader accustomed to an uninterrupted flow of narrative and dialogue, all prologues and poetry unnecessary to the main story have been deleted.

This selection of stories is based on *The Courtesan's Jewel Box: Chinese Stories of the Xth-XVIIth Centuries*, a volume of twenty stories translated by Yang Xianyi and Gladys Yang and published by the Beijing Foreign Languages Press in 1957. With the Yangs' encouragement and help I have chosen eight stories from that collection and added two previously unpublished translations by the Yangs of stories from Feng Menglong's *The Three Tales*. In making this selection I have made a small number of changes to the translations, added notes where necessary and converted the spelling of all Chinese words to the *Hanyu pinyin* system.

Geremie Barmé

April, 1980

十五貫戲言成巧禍

Fifteen Strings of Cash

from Tales to Awaken the World

It was during the reign of Emperor Gao Zong in the Song Dynasty (1127-1162) that the capital was moved south to Hangzhou, where it vied in wealth and splendour with the former capital in the north.[1] On the left of Arrow Bridge in Hangzhou lived a gentleman named Liu Gui. He came from a well-to-do family, but after he came into his inheritance, luck was against him; and although he studied at first, later he saw little hope of an official career and had to go into trade. As he was no professional, however, he had no head for business and soon lost his capital. He had to sell his big house and move to a small one where he lived in two or three rooms with his wife, a Miss Wang whom he had married in his youth, and a concubine whom he had married later as his wife bore him no son. The concubine's family name was Chen, and she was the daughter of a cake vendor. They called her Second Sister, and Liu had married her in the days when he was still comfortably off. His family consisted of just the three of them. Liu himself was a most agreeable man whom all his neighbours liked. They used to say to him:

"You are having a spell of bad luck, Mr. Liu. But better times are sure to be ahead."

This was what they all predicted, yet nothing of the sort happened; and Liu just stayed at home feeling thoroughly depressed, unable to find any way out of his difficulties.

One day he was sitting idly at home when Old Wang, his father-in-law's seventy-year-old servant, came in.

"This is our master's birthday, sir," said Old Wang. "He has sent me to invite you and the mistress over."

"So it is!" exclaimed Liu. "I've been so taken up with my own troubles that I actually forgot the old man's birthday."

He and his wife got out some clothes which they made up into a bundle and gave the servant to carry. Leaving the concubine in charge of the house, and telling her that they would not be able to come back that night but would return the next evening, they set out. Seven or eight miles from the city they came to Mr. Wang's house. Liu greeted his father-in-law; but as there were many other guests present, he could not talk about his poverty. When the guests had left, however, Liu's father-in-law asked him to stay in the guest room, and the next morning he had a talk with his son-in-law.

"You can't go on like this," he said. "You know the proverbs: A man who does nothing but eat can eat up a mountain, and a man's gullet is as deep as the sea, but time passes as quickly as a shuttle! You must think of some way of making a living. When my daughter married you, she expected you to provide her with food and clothing. This really won't do, you know."

Liu heaved a sigh and said: "You are right, sir. But it is easier to catch a tiger in the mountain than it is to find a friend in need. Who in the world will sympathize with me as you do, sir? We must resign ourselves to poverty: to beg for help would be labour wasted."

"There is something in what you say," agreed his father-in-law. "But I can't let things go on like this. Today I mean to lend you some money to start a grocery shop, so that you can make enough to live on. What do you say to that?"

"I am more grateful than I can say," replied Liu. "That will be the very thing for us!"

After the midday meal, Mr. Wang got out fifteen strings of cash[2] and gave them to Liu, saying: "Take these now to start a shop. When you've got everything ready, I shall let you have another ten strings. Let your wife stay here for a few days; and when you have settled on a day to open shop, I shall take her home myself to offer my congratulations, if you are agreeable."

After thanking his father-in-law again and again, Liu slung the money over his shoulder and left. It was already late when he reached the city; but, happening to pass the house of an acquaintance who wanted to go into business too, he thought he might as well stop to discuss the matter with him. He knocked at the door, someone answered within and his friend came out, greeted him and asked the reason for his call.

When Liu explained his plan, the other said: "I have nothing to do at present. If you can use me in your shop, I should be glad to help."

"Good," said Liu.

After they had talked business for some time, Liu's friend kept him to dinner; and, since wine and food were ready, he had a few cups. But Liu was not a good drinker, so presently, feeling the wine go to his head, he took his leave saying: "I've trespassed on your hospitality today. Please come to our humble house tomorrow to talk things over further." His friend saw him to the street corner where he said goodbye to him.

With his money on his back, Liu staggered home and knocked at the door. It was past the time to light the lamps and his concubine, left alone at home with nothing to do, after waiting for them till dark had closed the door and dozed off before the lamp; so she did not hear him knocking. He had to knock for a long time before she woke up and answered: "I'm coming." Then she got up and opened the door to let him in.

As she took the bag of money from him and put it on the table, the concubine asked: "Where did you get so much money? What are you going to do with it?"

Now Liu was slightly drunk, and he was also annoyed with her for taking so long to open the door; so he decided to frighten her.

"If I tell you, you will be angry," he said. "But I can't keep it from you: you will have to know. I'm so hard up right now, that I've had to pawn you to somebody. I don't want to let you go for good, though; so I've only asked him for fifteen strings of cash; and if I come into luck, I shall redeem you with interest. But if I remain as hard up as I am now, I'll have to let you go."

The concubine could scarcely believe her ears; yet there were the fifteen strings of cash confronting her. Liu had never said an angry word to her in his life, and her relationship with his wife was good too — what could have made him so cruel all of a sudden?

"Well," she said doubtfully, "you should at least have told my father and mother."

"If I had informed your parents, they would certainly have raised objections. Tomorrow when you've gone to that man's house, I'll send someone to convince your parents of the necessity for this. They won't be able to blame me."

"Where were you drinking today?"

"With the man to whom I pawned you. After drawing up the contract, I drank a few cups with him before coming back."

"Why is Elder Sister not back?"

"She couldn't bear the thought of parting with you like this; so she will come back after you have left tomorrow. This was the only way out for me, and it's all settled now." As he spoke, he was secretly laughing to himself. Then, without undressing, he lay down on the bed and fell asleep.

The young woman was very upset. "What kind of man

has he sold me to?" she wondered. "I must go home first
and tell my father and mother. If he's told that other man to
fetch me tomorrow, they can go to my home to settle matters
there."

After turning things over in her mind, she piled the
fifteen strings of cash by Liu's feet and, taking advantage of
the fact that he was drunk, quietly put together some clothes,
softly opened the door and tiptoed out, closing the door
behind her. She went to the house of a neighbour on their
left whose name was Zhu; and she slept that night with Mrs.
Zhu, whom she told:

"Today, for no reason at all, my husband has sold me; so
I must go home to tell my parents about it. I'll trouble
you to tell my husband tomorrow where I've gone. The
man who's bought me can come with my husband to my
parents' house to discuss the matter and arrange a proper
settlement."

"That's right," said Mrs. Zhu. "I'll give Mr. Liu your
message after you've gone."

The next morning the concubine set off for home.

Mr. Liu slept till midnight, when he woke to find the
lamp still lit and his concubine no longer at his side. Thinking she was in the kitchen clearing up, he called out to her to
bring him tea; but though he called several times, there was
no answer. He made an effort to get up, but because he was
still befuddled he dropped off again.

Just then a bad man happened to come along. Having
lost all his money through gambling, this rogue had slunk out
at night to steal something, and he came to Liu's house. Since
the concubine had only pulled the door to when she went
out, the thief was able to open it at a push and slip inside
unobserved. When he reached the bedroom, he found the
lamp still lit but could see nothing worth taking. As he
groped about the bed, however, he saw a man sleeping with
his face to the wall and a pile of cash at his feet. He was
taking a few strings, when Liu woke up and shouted:

"Hey! You can't do that! I have just borrowed that cash from my father-in-law to live on! What shall we do if you steal it?"

Without troubling to reply, the thief lunged out at Liu's face; but Liu dodged the blow and leapt out of bed to grapple with him. When the thief saw how active his opponent was, he fled from the room. Liu would not let him go, however, and followed him to the kitchen where he was about to shout to rouse the neighbours. The thief, being at a loss, suddenly caught sight of a bright axe lying close by. In desperation, he seized the axe and swung it at Liu's face, felling him to the ground. He followed up with another blow, and so the unhappy man was killed.

"There was no stopping once you forced my hand," panted the thief. "It was you who chased me, not I who wanted your life." Going back to the bedroom he took the fifteen strings of cash, tore up a sheet to wrap them in, fastened this loot on himself, and made off, pulling the door to behind him.

The next morning when the neighbours got up, Liu's door was still closed and there was not a sound from his room.

"Mr. Liu!" they called. "You've overslept!" But no one answered. Then they pushed open the door and went in, only to find Liu dead on the ground. His wife had gone home two days previously; but where was the concubine? There was a great uproar until Old Zhu, the neighbour in whose house the young woman had stayed the night before, said: "Yesterday evening the concubine stayed in my house. She told us Mr. Liu had sold her for no reason, so she was going back to her parents; and she asked me to tell Mr. Liu to take her new master there to settle matters with her parents. If we send to fetch her back, we should be able to get to the bottom of this. We must also fetch Mrs. Liu back before we decide on anything."

"You are right," they all agreed.

They first sent a messenger to Mr. Wang's house to break the bad news. The old man and his daughter wept bitterly, and Liu's father-in-law said:

"He was all right when he left yesterday, and I had given him fifteen strings of cash to start a business. How did he come to be murdered?"

"It was like this," said the messenger. "When Mr. Liu came home it was already dark and he was tipsy. None of us knew about his money, and we are not sure what time exactly he got back; but this morning we found his door ajar, and when we went in there he lay murdered on the ground, while the fifteen strings of cash were nowhere to be seen and the concubine had disappeared too. We made such a noise that Old Zhu from the house on the left came out. He told us that the concubine had stayed in his house yesterday, because she claimed Mr. Liu had sold her for no reason and she wanted to go and tell her parents. She spent the night there and left early this morning. We decided that we should let you know what has happened, and men have been sent, too, to catch up with the concubine. If they don't overtake her on the road, they will go all the way to her parents' house; but they must bring her back to find out the truth. You and your daughter had better come back now to avenge Mr. Liu." Old Mr. Wang and his daughter hastily made ready and, when the messenger had been given wine and food, hurried to the city.

Now the concubine had left Old Zhu's house early that morning to start home. She had walked only half a mile, though, when her feet started aching and she sat down by the roadside to rest. Presently a young man came down the road, wearing a cap with zigzag designs and a loose gown, clean socks and silk shoes. Over his shoulder he was carrying a bag containing cash. When he came up with the concubine he saw that, while no beauty, she had pretty eyebrows and good teeth, her face was rosy and her eyes inviting. In a word, he found her quite attractive.

He put down his bag, came up to her, made a low bow and said: "Are you all alone, ma'am? May I ask where you are going?"

With a curtsey, she answered: "I am going home to my parents. I felt tired, so I am taking a rest. Where are you from, sir, and where may you be going?"

Clasping his hands before him,[3] the young man answered respectfully: "I come from the country. I have just sold silk in the city and got some cash which I am taking to Chujiatang."

"Why, my parents live near Chujiatang. I would like it so much if you could walk with me for part of the way."

"Certainly, if you wish it," replied the young man. "I shall be delighted to accompany you."

They went on together; but they had gone less than a mile when two men came running after them, sweating and panting, with the fronts of their jackets open. "Stop, madam!" they shouted. "We've something to say to you."

Startled, the concubine and the young man came to a halt. When the two men caught up, they seized them both without a word of explanation, crying: "A fine thing you've done! Where do you think you are going?"

The concubine was taken aback, but she saw now that these were neighbours, one of them being the master of the house in which she had stayed the previous night.

"Didn't I tell you last night," she said, "that my husband had suddenly taken it into his head to sell me, so I was going home to tell my parents? Why have you come after me?"

"Never mind that story of yours," retorted Old Zhu. "Murder has been done in your house, and you must come back to clear yourself."

"My husband has sold me: he took home the money yesterday. What is this about murder? I'm not going back."

"So you're being stubborn, eh?" roared Old Zhu. "Well, if you won't come with us, we'll shout out that you're murderers and you should be arrested. Otherwise we'll find ourselves involved and you won't have any peace here either."

Seeing that things had taken an ugly turn, the young man said to her: "It looks as if you had better go back, ma'am. I'll leave you here."

But the two neighbours shouted: "If you hadn't been here, that would have been all right. But since you are travelling together, we can't let you go."

"How ridiculous!" protested the young man. "I just happened to meet this young lady on the road and walked a short distance with her. This can have nothing to do with me. What do you want me for?"

"Murder has been done," said Old Chu. "Do you expect us to let you go, and involve ourselves in a lawsuit with the accused absent?"

They ignored all the protests of the concubine and the young man.

By now a crowd had gathered, and people advised the young man: "You can't just make off. A man with a clear conscience needn't fear a midnight knock on his door. You'd better go along."

"If you refuse to go," said Old Zhu's neighbour, "that shows you have a guilty conscience. But we won't let you escape." They seized the young man and the concubine and hustled them off.

When they reached Liu's door, they found the house in a great hubbub. And when the concubine went in and saw Liu dead on the floor, killed by an axe, and realized that the fifteen strings of cash on the bed had vanished, her jaw dropped and she was too frightened to speak.

The young man was appalled, too, and exclaimed: "How unlucky I am! By happening to accompany this young lady, I've got myself mixed up with murder!"

In the midst of all this confusion, old Mr. Wang and his daughter limped in. They wailed over the corpse, then turned to the concubine and demanded: "Why did you kill your husband, steal the cash and fly? Heaven is just, and you have been caught. But what have you to say for yourself?"

"It's true that there were fifteen strings of cash," said the concubine. "But when he came back last night he told me that he was so pressed for money he had pawned me for fifteen strings of cash and that today I should have to go to that other man's house. Because I didn't know what sort of family he had pawned me to, I decided to tell my parents first; and late last night I put the fifteen strings of cash in one pile by his feet, then closed the door and went to stay in old Mr. Zhu's house, so that I could go home first thing this morning. When I left, I asked Mr. Zhu to tell my husband that since he had found me a new master they should go together to my family to settle the business. I've no idea how he got murdered."

"Well!" cried the wife. "Yesterday my father gave him fifteen strings of cash to bring home as capital to support us all. Why should he deceive you by saying it was money raised by pawning you? In the two days when you were alone at home you must have had an affair with a man. Seeing how poor we were, you didn't want to stick it out; and when you saw the fifteen strings of cash that put an idea into your head, so you killed my husband and stole the money. Then you deliberately stayed one night with the neighbours, after planning to run off with your lover. You were walking with a man today. What have you to say to that? Can you deny it?"

All agreed: "Mrs. Liu is right."

Then they asked the young man: "Didn't you plot Mr. Liu's death with his concubine, and secretly arrange to meet at some deserted place and escape together? What have you to say?"

"My name is Cui Ning," replied the young man. "I have never set eyes on this young lady before. Last night I came into town to sell silk — I have the money from the sale on me — and today on my way back I happened to meet this lady. When I asked her where she was going and why she was alone, she mentioned that she was walking my way; so I accompanied her. I know nothing of what has happened here."

Do you think they would listen to him? They searched his bag; and when they found there exactly fifteen strings of cash, not a coin more, not a coin less, they cried: "The guilty can never escape Heaven's justice! You murdered him, stole his money and his concubine and tried to make off, leaving us to be involved in a lawsuit in which the accused has fled."

Then the wife seized the concubine and old Mr. Wang seized Cui Ning. With all the neighbours as witnesses, they marched straight to the city magistrate's office. When the city magistrate heard that it was a murder case, he took his seat in the court and ordered the plaintiffs to state their case from the beginning. Old Mr. Wang was the first to speak.

"Your Honour," he said, "I am a native of this district, living in the country. I am nearly sixty and have only one daughter whom I married some years ago to Liu Gui who lived in this city. Later, as they had no son, Liu took a concubine from the Chen family. They called the concubine Second Sister, and the three of them got on quite well together and never quarrelled. The day before yesterday, since it was my birthday, I sent a man to fetch my daughter and son-in-law to stay for one night; and the next day, realizing that my son-in-law had no means of supporting his family, I gave him fifteen strings of cash to set up a business which would bring them in enough to live on. The concubine had stayed at home to look after the house. Last night when my son-in-law went home, she seems to have killed him with an axe and fled with a young man named Cui Ning; but they have both been caught. I beg Your Honour to take pity on my son-in-law's strange death. Here are the wicked man and the adulteress, with the stolen money as evidence. May it please Your Honour, in your wisdom, to pass sentence!"

Then the city magistrate called to the concubine. "Come here! How did you plot with your lover to murder your husband, steal the money and escape? What have you to say?"

"Though I was only Liu Gui's concubine," she replied, "he treated me well and his wife was good to me. Why should I want to harm them? But last night my husband came home half drunk, with fifteen strings of cash. When I asked him where the money came from, he said he had pawned me for fifteen strings of cash, because he couldn't support the family; and he hadn't let my parents know about it, but wanted me to go to the other man the next day. I was so upset that I slipped out that night to stay with a neighbour, and I set off early this morning for my parents' home. I had asked my neighbour to tell my husband to go with my new master to my parents' home to settle the business. I was on my way home when the neighbour I had stayed with caught up with me and dragged me back. I know nothing about my husband's murder."

"Nonsense!" shouted the city magistrate. "The fifteen strings of cash were given him by his father-in-law, yet you claim that he raised the money by pawning you: that is obviously a lie. And why should a woman slip out at the dead of night? You must have been planning to run away. You couldn't have done this alone: some man must have abetted you in this murder and robbery. Out with the truth now!"

Before the young woman could speak again, several neighbours stepped forward, knelt down and said: "Your Honour is as all-seeing as Heaven. The concubine did spend the night in the second house to the left of their house, going off this morning. When we discovered that her husband had been murdered, we sent men after her who overtook her on the road. She was walking with that young man and they refused to come back; they had to be dragged back by force. We also sent for Mrs. Liu and her father, and when they arrived Liu's father-in-law said he had given the dead man fifteen strings of cash yesterday to set him up in business; but now Liu was dead and the money gone! When we questioned the concubine, she said she had left the money piled on the bed; but we found the fifteen strings of cash on the young man. This proves that the concubine and the young man must have plotted the murder together. How can they deny it, with such clear evidence against them?"

The city magistrate believed all they said and, calling the young man forward, demanded: "Here, in the seat of the imperial government, how dare you act so lawlessly? Confess now how you made off with Liu's concubine, stole his fifteen strings of cash and murdered him, and where you were going together."

"My name is Cui Ning," said the young man, "and I live in the country. Yesterday I came into town and sold some silk: that's how I got these fifteen strings of cash. The morning I fell in with this young lady on the road; but I didn't even know her name, to say nothing of the murder."

In a towering rage, the city magistrate thundered: "Nonsense! How could there be such a coincidence: they lost fifteen strings of cash, and you got fifteen strings for your silk! You are obviously lying. Besides, a man shouldn't covet his neighbour's wife or horse: if she was nothing to you, why were you walking together and putting up together? No doubt a cunning knave like you will never confess unless I have you tortured."[4]

The city magistrate had Cui Ning and the concubine tortured until they fainted away again and again. Old Mr. Wang, his daughter and the neighbours insisted that the couple were guilty, and the city magistrate wanted to close the case, so the unfortunate concubine and Cui Ning were tortured until they broke down and agreed that they had been tempted by the money and killed Liu, then had taken the fifteen strings of cash and fled. The neighbours, acting as witnesses in the case, put their crosses to the confessions; Cui Ning and the concubine were pilloried and sent to the prison for those condemned to death; and the fifteen strings of cash were returned to Mr. Wang — who found they were not enough to pay the men in the yamen.[5]

The city magistrate drew up a report of the case which

he submitted to the imperial court; and after due consideration an imperial edict was issued to the effect that since Cui
Ning was guilty of adultery, robbery and murder, he should
be beheaded according to the law; while the concubine, who
had plotted with her lover to kill her own husband, was
guilty of the worst crime and should be sliced to death. The
confessions were then read out in court, after which Cui
Ning and the concubine were brought from the gaol to be
sentenced — he to decapitation and she to be cut into pieces.
Taken to the public square for execution as a public example,
they had no way to protest.

Now, worthy readers, if the concubine and Cui Ning had
really committed robbery and murder, would they not have
fled the same night? Why should she allow herself to be
caught by spending one night with a neighbour and setting
off to see her parents the next day? Anyone who thought
twice could see that injustice had been done; but the city
magistrate was a fool who, in his impatience to close the case,
did not stop to think that anybody will confess under torture.
And when a man commits injustice, either he or his descendants will suffer; for the wronged ghosts will not rest till they
are avenged. Thus a judge must not condemn people as the
whim takes him, nor torture prisoners as he pleases: justice
and wisdom are required. For the dead can never come to
life again, and the broken can never again be made whole.

Mrs. Liu stayed on in her husband's house, where she had
set up a shrine for him before which she mourned every day;
and when her father advised her to marry again, she said:
"Even if I don't mourn for the required three years, I ought
at lease to mourn for one."

Her father agreed and let her be. But time passed quickly,
and when she had eked out a miserable existence alone for
nearly a year, Mr. Wang saw that she could not carry on
much longer and sent Old Wang to fetch her, saying: "Ask
the mistress to pack up and come home. As soon as she has
observed the anniversary of her husband's death, she may

marry again."

Since Mrs. Liu was in difficulties, after careful thought she agreed with her father. Accordingly she made a bundle of her belongings which she gave to Old Wang to carry, and having said goodbye to her neighbours, left the city. It was autumn and, caught in a sudden squall on their way home, they had to leave the road to find shelter in the forest. They took the wrong path and as they were walking through the forest, someone shouted from behind them: "I am the king of the mountain! Stop and pay the toll!"

As the travellers stood there trembling, a man leapt out, wearing a red cap and a tattered old battle dress with a red silk sash and a pair of dark boots. He had a sword in his hand which he brandished as he advanced. Old Wang was fated to die, for he said: "Bandit! Skunk! I know your sort. I don't mind risking my old life to have it out with you." The old fellow charged at him, head down; but the bandit dodged and the old man fell flat on the ground.

In a rage, the bandit swore: "Surly old bull!" He ran the old man through and through with his sword, until Old Wang's blood was spilt on the ground and it was clear he was dead.

When Mrs. Liu saw how fierce this man was, she feared that she was lost as well; but hitting on a desperate plan to save herself she clapped her hands and cried: "Bravo!"

Glaring at her, the bandit stayed his hand to shout: "Who was he to you?"

"Unhappy that I am," she lied, "when my husband died I was tricked by the matchmakers into marrying this old man who did nothing but eat. Now you have killed him for me and rid me of a plague."

When the bandit saw that she was submissive and not bad looking, he asked: "Will you stay and be my wife?"

Knowing that she had no choice, she answered: "I would like to serve Your Highness."

Smiling now, the bandit sheathed his sword; and when he

had thrown the servant's corpse into a gully, he led Mrs. Liu towards a mean-looking cottage. He picked up a clod of earth and threw it at the roof, whereupon a man came out to open the gate and they went into the hall. The bandit had a sheep killed and wine heated, then married Mrs. Liu. After that they got on quite well together.

Curiously enough, in less than half a year after gaining Mrs. Liu, the bandit made several big hauls and became quite rich. Mrs. Liu, who was very intelligent, kept giving him good advice and told him: "The proverb says: An earthen pitcher will sooner or later be broken over the well, and a general is likely to die in battle. We have enough now to keep us in comfort for the rest of our life; but if you go on flouting the will of Heaven, you are bound to come to a bad end. Though an outlaw's life is good, it is not like having a home. Why don't you turn over a new leaf and start a small business to make an honest living?"

She pleaded with the bandit day and night, until she prevailed on him to abandon his wicked ways and rent a house in the city where he opened a grocery shop. During his leisure hours he would often go to monasteries to worship Buddha and observe fasts.

One day when he was resting at home, he told his wife: "Though I started life as a bandit, I knew that a man has to pay for his crimes, so it was just to make a living that I frightened people into handing over their money. Later, after I got you, I never did much; and now I have changed my ways. But it worries me sometimes to think how I killed two men wrongly in the past and ruined two other innocent people. I've never told you about this before; but I would like to atone for my sins by having sutras chanted for their spirits, to get them out of hell."[6]

"How did you kill two men wrongly?" she asked.

"One was your husband. You remember how he charged at me in the forest, and I killed him. He was an old man and I had no grudge against him, but I killed him and took his wife. He can't be resting easy in his grave."

"But if not for that," she said, "we wouldn't be together now. Don't worry over what's past and done with. Who was the other?"

"It was even more wrong of me to kill the other man," he said. "And two innocent people were involved who had to pay with their lives. It happened over a year ago. I had lost money in gambling and hadn't a cent left, so I slipped out one night to see what I could pick up. I noticed a door that was not locked, and when I pushed in there was not a soul there; but in the inner room I found a man drunk in bed with a pile of cash by his feet. I took some of the money and was leaving, when the fellow woke up and started crying: 'That cash was given me by my father-in-law to start a business. If you steal it, my whole family will starve,' Then he rushed to the door and was about to shout for help. Things were looking bad for me, when I saw an axe for chopping wood by my feet. In desperation, I picked up the axe, shouting: 'It's either you or me!' I cut him down with two strokes, then went back to his room and took all the fifteen strings of cash. Later I heard that his concubine and a young man named Cui Ning were wrongly accused of the robbery and murder and executed. Though I have been a bandit all my life, these two cases are the only ones that neither Heaven nor man could forgive; and I ought to sacrifice to the spirits of my victims."

When Mrs. Liu heard this, she moaned to herself: "So my husband was killed by this beast too! And Second Sister and that young man were innocent after all. Come to think of it, I was wrong to insist that they pay with their lives: they will never forgive me in the nether regions." She pretended, however, to be in the best of spirits, and said nothing.

The next day, she seized an opportunity to slip out, and went straight to the city magistrate's office to inform against her husband's murderer. A new city magistrate, who had taken up office only a fortnight before, was presiding over the court when the attendants took her in. When she came to the steps, she cried aloud. Then she denounced the bandit, describing how he had killed her husband Liu Gui, how the former city magistrate had not investigated the case carefully because he was eager to close the case, how the concubine and Cui Ning had forfeited their lives though they were innocent, and how later the bandit had killed her father's old servant and made her his mistress. Now that justice had prevailed and the criminal had confessed his guilt, she begged the city magistrate to pass judgement and right the past wrong. After she had spoken she wept again.

Moved by her words, the city magistrate sent men to arrest the bandit, and when he was tortured they found that his confession tallied in every point with her statement; accordingly he was condemned to death. The case was reported to the imperial court and, when the usual sixty days had passed, the emperor decreed that since the bandit had committed robbery and murder and caused the ruin of innocent people, he should be executed on the spot according to the law; the former city magistrate, who had passed a wrong sentence, should be dismissed from his post and struck from the official list; the families of Cui Ning and the concubine who had died unjustly should receive pensions from the authorities; and since Mrs. Liu had been forced by the bandit to become his wife and had avenged her husband's death, half of the bandit's property should be confiscated but half should be left to her to live on.

Mrs. Liu went to the execution ground to watch the sentence being carried out; and when the bandit's head had been cut off she took it and offered it as sacrifice before the shrines of her dead husband, the concubine and Cui Ning. After lamenting bitterly over them, she gave the property she had received to a nunnery, and she herself every morning and evening chanted Buddhist sutras for the souls of the dead until she died of old age.

Notes:

1. The Song dynasty was founded in 960AD with its capital at Kaifeng in present-day Henan. Due to the invasion of northern China by the Kitan and Nurchen tribes, the capital was moved south to Lin'an, now called Hangzhou, in the year 1127. The rule of the Song dynasty is thus divided into the Northern Song (960-1127) and the Southern Song (1127-79).

2. Chinese money was formerly minted with a square hole in the centre through which a string could be passed. In this way money could be carried as a chain either slung over the shoulder or tied to a belt. A 'string of cash' would consist of one thousand cash (*wen*).

3. Salutation in China used to consist of clasping or 'shaking' one's own hand at about chest level.

4. The use of instruments of torture for the extraction of evidence in Chinese courts was extremely prevalent and quite permissible.

5. 'Yamen' refers to any office of local government. What was originally the term for the entrance to an official government courtyard later became synonymous with the word 'government.'

6. The recitation of Buddhist texts (*sutra* or *jing*) was regarded as a meritorious act capable of absolving one's sins or counterbalancing bad *karma*.

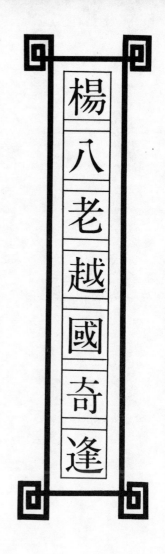

The Strange Adventures of Yang Balao

from Tales to Illuminate the World

In Xi'an, the provincial capital of Shaanxi, during the Zhi Da period (1308-11) of the Mongol Yuan dynasty,[1] there lived a man named Yang Balao, who was a native of Zhouzhi County. His wife's surname was Li,[2] and they had a precocious seven-year-old son. Needless to say, both parents doted on this child.

"I am nearly thirty," Yang Balao said to his wife one day. "Yet I have still not been able to pass the civil service examinations, and we've nearly reached the end of our resources. My family used to be traders in South China. What would you say to my raising some capital so that I could buy some goods to do trade with in the south?"

"It is said that a man should support a family with diligence and thrift," replied his wife. "It is not wise to sit by a tree and wait for a hare to run into it and die.[3] You should travel while you are still in your prime. My advice is that you pack and go without hesitation."

"That is all very well and good," said Yang. "But our son is still young, and you are delicate. How can I leave you with an easy mind?"

"He is no longer a child," she replied, "and I can see to

his education. My only thought is that the sooner you go, the sooner you'll return."

This decision having been reached, and an auspicious date chosen for the journey, Yang bid farewell to his wife, chartered a boat and travelled to the southeast, accompanied by a young servant called Suitong.

When Yang Balao reached Zhangpu in Fujian,[4] the destination of his trip, he put up at the house of a certain Mrs. Nie as a base from which to purchase Cantonese goods. Mrs. Nie's only child was a daughter of twenty-three, and the girl's husband, who had lived with them and helped support the family, had been dead for more than a year, leaving the young woman a widow. When Mrs. Nie saw that Yang Balao had plenty of money and seemed an honest, trustworthy and pleasant fellow, she became very attached to him, and wanted to marry her daughter to him. At first Yang declined, but Mrs. Nie wasn't one to give up easily.

"You're a stranger here, Mr. Yang, thousands of miles from home and with no close relatives here to look after you," she said. "My daughter is still young, and she'd make an excellent second wife for you here. When you go home you'll have your first wife to take care of you, and when you come to Zhangpu you'll have my daughter. So you don't have to feel lonely in either place during your trips, such an arrangement would be helpful to your business dealings as well. I'm not asking you to spend a lot of money on her. I'm only suggesting this because she's my only child, and I want her to marry a good man and have children, so that I'll have someone to depend on in my old age. If your wife knew of this, I'm sure she wouldn't object. After all, most men throw their money away on singsong girls when they are away from home, whereas this is a respectable alliance. Think it over carefully before you turn me down again."

Realizing that her proposal was reasonable, Yang Balao finally agreed, and chose an auspicious day on which to marry into the Nie family. Yang was very happy with his new wife, and soon she became pregnant. When a son was born to the couple, the whole family was delighted. There were the usual celebrations on the third day after the birth of the child, and at the end of the first month. Yet all this time Yang was longing for his young wife and son back in Xi'an.

He had meant to go back and see them after getting married, but he couldn't leave his wife while she was with child. And after the child was born his new wife wouldn't let him go. Time flew by until nearly three years had passed, and the boy was two years old. Since the name of Yang's first son was Shidao, he decided to call his second son Shide.[5] But the child took its mother's surname, and was thus called Nie Shide.

Finally Yang Balao told his second wife that he had to go back north to see his first wife and child. However, he promised to return soon. Unable to keep him with her any longer, she agreed. He packed his goods and made ready to leave, but as he and his servant were out collecting debts, Yang passed by the district yamen and saw an announcement warning all districts and counties to be vigilant as Japanese pirates were making raids along the coast.[6] It also declared that all travellers entering or leaving the city would be searched, and that a curfew would go into effect immediately. This quite took Yang by surprise and he thought to himself, "Just as I'm making ready to leave, they have this warning against pirates. If the Japanese do really carry out a raid, the gates will be closed and who knows how long it will take for things to get back to normal again? I'd better start out at once."

Yang decided to collect the rest of the debts when he returned, and headed straight for home. Fearing that he might meet up with pirates on the road, he decided not to take any merchandise with him. His wife could not bear to part with him, and when she learned that he planned to set out the next day she took her three-year-old child in her arms and said,

"My mother had me marry you so that we would have a man in the house to depend on. We've even been lucky enough to have this child. So be sure to come back soon for our little son's sake, if not for mine. We'll be anxious until you return." Then she started crying.

"Don't worry," replied Yang. "We've spent three years together as husband and wife, and I care for you deeply. You know I can't put this journey off, but I will be back with you in no more than a year."

That evening Yang's mother-in-law prepared a farewell feast for him. The next morning he got up at dawn, and after saying goodbye to his mother-in-law and wife, he set out with his servant Suitong. They had been travelling for less than two days when they came upon a scene of confusion. What they saw were crowds of country folk jostling each other in their panic to get to the towns for refuge. The news was that the Japanese were killing and burning everything along the road. The government troops were powerless to stop them, and even at that moment the pirates were approaching.

Frightened out of his wits, Yang dared neither to advance nor to turn back, instead he ran along with the rest of the crowd towards the city of Dingzhou. Three or four hours later, when he was about a mile from the city, he heard piercing shrieks and wails behind him — the pirates were upon them!

Many of the fleeing crowd were too terrified to move, but Yang dashed towards a wood he had spotted nearby, followed by a number of others. But the Japanese were not fools, and they fanned out around the forest to hide and wait. Suddenly, one Japanese leapt out into the open, and the country folk, thinking he was alone, were going to attack him. Just then he put a horn to his lips and blew, in a moment they were all surrounded by pirates brandishing long swords. But some of the tougher men who were used to

Japanese pirates come upon Yang

fighting tried to do their best against the Japanese with what weapons they had; but this was like throwing snow into a fire, or dust into the wind. The pirates hacked them down one by one, as if they were slicing melons. The rest of the captives fell fearfully to their knees and begged to be spared.

The Japanese pirates usually didn't kill all of the Chinese who fell into their hands during one of these raids. They raped the women they caught, but let them go when they got tired of them. Some of the more soft-hearted of them even gave the women presents. However, though they escaped death, such women were jeered at for the rest of their lives. As for the men, the old and weak were killed, while those in their prime were shaved bald and painted just like the Japanese.[7] In whatever future fighting took place these men were forced up into the front ranks. Since government troops were given a bounty for the head of each Japanese pirate they cut off, it often turned out that they killed Chinese citizens just for the sake of the reward. Anyway, they certainly didn't spare anyone captured in battle regardless of whether they were really Japanese or not. So the captured Chinese knew they couldn't escape death, and usually felt that by siding with the Japanese they might be able to postpone the inevitable. As a result, they fought as hard and as well as they could for the enemy. The real Japanese let their captives fight first before taking the field themselves, in this way they could trick the government troops and avoid defeat.

Captured by the Japanese, Yang and his companions were like turtles in a jar — unable to escape. Therefore they surrendered to save their lives. Suitong had disappeared, and Yang did not know whether he was dead or alive. Being in no position to protect himself at the time he could do little about his servant. We will not dwell on Yang Balao's distress at being taken prisoner, but turn rather to the pirates, who were very satisfied with the gold and jewels they had carried off. When they heard that the Yuan army was approaching, they seized a number of boats, hearded their captives aboard and set off happily for Japan.

The Japanese emperor was often quite ignorant of these pirate invasions of the Chinese mainland. The pirates were usually nothing more than the poor and destitute of outlying islands who banded together very much as pirates in China did. Their 'invasions' of China were to them just like business trips. During such expeditions they divided their forces, calling the leader of each group a prince. Upon their return to Japan, however, they dropped these titles. They divided their booty equally among themselves, sometimes giving one tenth or one fifth to the chief of their island to keep him quiet.

If any of the pirates were killed by the Chinese it meant a loss of capital to their 'business.' But they kept their healthy captives as slaves, making them shave their heads and go barefoot after the fashion of the Japanese, as well as giving them weapons and teaching them to fight in the Japanese way. Out of fear the Chinese captives obeyed, and after a year or so of life among their captors, they could speak Japanese and were accustomed to local practice, making them no different from the natives.

Time passed quickly, and Yang Balao found that he had spent nineteen years in Japan. Still he prayed secretly every night to the gods to keep him safe and allow him to return home to see his wives and children again.

During the Tai Ding reign period (1324-7) there was a famine throughout the islands of Japan, and the Japanese mustered a force to invade China again. Yang Balao was part of the force. This both pleased and disturbed Yang. At last he was going back to China, where he had his families in Shaanxi and Fujian. If Heaven protected him he might be able to return to his own people and be united with his loved ones. Yet he was distressed by the fact that he looked so thoroughly Japanese. He was shocked every time he looked at himself in the mirror. If he felt he looked strange, then how would his countrymen be able to recognize him? Besides, it was more than likely that he'd meet his death in the bloody fighting. But then again, better to be a ghost in one's own country than alive and well in a foreign land. If Heaven was merciful and the boats were blown close to Shaanxi or Fujian then there would be some hope. If they landed in some other province, then all would be lost.

When the Japanese crossed the ocean to China, they had to depend on both Heaven and the wind. If there was a northerly wind, then they would invade Guangdong, if it was a strong northeast wind blowing for several days, they northeast wind would carry them to Wenzhou in Jiangsu, while a southeast wind would land them in Yangzhou. As they set sail from Japan in the second month when there was a strong northeast wind blowing for several days, they travelled straight to Wenzhou.

The Mongol empire had long been at peace, hence its coastal defences were weak. Although the government did have a few ships and several hundred decrepit old soldiers manning them, these veterans took flight on first sight of the invaders. Having landed without meeting any resistance, the Japanese started devastating the area. Yang Balao, despite his reluctance, was forced to follow them. For some six months the Japanese pirates repeatedly defeated the imperial troops in combat. After plundering various towns they proceeded to Ningbo, Shaoxing and Yuhang in Zhejiang, where their cruelty defied description. The various districts and counties in the area petitioned the government for aid, and the emperor ordered the Board of War[8] to dispatch General Pu Hua of Pingjiang and his army to supress the invaders. Pu Hua was an able strategist, and had a handpicked group of officers under his command. He immediately advanced on Zhejiang ready to engage the enemy. When his scouts had located the pirates' headquarters at Qingshuizha near Shangyu County, he ordered the local militia to join him in his attack on land and by water.

The Japanese, who despised the Chinese troops, paid no attention to the force. But they were unaware that General Pu Hua had ten lieutenants of extraordinary courage, as well as cannon. The General concealed part of his force while the rest engaged the pirates in a fierce combat. Then the men waiting in ambush charged and the cannon roared. The Japanese, unable to flee, were completely routed. Over one thousand heads were taken and more than two hundred captured alive. Those who attempted to escape by ship were engaged by the navy and many of them drowned. The victorious general rewarded his troops, and sent out a force to make sure that none of the Japanese had escaped.

At Qingshuizha there was a temple named the Temple of Safe Crossing built for the worship of the saint Feng Jun. Feng had been a native of Qiantang. At the age of sixteen he had a dream that the Jade Emperor[9] had ordered celestial messengers to cut open his belly and change his vital organs. When he woke up he could still feel the pain. As he had never attended school he could neither read nor write, yet after this dream he became very wise and was able to read all manner of books, write fluent essays, and foretell the future. One day, waking from a long trance, he declared that he had just been feasting with the Dragon King of the Eastern Ocean,[10] but that he'd drunk too much. No one believed him until he vomited, and brought up strange seafood never before seen by men.

When he reached the age of thirty-six, Feng told his friends one day that the Jade Emperor had appointed him god of the river, and three days hence he was to take up his post. On the day appointed he died peacefully. The same day great waves welled up in the river, nearly causing passing boats to capsize. Then the boatmen saw red flags, dark canopies, and a god riding a white horse with red reins in the sky. This god rebuked the waves which thereupon subsided. When the boatmen questioned local people, they were told that judging by the appearance of this god it had to be Feng

Jun. So they set up a temple where he had lived and called it the Temple of Safe Crossing. During the Shao Ding reign period (1228-33) of Emperor Li Zong of the Song Dynasty, Feng Jun was given the title of Glorious Prince. He proved to be a very powerful deity.

During the Japanese occupation of Qingshuizha, Yang Balao prayed secretly in this temple, and was given a good omen. He then suggested to the other twelve Chinese captives that they surrender to the imperial troops, but they hesitated, fearing that the Chinese soldiers would cut off their heads regardless of whether they were really Japanese or not just for the sake of the reward.

On the twenty-eighth of the month, when the Japanese had been completely routed, Yang and his twelve companions were hiding in the temple not daring to come out when they heard shouting outside. It was old Wang Guoxiong, Commander of a Thousand, leading his troops in to search the place. The thirteen men were caught and strung up in the yard, vainly protesting that they were not Japanese. As it was already late in the day, Commander Wang decided to spend the night in the temple, and send his captives to the yamen the following morning for a reward. As luck would have it, Commander Wang had a servant by the name of Wang Xing who woke up during the night and heard the prisoners wailing in the yard. To his amazement one of the men was speaking like a native of Shaanxi; he quietly picked up a lantern to go and investigate. The sight of Yang Balao filled him with doubts.

"If you're not Japanese, then where are you from?" He demanded. "How did you come to join the pirates? And how is it that you look just like a Japanese?"

"These other men are all natives of Fujian," replied Yang, "but I come from Zhouzhi County in Xi'an Prefecture. Nineteen years ago, while on a business trip to Zhangpu, I was captured by the Japanese, who shaved my head and made me walk barefoot and suffer all kinds of hardship. These other men were all caught at the same time. We had originally come here to give ourselves up, but hesitated to do so because we feared that with our outlandish looks, unless we met someone we knew, nobody would believe us. Luckily our government troops have won the day and routed the pirates. We were hoping to live under our own sun and sky once more, never thinking that the old commander would have us all bound and hung up without even a trial. This means that when we are taken to army headquarters we shall be killed."

At that they all started weeping again. Wang Xing hastily gestured for them to be quiet.

"Shhh! Don't make such a noise!" he urged them. "If you wake the old commander you'll suffer for it. You, the man from Xi'an, what's your name?"

"Yang Balao. You have a northeast accent too, sir. Are you from the same prefecture by any chance?"

Wang stood there shocked,

"You must be my former master." he cried. "I am Suitong. Do you remember me?"

"Of course I remember you Suitong," said Yang, "but you've changed so much that I didn't recognize you. What happened to you after we were separated in Fujian?"

"That's a long story," Wang replied, "I don't have the time to tell it to you now. Tomorrow, when the commander orders you to be taken away, I shall stand beside him, then you can look over at me and call my name, and I will come forward and plead for you."

Having said this, he went back inside with his lantern. When the other captives questioned Yang, he explained briefly who Suitong was and they all took heart.

Suitong had been nineteen when he was serving Yang Balao. Now that another nineteen years had passed he was thirty-eight. So it is little wonder that Yang Balao did not recognize him. After being separated from his master, Suitong had hidden himself in a public lavatory where he was lucky enough to avoid capture. At the time, Wang Guoxiong, the Commander of a Thousand, was only the Commander of a Hundred Families, and was the local official in charge. When he met Suitong and saw that he seemed intelligent, he asked where he came from, and kept him as his servant. He also promised to make enquiries about the lad's master, but nothing more was heard of Yang. After Wang was promoted to be Commander of a Thousand and transferred to Zhejiang, Suitong, who had changed his name to Wang Xing,[11] remained with him as his favourite servant. Yet the fates had not decreed that Yang be left destitute and end his life as a captive of the Japanese. Once evil had played itself out, it was ordained that the master and servant would meet again. But that is enough of all of this.

The following morning, after Commander Wang had called the roll, he was about to order the captives taken to headquarters so he could claim a reward when one of the captives stared at his servant and cried,

"Suitong, I am your old master. Come and save me."

Wang Xing then pretended to recognize the prisoner suddenly, embraced him and wept. Since master and servant had been separated so many years ago, Commander Wang had forgotten what had happened. He hastily called Wang Xing over and questioned him.

"This is my old master," said the servant, "who was lost nineteen years ago. I didn't know he had been captured by the pirates. I was just thinking that his face looked familiar when he recognized me and called me by my old name. Please let me plead his innocence, sir, and have him released. Then, even though I would die before these very steps I would be doing so without regret."

At this he burst into tears, and all the other captives called out protesting their innocence while giving their names, native places and details of their lives.

"Well," said Commander Wang, "I have no authority to make a decision on a case like this. I will send them to the commander-in-chief to let them plead their own cases."

Suitong asked to be allowed to go with them as a witness. Commander Wang was unwilling at first, but he finally agreed to the servant's earnest plead. So the thirteen captives and Suitong were taken to General Pu Hua.

"Since they are Japanese prisoners," declared the general, "off with their heads."

At that the thirteen captives started protesting loudly. Suitong pleaded for them too, and Commander Wang knelt down to report what his servant had told him. Then General Pu Hua agreed to let Commander Wang take the men to the assistant prefect of Shaoxing, Yang Shidao, for trial. This assistant prefect was second in authority in the area and wielded great power, helping his superior with all of the business of the prefecture. It was an impressive sight that day when he ascended the court.

When Commander Wang had escorted the thirteen prisoners to the hall and reported the case according to the general's orders, the assistant prefect saw him out and then returned to his seat. First Suitong pleaded his former master's innocence, and all the captives wailed out loud. The assistant prefect then called Yang Balao forward to be questioned.

Yang gave his name and native place.

"So you're a native of Zhouzhi County," said the assistant prefect. "What was your wife's family name, and have you any children?"

"My wife was a daughter of the Li family in the East Village," replied Yang. "We only had one son named Shidao, who was seven when I went to Zhangpu on business. I stayed in the south for three years, after which I was captured by the Japanese on my way back to the north. Nineteen long years have since passed, and I've had no news from home. So I don't know whether my wife and child are alive or dead. If my son is still alive, then he should be twenty-nine this year. If you don't believe me, Your Honour, you can ask the Zhouzhi County authorities to look up the record of my family, for then my innocence will be proved."

Thereupon the assistant prefect questioned Suitong again, and all that Yang Balao had said was confirmed. The captives all started wailing once more, and when the assistant prefect examined them he found all the others to be natives of Fujian, captured the same time as Yang. After some thought, he ordered them to be taken to the gaol until reports could be obtained from their native places confirming their statements. With that the court was adjourned.

Muttering "How strange, how strange!", the assistant prefect returned to his residence and went to see his mother.

"What cases did you have today?" his mother asked him. "Why do you keep muttering the word 'strange'?"

"A certain Commander Wang brought in thirteen Japanese prisoners," her son told her, "all of whom turned out to be Chinese who had been captured by pirates, and are not real Japanese at all. One of them, whose name is Yang Balao and declares himself to be a native of Zhouzhi in Xi'an Prefecture, said that twenty-one years ago he left his wife, a daughter of the Li family, and went to Zhangpu to do business. Three years later, Japanese pirates overran that area of Fujian and carried him off. He said that when he left home he had a son aged seven, so now that would make him twenty-nine. You often told me in the past, mother, that when I was seven my father went to Zhangpu on business never to return. This man's name and birth-place are the same as that of my father, as is the family name of his wife, and I am just twenty-nine this year — can this merely be a series of extraordinary coincidences? Besides this, Commander Wang has a servant called Wang Xing who insists that Yang Balao was his former master, his original name being Suitong and that they were separated during the battle near Zhangpu. Well, Suitong *was* the name of my father's servant. That is why I think it is all so strange."

His mother agreed that it was indeed most extraordinary.

"All sorts of coincidence are possible," she said.

"But what makes this so remarkable is that every detail tallies. Try them again tomorrow, and I will listen behind the screen. Then we can make up our minds in no time."

Her son agreed. The next day he summoned the thirteen men for a further trial at which they repeated what they had said the previous day. Then the assistant prefect's mother called out from behind the screen,

"Yang Shidao, my son, doubt no more. This man from Zhouzhi is your father, and Wang Xing is Suitong."

The assistant prefect was so startled that he stumbled down from his seat to embrace Yang Balao and wept. Then he took him to a room at the back, to which Suitong followed them. There, father and son, husband and wife embraced each other and wept, feeling that their meeting again was like a dream. The servant shed tears as well. Then, when they had dried their eyes, the assistant prefect kowtowed to his father, and Suitong kowtowed to his former master and mistress.

"When I was in Japan," Yang told his son, "I prayed every night that I be given a chance to return home and see my wife and child again. Now Heaven has taken pity on me and granted my wish. I am very happy to find you so distinguished and noble, my son. But you must also acquit my twelve companions, for they are all from Fujian and were captured at the same time as I was, and, like me, were forced to serve the Japanese. Don't cause them further suffering by abandoning them."

In obedience to his father's wishes, the assistant prefect immediately released the other twelve captives, giving three taels of silver to each of them for their journey home, thereby winning their deepest gratitude. Then he ordered his clerk to write a report to General Pu Hua and prepared a feast to celebrate his father's return. A bath was made ready for Yang Balao, who then changed into new clothes, and an official cap and belt. Thereupon his son's wife came to pay her respects to her father-in-law and the whole family was happily reunited.

News of this reunion spread throughout Shaoxing prefecture, and Prefect Nie, hearing that his colleague had found his long-lost father, prepared mutton and wine and cake to congratulate them, and asked to be introduced to the old gentleman. Yang Balao came out of the inner quarters, and after he and the prefect had greeted each other, they sat down to chat. As Prefect Nie was so delighted by the family's reunion, Yang Shidao had him stay for more drink. While they were drinking, the prefect asked Yang Balao how he had come to stay so long in Fujian that he fell among pirates.

"My original intention was to stay for less than a year," replied Yang. "But I was lodging with a certain Mrs. Nie, who had a widowed daughter of twenty-three, and they wanted a man to marry into the family. So I married her and stayed there for three years."

"Did you have a son by her?" asked the prefect.

"Yes, it was because my wife had a son that I did not like to leave. Otherwise I would have returned home much earlier."

"What was your son's name?"

Not knowing the prefect's name, Yang Balao answered readily, "Because my first son was called Yang Shidao, I called my second son Shide to show that, despite their different surnames, they were related. I suppose that Nie Shide would be twenty-two this year. But I don't know whether he and his mother are alive or dead."

Yang Balao shed tears, and the prefect appeared to share his sorrow, for after a few more cups he took his leave.

When Prefect Nie got home he related all that happened to his mother.

"Mr. Yang said that he married a daughter of the Nie clan in Zhangpu," he told her. "That is your family, and the date is correct — could he be my father?"

"You had better invite him to a feast tomorrow and question him," said his mother. "Then I can find out by watching from behind a screen."

The next day, Yang Balao presented his card and returned the prefect's call. Nie Shide kept him to a feast, and Mrs. Nie watched him from behind a screen. Now that Yang was properly dressed, and no longer looked like a Japanese pirate, he was easy to recognize. So after listening to a few words, Nie's mother called out,

"Son, quickly invite your father into the inner chambers."

To Yang Balao's amazement, the prefect hastily knelt down before him.

"Forgive me, father," he cried, "I failed to recognize you."

Then he invited Yang inside to meet his mother, and they clasped each other and wept just as at the reunion in the assistant prefect's home. While they were talking Suitong arrived, sent by Yang Shidao to escort his father home. When the servant learned that Yang Balao was father to the prefect as well, in great amazement he hastened in to kowtow to Mrs. Nie, who immediately recognized him. Suitong described how he was separated from his master and met Commander Wang, the whole family was overjoyed. The prefect's wife also came out to pay her respects to her father-in-law and another feast was laid out. The assistant prefect was then invited over and told the news. Thus the two colleagues became brothers. The assistant prefect's wife was asked over as well and the whole family met together in great happiness.

During his nineteen years of hardship in Japan, Yang Balao had never dreamed that his first wife's son, Yang Shidao, and his second wife's son, Nie Shide, would grow up to pass the palace examinations in the same year and be appointed to posts in the same prefecture. Not only had Heaven delivered him from captivity, and brought his whole family together, but he found both his wives ladies and both of his sons officials — surely such a thing was never heard of before!

The next day all the officials in the prefecture knew of

Yang and his whole family rejoice at their reunion

this marvel and came to offer their congratulations, among them was Commander Wang. Because Suitong was Yang Balao's former servant, the commander let him go; and to please the prefect and the assistant prefect he sent Suitong's wife straight over to Yang's house.

The prefect and assistant prefect then wrote a joint report to General Pu Hua, informing him of their reunion with their father. When the general reported this to the government, the whole family received gifts from the throne. Nie Shide was renamed Yang Shide and entered his father's family, and Yang Balao enjoyed peace and dignity with his sons, living to be nearly eighty. This shows that our mortal lot is destined by Fate, and wealth and fortune are determined by Heaven. Human prosperity and misfortune, loss or gain, are decided by a man's stars, and nothing can change them.

Notes:

1. The Zhi Da period was the name of a four year period in the reign of one of the Yuan emperors. An emperor's name would never be used for a reign period, and the emperor could change the name of the reign period when he thought it necessary. The recovery from an illness, a reformed system of laws or a rare confluence of astrological forces could all result in a new reign period.

2. In China women do not change their surnames upon marriage.

3. This is a common expression in Chinese which is based on a story in the 'Five Pests Chapter' of the ancient philosopher Han Fei Zi ('Wu du,' in *Han fei zi*). The story tells of a peasant who sees a hare run into a tree stump and die. He thereupon puts down his tools and goes to the stump to wait for another hare to come along and run into the stump. The expression 'wait by a tree for a hare' (*shou zhu dai tu*) is used to describe someone who waits for gains without doing any work.

4. Zhangpu or Zhangzhou in southern Fujian province still plays a role in China's overseas trade today.

5. It is not uncommon for parents to give their children names with one common word or element. Thus, the word 'shi' in Shidao and Shide indicates that the two children are related.

6. Raids by individually organized groups of pirates along the Chinese coast were frequent during this period. The unsettled internal situation in Japan allowed the pirate gangs a free reign on the seas.

7. The Japanese shaved their crowns and painted them white.

44

8. The Board of War (*Bingbu*) was one of the six central government boards. It was responsible for the recruiting of soldiers, the army and the making of war.

9. The Jade Emperor (*Yuhuang*) is the highest diety of the Daoist celestial hierarchy. He was seen to be the emperor of heaven with power over all living and non-living things.

10. In Chinese mythology dragons were linked with water. All ponds and rivers were ruled by dragons. The Dragon King of the East Sea (*Donghai longwang*) was appointed by the Jade Emperor to rule over all terrestrial dragons.

11. A person would change their name (usually personal name and only rarely one's surname) when starting a new life, following a serious illness or any other time it seemed propitious to do so.

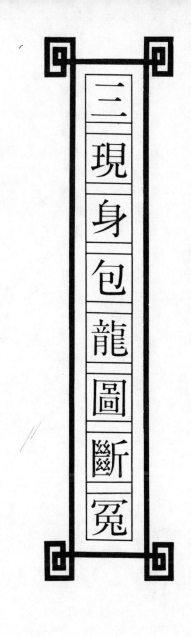

三現身包龍圖斷冤

The Ghost Came Thrice

from Tales to Warn the World

The story I will tell today is about a fortune-teller by the name of Li Jie who was a native of the Eastern Capital Kaifeng.[1] He travelled to Fengfu District in Yanzhou and set up a fortune-telling shop there. Outside the shop he hung up a sword covered with gilt paper with a trade-sign underneath it which declared: "Death to all unlearned fortune-tellers." He was obviously no charlatan.

Not long after he had put up his signboard a man came into the shop. Having greeted the fortune-teller this man who was quite well dressed gave his birth date and hour and cast lots.[2] The fortune-teller took one look and said curtly, "I can't tell you anything."

It turned out that the stranger was the first bailiff of the district by the name of Sun Wen. He asked:

"Why won't you tell me my fortune?"

The fortune-teller was adamant, and on repeated requests just said,

"Drink no more wine and ask not for bad news."

The bailiff replied,

"But I haven't been drinking, nor do I mind bad news."

At this the fortune-teller said,

"May I trouble you for the details of your birth again in case I made a mistake the first time."

The bailiff told him again, and casting the lots the fortune-teller said,

"Sir, ask me no more."

The bailiff said,

"I don't mind what it is, tell me."

The fortune-teller replied,

"The lots are bad." And with this he wrote down four lines, they were:

> *The white tiger is approaching*
> *Which means disaster;*
> *Before one o'clock tomorrow morning*
> *Your relatives will mourn for you.*

When the bailiff saw this he asked,

"What do the lots say?"

"To be direct, sir, it means you are going to die."

"But which year shall I die?"

"This year."

"Which month?"

"This month."

"On which day shall I die?"

"Today."

He then asked for the time of day, and the fortune-teller said:

"You shall die today at midnight."

"If I really die tonight, then that will be the end of the matter; if not, then I'll deal with you at the yamen tomorrow."

"If you do not die tonight, then you can come tomorrow and cut off my head with the sword which kills unlearned fortune-tellers."

When the bailiff heard this he was furious, and he threw the fortune-teller out of the shop.

Some attendants from the yamen came by and stopped the bailiff, and asked him why he was fighting. The bailiff replied:

"You ask me why I'm fighting? I asked this fellow to tell me my fortune, and he told me that I was going to die at midnight tonight. I'm not even sick, how could I die tonight? I'll take him along to the yamen and clear this all up."

Someone in the crowd said,

"If you believe everything a fortune-teller says then you'd end up selling your very house. The words of a fortune-teller are a bottomless measure."

Finally they managed to get the bailiff away, only to return and criticize the fortune-teller,

"Well, Mr. Li, we don't suppose you'll be doing business here any more now that you've offended the bailiff. It is easy to tell a person's wealth, but not the span of one's life. You're not a relative of the Judge of the Dead,[3] so how can you predict the very hour and minute of a person's death? You should be a little more general in your prophecies."

The fortune-teller retorted:

"If I only say what pleases people then I won't be telling the truth. Yet if I speak the truth then people are offended. If this is not a place for me to stay, then I will go somewhere else." Heaving a sigh, he put his things together and moved on.

After returning to his office, the bailiff felt very uncomfortable. He put down his work and went home still in an unhappy mood. His wife saw that he was looking worried and asked him,

"What's troubling you? I suppose it's some work that you didn't finish at the yamen?"

"No, it's not that. Don't ask me."

She persisted,

"Were you criticized by the magistrate for something today?"

"No."

"Well, did you quarrel with someone then?"

"No. Today, before going to the yamen, I went to have

my fortune told. The fortune-teller said that I will die
tonight at midnight."

On hearing this his wife stared at him in amazement,
and asked,

"How could a healthy man like you just up and die
like that? Why didn't you take him off to the yamen and
sue him?"

"I was going to, but I was stopped."

"Well, dear, you just stay here at home, and I'll go and
smooth things over with the magistrate. But first I'll go
and find that fortune-teller and ask him why you should
die at midnight. After all, you don't owe anyone money,
nor are you hard-pressed by official business."

"Don't go. If I don't die tonight then I'll deal with
him tomorrow. That'll be better than anything you can do."

It was getting late, so the bailiff said,

"Get me something to drink. I'll not be sleeping tonight."

After a few cups of wine he was quite drunk and only
semi-conscious, he started nodding off in his armchair. His
wife said,

"Dear, are you asleep?"

Getting no reply, she called for her maid Ying'er, and
told her to wake him. The maid shook him, and called out
to him, but all to no avail. In the end, the wife said,

"Come, Ying'er, let's carry him inside the room to
rest."

When the wife had seen him to bed, she told the maid to
put out the fire in the kitchen, and asked her,

"Did you hear father say that a fortune-teller told him
today that he'd die at midnight tonight?"

"Yes, mother,[4] I heard him say so. What a thing to say!"

"Well then, Ying'er let us do some sewing and see what
happens. If nothing comes of it all, then we'll deal with that
fortune-teller tomorrow. But be sure you don't go to sleep."

"I surely wouldn't dare to go to . . . . ."

Even before she'd finished speaking, she was fast asleep.

The wife called out to her,

"Ying'er, I told you not to go to sleep, and there you are sleeping already."

The maid replied,

"No, I'm not."

Though as soon as she'd finished she was dozing again. The wife called her to wake up, and asked her what time it was. Just then Ying'er heard the hour-drum of the yamen sound midnight. The wife said, "Ying'er, whatever you do, don't go to sleep now, for this is the fateful moment."

But the girl had dozed off again, and did not respond.

Suddenly the wife heard the bailiff jump out of bed, and the inside door open. She hastily called the maid up, and when they lit the lamp and looked out, the gate creaked open. Ying'er and the wife rushed out in pursuit with the lamp, and they saw a figure in white with one hand hiding its face. It moved outside and then there was a splash: the figure had leapt into the river. The river was a tributary of the Yellow River, and was flowing so fast that they had no way of finding the body.

The wife and maid stood at the river-side and burst out crying,

"Why have you jumped into the river, who'll support us now?"

Then they called up all of their neighbours, Mrs. Diao and Mrs. Mao from next door, and Mrs. Gao and Mrs. Bao from across the street. They all came out, and the bailiff's wife told them what had happened. Mrs. Diao exclaimed:

"How very odd this!"

Mrs. Mao declared,

"Why, I met the bailiff coming home from the yamen in his black clothes, with documents in his sleeve, and we greeted each other."

Mrs. Gao said,

"That's right, I greeted him too."

Mrs. Bao said,

"My husband had some business at the yamen today, and saw the bailiff fighting with the fortune-teller. Now look at this, he's actually dead."

Mrs. Diao said,

"Oh bailiff, why didn't you give us some reason? Why should you die?"

As she shed some tears, Mrs. Mao said,

"How can one help but feel sad when you think of the many kind things he did?"

She too cried, and Mrs. Bao called out,

"Bailiff, when will we see you again?"

Then they went to the yamen to report what had happened, and the wife performed the usual rites in mourning for the dead.

In no time, three months had passed. One day the wife of the dead bailiff and Ying'er were resting at home when two women lifted the curtain over the door and came in. They were both red in the face from drinking, the one on the right carrying a bottle of wine, and the one on the left holding two artificial flowers in her hand. The bailiff's wife immediately recognized them as the two well-known match-makers, Mrs. Zhang and Mrs. Li. She said,

"We haven't seen each other for some time."

"No, we didn't hear of your sad news until just recently, and so we didn't send over any incense or paper money, we hope you'll forgive us. When did your husband pass away?"

"It was the hundredth day just the day before yesterday."

"How time flies. So it's a hundred days already. He was such a good man when he was alive. Whenever I called out to him he would always reply in greeting. Now that he has been gone for such a long time you must be very lonely here. Don't you think it's time to be looking around for someone else?"

"Ah, where could I ever find a man as good as my husband?"

"That's no difficulty. We've got the very man for you."

"Say no more. How could he ever compare with my late husband?"

The matchmakers stayed for tea, and then departed.

A few days passed, and the matchmakers returned to talk to her again. But the wife was adamant and said,

"Don't make any more offers to me. Unless you can fulfil three conditions, I'll remain a widow for the rest of my life."

The matchmakers asked,

"What are the three conditions?"

The wife replied,

"First my husband's surname was Sun; if I am to marry again, the man must also be called Sun. Secondly, my former husband was the first bailiff in the district, so the man must have the same job too. Finally, I will not move in with his family, he must come and live in my house."

When the two matchmakers heard the conditions they said,

"Fine. So you want to marry a man called Sun, who has the same job as the former bailiff, and you want him to live in your house. If there are any other conditions there might be some difficulty, but if these are the only three, then we're agreed. Your late husband was the first bailiff, most people called him Big Bailiff Sun. After he died, the second bailiff was promoted to be the first bailiff. As it turns out this man is also called Sun. He's known as the Young Bailiff Sun. He is also willing to live in your house. So will you marry him?"

The wife declared,

"This is all too much of a coincidence, I can't believe it."

Matchmaker Zhang said,

"I'm an old woman of seventy-two. If we die may I be turned into seventy-two bitches and eat your family's shit."

"Well, if it really is the truth will you negotiate on my behalf and see whether it is all right?"

Old matchmaker Zhang said,

"Today is an auspicious day. Give me a note written on

lucky paper[5] from you to seal the deal."

"But I don't have any of the paper here at home."

Matchmaker Li spoke up,

"I've got some here," and she took some coloured paper with figures drawn on it from her apron. Then the bailiff's wife told the maid to bring pen and ink, and the note was written. With that the matchmakers were off.

After that followed the usual exchange of presents and messages, and in less than two months Young Bailiff Sun had come to live in the house. The couple were well matched and got on happily together.

One day the new husband and wife had had too much to drink, and they told Ying'er to make something hot for them to drink to get rid of their hangover. As Ying'er was going to the kitchen she grumbled to herself,

"When the old bailiff was alive I would have been in bed by now. But look at them, they want me to make drinks for them at this hour."

The bellows of the fire were clogged, and she couldn't get the stove to light. So Ying'er bent down to knock the bellows against the foot of the stove to clear them. She'd only knocked them a couple of times when the stove began to rise and hovered over one foot from the ground. Then she could see that a man was lifting the stove with his head. The wooden frame of the well hung around his neck, his hair was dishevelled, his tongue was sticking out, and blood was dripping from his eyes. He groaned,

"Ying'er, avenge your father!"

Ying'er was so frightened that she shrieked and fainted on the ground. Having heard her shrieks, the husband and wife rushed in and revived the girl, and gave her a sedative to drink. Then they asked her,

"What did you see just now that made you faint?"

Ying'er told the wife,

"Mother, I was making a fire in the stove when the whole thing started to rise slowly from the ground. Under it was the old bailiff with the well-frame on his neck with blood dripping from his eyes, and his hair all dishevelled. He called my name and then I fainted in fright."

When the wife heard this, she gave the girl a hard slap on the face and shouted,

"You wench, I told you to make us something hot to drink. You just made this story up to get out of doing any work. All right, put out the fire and go to bed." With that the young girl went off to bed.

When the husband and wife retired to their room, the wife whispered,

"Darling, now that the girl has seen that vision, we can't use her anymore. I'll have to get her out of my house."

"But where will you send her?"

"I have a plan."

The next morning, after the bailiff had gone to the office, the wife called Ying'er over to her and said,

"Ying'er, you've worked in my house now for seven or eight years. During that time I've treated you well. But now it's not like the old days when the former bailiff was master. I wonder if you've been secretly wishing to get married? Well, what I want to do is arrange a marriage for you."

"I never had such an intention", said the girl.

"Who do you want me to marry?"

Without giving the girl any choice in the matter, the wife married her off to a fellow named Wang Xing. This Wang Xing was nicknamed 'The Drunkard.' He was fond of drinking and gambling. Within three months of getting married Wang had used up all of Ying'er's dowry.

One day, Wang Xing came home drunk and cursed Ying'er,

"You damned bitch. See what a hard time I have. Why don't you go and ask your former master to lend us a few hundred cash?"

Given no respite from his cursing, she put on a skirt and went straight to Young Bailiff Sun's house. When the wife saw her she asked,

"Ying'er, you're a married woman now. What have you come back for?"

"Mother, the truth of it is that I've married a bad man. He drinks and gambles all the time, and in less than three months he's used up all I had. I've been forced to come and ask you for a loan of a few hundred cash to go into business with."

The wife replied,

"Ying'er, if your marriage is not a success, then it's your own affair. Now, I'll give you one tael of silver, but I don't want to see you back here again."

Ying'er took the silver, thanked her, and went home. But within a few days, the money was all gone. That evening Wang Xing came home rolling drunk, and staring at Ying'er, said,

"You bitch, see what a hard time I'm having. Why don't you go and ask your master for some help?"

Ying'er replied,

"Last time I went though I got a tael of silver, she gave me a lecture on how I shouldn't go back. How then can I go and ask for more?"

The drunk cursed her, saying,

"Bitch, if you refuse to go then I'll smash up your leg."

So Ying'er was forced to go to Bailiff Sun's house that night. When she reached the house, she found the door already locked. Though she wanted to knock, she was afraid of being yelled out. In her quandry she decided to walk back home again. After only having gone past a few houses someone called out to her, "Ying'er, here is something for you."

When Ying'er turned her head to look at the person who had called out to her she saw someone on the eave of a roof wearing an official cap, red gown with a belt with a horn clasp and carrying a scroll of writing. He said to her softly,

"Ying'er, I'm the former bailiff. I can't tell you where I am now, but put out your hand and I'll give you something."

Ying'er extended her hand and something was put into it.

In an instant the man in the robe and belt was gone. When she looked at the thing in her hand she discovered that it was a bundle of loose silver. She went back to her house and knocked on the door to be greeted by her husband's voice.

"Love, why have you been so long at your former master's house?"

Ying'er replied,

"Let me tell you: when I went to my mistress to borrow rice, I found her door closed. I dared not knock for fear that she would be angry. When I started walking back I found the former bailiff standing on somebody's roof. He was in an official cap, red robe and belt. He gave me this packet of silver."

When Wang Xing heard this, he said,

"You bitch, telling me all of these lies. Who knows where you got this packet of silver from. Get in here."

As Ying'er entered Wang Xing said,

"Love, I remember what you said before about the apparition of the dead bailiff under the stove. There is something suspicious about all this. I spoke to you roughly now because I was afraid the neighbours would hear you. Now put the silver away and I'll go to the magistrate tomorrow and make a complaint about them."

In the morning Wang Xing thought better of the matter — "I can't inform on them for two reasons. First, Sun is the senior bailiff in the yamen, so I can't risk making an enemy of him. Secondly, there is no definite proof of foul play. The silver will be confiscated, and I'll be involved in a hopeless lawsuit. I'd better go and get a few pieces of clothing out of hock from the pawnshop and buy some cakes to send as a present to Bailiff Sun's house. Maybe then I'll find out what's going on."

Having made up his mind, Wang bought two packets of cakes and sent them to the bailiff's as a present. Then he and his wife changed into clean clothes and went to the bailiff's as well. When the wife saw them all done up and with presents, she asked,

"How did you suddenly come into money?"

Wang Xing replied,

"Yesterday I got a bit of work to do and made myself a couple of taels of silver. So I decided to send you a gift. I've also given up drinking and gambling."

The bailiff's wife said,

"Wang Xing, you can go back home alone. But let your wife stay here with me for a couple of days."

When Wang had gone, the bailiff's wife said to Ying'er,

"I have promised to offer incense tomorrow at the temple on the Eastern Mountain. Let us go together."

After saying this they both retired for the night.

The next morning they got up, washed and dressed. The bailiff went off to the yamen, and the wife locked up the house and went with Ying'er to the temple on Eastern Mountain, and made an offering of incense. Once they'd finished in the main hall, they offered incense to the deities in the corridors. When they reached the shrine of the Judges of the Dead, Ying'er's skirt belt was loose, and she stayed back to tighten it. Suddenly, one of the effigies there, a judge wearing an official cap, red robe and horn belt, called out to her,

"Ying'er, I am the former bailiff, you must avenge me. Here take this."

Ying'er took the object and looked at it, saying to herself,

"How odd, even an earthen deity can speak. Now why has he given me this?" She hastily pocketed it, not wishing the bailiff's wife to see it.

After they had offered incense they went home. Later she told her husband what had happened. When Wang Xing asked to look at the thing the deity had given her, he found that it was a sheet of paper on which was written:

The big Sun, the small Sun,
One enjoys the fruit grown by the other.

If you will know what happened at midnight,
Put aside the fire and examine the water beneath.
Next year in the second or third month
'Ju Yi' will come and solve it.

When Wang Xing read this, he was at a loss. He told Ying'er not to tell anyone about it and to wait until the second or third month of the next year to see what would happen.

In no time it was the second month of the new year and the local magistrate was replaced. The new magistrate was a native of Jindou City in Luzhou. His name was Bao Cheng, who later became very famous in popular tales.[6] Because he was later promoted to be an imperial doctor,[7] he was known as Dr. Bao. The appointment he got as magistrate in Fengfu was his first official post.

Even in his youth Magistrate Bao was wise and just. He could probe into men's secrets and solve difficult cases. He had been at his new post only three days, and had not yet started examining cases. On the third night he had a dream in which he was presiding in court, and there was a couplet[8] before him. It reads:

If you will know what happened at midnight,
Put aside the fire and examine the water beneath.

The next morning when he went to the court he called all his secretaries and asked them to solve the riddle of these two lines. But none knew what it meant. Then he asked for a plain placard and had the couplet written on it. Little Bailiff Sun happened to be the one who did the writing. Magistrate Bao added on in red ink that if anyone could solve this riddle they would be rewarded with ten taels of silver. Thereupon, the placard was hung on the yamen gate.

Very quickly the announcement was surrounded by both government workers and private citizens, all attracted by the promise of the reward, and straining to get a better view. Wang Xing was just buying some date cake to eat near the front of the yamen when he heard about the mysterious placard hung out by the magistrate. He went over to take a look and found that the two lines were the same as those on the piece of paper that the Judge of Hell had given Ying'er. Quite startled he thought to himself, "Now, if I tell the truth I might offend the new magistrate who seems to be a fairly odd fellow. Yet if I don't speak up no one else will ever solve the riddle." He bought the date cake he wanted, and went home to tell his wife all about what had happened.

On hearing this Ying'er said,

"The former bailiff has appeared to me three times and told me to avenge him. He's also given me a packet of silver, yet I've done nothing for him. If you don't go and tell what you know then the ghost may blame you for it."

However, Wang Xing could still not make up his mind. He returned to the gate of the yamen where he came across his neighbour Secretary Pei. Wang knew Pei to be a sensible fellow, so he pulled him into a quiet alleyway to ask him his advice.

Pei inquired,

"What have you done with the sheet of paper from the Judge of Hell?"

"It's hidden in my wife's clothes' chest."

"All right then, while I go and report what you've told me to the magistrate, you go home, get the sheet of paper and bring it to the yamen. When the magistrate calls for you, you can take it out as evidence."

Wang went straight home and Pei went into the yamen and waited until the judge had finished holding court and Bailiff Sun was not around. Then, kneeling down before the magistrate he cried,

"Your honour, my neighbour Wang Xing says he knows the origin of the two lines of writing on the placard. He says they come from a sheet of paper he was given by an image in the temple. There are other things on the paper as well, and the couplet you dreamt are but two lines of the whole."

The magistrate asked,

"Where is this man Wang Xing?"

"He has gone home to fetch the sheet of paper."

Magistrate Bao ordered his runners to bring Wang Xing to the court immediately.

When Wang Xing had returned home and opened his wife's suitcase to get the sheet of paper out, he was flabbergasted to find that it was now only a sheet of white paper with no writing on it at all; so he stayed at home worrying about what would happen, not daring to go to the yamen.

Then the magistrate's runners came and told him that the magistrate wanted to see him urgently. He had no choice but to go to the court with the runners, his sheet of white paper in hand. They went straight into the inner court. Magistrate Bao sent away all of his attendants, leaving him alone with Wang and Pei. He then asked Wang,

"Pei has told me that you've got a sheet of paper from the temple. Show it to me."

Wang Xing then knelt on the ground and kowtowed,

"My wife went to offer incense in the temple on Eastern Mountain. When she passed the images of the Judges of the Dead, one of the deities gave her a piece of paper on which were written a number of words. Two lines from that paper have now been written on your lordship's announcement board. I have kept the paper in a chest since then, and when I just went to get it out I discovered that all of the words have disappeared. So now it is just a blank piece of paper, and here it is."

Magistrate Bao took the paper and looked at it. He then asked,

"Do you remember the words that were on it?"

"Yes sir, I do." Wang replied.

He then told the magistrate what had been written on the paper while the magistrate took what he said down. He then pondered over the meaning of the words and called to Wang,

"Wang Xing, let me ask you: when that deity gave this paper to your wife, did he say anything?"

Wang answered,

"He only told her to avenge him."

Angry Bao thundered,

"Nonsense. Why should a deity want to be avenged by a mere human? Why should your wife be the one avenge him. That he should ask for your help. What type of rubbish are you trying to tell me?"

Wang hastily kowtowed and said,

"Your honour, there is a reason for all of this."

The magistrate replied,

"Then tell me in detail. If you speak with reason then you'll be rewarded. If not then you'll be the first to be flogged today."

Wang spoke,

"My wife Ying'er used to work in the house of the former Bailiff Sun of this district. A fortune-teller had told the bailiff that he would die at midnight of that day. As it turned out he really did die. Later on the mistress of the house married the present Bailiff Sun, and married Ying'er off to me. Before we were married my wife saw an apparition of the late bailiff in the kitchen of the Sun's house. The dead bailiff had a wooden well-frame on his neck, his hair was all dishevelled, his tongue protruding, and his eyes were dripping blood. He cried out to my wife,

'Ying'er, revenge your father.'

"Then another time when she passed the Sun's house at night she met the former bailiff again all dressed in official garb. On that occasion he gave her a packet of loose silver. The third time that he appeared was at the temple in the shrine of the Judges of the Dead. That time he gave her this sheet of paper and told her to revenge him. This judge looked just like the late Bailiff Sun, my wife's former master."

When Magistrate Bao heard this he laughed out loud and cried,

"So, that's it." Whereupon he called to his attendants to have Bailiff Sun and his wife brought before him.

When they arrived, the magistrate thundered,
"A fine thing you two have done."
The Bailiff declared,
"I haven't done anything wrong."
Then Magistrate Bao explained the words on the paper,
" 'Big Sun and Little Sun,' that obviously refers to the two bailiffs. 'He enjoys the fruit grown by the other,' that means you've taken his wife and are enjoying his properties.

" 'If you will know what happened at midnight, put aside the fire and examine the water beneath,' now the former bailiff died at midnight. The next line explains how he died. The servant Ying'er had seen her former master under the stove with dishevelled hair, tongue protruding and blood dripping from his eyes. These are the signs of one who has been strangled. He had a well-frame on his neck as well. The well is the water, and the stove is the fire. The water is beneath the fire so that must mean that the stove was built over the well, and the corpse of the murdered man must be in the well.

" 'Next year in the second or third month,' that means now. 'Ju Yi will come to solve this,' the characters *ju* (句) and *yi* (巳) when put together make the character *bao* (包). That means that my coming here as magistrate will lead to the solution of this riddle and revenge for the dead bailiff."

Bao then ordered his attendants to go with Wang Xing and Bailiff Sun to the Sun house to search under the stove. For he was sure there would be a strangled body there. Everyone was still fairly dubious, but when they got to the Sun residence, they pulled up the stove and the slab of stone under it to find a well. Workers were then called to drain the well, and a man was let down to see if there was anything there. Sure enough he came up with a corpse. When they examined it, some declared they could recognize the features of the dead Bailiff Sun. Still on the neck of the body was the silk cloth that had been used to strangle him. The new Bailiff Sun turned white and stood there speechless.

Everyone else was pretty startled as well.

The 'Little Bailiff Sun' had in fact originally been a beggar boy that the old bailiff had found unconscious in the snow one winter. Seeing that he was a fine looking lad, the old bailiff took him home and taught him to read and write. Little did he know that his wife would end up having an affair with him. The day the bailiff had come home after seeing the fortune-teller, the young lover was hiding in the house. When he heard that the old bailiff had been told he would die at midnight that night, the lovers used the opportunity to get him drunk and strangle him, throwing the corpse into the well. Meanwhile, the young man had put on white clothes and covered his face. He ran to the riverbank and threw in a large stone, making out that the bailiff had drowned himself. Then they set the stove over the well and got married with the guileless help of the matchmakers.

The discovery of the body was reported back to the magistrate and the guilty couple confessed to their crime without undergoing torture. As a result they were both condemned to death. Thus was the former Bailiff Sun revenged. Nor did the magistrate break his word as regards the reward, and he gave Wang Xing ten taels of silver. Wang gave Secretary Bei three taels for his services. Having successfully solved this mysterious case in his first posting, Magistrate Bao's fame quickly spread throughout the empire. Even today people talk about him as a judge of men by day, and a judge of ghosts by night.

Notes:

1. The capital of the Northern Song dynasty, Kaifeng (or Bianzhou), was also popularly know as the Eastern Capital (Dongjing).

2. Fortune telling and the drawing up of a person's astrological chart required the year, month, day and exact hour of the birth of the person concerned. This information is called the 'eight characters' (*bazi*) of a person. For any important undertaking, an astrological calculation would have to be made on the basis of the 'eight characters' of the person.

3. The Judge or King of the Dead (*Yan wang* or *Yanluo wang*, from the Sanskrit *Yamarajá*) presided over the nether world. As judge of the dead he would sentence the deceased according to the number of good or bad acts they had done during their lives.

4. A servant would be completely bound to the master by both financial and moral ties. This relationship, though often cruel and exploitative, was usually expressed in terms of parent-child affection.

5. This is brightly coloured paper, usually red, with flecks of other colours on it. New Year cards are still written on such paper, as are wedding agreements and invitations.

6. Bao Cheng or Bao Qingtian (literally, 'Bao Clear-sky'), is a legendary figure embodying the spirit of traditional wisdom and justice. Tales surrounding Judge Bao have given rise to a considerable body of literature related to the many mysterious and deceptive cases the judge presided over and unravelled.

7. This refers to the scholars who became members of the Longtu Pavilion Imperial Academy established during the Song dynasty.

8. Couplets (*duilian*) were and are very common in China. They are written both as a literary exercise and for decoration. An appropriate couplet is sometimes seen as the best way to send a message or to comment on an inspiring scenic view or monument.

賣油郎獨佔花魁

The Oil Vendor
and
the Courtesan

from Tales to Awaken the World

At the time of the Song Dynasty in Anle Village outside Kaifeng, capital of the northern empire, lived a man called Xin Shan whose wife's maiden name was Yuan. They kept a grocery shop and made a comfortable living by selling grain, as well as flour, beans, tea, wine, oil, salt and other commodities. Xin Shan was over forty, but he had no sons and one daughter only — Yaoqin — a pretty and intelligent child. Sent to the village school at the age of seven, she soon became a great reader. At ten, she could compose poems. And at twelve she was an accomplished lyrist, chess-player, calligrapher and painter; while the skill with which she plied her needle astounded all who saw her. All these arts came to her naturally.

Since Xin Shan had no son, he looked forward to being supported by a son-in-law in his old age. But in view of his daughter's brilliance it was no easy matter to find a suitable husband for her; so he refused all the overtures of marriage that were made. Just at this time the Golden Tartars invaded China and besieged Kaifeng;[1] and, although reinforcements could have been summoned to the rescue of the capital, the prime minister, set on surrender, forbade them to advance.

Then the enemy's power increased, the capital was taken by storm, the emperor and his son were captured, and the people outside the city — frightened out of their wits — left their homes and fled with their old folk and children for their lives.

Xin Shan made off like the other refugees with his wife and twelve-year-old daughter, carrying their baggage on their backs. Fearfully as stray dogs, swiftly as fish escaping from the net, through cold and hunger they pushed desperately on. They were not overtaken by the Tartars; but they met some defeated government troops.

"The Tartars are coming!" cried these soldiers when they saw refugees with bundles on their backs. And they started fires to terrify the people.

Dusk fell as the panic-stricken fugitives scattered in all directions, each concerned only for himself; and the troops seized this opportunity to loot, killing those who refused to part with their goods. Thus confusion was added to confusion and sorrow piled on sorrow.

Pushed and jostled by the troops, Yaoqin fell down; and by the time she struggled to her feet her parents had disappeared. Not daring to call out, she passed the night by some deserted graves at the roadside; but the next morning when she came out of hiding there was nothing to be seen save wind-swept dust and corpses strewing the road. All the refugees with whom they had travelled the previous day had disappeared. Yaoqin cried bitterly for her parents, but did not know now to find them. She could only press on southwards, sobbing as she went. Hungry and wretched, she had walked less than a mile when she saw a mud hut and decided to ask there for a drink of water. When she reached the hovel, however, she found it dilapidated and deserted, its inmates having long since fled. Then she sat down by the mud wall and cried as if her heart would break.

At this juncture, as luck would have it, who should come by but one of Xin's neighbours! This was Bu Qiao, a loafer and wastrel. The government troops had separated him from the rest of his party too, so he was travelling alone; and when he heard sobbing he hurried over to see what was the matter.

Yaoqin had known this man since she was a child, and in her loneliness and distress any neighbour looked like a friend. Drying her eyes, she rose to greet him.

"Have you seen my parents, uncle?" she asked.

"Yesterday those soldiers stole my baggage, and I have very little money left," thought Bu. "Here is a heaven-sent means of support! She's worth her weight in gold."

"Your parents are very upset to have lost you," he lied. "They have gone on ahead; but they told me, 'If you find our daughter, be sure to bring her back to us.' And they promised to reward me well."

Though Yaoqin was an intelligent child, distress had made her over-credulous, and quite trustingly she attached herself to Bu.

"Your parents are travelling day and night," he told the girl, when he had fed her with some of his provisions. "If we can't overtake them on the road, we shall have to cross the river to Chiankang to find them. While we are travelling I shall treat you as my daughter and you had better call me your father; otherwise people may think I have been kidnapping little girls who have lost their way, and that wouldn't look good, would it?"

To this Yaoqin agreed; thus whether travelling on foot or by boat they passed for father and daughter. Upon reaching Chiangkang they learned that the Fourth Prince of the Tartars was about to lead troops across the river; so, fearing that Chiankang would not be safe and knowing that Prince Kang had ascended the throne at Hangzhou, now renamed Lin'an, they took a junk to Runzhou, then travelled by way of Suzhou, Changzhou, Jiading and Huzhou to the southern capital, where they put up at an inn.

Now in the course of this thousand-mile journey from Kaifeng to Lin'an, Bu had spent all his silver — he was even reduced to handing over his coat to settle the score at the last inn. All he had left was Yaoqin, and, eager to sell this living merchandise, as soon as he heard that a bawd at the West Lake named Mrs. Wang was buying girls, he brought her to the inn to inspect his goods and offer a price. In view of Yaoqin's good looks, Mrs. Wang agreed to pay fifty ounces of silver for her. Immediately Bu accepted the money and escorted the girl to the bawd's house.

"This is my own daughter, and it breaks my heart to have to part with her," the cunning man told Mrs. Wang. "If you treat her gently, she will do as you want; but you must be patient with her."

To the girl he said: "Mrs. Wang is a relative of mine. I am leaving you with her for the time being while I go to look for your parents; then I shall come to fetch you."

So Yaoqin went to Mrs. Wang quite happily.

Mrs. Wang made Yaoqin new clothes and lodged her in an inner chamber, giving her good food and tea every day and speaking to her so kindly that she soon felt quite at home. But when several days had passed with no news from Bu Qiao, Yaoqin started longing for her parents again, and with tears in her eyes asked Mrs. Wang:

"Why doesn't Uncle Bu come back?"

"What Uncle Bu?"

"The Mr. Bu who brought me here."

"He told me he was your father."

"His name is Bu, but mine is Xin."

Then she related how after losing her parents in their flight from the capital she had met Bu, who had reassured her and brought her to Lin'an.

"Well, I never!" exclaimed Mrs. Wang. "So you're an orphan, a crab without claws! I may as well tell you the truth: that fellow Bu has sold you to me for fifty ounces of silver. We are in the courtesan business here, and I already have three or four girls — none of them very much to look at. Because I've taken a fancy to you I mean to treat you as my own child; and once you grow up I guarantee you will live on the fat of the land."

When Yaoqin realized that Bu had deceived her, she burst out crying and for a long time was inconsolable.

After that Mrs. Wang gave her a new name, Wang Mei, and everybody in the house called her by this name. Taught music, dancing and singing, she excelled in all these arts; and by the time she was fourteen she was so lovely that all the young gallants of Lin'an brought her rich presents, marvelling at her beauty. There were others who admired genius in a woman, and when it was known that she was a skilled calligrapher and writer, every day men thronged the door asking for her calligraphy or poems. So she grew famous, and became known as The Flower Queen. And some young men on the West Lake composed the following verses about her:

> What other maid can compare with The Flower Queen?
> She is poetess, painter, skilled calligrapher,
> And unequalled too in dancing, singing and music.
> We often compare the West Lake to the beauty Xi Shi[3];
> But no beauty of old can compare with this worlderful girl.
> Happy the man who is lucky enough to possess her!
> Who would not be willing to die for such delight?

Since Yaoqin was so famous, by the time she was fourteen men came to negotiate for the first night with her; but she refused them all. As for Mrs. Wang, she valued the girl as if she were made of gold, so when she saw that The Flower Queen was unwilling, she dared not cross her.

Another year passed. Mrs. Wang asked Yaoqin to receive clients, but the girl was adamant.

"I will agree to it only after I have seen my parents and gained their consent," she declared.

While secretly indignant, Mrs. Wang did not want to offend the girl, so she let the matter drop. One day, however, a rich man named Jin offered three hundred taels of silver for the first night with The Flower Queen, and this great sum of money induced Mrs. Wang to think of a plan, to which Jin agreed. On the evening of the Moon Festival,[4] The Flower Queen was invited to the West Lake to watch the tide from a boat. Then three or four of the bawd's accomplices played drinking games with the girl until she was drunk, after which they carried her back to Mrs. Wang's house and laid her on the bed; and when she woke at dawn the next day she realized that she had been tricked into losing her maidenhood. Lamenting her unhappy fate she rose and dressed, then threw herself down on a bamboo couch near the bed with her face to the wall and wept silently. When Mr. Jin came up to her, she scratched his face till the blood came. And since this was more than he had bargained for, he took his leave as soon as it was light. By the time Mrs. Wang emerged from her room to beg him to stay, he was gone.

Now it is customary for men who enjoy the first night with a courtesan to receive congratulations from the girl's mistress the next morning, and for all the other bawds to compliment him too. There is usually feasting for several days, while the young man often stays in the house for one or two months, or at least twenty days or a fortnight. So Mr. Jin's departure so early the next morning was quite unheard of. Uttering exclamations of dismay, Mrs. Wang threw on her clothes and hurried upstairs, where she found Yaoqin lying on the couch bathed in tears. Because she wanted to induce the girl to accept more clients, Mrs. Wang apologized profusely; but The Flower Queen said not a word, and finally the bawd had to leave her alone.

Yaoqin cried for a whole day, took neither bite nor sup, and declared that she was too ill to go downstairs or see callers. Mrs. Wang had no patience with such behaviour and wanted to punish her, but feared this would only make the high-spirited girl more stubborn. Yet if she gave way to her, instead of making money Yaoqin would receive no one, in which case she would be useless even if she stayed there for a hundred years. After racking her brains fruitlessly for several days, Mrs. Wang remembered a sworn sister of hers, Mrs. Liu, who was a frequent visitor to her house.

"Mrs. Liu has the gift of the gab, and she's on good terms with Yaoqin," thought the bawd. "I'll ask her to speak to the girl. If she can make her see reason, so much the better!"

She sent a maid to invite Mrs. Liu over; and when her friend had arrived and sat down in the front room, Mrs. Wang explained her problem.

"I can make even angels and goddesses lovesick," declared Mrs. Liu. "Just leave this to me."

"If you can do this," said Mrs. Wang, "I'll gladly kowtow to you. Have some more tea before you go to see her, so that talking won't make you thirsty."

"My mouth is like the sea," boasted the other "I can talk all day without feeling dry."

After a few cups of tea Mrs. Liu went to the inner quarters, where she found Yaoqin's door locked. She knocked lightly and called: "Niece!"

Recognizing Mrs. Liu's voice, Yaoqin opened the door and they greeted each other. Then Mrs. Liu sat down beside the girl at the table on which she noticed a piece of silk with a woman's face drawn but not yet coloured on it.

"What a wonderful sketch!" she cried. "How clever you are! Lucky Mrs. Wang, to get such an intelligent girl as you — so good-looking and so accomplished! One could offer thousands of ounces of gold and search the whole capital without finding another like you."

"Don't tease!" protested Yaoqin. "What good wind has blown you here today?"

"I've been wanting to call for a long time," replied Mrs. Liu, "but there's too much to do at home. I made time today, though, to come over and congratulate you, because I hear you are a woman now."

Yaoqin blushed scarlet and lowered her head without a

word. Knowing that she felt ashamed, Mrs. Liu moved her chair nearer and took the girl's hand.

"You're not a soft-shelled egg, child," she said. "Why be so squeamish? If you remain so bashful, how are you to make big money?"

"What do I need money for?"

"Even if you don't want money, child, your mistress expects a return on all she's spent on bringing you up. Those who live by a mountain depend on the mountain for a living, and those who live by water depend on the water. Not one of Mrs. Wang's other girls is a patch on you. You're the best melon in her garden, and she treats you better than the rest. An intelligent girl like you should understand that. Yet I hear since you had your first customer you've been refusing to see anybody else. What do you mean by such behaviour? Who would feed silkworms mulberry leaves if they refused to spin silk? Since your mistress shows you special consideration, you should do something for her too, instead of giving the other girls reason to find fault."

"Let them find fault. What do I care?"

"Well, of course, talk is a small matter. But don't you know our ways?"

"What do you mean?"

"You girls are food, clothes and money to people in our profession. When we are lucky enough to get a good-looker, it's like a rich family acquiring a good piece of land. If the girl is still young, we hope she will grow up quickly; because once she's had her first man she's like a crop ready to be harvested — we can expect the money to start rolling in! As one man leaves by the back, another comes in by the front. Mr. Zhang sends rice, Mr. Li fuel; and clients just flock to our doors. That's what we call a successful house."

"You make me blush," said Yaoqin. "I'm not going to do anything like that."

Putting her hand to her mouth, Mrs. Liu crowed with laughter.

"You're not, eh?" she cried. "You won't have any say in the matter, miss! Mrs. Wang is head of this house, and if you don't obey her she can beat you within an inch of your life. Then you'll have to do as she wants. Your mistress has never treated you harshly because you're intelligent and pretty and used to kindness and she wanted to save your face and leave you some self-respect. But just now she was telling me that you don't appreciate your own luck: you don't know that eiderdowns are light and millstones heavy. So now she's angry and has asked me to speak to you. If you persist in being stubborn she may lose her temper, and then you'll be cursed and beaten. You can't escape. But don't make a bad start; because once you begin wrangling you may go on all day and every day, until you can't stand it any more and have to receive men. By then, though, you'll have lost your privileged position and the other girls will laugh at you. Take my advice: since you're in her power, you'd better do as your mistress says; then you'll find life very pleasant."

"I belong to a good family," said Yaoqin. "I was tricked into coming to this brothel. If you'll help me to find a proper husband, aunty, you'll be doing a better deed than building a nine-storeyed pagoda. But I'd rather die than prostitute myself."

"To get married is only right and proper, child," replied Mrs. Liu. "Of course I won't gainsay that. But there are different kinds of marriage."

"What do you mean by different kinds of marriage?"

"There's true marriage, sham marriage, sad marriage and happy marriage; there are marriages that are timely and marriages of necessity; marriages that end well and marriages that end badly. Now, child, be patient while I explain this to you.

"What do we mean by true marriage? Well, the ideal match is between a brilliant scholar and a beautiful girl; but such marriages are rare. When two such people meet and fall in love, they can't bear to be separated for a moment and long to marry each other. They are like two moths clinging together till death. This is true marriage.

"What is sham marriage? It's when a young man loves a girl who doesn't want to marry him, but tricks him into spending a lot of money on her. When the wedding day is fixed, she backs out. But though the fool knows that she doesn't love him, he insists on marrying her and offers her mistress a bribe she can't resist, so that the girl's wishes are over-ridden. Carried against her will to his house, she deliberately breaks the family rules, makes scenes or even carried on with other men, until her husband finds it impossible to keep her. In six months or a year he lets her go back to the brothel. Such a marriage is just a way of making money; that's why we call it sham.

"What is a sad marriage? It's when a man loves a girl who doesn't care for him, and uses his position to force the mistress of the house— who is afraid of trouble — to consent to the match. With tears in her eyes, the girl is compelled to go with him. But once in his house she feels as if she were at the bottom of the ocean, for his family rules are so strict that she dare not lift her head; and she leads a miserable life, half as concubine half as servant. This is a sad marriage.

"What is happy marriage then? It's when a girl can choose her husband and has come across someone rich and gentle, whose wife is kind too but has no children. He takes the girl in the hope that she will bear him a son; and if she does, she is treated as one of the mistresses of the family. So she has a comfortable life and good prospects. That is a happy marriage.

"What is meant by a marriage which is timely? It's when a courtesan who is still famous and sought after has had her fill of love and pleasure and chooses a really satisfactory husband. By stopping at the height of her success, she can make sure that no one will despise her. Such a marriage is timely.

"What is a marriage of necessity? It's when a girl has no desire to get married, but is forced to by the authorities, blackmailed into it, or disposed of in payment of a debt. In such cases she has no choice but to marry, whether the man is good or not; and all she can hope for is peace and quiet and a roof over her head. This is a marriage of necessity.

"What do I mean by a marriage that ends well? It's when a courtesan who is no longer young and has been through a great deal meets an honest fellow, and they are attracted to each other. Then she may hoist sail and go to live with him till old age. This is marriage that ends well.

"What do I mean by a marriage that ends badly? It's when a couple fall passionately in love, only to cool before long. Or when a man's parents are difficult or his wife jealous, so that after several quarrels he sends the girl back and demands the return of his dowry. Or when the man becomes too poor to keep her, so that if she can't bear hardships she must leave him and take up her old trade again. These are marriages which turn out badly."

"What must I do now if I want to marry?" asked Yaoqin.

"Listen to me, child, and I'll tell you."

"I shall be indebted to you for ever for your advice."

"Marriage is a serious step," began Mrs. Liu. "Besides, you have already slept with a man, so that even if you marry tonight you won't be a virgin. It was a mistake to come here at all, but that was your fate; and now that your mistress has been to so much trouble to bring you up, she certainly isn't going to let you go until you have helped her for a few years and earned her a few thousand taels of silver. Besides, before marrying you must find a good man. You wouldn't want an ugly, stinking fellow, would you? But if you don't receive clients, how are you to find a man you like? If you refuse to admit anyone, your mistress will be forced to find some rich man to buy you as his concubine. That is another kind of marriage. But your husband may be old or ugly, or some illiterate country bully, in which case you will lead a wretched life. It would be better for you to be thrown into the river, for then at least there would be a splash and people would pity you. So I advise you to do as your mistress says and receive clients. Since you are so beautiful and accomplished, ordinary fellows won't dare approach you, but only the sons of rich and aristocratic families who won't disgrace you. While you enjoy love and pleasure in your youth you will be helping your mistress in her business, and putting something aside so that you don't have to ask help from anyone in future. Then, in five or ten years, when you come across someone you like, I shall act as your go-between and see that you marry in style; and by that time Mrs. Wang will be willing to let you go. Isn't this best for both parties?"

When Yaoqin smiled and said nothing, Mrs. Liu realized that she was convinced.

"It's sound advice I've been giving you," she concluded. "You'll live to thank me for it." Then she rose to go.

Mrs. Wang outside the door had heard every word and when the girl saw Mrs. Liu out and came face to face with her own mistress, she retreated blushing into her room. The two bawds returned to the front of the house and sat down.

"She's a very stubborn girl," said Mrs. Liu. "But thanks to my persuasion the iron is melting. If you lose no time in finding another client for her, she should be agreeable; and then I shall come again to congratulate you."

Mrs. Wang thanked her friend profusely, and treated her to a meal and wine before letting her go.

After her talk with Mrs. Liu, Yaoqin accepted customers willingly; and soon so many were flocking to her she had not a moment to herself. She became so famous that Mrs. Wang charged ten taels of silver for a night with her; but even at that price men fought for her. Mrs. Wang was overjoyed to be making so much money, and Yaoqin was looking hard for a man she could love; but not one could she discover. As the proverb says: 'It is easier to find a priceless jewel than a true lover.'

Our story brings us now to an old man named Zhu who kept an oil shop outside Qingbo Gate in Hangzhou. Three years before this he had adopted a young refugee from Kaifeng called Qin Zhong. This lad's mother had died when he was a child; and when he was thirteen his father, Qin Liang, had abandoned him to become a monk at Tian Zhu Monastery. A childless widower, Old Zhu treated Qin Zhong as his own son, changing his name to Zhu Zhong and keeping him in the shop to learn the trade. And at first all went well. But then Old Zhu developed kidney trouble, which meant that instead of working he had to sit or lie down all the time; so he engaged an assistant named Xin Quan to help with the business.

Four years passed in a flash, until Zhong was a handsome young man of seventeen; but though of age, he had not married. A maid of over twenty in the household, called Orchid, had her eye on him and tried several times to hook him; but he was an honest lad. Besides, she was such an ugly slut that he was not interested. So one side was willing but the other was not.

When Orchid saw that she had made no impression on the young man, she started angling for the assistant, Xin Quan. A bachelor of nearly forty, he jumped at the bait at once and often lay with the maid in secret. Later however, they felt Zhong was in their way, and plotted together to have him driven out.

One day, the picture of injured innocence, Orchid complained to Old Zhu: "Master Zhong has tried several times to seduce me. He's a bad young fellow."

Old Zhu had trifled with the maid himself, so he could not avoid a twinge of jealousy.

Then Xin Quan stole some silver from the shop.

"Master Zhong has been gambling outside," he told the old man. "He has taken money several times from the till."

At first Old Zhu did not believe them. But because he was growing senile they succeeded in convincing him. Then he called Zhong and rated him soundly.

Zhong was smart enough to realize that he had Xin Quan and Orchid to thank for this. But any attempt to clear himself would only stir up trouble and, if Old Zhu did not believe him, would make matters worse. He took another line.

"There is not enough business to keep both Mr. Xin and me busy," he said to Old Zhu. "Let him look after the shop while I go out as an oil vendor. The money I make every day should double our turnover."

The old man would have agreed but for Xin Quan.

"It's not that he wants to be an oil vendor," said Xin, "but after stealing from you all these years he has quite a tidy sum tucked away. And because he bears you a grudge for not finding him a wife, he doesn't want to work here. He would like to set up on his own, so that he can marry and start a family."

"I've treated him as my own child, but he has no sense of gratitude," sighed Old Zhu. "May Heaven curse him! Very well. Since he is not my own son and we don't seem able to get on together, I had better let him go."

He gave Zhong three taels of silver and told him to go away, letting him take his clothes and bedding, however, which shows that after all the old man had a kind heart. When Zhong saw that his foster-father would not keep him any longer, he bowed four times and left, sobbing bitterly.

Now when Zhong's father left for Tian Zhu Monastery, he had not told his son where he was going; so as soon as the lad quit Old Zhu's house he rented a small room by Zhongan Bridge, put down his luggage there, bought a padlock and locked the door, then trudged through the highways and byways in search of his father. But after searching several days to no purpose, he had to give up. During his four years in Old Zhu's house, the lad had been so loyal to his foster-father that he had not put by a cent for himself; hence all he possessed was the three taels given him when he left, and this was not enough to start any business. After cudgelling his brains, he decided that since oil was the only trade with which he was familiar, and the oil shops knew him, that would be the safest trade for him. So he bought a pole and casks, and spent what was left of his money on oil.

The merchant who sold oil to Zhu knew Zhong for an honest fellow, and pitied him because another man's slander had cost the lad his job as shop assistant and reduced him to selling oil in the streets. To help him, this merchant chose the purest oil for him and gave him better weight than anyone else; and with these advantages Zhong was able to give his customers better measure too. So he sold more oil than other vendors, and made a profit every day. But he lived frugally, saving his money or using it only to buy necessities. The one thing that worried him was the thought of his father.

"My foster-father changed my name to Zhu," he reflected. "How can people know that my real name is Qin? If my father looks for me, he won't be able to find me."

So he decided to use his original surname once more.

If an upper-class gentleman with a fine future wants to change his name, he can send a petition to the government or notify the Board of Ceremony or the Imperial College, for then an announcement will be put on the census list so that everybody knows of it. But how was a mere oil vendor to make his change of name known? Zhong found a way. In large characters he wrote 'Qin' on one of his oil containers and 'Kaifeng' on the other, so that all could tell his surname and place of origin. And eventually everybody in the market came to know him by his true name, calling him Oil Vendor Qin.

It was then early spring, when the weather was neither too hot nor too cold. Hearing that there was to be a nine-day mass in Zhao Qing Monastery and calculating that a great deal of oil would be needed, thither Zhong carried his casks.

And the monks, who knew his name and had heard that his oil was better and cheaper than anyone else's, gave him all their custom. So for nine days in succession Zhong carried his wares to the monastery.

It was fine on the ninth day when Zhong carried his empty casks out of the monastery, and there were many sightseers about. Walking along the lake-side, the young man feasted his eyes on the peach blossom, willows and painted barges with flutes and drums which were plying to and fro on the lake. And presently he set down his casks and pole in a clearing to the right of the monastery, and sat on a rock to rest. Nearby, overlooking the lake, was a house with a fence and a gilded gate behind which grew some dwarf bamboos enclosed by a vermilion balustrade; while the front court, which was all that could be seen of the interior, was neat and clean. From this house now emerged several men in caps, accompanied by a girl. When they reached the gate the men bowed and walked off, and the girl went in again.

Zhong's eyes had been riveted upon this girl, for never in his life had he seen so dainty a beauty. He sat there like one in a dream, unable to move. The simple lad had no experience of courtesans, and he was just wondering whose house this could be when a middle-aged woman and her maid came out.

"I was just going to send out for some oil!" exclaimed the woman at the sight of his casks. "And here is an oil vendor. Let's buy from him."

Then the maid walked over.

"Are you selling oil?" she asked.

"I've none left, ma'am," replied Zhong. "But I can bring you some tomorrow."

The maid could read, so when she saw the characters on the casks, she told her mistress: "This oil vendor's name is Qin."

The woman had heard of this honest Oil Vendor Qin.

"We need oil every day," she told him. "If you will bring

it here, we shall buy from you."

"Thank you, ma'am," replied Zhong. "I'll come without fail."

Then the woman and her maid went in.

"I wonder what relation that woman is to the girl?" mused Zhong. "I don't care if I make no profit each time I come, so long as I can have a good look at that girl."

He was picking up his pole to go, when a sedan chair with a blue silk canopy and two pages running behind it stopped at the gilded door. The chair was set down, and the two pages went into the house.

"Strange," thought Zhong. "Whom are they coming to fetch?"

Presently two maids came out, carrying a bundle in a crimson rug and an inlaid bamboo box. When they had given these to the chair bearers to put under the seat, the wonderful girl came out. At her heels were the two pages, one with a lyre in a case, the other with some scrolls and a jasper flute hanging from his wrist. The girl mounted the chair and the bearers carried it once again along the way they had come, while the maid and pages followed behind. After this second and closer look, Zhong wondered even more who the girl could be as he walked slowly off, his pole over his shoulder.

A few paces brought him to a tavern by the lake. He seldom drank, but today the sight of the girl had filled him with a pleasant melancholy; so putting down his pole he walked into the tavern, chose a table for one and sat down.

"Will there be other guests, sir?" asked the waiter. "Or are you drinking alone?"

"I am on my own," replied Zhong. "Bring the best wine you have and some fresh nuts. I don't want any meat dishes."

As the waiter was pouring wine for him, Zhong asked: "Whose is that house over there with the gilded gate?"

"That is Lord Qi's house," was the reply. "A Mrs. Wang is living there now."

"Who is the girl who just went by in that sedan chair?"

"That is the famous courtesan Yaoqin whom people call The Flower Queen. She comes from Kaifeng, but was stranded here. She is good at music, singing, dancing, chess, lyre-playing, calligraphy and painting; and she receives only grandees. A night with her costs at least ten taels of silver; so ordinary fellows don't get a look in. She used to live outside Yongjin Gate, but the place was too small; and six months ago Lord Qi, who is a friend of hers, lent them this house and garden."

When Zhong heard that The Flower Queen came from the north too, he was reminded of his old home and felt even more drawn to her. After drinking a few cups, he paid the bill, took up his pole and left.

"What a pity that a beautiful girl like that should become a courtesan!" he thought. "If she hadn't, though," he reflected with a smile, "I would never have seen her. Life is short" — his imagination was running away with him — "and if I could hold such a beautiful girl in my arms for one night, I would die content. But even if I peddle oil all day, I make only a few cents. She's not for the likes of me. I'm worse than the toad in the cesspool who longed to eat a swan. All her friends are young noblemen. Even if I saved enough silver, she would turn me away because I'm only an oil vendor."

But then he thought: "I've heard that the mistresses of such houses will do anything for money. They would admit even a beggar if he could pay, so why not a respectable tradesman? Yes, if I had the silver, I'm sure they'd accept me! . . . . . The question is — how to get it?"

So he muttered to himself all the way back, giving free rein to his fancy.

Was there ever such a madman? A small tradesman whose whole capital was barely three taels of silver — how could he dream of spending ten taels for one night with a famous courtesan? But where there's a will there's a way. After long consideration he came to a decision.

"Starting from tomorrow, when I've got back my outlay I'll put what's pure profit aside," he vowed. "If I make one cent's profit a day, in a year I shall have three taels and sixty cents; and in three years I shall have enough. If I make two cents a day, I shall need only a year and a half. If I make more, I shall have the sum in about a year."

Occupied with these thoughts he reached home, unlocked his door and went in. But after the daydreams in which he had indulged on the road, the sight of his bed filled him with melancholy; and he lay himself down without any supper to toss sleepless through the night, thinking of the beautiful girl.

At dawn Zhong rose to fill his casks and breakfast, then locked his door and carried his oil to Mrs. Wang's house. Once at her gate, however, he dared not go in, simply putting his head inside to look round. Mrs. Wang, who had just risen but not yet combed her hair, was telling her maid what provisions to buy. And, recognizing her voice, Zhong called her name.

When the bawd saw who it was, she laughed.

"Good man!" she cried, "you have kept your word."

Then calling him in, she bought a jarful of oil — about five catties. She offered a fair price, and when Zhong did not dispute it she was very pleased with him.

"This jar will not last more than two days," she said. "If you come every other day. I won't buy from anyone else."

Zhong assented, shouldered his load and left, regretting that he had not seen the girl. He was happy, though, to have made a regular customer of Mrs. Wang, for that meant that although he had not seen The Flower Queen this time, he might see her the next time or the time after. Still, to go all that way just for one customer was not good business.

"Zhao Qing Monastery is near here," he thought. "And though they aren't celebrating any special mass, they must need oil just the same. I had better take my casks there. If I get several customers, I can sell all my oil in one trip."

The monks were very pleased to see him. They all bought from him, and Zhong arranged to bring them oil every other day. As that day was an even number, he decided to come out this way on the days which had even numbers, and to sell his oil in the city on the odd days. After this, whenever Zhong left the city he made straight for Mrs. Wang's house, ostensibly to sell oil but actually to see The Flower Queen. Sometimes he saw her and sometimes he did not. When he missed her it made him sad; yet seeing he made him sad too, for then he longed for her all the more.

After he had been there several times, everybody in Mrs. Wang's household knew Qin the Oil Vendor. Soon more than a year had passed, and every day Zhong put aside some pure silver — sometimes three cents, sometimes two, never less than one — and when he had a certain amount he made it up into a packet. Bit by bit he accumulated a large parcel of silver, how much exactly he did not know.

One day — it was an odd day and raining so heavily that Zhong could not do business — pleased at the sight of his big bundle of silver, he decided to have it weighed and see how much it came to. Taking an umbrella, he walked to the silversmith's across the road and asked if he could borrow their scales.

"How much silver can an oil vendor have?" thought the silversmith, eyeing him contemptuously. "The small balance for less than five taels will be more than enough for him!"

But when Zhong undid his bundle and showed his silver — which being in pieces looked even more than it was — the silversmith, who was a mean, obsequious fellow, regarded him quite differently.

"It's true that you can't judge by appearances!" he thought.

Hastily setting up the balance, he produced all his weights, large as well as small. And Zhong found that he had exactly sixteen taels, not a cent more, not a cent less: in other words, a whole catty!

"If I set aside three taels as capital," though Zhong, "I shall still have more than enough for a night in the courtesans' house. But if I gave them all this loose silver, they will laugh at me. I'll have it cast into ingots while I'm here. That will look better."

He weighted out ten taels for a large ingot, and one tael and eightly cents for a small one, then paid the silversmith with a piece from the four taels and twenty cents that were left. After this, he laid out a few dozen cents on new shoes, socks and a new cap, went home to wash and starch his gown, and last of all bought some Persian incense to scent his clothes. On the next fine day he dressed himself up.

He put the silver in his sleeve, locked his room and went straight to Mrs. Wang's house, feeling as if he were walking on air. But once at her gate his courage failed him.

"I usually come with my pedlar's kit to sell oil. How can I explain that I'm here today as a customer?" he wondered.

As he stood there hesitating, the gate creaked and Mrs. Wang came out.

"Aren't you doing business today, Master Qin?" she asked. "Where are you off to, dressed up so smartly?"

Zhong had to pluck up courage to step forward and bow, and Mrs. Wang returned his greeting.

"I have come specially to see you, ma'am," he murmured.

The bawd was experienced enough to read his mind.

"Here is Qin Zhong all dressed up and paying me a visit," she thought. "He must have taken a fancy to one of my girls; I suppose he wants to spend a night or an hour with her. Well, he's no millionaire, but whatever's in the basket can be used as food. We can make enough out of him to buy garlic."

So, beaming she asked: "Are you giving us your patronage, Master Qin?"

"I want to make a bold request. But I don't know how

to begin."

"Don't be afraid. Come in and sit down, then we can talk."

Though Zhong had often been to the house to sell oil, this was the first time he had been offered a seat. But since he was here today as a client, Mrs. Wang took him to the reception room, made him sit in the place of honour, and called for tea. When the maid came in with tea, she was so surprised to see Qin the Oil Vendor here as a guest that she lowered her head to giggle.

"What are you sniggering at?" demanded Mrs. Wang. "Where are your manners?"

Then, with a straight face, the maid carried out the used cups.

"Now, Master Qin," prompted Mrs. Wang. "What was it you wanted to say?"

"I just wanted to invite one of your young ladies to have a drink with me."

"Nothing but a drink? Surely you want to make love to her too!" declared the bawd. "You are an honest fellow — what put such romantic ideas into your head?"

"I have been dreaming of this for a long time."

"Well, you know all my girls. Which one do you fancy?"

"I want to spend one night with The Flower Queen."

"Don't talk nonsense!" Mrs. Wang was annoyed, for she could not believe he was serious. "Are you trying to make fun for me?"

"I mean what I say," protested Zhong. "I wouldn't lie to you."

"Even a chamber pot has ears: haven't you heard what her price is? All your oil couldn't buy half a night with her! You had better pick one of the others."

"Whew! True sales talks!" Zhong showed his tongue incredulously. "May I know how many thousand taels you ask for a night with The Flower Queen?"

When Mrs. Wang saw that he was joking, her face cleared.

"Not so much!" she said with a laugh. "Only ten taels, plus miscellaneous expenses."

"That's nothing, then," replied Zhong, and produced from his sleeve the large ingot of bright silver. "Here is a good ten taels for you. And here" — handing her the smaller ingot — "is about two taels with which I'll trouble you to prepare a meal. If you will help me, I shall be indebted to you for ever and shan't forget to show my gratitude."

Mrs. Wang was unable to resist the large ingot. Fearing, however, that the oil vendor was acting on a sudden impulse which he might regret later, she felt she should sound him out.

"It's not easy for a tradesman to save up ten taels of silver," she said. "You had better think again."

"My mind is made up," replied Zhong. "Don't worry, ma'am."

"Even so," said Mrs. Wang, as she put the silver in her sleeve, "there are other difficulties."

"What difficulties can there be since you are mistress of the house?"

"The young gentlemen who come to see The Flower Queen are from rich and aristocratic families. They are all scholars too; there's not an ordinary citizen among them. If she recognizes you as Master Qin the Oil Vendor, she will never receive you!"

"Please think of some way to get round her, ma'am," he begged. "If you help me I shall never forget your kindness."

When Mrs. Wang saw how determined he was, she frowned thoughtfully.

"I have it!" she cried at last with a smile. "With any luck you may succeed; but if you fail don't blame me. The Flower Queen hasn't come back yet from a feast she went to yesterday in Academician Li's house. Today Lord Huang has invited her to go boating. Tomorrow Mr. Zhang the poet and some others are asking her to a poetry meeting; and the day after was booked by Minister Han's son some time ago. So you'd better come the day after that. And you'll make a better impression if you don't come here this week to sell oil. Another thing: you don't look like an upper-class customer in that cloth gown. Wear silk or satin next time you come, so that the maids won't recognize you. Then it'll be easier for me to spin some kind of yarn about you."

"I shall remember all you've told me," promised Zhong as he took his leave.

For three days he stopped selling oil, and strolled about the streets in a second-hand silk gown he had bought at a pawnshop, to practise carrying himself like a scholar and a gentleman.

On the fourth day Zhong went so early to Mrs. Wang's house that he found the gate still closed. He decided to take a stroll; but, not daring to pass the monastery for fear the monks would laugh at his fine clothes, he walked in another direction. Upon his return he found the gate open; but there was a carriage outside and a number of footmen were sitting in the courtyard. Though Zhong was a simple lad, he had all his wits about him; so instead of going in he beckoned quietly to the coachmen.

"Whose carriage is this?" he asked.

"Minister Han's," was the reply. "We've come to fetch our young master."

When Zhong realized that the minister's son had not yet left, he went to an inn for a meal. By the time he returned the carriage had gone, and as he entered the gate he met the bawd herself.

"I'm very sorry," she told him. "But The Flower Queen is not free today. Just now Master Han begged her to go with him to East Village to enjoy the early plum blossom; and he is such an old customer that I couldn't refuse him. He wants to take her to Ling Yin Monastery tomorrow, too, for a chess tournament. Lord Qi has also asked for her several times; and since he is our landlord we can't very well refuse him either. He often stays three or four days when he comes, so I can't tell when he will leave. If you really want a night with her, you must wait a little longer. Otherwise I can refund you the money you gave me the other day."

"The only thing I'm afraid of is losing your help, ma'am," replied Zhong. "I don't mind waiting ten thousand years if I can have her in the end."

"That's all right, then," said the bawd. "And there's another thing, Master Qin," she added as he was leaving. "Come at about four in the afternoon next time instead of in the morning. Then I can tell you whether she is booked or not. In fact, the later you come the better. Don't take offence if this is all I can do for you."

"Indeed not," he protested.

Zhong did no business that day, but went out the next morning with his pedlar's kit to sell oil inside the city, giving Qiantang Gate a wide berth. And every evening, after his work was done, he dressed himself neatly and went to Mrs. Wang's house. But The Flower Queen was never free, and he waited for more than a month in vain.

On the fifteenth of the twelfth month it snowed heavily, and when the snow stopped the wind whistled over the snowdrifts till they turned to ice. It was bitterly cold, but the ground was dry. After plying his trade for the greater part of the day, Zhong dressed himself as usual and went to see what news there was for him. Mrs. Wang greeted him with a beaming face.

"Today you have a ninety-nine per cent chance!" she said.

"What is it that is still uncertain?" he asked.

"The fact that she is not back yet."

"Will she be coming back?"

"Today Marshal Yu invited her to his home to enjoy the snow, and then they feasted on a boat in the lake. The marshal is seventy, so of course he won't be making love to her, and he said he would send her back this evening. Why don't you go to her room and have a cup of wine to warm you up while you wait for her?"

"Please lead the way, ma'am!"

Mrs. Wang led him through several winding passages and halls to a clean and airy building and two small chambers as wings. On the left was a room for the maids with little in it but a bed, table and chairs. On the right was The Flower Queen's bedroom, which was locked. In the sitting room in the middle hung a painting by a famous artist, while ambergris was burning in an old bronze censer on the table. The writing tables on two sides of the room were laden with curios, and the walls were hung with poems; but, ashamed that he was no scholar, Zhong did little more than glance at them.

"If her sitting room is so elegant, her bedroom must be simply magnificent!" he thought. "And tonight I shall enjoy it to the full! Ten taels a night is really not too much."

Mrs. Wang offered him a seat and acted as hostess while maids brought in a lamp and laid a square table with six bowls of nuts and cakes and one hamper of delicacies. Even before tasting the wine you could smell its bouquet!

"Today all my girls are engaged, so there is no one but me to keep you company," said the bawd as she offered him wine. "Please drink a few cups and make yourself at home."

But Zhong was not a good drinker, and he had too much on his mind to finish even one cup.

"I expect you are hungry," said Mrs. Wang. "Have some food before you go on with your wine."

A maid brought in two bowls of rice which she placed before him, with a bowl of soup. Mrs. Wang was a good drinker and she did not touch the rice but kept the young man company with wine. After finishing one bowl, he laid down his chopsticks.

"The night is long," said Mrs. Wang. "Have some more."

So he ate another half bowl.

Presently a maid came in with a lantern.

"Your bath is ready, sir," she said.

Although Zhong had bathed before coming out, he dared not refuse, but went to the bathroom to wash, soap and scent himself again, then came back to the table. Mrs. Wang had ordered the food to be removed, keeping only the wine and a small stove to warm it. It was now after dusk and the bells in Zhao Qing Monastery had stopped tolling; but there was still no sign of The Flower Queen.

What can be more trying than waiting? As the girl failed to appear, Zhong began to lose heart; but the bawd kept up a flow of banter and pressed him to drink until two or three hours had passed. Then they heard a commotion outside. The Flower Queen was back! When the maid announced her return, Mrs. Wang hurried out to meet her, and Zhong stood up. Then Yaoqin was helped in, very drunk, by her maid. She halted at the threshold to gaze with drunken eyes at the bright candles, cups and dishes in the room.

"Who is drinking here?" she asked.

"Child," said Mrs. Wang, "this is the Master Qin I've told you about, who has admired you for so long and sent presents over. Because you were never free we have kept him waiting for over a month. But this evening luckily you have no engagements, so I asked him here to meet you."

"I've never heard of any Master Qin," retorted Yaoqin, turning away. "I won't see him."

Mrs. Wang put out both hands to stop her.

"He's a good man!" she declared. "I'm not fooling you."

So Yaoqin had to turn back. But as soon as she stepped into the room and saw Zhong she recognized him, though she was too drunk to remember his name.

"I know this man, mother," she said. "He's not a respectable gentleman. If I admit him, I shall be laughed at."

"Child!" protested Mrs. Wang. "This is Master Qin who owns a shop inside Yongjin Gate. You must have seen him when we lived in that part of the city; that's why you know his face. Don't go mixing him up with other people! He begged so hard that I let him come, and I can't go back on my word. So please put up with him for one night for my sake. I know I shouldn't have done this, and I'll make it up to you tomorrow."

She pushed Yaoqin into the room, so that the girl had to greet Zhong, who pretended not to have heard a word. Yaoqin curtseyed to the young man and sat down beside him; but the more she looked at him the more annoyed and suspicious she felt. At length she broke her silence to call for wine, which she poured into a large cup. Instead of offering this to the guest as Mrs. Wang expected, she drank it straight off herself.

"Child, you've already had too much!" protested the bawd. "Don't drink any more."

But Yaoqin would not listen.

"I'm not drunk!" she retorted, then drained ten cups in succession.

If she had been drunk before, she was now much more so. She ordered a maid to unlock her room and light the lamp so that she could lie down. Then without letting down her hair or removing her clothes, she kicked off her embroidered slippers and threw herself on the bed to sleep.

"She's a spoilt, self-willed girl," said Mrs. Wang, much embarrassed. "Something must have happened today to upset her; but it's nothing to do with you. I hope you will excuse her."

"That's quite all right," Qin assured her.

After drinking a few more cups he begged to be excused, and Mrs. Wang saw him to Yaoqin's bedroom, whispering: "Don't be too rough — she's drunk."

To Yaoqin she called: "Get up, child, and undress so that you can sleep properly."

But Yaoqin was already sound asleep. So the bawd had to leave them.

A maid cleared the table, then suggested: "Why don't you go to bed now, Master Qin?"

"I'd like a pot of hot tea, if there is any," he said.

The maid brewed a pot of strong tea and brought it in, then closed the door and went to her room. Turning to look at The Flower Queen, Zhong saw that she was fast asleep on her silk quilt, with her face to the wall. Although afraid she might catch cold after drinking, he did not like to disturb her; but, noticing another red silk quilt on the bedstead, he spread that gently over her. Next he trimmed the lamp, took off his shoes and lay down beside her, the tea pot in the crook of his left arm, his right arm over her waist. And not for a moment dared he close his eyes.

In the middle of the night Yaoqin awoke, overcome with nausea, and sat up shuddering. Putting down his tea pot Zhong hastily sat up too, and supported her while she was very sick; holding the sleeve of his gown before her to avoid dirtying the bedding. Presently, her eyes still closed, she asked for tea to rinse her mouth. At that, the young man gently removed his gown and tossed it on the floor; then, happy to find the tea still hot, poured her a cup of the strong, fragrant brew. After two cups she felt much better and lay down again, quite exhausted, to sleep with her face to the wall. And Zhong, having rolled up his soiled gown and put it in a corner, lay down once more beside her.

Yaoqin did not wake till the morning, when she turned over to discover someone lying beside her.

"Who are you?" she asked.

"My name is Qin," he said.

"Last night I was very drunk, wasn't I?"

She had only a hazy recollection of what had passed.

"Not very," he lied.

"Was I sick?"

"No."

"Well, that's not too bad."

But after a little reflection she said: "No, I remember being sick and drinking some tea. Surely I couldn't have dreamed it?"

"Well," admitted Zhong, "as a matter of fact you're right. I saw that you had had too much to drink, so I kept the tea pot warm for you. After being sick you asked for tea, and I poured you two cups."

"Was I sick on the bed?" demanded Yaoqin in dismay. "How disgusting!"

"I was afraid your bedding might be soiled, so I held out my sleeve."

"Where is your gown now?"

"Over there."

"What a shame to spoil your clothes!"

"My clothes are lucky to have been of service."

"What a nice, considerate man!" thought Yaoqin, who was beginning to like him.

By this time the day was bright, and the girl got up. Suddenly she recognized the oil vendor.

"Tell me truly, now," she said, "who are you and what brought you here last night?"

"I can't lie to The Flower Queen," was the reply. "I am Qin Zhong, who used to sell oil at your door."

He described how he had first seen her escorting a guest to the gate and getting into the sedan chair; how much he had admired her and how he had saved up the money for a night with her.

"Because I was able to sleep beside you last night I count myself the happiest of men," he concluded. "I am quite content."

Yaoqin was very moved.

"Last night I was too drunk to entertain you, so you spent all that money for nothing," she said. "Don't you feel bad about it?"

"You are my goddess," replied Zhong. "I'm afraid I didn't look after you well enough, and I am very lucky not to have made you angry. What more dare I hope for?"

"You are in business," she answered. "When you make money, why don't you keep it for your family? You shouldn't come to a place like this."

"I have no wife or children," was the rejoinder. "I am all alone."

"Will you ever come back?" she asked after a moment's silence.

"Last night the dream of my life came true, when I was able to be near you. How dare I hope for more?"

"What a wonderful man!" thought Yaoqin. "So sincere and honest! So kind and considerate too! He's one in a thousand. What a pity that he's a tradesman. If he were a gentleman, I would like to marry him."

Just then her maid brought in a basin of water and two bowls of ginger soup. Zhong washed, but since he had not taken off his cap the previous night he did not have to do his hair. After drinking a little soup he stood up to take his leave.

"Don't go yet," said Yaoqin. "I want to talk to you."

"I admire you so much I would like to stay here a little longer," he replied. "But a man must know his place. I took a great liberty in coming here last night. If people hear of it, your reputation may suffer. So I had better leave early."

Yaoqin nodded. Then, dismissing her maid, she hastily opened her jewel box and took out twenty taels of silver.

"I behaved too badly last night," she said. "Take this for your business; but don't tell anyone I gave it to you."

Zhong, of course, would not accept the money.

"I make money so easily," insisted the girl. "And this is just to thank you for your kindness last night. You mustn't refuse it. If ever you are short of cash, you must let me help you. You had better leave that soiled gown here, and I'll tell my maid to wash it for you."

"Please don't trouble," he replied. "I shall wash it myself. How can I take money from you?"

"Don't say that!" she protested. And thrusting the silver into his sleeve she gave him a little push. Seeing that he could not refuse, Zhong accepted the money with a deep bow, then rolled up his soiled gown and went out past Mrs. Wang's room.

"Master Qin is leaving, madam!" called a maid when she saw him.

"Why are you leaving so early, Master Qin?" cried Mrs. Wang from her room.

"I have some business," he answered as he left. "I shall come to thank you another day."

Now though Yaoqin was not really interested in the oil vendor, she was touched by his devotion. Still suffering from the effects of wine, she rested that day instead of receiving guests, and her thoughts ran not on her other admirers but on Zhong.

Let us go back now to Old Zhu. When Xin Quan and Orchid saw that the old man was bed-ridden, they began to carry on together quite openly. And after several disputes with him they decided to quit. They slipped away one night taking all the money in the shop with them.

The next morning when Old Zhu discovered his loss, he asked his neighbours' help; but although they posted up a notice and an investigation was made for several days, it came to nothing. By now, of course, the old man saw matters in their true light and repented of listening to Xin Quan and driving Zhong away. Learning that the youth was living near Zhong'an Bridge as an oil vendor, he decided to invite him back as a support for his old age. And fearing that Zhong might bear him a grudge, he asked the neighbours to plead with the young man to return. Zhong then packed up his things and went back to Old Zhu's house, where both of them wept at their meeting.

Old Zhu entrusted all his property to his foster-son, and by using his own twenty taels of silver Zhong was able to get the shop in good shape again. Once more he sold oil over the counter and called himself Zhu Zhong.

When, in less than a month, Old Zhu's illness took a turn for the worse, physic proved useless and he died, Zhong beat his breast and wept as bitterly as for his own father. And the funeral, sacrifice, and interment of the coffin in the Zhu family graveyard outside Qingbo Gate were just as they should be, winning Zhong great praise from his neighbours. When all this was over, he resumed business. His shop was an old firm which had done good business until Xin Quan's niggardly dealings drove customers away; but now that Zhong was in charge all the old customers came back; so business was better than ever.

Since Zhong was all on his own, he urgently needed an honest assistant, and one day a middleman introduced to him a man over fifty. This was none other than Yaoqin's father, Xin Shan. Lonely and helpless, he and his wife had wandered from place to place for several years, living from hand to mouth. Now, hearing that the southern capital had grown prosperous and most of the refugees from the north had settled there, they had come to Lin'an to search for their lost daughter. They could get no news of her, however, and soon all their money was spent and the innkeeper pressed them every day for payment. When they heard that an assistant was needed for an oil shop whose young manager, Zhu, also came from the northern capital, Xin Shan asked the middleman to recommend him. He knew the business, having once owned a grocery himself. And Zhong was very sympathetic when he heard his fellow-townsman's story.

"Since you have nowhere to go, why don't you and your wife stay with me?" he suggested. "After all, we are virtually old neighbours. You can continue making inquiries about your daughter from here."

He gave Xin Shan two strings of cash to pay his bill at the inn. Then Xin brought his wife to meet Zhong, who cleared out a room for the old couple and was pleased to find them a real help in the shop.

Swift as an arrow another year passed. It was high time for Zhong to marry, and because he was well off and honest into the bargain, many families offered him their daughters for nothing. But after meeting an enchantress like The Flower Queen, Zhong could take no interest in ordinary girls and determined to wed none but a beauty. So day after day slipped by, but brought him no nearer to marrying.

Meanwhile, in Mrs. Wang's house, Yaoqin enjoyed such fame and pleasure that she had all the silks and satins and delicate fare she could desire. Yet whenever anything went wrong, when her admirers became jealous and quarrelled, or when she woke in the middle of the night drunk or unwell and found no one to care for her, then she would remember Master Qin's sterling qualities and wonder if they would ever meet again.

A year later, however, something happened to change her whole life.

There lived in Lin'an a young man named Wu, the eighth son of Wu Yue, Governor of Fuzhou. Thanks to his father's position Master Wu had plenty of money; and he liked to gamble, drink and amuse himself with singsong girls. He knew The Flower Queen by reputation; but although he sent several times to engage her for a night, she had heard such ill reports of him that she invariably excused herself. He called more than once with some other wastrels at Mrs. Wang's house; but still Yaoqin would not receive him.

Soon the Spring Festival arrived, when folk visit their family graves or go sightseeing. After several days of outings, Yaoqin was tired. Moreover, she had promised poems and paintings to a number of friends; so, ordering her maids to inform all callers that she was out, she closed her door, lit some fine incense, and set her desk in order. She had just taken up her brush when she heard shouting outside — it was Master Wu who had come with a dozen ruffians to demand that she accompany him to the lake. Refused once more by Mrs. Wang, he started smashing furniture in the hall, then charged straight for The Flower Queen's door, only to find it locked.

One way for a courtesan to avoid guests is to have

someone lock her door from outside and say that she is out. But whereas simple customers can be fooled in this way, an old hand like Wu was not deceived by such a trick. He ordered his servants to smash the lock and kick open the door; Yaoqin was unable to hide herself; and Wu, shouting curses, bade two of his men drag her out. Mrs. Wang wanted to intervene and apologize; but the ugly turn things were taking made her slip away, and her whole household promptly went into hiding. Then with no consideration for Yaoqin's tiny bound feet, Wu's bullies hustled her out of the gate and through the streets, while their master swaggered behind. Only when they reached the West Lake and pushed her on the boat did they let go of her.

Clothed in silks and prized like a jewel, The Flower Queen had been pampered and cosseted ever since she came to Mrs. Wang at the age of twelve. Never before had she been so roughly and rudely treated. Once aboard, she turned towards the stern, hid her face in her hands and started sobbing. But instead of relenting, Wu nearly burst with rage. Fierce as the God of War, he jerked his chair round to face the shore, sat down with his bullies ranged beside him, and ordered the boatmen to cast off.

"You bitch!" he cursed. "You don't know how to appreciate an honour! If you don't stop crying, you whore, I'll have you whipped!"

Not to be frightened by this, Yaoqin went on sobbing. When the boat reached a pavilion in the middle of the lake, Wu went ashore, ordering the food to be served in the pavilion. But when he told his men to fetch The Flower Queen to amuse him, she clung fast to the railing of the boat, crying bitterly, and would not let go. So all Wu's pleasure was spoilt. After drinking a few cups of wine alone, he went back to the boat to drag the girl from the railing; but she stamped and screamed until the furious bully ordered his servants to remove her hairpins and trinkets. Then, with dishevelled hair, Yaoqin ran to the end of the boat to throw herself into the water. But the men stopped her.

"Are you trying to frighten me?" demanded Wu. "Even if you kill yourself, it will only cost me a few taels of silver. Of course, I don't want you to do away with yourself here; so if you stop that noise, I'll let you go."

When Yaoqin heard this, she stopped crying; and Wu ordered the boat to moor at a quiet spot outside Qingbo Gate. There he had the girl's embroidered slippers torn off.

"Walk home if you can, you bitch!" he jeered, ordering his ruffians to set her ashore. "Nobody's going to see you back."

Then the boat cast off again and steered for the middle of the lake.

How could Yaoqin walk on her tiny, bare feet? Though she had talent and beauty, she reflected, she was a despised courtesan and not one of her rich and aristocratic admirers would be willing to help her now.

"How can I face the world again, even if I do get back?" she thought. "It would be better to die. But what a futile death! For all my reputation, any peasant woman is luckier than I. It's all thanks to Mrs. Liu, with her sugared tongue, that I'm in this fix today. Has there ever been a woman as unhappy as I?"

She felt more and more wretched, and finally broke down and cried as if her heart would break.

Now it happened that Zhong had gone that day to sacrifice at Old Zhu's grave outside Qingbo Gate. Having sent the sacrificial vessels back by boat, he was walking home alone when he heard a girl crying. And drawing nearer he recognized the beauty at once, in spite of her dishevelled state.

"What has happened, Flower Queen?" he demanded, aghast.

When Yaoqin heard a familiar voice, she stopped crying and looked up to see that understanding, considerate Master Qin. Here was a friend in need! She poured out her whole unhappy story, and Zhong, touched to the quick, shed tears of sympathy. From his sleeve he took a white silk handkerchief over five feet in length, which he tore in half and gave to the girl to bind round her feet. He then wiped the tears from her face and fastened up her hair, comforting her as he did so. As soon as her sobs ceased he called a sedan chair, asked her to be seated, and escorted her himself on foot to Mrs. Wang's house.

Now the panic-stricken bawd, not knowing what had become of the girl, was sending out everywhere to make enquiries, when who should arrive but Master Qin with The Flower Queen! Mrs. Wang was as pleased as if someone had returned her a gem of the first water. Besides, the young man had long since stopped peddling oil at her door and she knew that he had taken over the Zhu Family Shop and was doing well. Now that he was a substantial citizen, her attitude to him had naturally changed. And when she saw the state Yaoqin was in, learned what a terrible experience she had been through and that it was Master Qin who had rescued her, the old woman could not thank him enough. She insisted that he stay to a meal.

Late in the afternoon, when Zhong had drunk a few cups, he rose to go. But The Flower Queen would not hear of his leaving.

"I have often thought of you, and longed to see you again," she said. "I'm not going to let you leave like this."

Mrs. Wang also urged him to stay.

Never had Zhong been so happy. That evening Yaoqin played, sang and danced for him, using all her art to please him, until the young man felt he was in paradise and could scarcely contain himself for joy. And as night fell they went arm in arm to her bed-chamber, where Zhong's bliss can be imagined.

"I want to speak to you from my heart," said Yaoqin later that night. "You mustn't refuse what I ask!"

"I'd gladly go through boiling water or fire to serve you,"

declared Zhong. "How can I refuse you anything?"

"I want to marry you."

Zhong laughed.

"Even if you married ten thousand times, you would never choose a poor fellow like me," he replied. "Don't joke about such a thing. I am too far beneath you."

"I am perfectly serious," insisted Yaoqin. "When I was fourteen and they made me drunk to start me on this life, I wanted to marry but knew of no one suitable. I couldn't tell who would make a good husband, and was afraid of making a mistake I would regret all my life. Later, though I met many men, they were all rich young gallants who gave their time to wine and women because they cared only for pleasure. None of them had any real feeling for me. I've met no other man so trusty and true as you, sir. Besides, I understand you are not yet married; and if you don't despise me because of my profession, I would like to serve you all my life. If you refuse, I shall hang myself here with three feet of white silk to prove my sincerity. That will be better than dying miserably as I might have done yesterday at the hands of those boors, jeered at by everyone."

Having said this, she started sobbing.

"Don't distress yourself so," Zhong entreated her. "It's beyond my wildest dreams that you should love me. How dare I refuse you? But how can a poor man like myself pay the thousand of taels needed to redeem you? Much as I long to, it's not in my power."

"That need not hinder us," she replied. "As a matter of fact, I have saved up money and valuables for my marriage and left them with friends. I needn't trouble you for a cent."

"Even if you redeem yourself, you are used to living in a large house and enjoying the best of everything. How will you manage in my house?"

"With you I shall be happy wearing cotton and eating the plainest food."

"And what if your mistress objects?"

"I can get round her."

So they chatted till dawn.

Yaoqin now collected the boxes which she had deposited with the sons of Academician Huang, Minister Han, Marshal Qi and others, and asked Zhong to take them home. This done, she took a sedan chair to Mrs. Liu's house and told her that she wished to marry.

"Yes, that was my advice to you, wasn't it?" said Mrs. Liu. "You are still young, of course; but who is the man?"

"Never mind who he is, aunty. But I am acting on your advice, and this is going to be a true, happy marriage which ends well, not one of your sham, unhappy marriages which end badly. And if you will take my side, my mistress is bound to agree. I have nothing worthy to offer you; but as a sign of my gratitude here are ten taels of gold to make trinkets. Do help me by talking my mistress round! If you succeed, I shall give you another present for acting as my go-between."

When Mrs. Liu saw the gold, she smiled till her eyes seemed like two slits.

"You are like a daughter to me, and you are doing the right thing!" she cried. "How can I accept a present from you? I shall just keep this gold for the time being to look after it for you. You can depend on me. But your mistress considers you a money-tree which needs only be shaken to shower down gold. She won't want to let you go, and will probably ask at least a thousand taels for you. Is he willing to pay that much? I'd better have a talk with him first."

"Never mind about that, aunty. Let's assume that I'm redeeming myself."

"Does your mistress know you are here?"

"No."

"Well, you stay here for lunch while I go to have a talk with Mrs. Wang. I'll let you know when I come back if she's agreeable or not."

Mrs. Liu took a sedan chair to Mrs. Wang's house and was

invited in. When she asked about the trouble with Master Wu, Mrs. Wang told her the whole story.

"In our profession it is safer and more profitable to keep more ordinary girls," said Mrs. Liu. "They aren't particular about whom they receive, and they admit clients every day. That Flower Queen of yours has become so famous that she's like a piece of dried fish on the ground — every ant wants a bite! Though she's a great attraction, she must cause you a lot of worry. And though you charge ten taels a night for her, she brings you more fame than money; because whenever those young lords come they bring friends who stay all night and make an immense amount of work. There are all their servants, whom you have to treat well, too. If you don't do exactly what they want, they start using foul language and smashing things up; and you can't complain to their masters either. Then there are the scholars and poets and chess-players, who demand several days of her time every month. And the sons of the best families keep fighting for her. If she accepts Zhang, she offends Li. When one man is pleased, another is sure to grumble. Take this trouble with Master Wu for example. What a fright it must have given you! Because if anything were to go wrong, you would lose your capital. You can't bring a lawsuit against an official family; you have to put up with whatever they do. Luck was with you this time, and the stormclouds have blown over, but if anything unfortunate were to happen, you could do nothing but wring your hands. I hear, too, the Wu means mischief, and is likely to make more trouble for you. And Yaoqin is a quick-tempered girl, who won't flatter people. She's bound to come to grief."

"That's what worries me too," replied Mrs. Wang. "This young Wu comes of a rich, powerful family — he's not just anyone — yet she wouldn't hear of admitting him. That's how all this trouble started. She was easier to manage when she was younger; but now that she's so well-known and all those rich gentlemen make so much of her, she's grown spoilt and insists on having her own way. She receives only the customers she likes; and if she's unwilling, nine bulls can't budge her."

"The least bit of fame goes to these girls' heads," agreed Mrs. Liu.

"I want your advice," said Mrs. Wang. "If a man could be found willing to pay, wouldn't it be better to sell her? That would simplify matters and save me a lot of worry."

"You're quite right. If you sell her, you'll make enough to buy five or six others. In fact, if you drive a good bargain, you may even get ten girls for the money. It's well worth your while."

"I've been thinking it over. Those high officials never pay much: they expect to get everything cheap. But she's so particular that when someone's found who'll pay the right price, she may go into one of her tantrums and refuse. So if you come across a good customer, my dear, do act as go-between and help us. And if the girl refuses, I hope you'll make her see reason. She won't listen to me; but she trusts you, and you can get round her."

Mrs. Liu went into a peal of laughter.

"I am here now as a go-between!" she cried. "How much do you want for her?"

"Well, sister, you know how things are. In our profession we buy cheap but sell dear. Besides, look how famous she has been for the last few years. Is there anyone in the capital who hasn't heard of The Flower Queen? So how can I let her go for a beggarly three or four hundred taels? No, I want at least a thousand."

"Let me go and tell him," said Mrs. Liu. "If he's willing to pay so much, I'll come back. If not, I won't." Then, getting up to leave, she asked: "Where is the girl today?"

Mrs. Wang sighed.

"Since Wu insulted her that day," she said, "she's been afraid that he may come back to make more trouble; so she takes the sedan chair every day to different houses to complain. The day before yesterday it was Marshal Qi; yesterday it was Academician Huang. Heaven knows where she is today."

"If you make up your mind and are firm with her, she will have to agree," said Mrs. Liu. "If she doesn't, I shall talk her round. But don't make any difficulties, now, if the man is willing!"

"I've given my word," replied Mrs. Wang. "I shan't go back on it."

Then she saw her friend to the door, and Mrs. Liu after a hasty leave-taking mounted her chair and was carried away.

Once home Mrs. Liu told Yaoqin: "Well, I've won your mistress over. She's given her consent. The moment you produce the silver, it can be settled."

"The silver is ready," replied Yaoqin. "Will you promise to come to our house tomorrow, aunty, please, to get this settled? We must strike while the iron's hot."

"Since it's all arranged, I'll certainly come," promised Mrs. Liu. Yaoqin then said goodbye and went home, but did not breathe a word of this to anyone.

At noon the next day, Mrs. Liu arrived.

"How about it?" asked Mrs. Wang.

"It's ninety per cent certain. But I haven't spoken to the girl yet."

Mrs. Liu went to Yaoqin's room and, when they had greeted each other and chatted for a little, asked: "Did your man turn up? Where is the money?"

"In those leather cases."

Yaoqin pointed to the head of her bed, then opened five or six cases and took out thirteen or fourteen packets containing fifty silver taels each. With the gold, gems and jade which she produced as well, she had not less than a thousand tael's worth.

Mrs. Liu's eyes sparkled at this sight, and her mouth watered.

"How smart the girl is for her age!" she thought. "How

did she manage to save up so much? The girls in my house receive guests too, yet none of them has come anywhere near this. Whenever they have a little money in their pockets they spend it on nuts and sweets instead of saving it; so if their foot binding is worn out, I have to buy new for them. Mrs. Wang was really in luck to get a girl like this, who could bring in so much money and save so much to redeem herself. It's all here ready!"

Yaoqin guessed what was in Mrs. Liu's mind, and quickly fetched four rolls of Luzhou silk, two bejewelled hairclips, and two phoenix hairpins of jade.

"Here are a few presents for you, aunty," she said, putting them on the table. "I must thank you for acting as my go-between."

Then, beaming with joy, Mrs. Liu went back to Mrs. Wang.

"She wants to redeem herself for the amount you fixed, not a cent less," she said. "This is better than if some man were to buy her, because it means there are no middlemen asking for wine and tea, who have to be paid one or two per cent of the price."

Mrs. Wang was rather vexed, however, to learn that the girl had so much money in her cases. The fact is, these bawds are pleased only when all the extras their girls make come to them. If they suspect that a girl is keeping a private hoard, they will wait till she is out, then unlock her door and ransack her room. Because Yaoqin was well-known and her friends were all important men, and because she was making a great deal of money for her mistress and had a hot temper, Mrs. Wang had tried not to offend her. So she had never entered Yaoqin's room, not realizing that the girl had put by so much.

Mrs. Liu understood why Mrs. Wang's face had clouded.

"Now, sister, stick to your word!" she said. "These are her own savings, not money that should have come to you. She could have spent it all. Or if she were a bad girl she could have given it all to some lover, and you'd have been none the wiser. It's a good thing that she put it by. Besides, if she hadn't saved a cent, you couldn't have let her leave your house naked, could you? You'd have had to fit her out decently before marrying her off. But now that she has produced all these things, I'm sure she won't ask you for so much as a thread. You can keep the whole of this sum to line your purse. And though she is getting married, she is still your daughter. If she does well, she is bound to send you presents during festivals; and, since she has no parents, you will be her husband's mother-in-law. There'll be plenty of good things coming to you."

Consoled by this reasoning, Mrs. Wang gave her consent. Then Mrs. Liu brought out the silver, weighed it packet by packet, and gave it to Mrs. Wang. This done, she went through the gold, jewels and jade to reckon the value of each piece.

"I am deliberately marking them down," she told Mrs. Wang, "so that when you sell them you can make a few dozen taels extra."

Though a bawd, Mrs. Wang was fairly honest, and she agreed to all her friend's estimates. And when Mrs. Liu saw that she was won over, she told her pander to draw up a marriage agreement for Yaoqin.

"I had better say goodbye to my mistress and leave with you, aunty," said the girl. "Will you let me stay with you for a couple of days, until we have chosen an auspicious date for the wedding?"

After receiving so many presents from Yaoqin, Mrs. Liu did not want Mrs. Wang to change her mind and keep the girl after all. Anxious to see the matter settled, she agreed.

Yaoqin promptly packed her toilet case, jewel boxes, chests, bedding and other belongings, without taking a single object belonging to Mrs. Wang. Leaving her room with Mrs. Liu, she said goodbye to the other girls and to her mistress, who shed a few conventional tears. Then Yaoqin had her baggage carried to the sedan chair and went off happily with Mrs. Liu, who cleared a good, quiet room for her and her chests. And all the girls in Mrs. Liu's house came to congratulate her.

That evening when Zhong sent Xin Shan to Mrs. Liu to ask for news, he learned that the business was settled. Then, with Mrs. Liu as go-between, an auspicious day was chosen, the wedding was celebrated with flutes and drums, and great was the young couple's happiness on their wedding night.

The following day, when Xin Shan and his wife were introduced to the bride, they were amazed to recognize their child; and when they had exchanged their stories they embraced with tears of joy. Then Zhong asked his father and mother-in-law to be seated so that he and Yaoqin could pay their respects. All their friends marvelled, and a feast was held to celebrate this double happiness.

Three days after the wedding Yaoqin asked her husband to send rich presents to the friends who had stored her cases, and to tell them that she was now married, thus showing that she had a sense of gratitude. She also sent additional gifts to Mrs. Wang and Mrs. Liu, to the delight of both.

After the honeymoon, Yaoqin opened her chests to disclose gold, silver and hundreds of lengths of silk and embroidery from Suzhou and Chengdu, worth more than three thousand taels. She gave the keys of her chests to her husband, who gradually bought houses and land and expanded his business, leaving the management of the oil shop to his father-in-law. In less than a year the family was wealthy enough to live in style with plenty of servants.

One day, to express his gratitude to the gods, Zhong vowed to present all the temples and monasteries in the city with sufficient candles and oil for three months. He also undertook to burn incense, offer prayers, observe fasts and purify himself. Starting with Zhao Qing Monastery, he went by turn to Ling Yin, Fa Xiang, Jui Ci and Tian Zhu monasteries.

Now Tian Zhu Monastery, which is devoted to the worship of Guanyin,[5] consists actually of three monasteries: Upper Tian Zhu, Middle Tian Zhu and Lower Tian Zhu, all of which are important centres of worship but can be reached only by mountain paths, not by boat. Bidding his servants carry up one load of candles and three of oil. Zhong set off up the mountain by sedan chair.

He went first to Upper Tian Zhu Monastery, and was welcomed by the monks in the hall where his father lit candles and tended incense. Now that he was prosperous and well fed, Zhong had grown stout and changed so much that Old Qin did not recognize him. On one oil cask, however, the old man saw the word 'Qin,' and on the other 'Kaifeng'; and that set him thinking. What a strange coincidence, indeed, that these two oil casks should be brought to this monastery! After Zhong had offered incense, Old Qin brought in a tea tray and the chief monk offered their patron tea. Then Old Qin spoke up.

"May I ask, sir, why you have these words on your casks?"

"Why do you ask?" inquired Zhong, interested to hear a northern accent. "Are you from Kaifeng too?"

The old man replied that he was.

"What is your name?" asked Zhong. "Why did you join this order? And how long have you been here?"

The Old Qin told him his name and place of origin.

"When I reached here after escaping from the soldiery, I had no means of support," he said. "So I let my thirteen-year-old son be adopted by a Mr. Zhu. Eight years have passed since then, but being old and infirm I have never left the mountain to ask news of him."

Zhong threw his arms round the old man and wept.

"I am your son!" he cried. "I used to sell oil for Mr. Zhu. It was because I wanted to find you, father, that I wrote these words on the oil cask. Who would have thought that we should meet here! This was surely ordained by Heaven!"

The monks, too, exclaimed in wonder.

After spending that day at the monastery with his father talking of the past, Zhong changed the name on his written invocations to the gods of the two remaining monasteries from Zhu Zhong back to Qin Zhong. Having offered incense in Middle Tian Zhu and Lower Tian Zhu, he returned to ask his father to accompany him home, so that he could be well looked after. But Old Qin had lived so long as a monk that he was used to observing fasts and unwilling to leave.

"We have been separated for eight years," protested Zhong, "and all that time I have been unable to look after you. Besides, I have just married, and my wife ought to pay her respects to her father-in-law."

Then Old Qin had to agree.

Zhong had his father carried in the sedan chair while he walked on foot. Once home, he brought out new clothes for the old man and asked him to be seated in the hall while he and Yaoqin paid their respects. Her parents were introduced too.

That day a great feast was spread; but Old Qin would not touch the meat or wine. And the following day all their neighbours brought presents to congratulate the family on their fourfold happiness: Zhong's marriage, the reunion of Yaoqin's family, the reunion of Zhong with his father, and the restoration of the Qin family name. So they feasted for several days.

Then Old Qin chose to return to his monastery; and Zhong, not daring to thwart his father's wishes, spent two hundred taels to build a lodge there for him. Every month Zhong sent him provisions and money, and every ten days he went to see the old man, while Yaoqin visited her father-in-law four times a year. He lived to be over eighty, dying peacefully one day during his yoga exercises. In accordance with his wishes, he was buried on the mountain near the monastery.

As for Zhong and Yaoqin, they lived happily together till old age, and had two sons both of whom became famous scholars.

And even to the present day, when singsong girls want to praise a man for showing consideration, they call him 'a Master Qin' or 'an oil vendor.'

Notes:

1. The Golden Tartars or Jin were members of the Nurchen (Nuzhen) tribe. Responsible for the fall of the Northern Song dynasty, the Jin set up a dynasty in the north of China which lasted from 1115 to 1234.

2. Courtesans and their less talented fellows were in China, as in other countries, sold into service. To regain their freedom they had to pay an amount equivalent to a few years earnings to their owners.

3. Xi Shi was a legendary beauty of the State of Yue at the end of the Spring and Autumn Period (770-467BC).

4. Also known as the Mid-Autumn Festival (*Zhongqiujie*). This festival takes place on the 15th day of the eighth lunar month and is accompanied by the eating of moon cakes, and viewing the full autumn moon. It has traditionally been an ideal occasion for the display of literary accomplishment, the writing of poems and various literary games being very popular during the celebrations.

5. Guanyin is the 'All-seeing Boddhisattva' (*Avalokiteśvara*) who sprouted extra eyes to see the sufferings of all sentient beings and extra arms to offer succour to all. As the embodiment of compassion, Guanyin was and still is a favourite Buddhist deity in Asia.

沈小霞相會出師表

大小篆隸四體千字文

A Just Man Avenged

from Tales to Illuminate the World

During the Jia Jing period (1522-1566) of the Ming Dynasty, a wise emperor was on the throne, the elements were propitious, the country prospered and the people were at peace. But then the appointment of one evil minister corrupted the entire government and endangered the security of the state. Who was this evil minister? He was Yan Song, a native of Fenyi in Jiangxi Province. Having won favour by flattery and ingratiating himself with the eunuchs, he sacrificed as a Daoist[1] and made a great show of writing invocations and fasting to please the emperor. So he was rapidly promoted to a position of authority. A circumspect manner cloaked his vindictive nature; and after slandering and ruining the prime minister, Xia Yan, he stepped into his shoes. Then, exalted and powerful, he was feared by officials and common citizens alike.

Yan Song's son, Yan Shifan, who rose gradually from the rank of a college student to be vice-minister of the Board of Works,[2] was even craftier than his father. Since he combined talent with extensive knowledge, a good memory and a cool, calculating brain, the prime minister listened readily to his advice and consulted him whenever he was in doubt.

Thus they were known at court as the Old Prime Minister and the Young Prime Minister.

Working hand in glove, these evil men seized power, accepted bribes and sold government posts and titles. Any official who wished for promotion had only to bribe the prime minister well and beg to become his godson to be appointed to an important post. So the most despicable hangers-on flocked to them, until all ministries and offices were filled with their men; while all who opposed them came to grief, being beaten, banished or killed. The result was that only those prepared to sacrifice their lives dared to protest against the Yans' injustice, and all but the most devoted patriots preferred to see the country ruined rather than offend the prime minister. As an anonymous poet of the period wrote:

Why study hard in your youth,
When gold will carry you to a high position?
Look at Prime Minister Yan:
He always appoints the rich to official posts.

Another verse ran:

The Son of Heaven trusts the powerful,
And any remonstrance will only lead to trouble;
Thus everything else today takes second place,
But flattery is the thing.

Yan Song and his son took advantage of the emperor's favour to fleece and oppress the people, until their sins were mountain-high. Then a loyal subject did a remarkable deed and left a stirring tale behind him. Though he died, his name will live for ever.

This man was called Shen Lian, and he was a native of Shaoxing in Zhejiang Province. Well versed in all the arts of peace and war, his ambition was to serve his country and people, and from boyhood he had the greatest admiration for Zhuge Liang,[3] and especially for the two memorials his hero had written while on his way to the front. He made several hundred copies of these to paste over his walls, and after drinking would recite them at the top of his voice. More-over, when he reached the line: 'I devote myself heart and soul to affairs of state, and shall do till I die,' he would sigh and shed tears. He did this so often that everyone considered him eccentric.

In 1538, Shen Lian passed the palace examination and was made a county magistrate. He served three terms as a magistrate, acquitting himself well.

Because of his integrity and refusal to fawn on his superiors, Shen Lian was transferred to the capital as secre-tary of the Imperial Constabulary and there he saw with indignation the crooked ways and ill-gotten wealth of the Yan family. One day at an official banquet he was disgusted by Yan Shifan's arrogance. In the middle of the feast Yan began to shout in the most ill-mannered way, and calling for a big goblet, penalized those who would not drain this when he proposed a toast. This goblet contained over a pint, yet the other guests dared not cross Yan. There was a Censor Ma present, however, who was physically incapable of drink-ing. When Yan deliberately sent the goblet to him, he begged repeatedly to be excused; but Yan would not let him off. After one sip, the censor flushed crimson and showed signs of acute discomfort. Then Yan strode over to his table, seized the unhappy man by one ear and poured the contents of the goblet down his throat. After forcing himself to gulp down the wine, Censor Ma felt dizzy and the walls began to revolve around him. His head was heavy, his feet light; and as he staggered and fell, Yan clapped his hands and roared with laughter.

Shen Lian could contain himself no longer. Rolling up his sleeves, he seized the goblet, filled it to the brim, and carried it to Yan.

"You did Censor Ma the honour of inviting him to drink," he said. "Since he is too drunk to return your courtesy, let me invite you in his stead!"

Taken aback, Yan was raising his hand to decline, when

沈青霞酒灌嚴也蕃

Shen Lian pours the wine down Yan Shifan's throat

Shen Lian bent an angry look on him.

"If others can drink this, so can you!" he thundered. "Others may be afraid of you, but I am not!"

Seizing Yan by one ear he poured the wine down his throat, then threw the goblet on the table, clapped his hands and roared with laughter. All the officials present turned ashen pale, and lowered their heads in terrified silence. But when Yan left on the pretext that he had drunk too much, Shen did not rise to see him off.

"Loyal men and traitors cannot work together," he sighed. "They cannot work together."

He repeated this sentence, which was another quotation from Zhuge Liang, seven or eight times, likening Yan Song and Yan Shifan to Cao Cao[4] and his son. And though the others sweated for fear Yan Shifan should hear him, Shen ignored them completely. After draining several cups of wine in swift succession, he went home and slept soundly till dawn.

When he awoke he remembered what he had done.

"In a fit of temper I forced that accursed Yan Shifan to drink," he reflected. "He will certainly try to get even with me; and since I have offended him anyway, I may as well get in first if I can. Their crimes are hated by both gods and men; but they are high favourites at court, and my position is too low for my words to carry any weight. I meant to look for a suitable occasion to denounce them, but now I cannot wait . . . ."

His head on the pillow, he mentally drafted a memorial to the emperor until it was light; then got up, burned incense, washed his hands and wrote a memorandum describing the many evil deeds of Yan Song and Yan Shifan, and how they were seizing power and accepting bribes. He enumerated ten great crimes whereby they had deceived their sovereign and endangered the realm, and begged the emperor to have them executed in the interests of the state.

Then the following edict was issued: "Shen Lian has

been found guilty of slandering high officials in order to increase his own reputation. Let him be given a hundred strokes in the Imperial Constabulary, deprived of his official rank, and banished to the northern frontier."

Yan Shifan sent men to urge the constables to beat Shen Lian to death; but fortunately Lu Bing, the officer in charge, had a sense of justice. He had always admired Shen Lian's integrity and been on good terms with him; therefore he did what he could for his superior by pretending to beat him hard while actually giving him light strokes.

The Board of Civil Affairs then registered Shen Lian as a common citizen of Bao'an, and with his wounds still unhealed he was forced to pack up immediately, hire a carriage and set out with his wife and children on a long, hard journey. He had four sons, the eldest of whom, Shen Xiang, was a stipendiary scholar who had remained in Shaoxing; but the three others had accompanied their father to Beijing. Shen Gun and Shen Bao had studied in the capital, while Shen Zhi was only one year old; and these three left now with their parents. But for fear of the Yan family, none of the government officials dared see them off.

After many hardships on the road, at last they reached Bao'an in the Xuanfu Military Area, a frontier outpost with none of the luxuries of the cities of the interior. The unfamiliar landscape depressed them; for after several days' rain the place looked unusually dark and gloomy. Shen Lian wanted to rent a house, but having no acquaintances there did not know how to set about it. As he was wondering what to do, a passer-by carrying a small umbrella stopped at the sight of the baggage by the roadside, struck by Shen's distinguished air.

"May I ask your name, sir, and where you come from?" he asked.

"My name is Shen, and I come from the capital."

"I hear there was a Secretary Shen in the capital who memorialized the throne requesting the execution of Yan

Song and his son. Could you be he?"

"I am."

"I have long admired you and am most fortunate to have met you, but we cannot talk here. My humble home is not far away. Will you condescend to bring your honourable family to stay with me for a while before you make other plans?"

Impressed by such sincerity, Shen Lian agreed. And they soon reached the stranger's house which, though no mansion, was clean and pleasant. The stranger invited Shen into the hall, then kowtowed to him, and Shen hastily returned his greeting.

"Who are you?" he asked. "Why are you so good to us?"

"My name is Jia Shi," replied the other. "I am a guard in the local garrison. My brother was a lieutenant here, and when he died leaving no son I stepped into his position. But as soon as that traitor Yan seized power, all those with inherited ranks had to pay heavy bribes. I had no desire to be an official, and luckily my ancestors have left me a few acres of land, so I live as a peasant. Some days ago, I learned that you had impeached the Yans, and knew you must be a just man and a loyal minister. When I heard that you would be coming here, I longed to meet you. And now that Heaven has granted me my wish, I count myself most fortunate."

After this speech he prostrated himself.

Shen Lian helped him to rise, then called Shen Gun and Shen Bao forward to greet their host. Jia Shi told his wife to take Mrs. Shen to an inner chamber to rest; and when the luggage had been brought in and the coachman paid and dismissed, he ordered his men to kill a pig and prepared wine for the guests.

"It is raining hard, and I don't suppose you have found lodgings yet," said Jia. "You had better stay in my humble house. Please make yourselves at home and have some wine to refresh yourselves after your hard journey."

"Meeting by chance, how can I impose on your

hospitality?" rejoined Shen after thanking him.

"Our country ways are rough," replied Jia. "Please do not think us remiss."

After toasting each other they fell to deploring current events, and found so much in common that they regretted not having met earlier.

The next morning Shen said to his host: "May I trouble you to help me find a house for my family?"

"What kind of house?" asked Jia.

"If I could find one like yours, I should be very satisfied. As for the rent, I leave that entirely to you."

Jia went out to look for a house, and returned some time later.

"There are plenty of houses for rent," he announced, "but they are all damp and dirty. It will be hard to find anything suitable at short notice. Your best course will be to stay here for the time being, while I take my family to live with relatives until you return to the capital. What do you say?"

"You are too good," replied Shen Lian. "But how can we turn you out of your house? That is quite out of the question."

"Though I am only a peasant I know right from wrong," protested Jia. "I admire you as a true gentleman, sir, and have been longing to serve you; and at last Heaven has given me this chance. By lending you these few poor rooms I am simply showing my respect. You mustn't refuse them!"

Then and there he ordered his men to bring out the cart, horse and donkey, to move away his family's personal belongings, leaving the furniture and household utensils for Shen Lian. Deeply moved by such generosity, Shen asked Jia to become his sworn brother.

"I am a common peasant," demurred Jia. "And you are a gentleman."

"When a true man finds a friend after his own heart, there is no distinction between high and low," replied Shen.

Since Jia was the younger by five years, he addressed

Shen as his elder brother, and Shen bade his sons address Jia as their uncle. Then Jia presented his wife, and they feasted together as relatives, after which Jia moved out to live with his brother-in-law, while Shen Lian stayed on in his house.

When the elders of Bao'an heard that Secretary Shen had been banished to their district for impeaching Prime Minister Yan, they admired him so much that they all wanted to meet him. Some sent him rice and fuel, others wine and dishes, yet others sent their sons and younger brothers to be his pupils. Every day Shen would discuss loyalty and piety with the local people, or tell stories of just and true men in history, pounding the table indignantly as he described their misfortunes. At other times he would sing tragic songs, sigh or shed tears. The old and young of Bao'an listened spellbound, and joined in when he cursed the Yan family. In fact, anyone who remained silent during these tirades was abused for his lack of humanity and justice. They took such pleasure in his company that, when they learned that Shen Lian also excelled in military arts, they asked him to join in their archery contests.

Then Shen Lian bade them make three men of straw. On one he wrote Li Linfu, the Tang Dynasty traitor; on another Qin Hui, the Song Dynasty traitor; and on the third Yan Song, the Ming Dynasty traitor; and he used these three straw figures as targets.[5]

"You traitor!" he would cry, when shooting at these figures. "Here comes my arrow!"

The honest northerners enjoyed this sport with him, not caring whether the Yan family heard of it or not. But as the proverb says: All powerful men have their informers. When someone reported to Yan Song and his son what was happening, they racked their brains furiously for some excuse to have Shen Lian killed.

There was then a vacancy for a military governor in Xuanfu and Datong, and Yan Song made the Board of

Civil Affairs appoint his godson, Yang Shun. When Yang Shun went to take his leave of his patrons, Yan Shifan entertained him to a feast, during which he dismissed the attendants and privately directed Yang to find some way to put Shen Lian publicly in the wrong. After assenting readily, Yang left.

Soon after Yang Shun reached his post, Altan Khan, the Tartar chief at Datong, invaded China.[6] He took over forty strongholds in Yinzhou by storm and captured many prisoners; but Governor Yang dared not resist him. Only after the enemy had left were Chinese troops sent in pursuit, who beat gongs and drums, waved flags, fired guns and raised pandemonium, without seeing so much as the shadow of a Tartar! Then, realizing that he had blundered and might be punished, Governor Yang secretly ordered his men to seize the common people who were fleeing before the soldiery, shave and cut off their heads, and send them to the Board of War as Tartars' heads, for which a reward was given. Thus many innocent people were massacred.

As soon as Shen Lian learned of this he blazed with indignation, and wrote a letter which he asked a lieutenant to hand to Governor Yang. Regarding Shen as a trouble-maker who was capable of writing anything, the lieutenant refused to accept the letter, whereupon Shen put on dark clothes and a private citizen's cap and waited outside the yamen for Governor Yang, then handed him the letter himself.

"Personal achievement and fame mean little," read the governor, "but the people's lives are of paramount importance. How could you have the heart to kill common citizens to gain false credit? The Tartars merely rob our people and carry them off captive, whereas our own troops kill them. Thus our officers are more to be feared than the Tartars."

And the following verse was appended to the letter:

> Did you kill to report your achievements to your
> sovereign,
> To win credit at the price of ten thousand lives?

> *Listen, some stormy night on the battlefield:*
> *The unjustly slain are calling for their heads.*

The governor tore up this letter in fury.

Then Shen Lian wrote a dirge and went with his young men to sacrifice to the spirits of those unjustly killed. He also wrote these two verses on frontier warfare:

> *As the enemy's beacon fires flare high at the frontier,*
> *How hard the Chinese general exerts himself!*
> *He kills not the khan but our people,*
> *Staining his sword with the blood of the wrongly slain.*

And:

> *They fled from the Tartars, hoping to save their lives;*
> *But instead they met their death.*
> *Had they known that their heads would be sent in as enemy heads,*
> *They would surely have chosen surrender to the khan.*

When the governor's trusted lieutenant made copies of these poems and the dirge and sent them secretly to Yang Shun, the latter's rage knew no bounds. He altered the first verse to read:

> *As the enemy's beacon fires flare high at the frontier,*
> *The Chinese general exerts himself in vain.*
> *Would that the khan would kill this flattering minister;*
> *For then there would be no need for the emperor's sword!*

He wrote a letter enclosing these verses, sealed it, marked it confidential, and sent it to Yan Shifan. In this letter he declared that Shen Lian was secretly gathering assassins to kill Yan Song and his son in order to wreak his hatred; and during the Tartar invasion he had written these poems urging the khan to kill the prime minister — in other words, he was guilty of treason.

When Yan Shifan read this, he was startled and consulted his trusted censor, Lu Kai.

"If I am sent to inspect that district," said Lu, "I can settle this for you."

Yan Shifan was delighted and ordered the Court of Censors to despatch Lu to that area; then, on the eve of the censor's departure, invited him to a farewell feast.

"Convey my regards to Yang Shun," he said. "I hope you will co-operate with him. If you can rid me of this thorn in my flesh, I shall certainly not let either of you down, but reward you with some noble rank."

Lu assented. A day or two later he left with his credentials for Xuanfu, where he met Governor Yang and told him of Yan Shifan's instructions.

"This has been rankling with me day and night, so that I have not been able to sleep or eat," said Yang. "But I have not yet hit on a good plan for killing him."

"We should both keep our eyes open," said Lu. "We must not disappoint the prime minister, and it would never do to let slip this chance of advancing ourselves."

"You are right," agreed Yang. "If either of us finds an opportunity, he should let the other know."

After they parted, preoccupation with what Lu Kai had said kept Governor Yang awake all night. The next morning when he went to his yamen his lieutenant reported:

"Two rebels caught in Weizhou have been sent here for Your Excellency to sentence."

"Bring them in," ordered Yang.

The escort came in, paid his respects and presented an official document. When Governor Yang opened and read it he laughed for joy; for these two rebels, Yan Hao and Yang Yinkui, were followers of the sorcerer Xiao Qin, leader of the White Lotus Sect,[7] who travelled constantly into Tartar territory and deceived people with his superstitious rites. He had assured Altan Khan that he had magic means to kill men and cause city walls to crumble; and the khan, foolish enough to believe him, had given him the title of Great Master. Xiao Qin had several hundred followers, who formed a separate unit in the Tartar army and acted as guides each time Altan Khan raided the border; thus they had done China great harm. Yang's predecessor, Governor Shi, had sent envoys with gifts to the Tartar chief, Tuotuo, the inform him:

"The Son of Heaven is willing to make peace with you and establish a system of barter whereby we exchange cloth and grain for your horses. A cessation of hostilities and a period of peace would be beneficial for both our countries; but we fear Xiao Qin may attempt to obstruct a settlement and stir up strife. This Xiao Qin is a rogue and a charlatan, who has no magic powers but has been tricking you into carrying out raids for his own selfish ends. If you doubt this, ask him for some proof of his boasted arts. If he can indeed make walls crumble and kill men by witchcraft, by all means treat him well. If he cannot, then he has deceived you, and you had better deliver him to us in chains. Then our celestial court, pleased with your help, will reward you handsomely; and once the horse barter is established you will reap endless profit year after year. Would that not be much more advantageous than pillage?"

Tuotuo approved of this proposal and reported it to Altan Khan, who was also favourably impressed, and told Xiao Qin that a thousand horsemen would follow him across the frontier to test his skill in causing walls to crumble. Then Xiao, knowing that he was doomed to exposure, disguised himself and fled by night. He was challenged and seized by the garrison at Juyong Pass, then taken to Governor Shi; and when he confessed that he had many followers in the west and south, orders were given for their arrest. Since the names of the rebels Yan Hao and Yang Yinkui were on Xiao Qin's list, Governor Yang was delighted that they had been arrested, for he felt their capture reflected credit on him and he could make use of them to trap Shen Lian. That same evening he invited Censor Lu to discuss the matter in one of his inner chambers.

"We cannot get Shen on any other charge," said Yang, "but there is nothing the emperor dislikes more than this treasonous alliance between the Tartars and the White Lotus Sect. Now we can make these two men write in their confession that they were Shen Lian's pupils, and that after he lost his post he became discontented and incited them to practise sorcery and ally with the Tartars to overthrow their own country. Since Heaven has decreed their capture, we can ask His Majesty's permission to execute Shen Lian in order to avoid further trouble, after first writing privately to the Yans urging them to order the Board of Justice to report this promptly to the imperial court. Then Shen Lian will not escape."

Lu clapped his hands in approval. Then and there, the two of them decided on the contents of the reports and arranged to send them in together. When Yan Song received these reports, he told his son to inform the Board of Justice. The minister, Xu Lun, was a cowardly, incompetent old man, who after receiving the prime minister's order lost no time in addressing a memorial to the throne along the lines proposed by Yang and Lu. Then an imperial edict was issued ordering the immediate execution of the sorcerer Shen Lian by the local authorities; Yang's son was appointed a lieutenant, and Lu was promoted three ranks and promised a new post in the capital as soon as there was a vacancy.

Once Governor Yang had sent in his report, he ordered his men to seize Shen Lian and throw him into gaol. Shen's wife and sons were frightened out of their wits, and the two lads took counsel with Jia Shi.

"Those scoundrels Yang Shun and Lu Kai must have done this to please the prime minister," said Jia. "And the fact that your father has been thrown into gaol means they have certainly charged him with some serious crime. You two young gentlemen had better go as far away as you can and remain in hiding until the Yans have fallen from power. If you stay here, they will kill you too."

"How can we leave without waiting to see what becomes of our father?" asked Shen Gun.

"Now that your father has fallen into his enemies' hands, he is beyond help," replied Jia. "It is more important to continue your family line than to throw away your lives for the sake of filial piety, and you had better advise your mother to save herself too. As for your father, I shall see that he is properly looked after. You needn't worry on that score."

When the two brothers went in to tell their mother this, however, she raised objections.

"Your father is innocent," she said. "How can we abandon him now that he is in gaol? Though Uncle Jia has been so good to us, he is not a kinsman after all. I am sure those two scoundrels Yang and Lu are angry only with your father; they can't possibly involve us in this. If you run away because you are afraid, and your father dies, there will be no one to bury him and you will be condemned for ever as unfilial sons. How could you hold up your heads again?"

After saying this she wept bitterly, and her sons shed tears too. As for Jia Shi, when he heard that Mrs. Shen would not listen to reason, he sighed and left. A few days later he received reliable information that Shen Lian had been condemned to death as a member of the White Lotus Sect. Shen Lian kept cursing his enemies loudly in gaol, and Governor Yang, who knew that injustice had been done and feared that he might lose face if the prisoner denounced him publicly on the way to the execution ground, ordered the gaoler to report that Shen Lian had died of illness, then had him murdered.

When Jia Shi broke this news to Mrs. Shen, it goes without saying that she and her sons lamented bitterly. Jia, who had many connections, succeeded in buying Shen's corpse by persuading the gaoler to produce a false corpse if the head had to be publicly exhibited. Then, unknown to the Shen brothers, he buried his old friend's body with due rites in a spare plot of ground.

"I have saved your father's body and shall show you his grave when the trouble is over," he told them. "For the present, though, I must keep it a secret."

The young men thanked him again and again, while Jia urged them once more to leave that district.

"We know that we have occupied your house for a long time, uncle," said Shen Gun, "and we feel very bad about it. But our mother wants to remain here till our father's name is cleared, then move his coffin to our ancestral grave-yard. That is why we want to stay on."

"I always advise people for their own good," replied Jia angrily. "I urged you to move for your own sake, not because I want my house back. Since your respected mother has made up her mind, I cannot insist. But I myself find it necessary to leave home for a year or so. Stay here by all means as long as you please."

Just then he caught sight of two of Zhuge Liang's memorials in Shen Lian's handwriting on the wall.

"May I have these two scrolls as a memento?" he asked. "Then, when we meet again, we shall know each other by them."

Shen Gun took down the scrolls, rolled them up and gave them to Jia Shi, who put them in his sleeves and left, shedding tears. Jia knew that Governor Yang and Censor Lu were wicked men, who would not rest content with murdering Shen Lian, and that as Shen's friend he was likely to be involved. So he fled to Henan to stay with a kinsman there.

When Censor Lu received the imperial edict based on the report from the Board of Justice, he had the rebels Yan Hao and Yang Yinkui executed, and gave orders for Shen Lian's head to be displayed with theirs. By this time, how-ever, Shen's corpse had been bought by Jia Shi, and the censor did not realize that another corpse had been sub-stituted for it. But when Governor Yang saw that his sole reward was an official rank for his son, he felt resentful.

"Yan Shifan promised to make me a noble," he told Lu. "I wonder why he has not kept his word?"

"Shen Lian was the Yans' arch enemy," replied Lu after some thought. "Though he is dead, his sons are still alive. It is no use cutting grass unless you pull out its roots. No doubt the prime minister is not completely satisfied."

"That is easy," replied Yang. "We can send in another memorial reporting that Shen Lian has been executed, but it appears his sons are in the plot too, and they ought to be punished and their property confiscated as an example to all evil-doers. We should also arrest those wild young men who practised archery with Shen Lian, as well as the fellow who lent Shen his house, and have them all punished. Then the prime minister's vengeance will be complete, and he can hardly fail to keep his promise."

"That is an excellent plan," approved Lu. "But there is no time to be lost. If we can seize them all while his family is still here, so much the better. I am only afraid Shen's sons may scent danger and fly, in which case we shall have trouble."

Yang Shun agreed. They sent a memorial to the throne and a letter to the Yan family pledging their loyalty. At the same time they ordered the prefect of Bao'an to watch the culprits well and not allow them to run away, for as soon as an edict was issued they would have to be arrested.

Within a few days the imperial edict arrived and the local authorities issued warrants for the arrest of Shen Lian's family and all his friends. Jia Shi alone had left home, and they had to report that he had escaped.

Governor Yang tried Shen's sons himself, ordering them to confess that they had worked for the enemy. And when they protested that they were innocent, he had them tortured until their bones were broken, their flesh torn, and they died in agony under the rods, their spirits taking flight to the nether regions. Dozens of others who had been arrested with them were also executed as their accomplices. Shen

Lian's youngest son, Shen Zhi, was spared because he was still a child; but he and his mother were banished to the outpost of Yunzhou.

Then Censor Lu said to Governor Yang: "Shen's eldest son, Shen Xiang, is a well-known scholar in Shaoxing. Once he passes the official examinations he will try to pay us back. We had better get rid of him now, to avoid trouble in future. The prime minister will approve of our caution."

Yang agreed, and wrote to the authorities in Zhejiang Province asking to have Shen Xiang sent to his district for trial. Then he bade his trusted secretary, Jin Shao, select able runners who would take the letter to Shaoxing and murder Shen Xiang on the way back. If they could procure a certificate from the local authorities stating that Shen had died of illness, to close the affair, he promised to reward them well and to recommend Jin for promotion. The secretary was delighted. He made a careful choice of two experienced runners, Zhang Qian and Li Wan, invited them to his quarters for a good meal, and presented them with twenty taels of silver from his own pocket.

"How can we accept this when we have done nothing for you?" protested Zhang and Li.

"This silver is not from me but from Governor Yang," replied Jin. "He wants you to take a summons to Shaoxing to arrest Shen Xiang. Be very strict with him on the way; and if you see that he does not reach here alive, you will be well rewarded. If you fail, you will find that the governor is no person to trifle with. You will be held fully responsible."

"How dare we disobey the governor's wishes?" replied Zhang and Li. "Your instructions shall be faithfully carried out."

They pocketed the silver, thanked Jin, took the summons from the prefecture, and travelled with all speed southwards.

Now Shen Xiang was a stipendiary scholar of Shaoxing Prefecture. When he heard that his father had been deprived of his official rank and banished to the frontier, he was very worried and wanted to go to Bao'an. He could not leave, however, because he had no one to whom to entrust his family. Now suddenly men from the prefect's yamen loaded him with chains and took him without a word of explanation to court, where the prefect showed him the summons and handed him over with the official reply to the runners from Bao'an, charging them to be careful on the way. Realizing that his father and two younger brothers had been killed and his mother exiled to a lonely outpost, Shen Xiang cried aloud all the way out of the court, and at the gate he found his whole family waiting in tears. The authorities had ordered the confiscation of his property, and the prefect had sent constables to seal up his house and drive out the inmates. This so added to Shen Xiang's grief that he wailed till he was out of breath. Then his relatives came to bid him farewell, proffering a few words of comfort though they knew they would probably never see him again. His father-in-law, Meng Chunyuan, offered a packet of silver to the runners and begged them to look after Shen Xiang well on the road; but they refused to accept the money until his wife added a pair of gold hairpins.

"The odds are that I shall be killed," Shen Xiang told his wife with tears. "Don't grieve for me, but consider yourself a widow and go back to live with your parents. You come from a good family, so there need be no question of your remarrying and I can set my mind at rest."

Then he pointed to Wen Shunu, his concubine.

"She is very young," he told his wife, "and has no family to which to return. I should bid her marry again, but I am thirty now and have no son, and she is two months pregnant. If she gives birth to a son our ancestral sacrifices can be continued. So for my sake, wife, will you take her to your home for a while? You can send her away after she has given birth if you wish."

"How can you suggest such a thing, husband?" put in Shunu before he had finished. "If we let you go hundreds of miles away with no one to look after you, we can never rest easy in our minds. Our mistress may go back to her own family, but I shall go with you, shabby as I am. Then you will have someone to keep you company, and our mistress need not worry so much."

"Of course I would like to have a companion," rejoined Shen Xiang, "but this journey is not likely to end well. Why should I involve you and perhaps cause your death in a strange province?"

"Everyone knows that you were at home all the time your father was in the capital," said Shunu. "Even if they slander your father, they can hardly accuse you of being his accomplice when you were so far away. I shall go with you to the capital to plead your innocence, and I am sure you will not be condemned to death. And if they throw you into gaol, I shall be near enough to look after you."

Shen Xiang's wife was concerned for him too, so because there was reason in what Shunu said she urged him to take the concubine with him. And since Shen Xiang had always liked Shunu for her talent and wit, now that his wife supported her proposal he agreed to take her. That night they stayed with his father-in-law, and the next morning when the two runners Zhang Qian and Li Wan pressed him to set out at once, Shunu changed into cloth garments and a black kerchief, said goodbye to Shen Xiang's wife, shouldered her baggage and walked out behind her husband. The family's grief at parting can be imagined.

During the journey Shen Xiang's concubine stirred not a step from his side, and served him his food and drink herself. At first Zhang and Li treated them well; but once they had crossed the Yangzi River and were continuing on foot from Xuzhou, far from Shen's home, the runners began to grow rough, shouting curses and making things more difficult for their prisoner. Shunu noticed this.

"Those wicked men mean mischief," she whispered to her husband. "I am only a woman, and I don't know the way. But if we pass through wild, lonely country, you must be on your guard."

Shen Xiang nodded, although he was confident that all would be well. When a few more days had passed, however, and he noticed that the two runners kept laying their heads together in a suspicious manner and that they had a glittering Japanese sword in their baggage, he began to be afraid.

"You said these runners are plotting mischief," he told Shunu, "and I am inclined to agree with you. After crossing the boundary of Jining Prefecture tomorrow we shall reach the Taihang and Liang Mountains, and that is wild, bandit-infested country. If they attack us there, we shall have no means of defending ourselves. What shall we do?"

"If you know of a way to escape, please take it and leave me to shift for myself," begged Shunu. "They can't eat me."

"Inside the East Gate of Jining lives a certain Secretary Feng, who has retired from office because he is in mourning for his father," said Shen Xiang. "He is a gallant man, and my father's classmate and good friend. If I call on him tomorrow, he will certainly take me in. But how can a woman deal with these two ruffians? I'm afraid they will hold you responsible for my escape, and I don't like the idea of that. If you feel confident that you can deal with them, I shall go with an easy mind. Otherwise, let us live or die together as fate decrees. I shall meet death without regret."

"You must escape if you can," replied Shunu. "I shall be able to cope with them. Don't worry."

Thus husband and concubine deliberated in secret, while the two runners snored away after a hard day's journey capped by heavy drinking. The next morning when they set out again, Shen Xiang asked Zhang Qian: "How far are we from Jining?"

"Only twelve or thirteen miles," replied Zhang. "We shall be there before noon."

"Inside the East Gate of that town lives a Secretary Feng

who used to be my father's friend," said Shen. "While in the capital he borrowed two hundred taels[8] of silver from my father, and I have his note of hand with me. He used to be in charge of the Beixin Customs, so he has plenty of money, and I am sure he will repay me now that I am in trouble if I ask him. This money would give us ample to spend on the road, and we could travel in comfort."

While Zhang Qian hesitated, Li Wan immediately approved of this scheme.

"Shen seems an honest man," he whispered to Zhang. "Besides, his baggage and concubine are here — what can go wrong? Let him go and get the money, I say. It will all be ours, won't it?"

"Very well," replied Zhang. "But wait till we've put down our baggage in an inn. Then I can keep an eye on the woman there while you follow Shen. That should be safe enough."

By ten o'clock that morning they reached Jining, and deposited their baggage in a clean inn outside the city.

"Which of you will come with me to the East Gate?" asked Shen. "We can have our midday meal when we get back."

"I'll go with you," said Li. "They may invite us to a meal with wine."

"You know the proverb," said Shunu to her husband, "the world is full of fair-weather friends, who look down on you when you're down on your luck. Though Secretary Feng owes your family money, now that your father is dead and you are in difficulties he may not feel like paying you back promptly. Most likely he will refuse to see you. Better have a meal and go on."

"It's not far from here to the East Gate," countered Shen. "We can't lose anything by calling on him."

Li Wan, who was eager to lay his hands on that two hundred taels of silver, urged Shen on.

"Wait for me here," said Shen to his concubine. "If we

are back soon, it will mean our trip was in vain; but if he keeps us to a meal, he is bound to pay me something. Then tomorrow we can hire a sedan chair for you. You must have found it hard all these days on that donkey.''

"Very well," said Shunu with a meaning glance at her husband. "Come back as soon as you can. Don't keep me waiting too long.''

"How long do you think he'll be anyway?" asked Li Wan with a laugh. "Can't you let him out of your sight for a moment?''

As Shen Xiang was leaving, Shunu deliberately called Li back.

"If Secretary Feng invites you to a meal, please don't let him keep you too long," she said.

"Don't you worry," replied the runner.

By the time Li Wan walked down the steps of the inn, Shen Xiang had a good start of him. The runner was a careless fellow. He was quite familiar with this town, having often been here before, and even knew which was Secretary Feng's house. He was therefore not in the least anxious. After walking a few yards he looked round for a public latrine, then strolled slowly towards the East Gate.

When Shen Xiang saw that Li was not following him, he ran straight to Secretary Feng's house, where he was lucky enough to find Feng alone in the sitting room. They had been old friends in the capital, and Feng was delighted by this unexpected visit. But instead of greeting him Shen pulled at his sleeve.

"May I speak to you in private?" he begged.

Realizing that the situation was serious, Feng led him to the library, where Shen burst into tears.

"My dear nephew, what is the matter?" inquired Feng. "Don't waste time weeping if prompt action is needed.''

"I expect you know how my father was done to death unjustly by that traitor," said Shen. "Now my two younger brothers who were with him have been murdered by Yang

Shun and Lu Kai. I was the only one left at home, but they sent a warrant to our district and runners to take me to Bao'an. It looks as if our whole family is to be wiped out. The two runners escorting me mean mischief: I suspect they have orders to murder me when we reach the Taihang and Liang Mountains which are just ahead. So I have tricked them, and come to throw myself on your mercy. If you can protect me, my father's spirit will be grateful to you in heaven. If you cannot, I shall dash my head against the stone steps and die here rather than at the hands of those traitors."

"Don't worry," said Secretary Feng. "I have a double wall behind my bedroom where you can hide and no one will find you. You had better stay there for a few days. I have a plan, if you will only wait."

"You are a second father to me!" cried Shen, bowing to express his thanks.

Then Feng took him by the hand and led him to the back of his bedroom, where he removed some planks from the floor to reveal an underground staircase. After fifty or sixty steps, they saw light and came upon three small rooms walled in so that no one could reach them. Every day Feng himself brought tea and food to Shen here; and because his household discipline was strict no one dared disclose the fugitive's presence.

Meanwhile Li Wan was proceeding in a leisurely fashion towards Secretary Feng's house at the East Gate.

"Is your master in?" he asked at the door.

"Yes," replied the old door-keeper. "He is."

"A gentleman in white called to see him. Did Secretary Feng admit him?"

"Yes. He has asked him to stay for lunch in the library."

Hearing this, Li settled down to wait with an easy mind; and at two in the afternoon a man in white came out. But when Li stepped forward hastily to accost him, he discovered this was not Shen but a stranger. By now the runner was both hungry and impatient, so he questioned the old doorkeeper again.

"Why doesn't the gentleman your master is keeping for a meal come out?"

"He did come out just now."

"Doesn't your master have another guest in the library?"

"Not that I know of."

"Who was that gentleman in white who just left?"

"That is our master's brother-in-law, who often calls."

"Where is your master now?"

"He always has a nap after lunch. He must be sleeping now."

The fact that he was receiving the wrong answers to all his questions began to make Li worried.

"The truth is that I am here on business for His Excellency the Governor of Xuanfu and Datong," he said. "I have been escorting a state prisoner named Shen Xiang, a young gentleman from Shaoxing who said he was connected with your master and wanted to call on him. I followed him to your house, and he went in; but although I have waited all this time he has not come out yet. I suppose he is still in the library, though you don't know it. Please ask him to hurry up and come out, because we must be on our way."

"What are you talking about?" demanded the old man, feigning complete bewilderment. "I don't understand a word you say."

When Li suppressed his anxiety to explain the situation again in detail, the old man spat at him.

"You've been seeing ghosts!" he swore. "No Mr. Shen has been here! My master is in mourning, so he doesn't receive anybody outside the family. I am in charge of the gate and I announce everyone who goes in. How can you spin a yarn like that to me? I suppose you are one of those thieves who sneak around in broad daylight pretending to be government runners. Get out now, and don't pester me any more."

At this Li became really worried, and flew into a rage.

"Shen Xiang is an important state criminal!" he bellowed. "This is no joking matter. Please ask your master to come out, so that I can speak to him."

"Secretary Feng is sleeping now, and I dare not disturb him for no reason. You northern barbarians are fools!"

With that the door-keeper walked slowly off.

"The old idiot!" swore Li. "Why should he lose his temper just because I asked him to send in my message? Shen Xiang *must* be inside. I have the warrant on me, and this is not private business. I may as well go straight in."

He marched boldly into the hall and banged on the screen.

"It's time to go, Mr. Shen!" he shouted.

When there was no answer, he went on shouting until a servant-boy came out.

"Where is the door-keeper?" demanded the boy, staring at the runner from behind the screen. "Who let this fellow in to make so much noise?"

Before Li could call to him to stop, the boy walked out towards the west.

"Maybe the library is there," thought Li. "I'll have a look."

He turned west from the hall and headed down a long, deserted corridor till he came to a number of rooms which were obviously the women's quarters; then he dared go no further, but returned to the hall. At this point he heard shouting outside, and upon going to the gate found that Zhang Qian had come to look for him and was swearing at the door-keeper. The moment Zhang caught sight of Li, he started abusing him.

"A fine fellow you are!" he cried. "All you care about is food and wine, not how to do your job properly. You came into town at ten o'clock, and now it is nearly five in the afternoon; yet you are still hanging about here instead of making the criminal get a move on. What are you waiting for?"

"Curse it!" retorted Li. "What food have I had? I can't find him!"

"But you came with him into town."

"I stopped for a second at a latrine on the way. Then that damned southerner went ahead, and I couldn't catch up with him. I followed him all the way here, and the gateman told me a gentleman in white had been kept for lunch in the library; so I took it for granted it must be him. But though I've waited all this time, he still hasn't come out, and the gateman won't announce me. Not a drop of water has passed my lips, brother. Please wait here a few minutes while I fill my belly."

"How could you be such a fool?" exploded Zhang. "How dare you let a criminal like that out of your sight? Even if he did go to the library, you ought to have followed him in. Now who knows whether he is inside or not? Yet here you are talking as if nothing had happened. Well, you're responsible for this; it's nothing to do with me."

He started walking off, but Li hurried after him and caught hold of him.

"The fellow must be inside," insisted Li. "I'm sure he can't get away. We should both try to get him out, and you've had your meal — what's the hurry?"

"His concubine is still in the inn," replied Zhang. "Though I've asked the landlord to keep an eye on her, I don't feel happy about leaving her. She's the rope through the ox's nose: as long as she's there, we may be sure he'll come back."

"Right," agreed Li.

When Zhang had left, Li waited with an empty stomach till evening without seeing any sign of Shen. By sunset he was ravenous. Noticing a pastry shop next door, he went to pawn his coat for a few coins to buy dumplings. But although he was only away for a few minutes, he heard the sound of a gate being barred, and when he ran back he found Secretary Feng's house locked.

"Never have I been treated like this in all my years as a

runner!" swore Li. "How high does he think a secretary's rank is, to put on such airs? Shen Xiang is the limit too. His concubine and baggage are in the inn, so even if he wants to spend the night here he ought to send us word. Well, it can't be helped; I'd better pass the night as best I can under the eaves. At daybreak I shall get hold of a more intelligent servant to talk to."

It was then the tenth month, and not too cold; but a wind sprang up in the middle of the night and rain fell. Soon Li's clothes were wet, and he shivered miserably. At dawn the rain stopped and Zhang Qian turned up again, sent by Shunu.

He had with him the official despatch and summons, and they agreed that as soon as the gate opened they should push their way in. This they did. The old gateman could not stop them, and they created a great uproar in the hall. Presently the whole household had gathered round and begun shouting too, making the noise even worse; and when passers-by heard the din they clustered outside the gate to watch. Finally Secretary Feng walked out to see what the clamour was about. The servants heard him cough as he approached.

"The master is here!" they cried, hastily ranging themselves on both sides of the room.

"What is all this noise?" demanded Feng, entering the hall.

The two runners stepped forward to pay their respects.

"Sir," they said, "we are here on a mission for the Governor of Xuanfu and Datong. We arrested the state criminal Shen Xiang at Shaoxing, and were escorting him through your district when he said he was related to you and wanted to call on you. Not daring to refuse him, we let him come. But that was yesterday morning, and he has still not come out. This is holding up our journey, yet your servants would not announce us. We hope, sir, you will kindly urge him to leave now."

Then Zhang Qian took from his wallet the warrant and

the official despatch.

"Is this Shen Xiang the son of Shen Lian?" asked Feng, after reading these documents.

"Yes, sir," replied Li.

Feng put his hands over his ears and thrust out his tongue in dismay.

"What criminal negligence!" he exclaimed. "Shen Xiang is not only a state criminal, but the enemy of the prime minister. Who would dare shelter such a man? When did he come to my house, pray? You are raving! If this rumour reaches the authorities and they inform the Yan family, what will become of me? I would like to know how large a bribe you irresponsible scoundrels took to let such an important criminal go. And now you are trying to shift the blame on to me! Throw them out, men, and bar the gate; otherwise we shall find ourselves involved. It will be no joke if the Yan family hears of this."

Still swearing, he went back to his room, while the servants pushed and shoved the two runners out and closed the gate behind them, still cursing them from inside. Zhang and Li stuck out their tongues and gaped at each other in consternation. "Yesterday you urged me to let him come to town," accused Zhang. "Now it's up to you to find him."

"Stop grumbling and let's go back to question his concubine," said Li. "She ought to know where he is. Then we can come back to get him."

"All right," said Zhang. "They are certainly devoted to each other. Yesterday when he didn't show up she went on crying for hours and insisted on waiting up for him. She must know where he is."

As they were talking, they hurried back to the inn. And the moment Shunu heard their voices from her room she ran to the door.

"Where is my husband?" she demanded.

"Ask him!" Zhang pointed at Li.

Li told her all that had happened the previous day.

"This morning I hurried to town without my breakfast but got nothing for my pains," said Zhang. "It doesn't look as if your husband can be with Secretary Feng, but in that case he must have gone somewhere else. He must have told you his plans, ma'am. If you tell us, we can go to look for him."

Before he had finished speaking, tears sprang to Shunu's eyes and she seized the two runners.

"Give me back my husband!" she cried.

"Your husband asked us to allow him to call on a relative, and we were good enough to let him go," they protested. "Now he's disappeared, and left us in this fix, yet you act as if we had hidden him somewhere. This is ridiculous!"

They undid their shirts to cool off and sat down sulkily together.

Shunu ran to the door to bar their escape, then stamped her feet and screamed that injustice had been done. The old innkeeper hurried over to see what the matter was.

"Let me tell you what's happened, uncle," said Shunu. "My husband still had no son at thirty, so he took me as his concubine, and I have been with him for two years. Because I have been with child for more than three months, he could not send me away; and I have followed him all this way, not letting him out of my sight once. Yesterday, because we were short of travelling money, he wanted to call on a friend; and that runner, Li, went with him. When he didn't come back last night, I began to have my suspicions; and now that these two have come back without him, I know they must have murdered him. Please help me, sir, and make them give me back my husband!"

"You mustn't jump to conclusions, ma'am," said the innkeeper. "These officers are not your husband's enemies. Why should they kill him?"

At that Shunu wept more bitterly than ever.

"I can tell you why," she sobbed. "My husband is hated

by Prime Minister Yan, and these two men must have been
sent by the Yan family or decided to ask for a reward from
them. Just think, sir! Why should my husband suddenly
go off without a word after bringing me all this way? And
even if he wanted to, would Li Wan let him go? No, to
curry favour with the prime minister these wicked men have
made away with my husband. And what can a poor, lonely
woman do? Please seize these murderers for me, uncle!
Then I shall lodge a complaint at the yamen."

As she wept and stormed, Zhang and Li had no answer to
make. Then the old innkeeper thought there must be something in what she said, and pitied her.

"Even if this is true, ma'am," he said, "your husband
may not be dead. Why don't you wait another day?"

"It's all very well to tell me to wait another day, but who
will be responsible for these two murderers? They may seize
the chance to run away."

"If we had really murdered your husband and wanted to
run away," declared Zhang, "why should we have come back
here?"

"You counted on the fact that I am a helpless woman,"
retorted Shunu. "I suppose you thought you would kidnap
me. Tell the truth now: where is my husband's body? You
will have to confess when we go to court."

Hearing how convincingly she spoke, the innkeeper dared
say no more. Meanwhile forty or fifty people had gathered
round, and when they learned the concubine's sad story they
were furious with the two runners.

"If you want to lodge a complaint, ma'am, we'll take you
to the military commissioner," they offered.

Shunu bowed deeply to them, weeping.

"Thank you for your kindness," she said. "Have pity on
a lonely woman in distress and help me! Take these two
murderers with you, and don't let them escape!"

"Never fear," they replied. "You can depend on us."

When the runners attempted to explain matters, they

were silenced.

"There is no need for explanations," said the crowd. "Truth will always out. If you are innocent, why should you mind going with her to the yamen?"

Shunu shed tears as she went, and the crowd dragged Zhang Qian and Li Wan with them to the military commissioner's office. It was still too early, however, for that day's morning session.

Then Shunu, who had put on a white mourning apron, darted inside the palisade to where there was a big drum near the gate with a drum stick hanging from its frame. She seized the stick and beat the drum as loudly as she could. Shocked and startled, the yamen attendants and gate-keeper rushed forward and bound her.

"How dare you, woman!" they shouted.

Shunu fell sobbing to the ground, where she cried that she had been cruelly wronged. Then a shout was raised inside, the gate opened, and the military commissioner took his seat in court and asked who had beaten the drum. His lieutenant brought in Shunu, who wept as she related the misfortunes that had befallen her family and described in detail how Shen Lian and his sons had been killed, leaving only her husband, who had been murdered the previous day by the runners. She gave circumstantial evidence, and when the commissioner questioned Zhang and Li she pulled all their arguments to pieces. Moreover, she spoke so convincingly that they could not refute her.

"The prime minister is powerful and often plots the death of innocent men," reflected the commissioner. "What she says may be true."

He bid his lieutenant take Shunu and the two runners to the local Prefect He.

As soon as the prefect received this case, he sent for the innkeeper and cross-examined the four of them. The woman insisted that the two runners had murdered her husband, Li declared that he had been delayed by going to the latrine and lost his man, and Zhang and the innkeeper stated the facts as they knew them. The prefect did not know which of them was telling the truth. Shunu was so sad that it seemed her story must be true, yet Zhang and Li would not admit to murdering Shen Xiang. Finally Prefect He decided to detain the four of them while he went by sedan chair to find out what Secretary Feng thought of the case. When Secretary Feng heard that the prefect had come, he hastily invited him into his sitting room, where they drank tea. But as soon as Shen Xiang's name was mentioned, Feng clapped his hands over his ears.

"That man is the prime minister's enemy," he declared. "Though I knew him in the capital, we were never close friends. Please don't mention Shen Xiang to me. If the Yans hear of this, they may make trouble for me."

Then he stood up.

"Since you have public duties to attend to, sir," he said, "I dare not detain you any longer."

After such a rebuff, the prefect had to leave.

"Judging by Feng's fear of the prime minister, he can hardly be sheltering Shen Xiang," he thought on the way back. "Perhaps the man was murdered by those runners after all. Or he may have called on Feng and been refused admittance, then gone to somebody else he knew."

Upon his return to the yamen, he summoned the four people in the case again.

"What other friends did your husband have in this district apart from Secretary Feng?" he asked Shunu.

"None, Your Honour."

"When did your husband leave? And when did they tell you he had disappeared?"

"My husband left the inn yesterday before lunch with Li Wan. At about four in the afternoon Zhang Qian went into town saying he was going to fetch them, and didn't come back till after dark. 'Brother Li is staying with your husband in Secretary Feng's house,' he told me. 'I shall go early tomorrow morning to call for them.' Today Zhang was out all morning, but he and Li came back without my husband. They must have murdered him! If my husband wasn't at Secretary Feng's house yesterday, Li should surely have looked for him and Zhang should have been worried too. Why should they reassure me? It's obvious what must have happened. They arranged on the road for Li to kill him that night, and this morning Zhang went back to town to help bury the corpse; then they returned to tell me my husband was missing. Avenge an unhappy woman, Your Honour!"

"I believe you are right," said the prefect.

And when Zhang and Li protested, he silenced them.

"Fine runners you are!" he exclaimed. "If you didn't plot his death, you allowed yourselves to be bribed into letting him escape. What more have you to say?"

He ordered his men to give them thirty strokes with the heavy bastinado;[9] yet even when bleeding and torn they would not confess. Shunu was weeping bitterly, and pity for her made the prefect have the runners put to torture; but naturally they would not admit to a murder they had not committed, and though they were tortured twice they maintained a stubborn silence. When the prefect ordered them to be tortured again, however, they knew they could not stand any more.

"Shen Xiang cannot be dead, Your Honour," they pleaded. "If you will send officers with us, we promise to find him within a certain time and restore him to his wife."

Because the prefect was not certain of their guilt, he agreed. Shunu was sent to stay in a nunnery, while Zhang and Li were chained and despatched with four militiamen to find Shen, being ordered to report at the yamen every five days. The innkeeper was released, and a full report of the case was sent to the military commissioner.

Zhang and Li were loaded with chains and watched in turns by the four militiamen, who took their few taels of travelling money for food and drink, and sold their sword for liquor too. In a large district like this, through which travellers were constantly passing, they had not the slightest hope of finding the missing man. The search was simply a means of escaping torture.

Shunu, who was staying in the nunnery, went every few days to weep and wail in the yamen and threaten to commit suicide. And since the prefect could not solve the case, he demanded that the runners find Shen by a certain date. He called Zhang and Li in dozens of times and gave them so many strokes with the bastinado when they failed to find their prisoner that they could hardly move. At last Zhang Qian fell ill and died. And Li Wan, left alone, went to the nunnery to plead with the concubine.

"I am desperate," he told her, "so I will tell you the truth. Before we left Xuanfu, Secretary Jin Shao told us that Governor Yang had ordered us to kill your husband on the way, then get a certificate from the local authorities to close the matter. But although we agreed, naturally we would never have done such a cruel thing. As Heaven is my witness, however your husband escaped we had nothing to do with his disappearance; and if that is not the truth may my whole family perish! Now every five days the prefect summons me to demand the prisoner, and Brother Zhang has already been beaten to death. How unfair it will be if I die too! For your husband is *not* dead, and you are bound to meet again. So please have pity on me, ma'am, and stop weeping at the yamen. Give me a little more time in which to find him. You will be doing a good deed if you save my wretched life."

"I find it hard to believe that you have not murdered my husband." replied Shunu. "But since you say so, I'll stop going to the yamen and let you take your time looking for him. Mind you search hard, though, and leave no stone unturned."

Li Wan assented and left.

The prefect had set a time limit for the recapture of Shen

Xiang and summoned the runners constantly because Shen was an important criminal wanted by Governor Yang, and because his concubine kept coming to beg that justice be done. At last, however, Li Wan's luck turned, and something happened to save his life. Governor Yang and Censor Lu had been taking counsel day and night how best to flatter the Yan family, in the hope that they might soon be ennobled; but now Secretary Wu Shilai in the Board of War heard of Yang Shun's slaughter of innocent people to gain credit, and presented a memorial denouncing him indignantly and accusing Lu Kai of abetting him in his evil courses. The emperor, who was then offering sacrifices to invoke the blessing of Heaven, was furious to hear of this massacre for it meant that the harmonious influences must have been impaired. He ordered the imperial police to arrest the culprits and bring them to the capital for punishment. Since the emperor was angry, Yan Song could not save his protégés entirely; but by putting in a good word for them he contrived that they should merely be deprived of their ranks instead of executed. Thus Yang Shun and Lu Kai, who had killed innocent citizens to curry favour with the mighty, simply covered themselves with shame.

When the Prefect of Jining heard that Yang Shun had been dismissed from office, he was willing to let Shen Xiang's case drop; the more so since Shunu had stopped coming to beg him to take action, and one of the runners was dead while the other kept entreating him to be merciful. So the prefect freed Li Wan from his chains and gave him a writ ordering him to make a careful search for the missing man, which was tantamount to releasing him. Li Wan felt as relieved as a criminal who receives an amnesty. After kowtowing again and again, he left the yamen and made off as fast as he could. Since he had no money left, he begged his way home.

Meanwhile Shen Xiang had been staying in Secretary Feng's secret chamber for many months, learning all that was happening outside from his host, and rejoicing to think that Shunu was still in the nunnery near by. After a year, when Zhang Qian had died, Li Wan had fled, and the case was dropped, Feng vacated three inner chambers for Shen Xiang so that he could study in the house, but would not allow him out nor let outsiders know of his presence. And because he was harbouring an outlaw in his house, Feng did not take up office again after completing his three years of mourning.

Time sped like an arrow, and soon eight years had passed. Yan Song's wife died, but instead of accompanying his mother's coffin to their home in the country Yan Shifan persuaded the prime minister to obtain permission for him to remain in the capital "to wait on his father." In fact, however, he spent the whole period of mourning drinking and enjoying himself with his concubines; and because the emperor was himself a dutiful son, when he heard of this he was displeased. There was a priest at that time named Lan Daoxing, who was able to commune with spirits, and the emperor summoned him to ascertain whether his ministers were good or bad.

"I summon only real deities from the upper regions who speak the truth and cannot flatter," said the priest. "If the oracle happens to offend Your Majesty, I hope you will pardon me."

"I desire to hear the truth from Heaven," replied the emperor. "This in no way concerns you, and I shall certainly not be angry with you."

Then the priest traced a charm and read an incantation, whereupon the sand on his tray began to move and the following lines appeared on it:

On a high hill grows foreign grass;
Both father and son are ministers of state;
The sun and moon have lost their brightness,
And heaven and earth are upside-down.

"Can you explain this to me?" asked the emperor.

"I am an ignorant man," replied the priest. "I cannot understand it."

"*I* understand it," said the emperor. "A *high* (高) *hill* (山) stands for the character *Song* (嵩), and *foreign* (番) *grass* (草) for *Fan* (蕃). This is therefore a reference to Yan Song and Yan Shifan. I have long suspected that they were usurping authority and injuring the state, and now that Heaven has confirmed this I shall know how to deal with them. See that you do not say a word of this to others."

The priest kowtowed.

"I shall not speak of it to anyone," he promised. Then, taking his reward, he left.

After that the emperor began to treat Yan Song coldly, and a censor named Zou Yinglong took this opportunity to present a memorial to the throne impeaching the prime minister and his son. He pointed out that Yan Shifan had taken advantage of his father's position to sell official posts and ranks and commit other crimes, and urged that he should be executed. He also recommended that since Yan Song had encouraged his profligate son and gathered a clique to injure good people, he should be dismissed from his post in order to reform the government. The emperor was delighted to receive this memorial. He promoted Zou to the rank of an advisor to the Board of Transmission and sent Yan Shifan to be tried by the chief justice, who banished him to the frontier. Yan Song was ordered to retire to the country too. Soon after this the Inspecting Censor of Jiangxi, Lin Run, reported that Yan Shifan had refused to do military service but was acting as a local despot, seizing people's property, sheltering outlaws, making secret overtures to the Japanese pirates and plotting high treason. The emperor decreed that the case should be investigated, and when the chief justice reported that the charges were true Yan Shifan was promptly executed and all his property confiscated. As for Yan Song, he ended his days in an old men's home, while all those who had suffered at his hands had their property and posts restored.

When Feng heard this good news, he lost no time in telling Shen Xiang that now he could go out, and Shen hurried to the nunnery to look for Shunu. After embracing each other they wept. At the time of leaving Shaoxing, Shunu was nearly three months gone with child, and she had given birth to a son in the nunnery who was now ten years old. Shen was happy to find she had taught the boy herself, so that he could already read the Five Classics.[10]

Feng decided to go to the capital to apply for an official post, and he advised Shen to accompany him to clear his father's name, leaving his concubine for the time being with the Feng family. Shen took his advice, and they travelled to Beijing. When Feng called on Advisor Zou, told him of the injustice done to Shen Lian and his sons, and showed him a report written by Shen Xiang, Zou promised to take the matter up. The next day Shen Xiang sent in his report; and soon an imperial decree was issued stating that since Shen Lian had been killed on account of his loyalty to the state, his official status should be restored and he should be posthumously promoted one rank to commend his virtue. His wife and son should return home, and their confiscated property should be returned in full by the local authorities. Shen Xiang, who had long been a government stipendiary, was now appointed a magistrate.

Then Shen Xiang addressed the following memorial to the throne:

"When my father, Shen Lian, was at Bao'an and saw Governor Yang Shun slaughter innocent people for the sake of personal aggrandizement, he wrote verses to express his indignation. Then the censor Lu Kai, acting on secret instructions from Yan Shifan, inspected the area and conspired with Yang to execute my father and kill my two brothers. I myself barely escaped with my life. Thus the unjustly slain received no burial, and our family was nearly wiped out. No other family can have suffered as much as ours! Now Yan

Shifan has been punished; but as long as Yang Shun and Lu Kai remain alive, those wrongly slain at the frontier have not been avenged, and the three murdered members of my family must be wailing in the nether regions. I fear this is not in accordance with the requirements of law and justice."

The emperor sanctioned Shen's request, and Yang and Lu were taken to the capital, condemned to death, and sent to gaol to await execution. Then Shen Xiang went to take his leave of Feng before going to Yunzhou to escort his mother and youngest brother back to the capital to live near his friend. After that he intended to go to Bao'an to find his father's remains and take them home for burial.

"I have received news of your mother from Yunzhou," said Feng. "She is well, and your youngest brother is already studying in the district school. Let me send someone to fetch them, while you go in search of your father's remains that is your most important task. You can join your mother when that is done."

Shen agreed and travelled with all speed to Bao'an, where he searched for two days without finding a single clue. On the third day he was sitting down to rest by the roadside when an old man came out of a nearby house and invited him in to have some tea. Shen saw a scroll hanging on the wall on which were mounted two memoranda of Zhuge Liang bearing a date, but no signature. He gazed at this intently, as if unable to tear his eyes away.

"Why are you so interested in that scroll?" asked the old man.

"May I ask who wrote it?" inquired Shen.

"It was written by my deceased friend, Shen Lian."

"Why do you keep it?"

"My name is Jia Shi. When Mr. Shen was sent to stay here he lodged in my house, and we became sworn brothers. When tragedy overtook him I was afraid of being involved, and fled to Henan; but I took these two pieces of writing with me and mounted them on one scroll. Whenever I look at it, I feel as if I were seeing my old friend again. Only after Governor Yang was dismissed dared I return here. Shen Lian's wife and his youngest son, Shen Zhi, have moved to Yunzhou, where I frequently go to see them; and I have just sent a man to tell them that the Yans have fallen and Mrs. Shen's wrongs can now be avenged. I expect young Mr. Shen will come before long to fetch his father's coffin; so I have hung this scroll in the hall, in order that he may recognize his father's writing."

Shen Xiang hastily kowtowed, addressing Jia Shi as his uncle and benefactor.

"Who are you?" asked Jia, having helped him to rise.

"I am Shen Xiang, and this is my father's writing."

"I heard that Yang Shun sent runners to your district to seize you, so that he could destroy your whole family," said Jia. "I thought you had been murdered by him. How did you escape?"

As Shen told him all that had happened in Jining, Jia exclaimed in pleasure and surprise, then told his servants to prepare a meal for his guest.

"You must know where my father was buried," said Shen Xiang. "Will you show me the place so that I can pay my respects?"

"After your father was murdered in gaol, I stole his body and gave it burial," replied Jia. "But I have never dared speak of this before. Now you can take his remains to your home, and my efforts will not have been wasted."

They were on the point of leaving when a young gentleman rode up.

"What a coincidence!" cried Jia, pointing to the newcomer. "Here is your younger brother."

And indeed it was Shen Zhi who alighted to greet them.

"This is your eldest brother, Shen Xiang," Jia told him.

The brothers felt as if they were meeting in a dream, and embracing each other they wept. Then with Jia leading the way, the three of them went together to Shen Lian's

小霞相會拜師表

Shen Xiang kowtows to Jia Shi

grave — a mound covered with wild brambles and grass. The old man bade them kowtow, and they fell crying to the ground. But soon Jia urged them to rise.

"We must discuss important business now," he said. "Don't give way to grief."

At that the brothers dried their tears.

"When your two brothers were unjustly killed," Jia told them, "there was a kind gaoler with a sense of justice named Mao, who pitied them and buried them west of the city. Though Mao is dead now, I know the place. You had better take their remains with your father's coffin, so that the sons' spirits can dwell with their father's. What do you think?"

"We could ask nothing better, uncle," they replied.

That same day they went with Jia to the west of the city and were overcome with grief at the sight of the place. The next day they prepared coffins and chose an auspicious date on which to open the graves and remove the three corpses, which, due to the loyalty and integrity of the dead men, had not decomposed in the least. After shedding more tears, the brothers ordered a carriage to take the three coffins away, then said farewell to Jia Shi.

"I would like to have this scroll to hang in our ancestral temple," said Shen Xiang. "I hope you will agree, uncle."

Jia thereupon gave them the scroll, and when they had thanked him with tears in their eyes they left. Shen Zhi took the coffins to Zhangjiawan, whence they would be conveyed by boat, while Shen Xiang went back alone to Beijing to see his mother. Then, after making his report to the authorities, he thanked Feng for his assistance and left for home.

All the officials in the capital were full of praise for Shen Lian's loyalty and justice, and admired the brothers for travelling so far with the coffins; therefore they sent them gifts, money and travelling credentials. Shen Xiang, however, accepted only one credential. When he reached Zhangjiawan he chartered a large junk, which a hundred men towed rapidly along. In a few days they reached Jining, where Shen Xiang had the junk moored while he went alone into the city to let the Feng family know that all was well; then he escorted Shunu and her ten-year-old son to the boat. They paid their respects first to Shen Lian's coffin, then to Shen Xiang's mother; and when the old lady saw how big her grandson was, she was overjoyed. She had believed the whole family destroyed; but now she had her sons and grandson with her, while all their former enemies had died in misery. This shows that the wicked invariably come to a bad end, whereas the good prosper at last.

When they reached Shaoxing in Zhejiang Province, old Mr. Meng and his daughter, Shen Xiang's wife, welcomed them six or seven miles outside the city. Thus the whole family was reunited, joy mingling with their sadness. As the boat moored at the harbour, the local officials came to pay their respects to the dead; all the former property of the Shen family was restored; and after the two brothers had go to our respective posts."

interred the coffins in their ancestral graveyard, they observed three years of mourning so dutifully that their praise was on everyone's lips. The local governor also had a temple built for Shen Lian, where sacrifices were held in spring and autumn; and the scroll with his handwriting has been kept there to this day.

After the three years of mourning Shen Xiang went back to the capital and was appointed a magistrate. Since he proved a good official, he was soon promoted to a prefectship. Shunu's son passed the examinations early in his career, and became a palace graduate during the same year as his uncle, Shen Zhi; and all their descendants were scholars. Because Feng had saved Shen Xiang's life, the whole capital praised his gallantry, and he was appointed Head of the Board of Civil Affairs. One day he dreamed that Shen Lian called on him and said: "Because I am loyal and just, Heaven has made me the guardian spirit of Beijing. You are to be the guardian spirit of Nanjing.[11] Tomorrow at noon we must go to our respective posts."

Feng woke up puzzled. But the next day at noon he suddenly saw carriages coming to welcome him, and passed away peacefully. Thus the two friends became deities.

Notes:

1. A follower of Daoist teachings based on the writings of the philosophers Lao Zi, author of *The Way* (*Daodejing*), and Zhuang Zi. In reality, the word 'Daoist' covers anything from a hermit striving for immortality to a priest conversant in making offerings and talismans with his eye set on physical comfort in the present life.

2. Established as one of the six boards or ministries of the central government in the 7th century, the Board of Works supervised construction, agricultural levies, irrigation works and transportation.

3. Zhuge Liang (181-234AD) was a politician and strategist of the Three Kingdoms period. Renowned as the chief strategist and general of the State of Shu, Zhuge Liang was regarded as an example of justice and loyalty by later generations. The two memorials Zhuge wrote on the way to the front are examples of literary clarity and political integrity still much admired in China.

4. Cao Cao (155-220AD), one of the ablest generals at the end of the Han dynasty, has been traditionally regarded as a usurper. His son, Cao Pi, was the first king of the Kingdom of Wei and a noted writer.

5. Li Linfu, Qin Hui and Yan Song were infamous traitors of the Tang, Song and Ming dynasties respectively. Even in China today they are the object of censure in both literature and politics.

6. Altan Khan (1507-1581) was a Mongolian leader who had his base in present-day Huhehot, Inner Mongolia. In the year 1570 he was enfiefed by the Ming court. His support was crucial to the establishment of Tibetan Buddhism in Mongolia.

7. The White Lotus Sect (*Bailian jiao* or *Bailian she*) was a secret religious organization that originated in the Song dynasty and which combined elements of Buddhism, Zoroastrianism and the Sect of Maitreya (the 'Future Buddha'). Banned in the Mongol Yuan dynasty, the White Lotus Sect developed into a clandestine political organization that led many peasant rebellions against the dynastic governments of the Yuan, Ming and Qing.

8. A tael is a Chinese ounce (*liang*) equal to fifty grams. Silver and gold were used according to weight along with officially minted coins.

9. Beating with a bamboo or birch plank on the body or soles of the feet was a common form of punishment. A number of strokes with a bastinado were the equivalent to a court fine. Beating was also a popular method used for the

extraction of confessions.

10. The Five Confucian Classics were first recognized as the basic writings of Confucianism at the time of the Emperor Wu of the Han dynasty in the 1st century B.C. The Five Classics are, *The Book of Poetry* (*Shi*), *The Book of History* (*Shu*), *The Book of Rites* (*Li*), *The Book of Changes* (*Yi*), and *The Spring and Autumn Annals* (*Chunqiu*).

11. Beijing (Peking) means literally 'Northern Capital' and was the capital of China for both the Ming and Qing dynasties. Nanjing (or Nanking) means 'Southern Capital' and was the capital at various times throughout Chinese history. While Beijing was the political centre of the Chinese empire in the Ming and Qing, Nanjing was still important as a cultural centre.

金玉奴棒打薄情郎

The Beggar Chief's Daughter

from Tales to Illuminate the World

During the Shao Xing period (1131-1162) of the Song Dynasty, though Hangzhou was the capital of the empire and a wealthy city it abounded in beggars. The beggars had a chief whom they addressed as 'Master,' who controlled all their activities and levied a daily tribute on all the alms they received. If rain or snow prevented them from begging, he would prepare gruel to feed them; he also provided them with tattered clothing. So, like slaves who dared not offend their lord, the beggars obeyed their chief implicitly.

With the regular tribute the chief received from his followers, he practised usury; and if he did not gamble or squander his money on singsong girls, it was easy for him to become a man of substance. The post was such a reliable source of income that no man in his senses would think of relinquishing it. But it had one drawback: the title 'Beggar Chief' did not sound respectable. No matter how much property a beggar chief might acquire or how many generations of wealthy forbears he could boast, he was king solely among beggars and beyond the pale for ordinary citizens. No one outside his family would respect him. He could act the great man only in his own home.

Our story is about a beggar chief in Hangzhou named Jin Laoda, whose forefathers had followed the same profession for seven generations. A man of property, Jin had fine houses, fertile fields, handsome clothes, good food, grain to fill his granaries, money to fill his pockets, and a troop of servants and maids to wait on him. Though not the richest, he was one of the wealthiest men in the capital. And because Jin aspired to respectability, he ceded his title to a fellow clansman named Scabby in order to retire and live in comfort, severing his disreputable connection with all the beggar tribe. Such is the force of habit, however, that people in that district persisted in referring to him as the beggar chief. He could not rid himself of the name. Jin was now over fifty and his wife had died leaving him no son but an only daughter named Yunu, a girl of remarkable beauty.

Jin prized his daughter above jewels. He had her taught to read while yet a child, by the age of sixteen she could write poems in various metres or dash off impromptu verses. She was a fine needlewoman too, and a skilled performer on many musical instruments; for she excelled in everything she did. And Jin had set his heart on marrying this paragon to a gentleman. But though it was not easy to find a girl like this even in famous old families, because she was the daughter of a beggar chief she was not approached by eligible suitors. And as her father would not marry her to a common tradesman, at eighteen she was not yet betrothed.

One day a neighbour called and told Jin: "By Taiping Bridge there lives a handsome, learned young scholar of twenty named Mo Ji. Because both his parents have died and his family is poor, he is still unmarried: but recently he passed the examination qualifying him to join the Imperial College, and he would be willing to live with his wife's family after marriage. Why don't you ask him to be your son-in-law?"

"That is a very good suggestion," said Jin. "May I trouble you to be the matchmaker?"

The neighbour consented, and went straight to Taiping Bridge to find the young scholar.

"I'll be frank with you," he told Mo Ji. "Their ancestors were beggar chiefs, but Mr. Jin gave that up long ago. She's a good girl, and the family is rich. So if you don't think it beneath your dignity, I'll help to arrange a match between you."

Mo Ji was silent.

"I can neither support myself nor find a wife," he was thinking. "If I stoop to marry this girl and live with her family, I shall be killing two birds with one stone. I am in no position to care if others laugh at me."

"Yours is an excellent proposal, sir," he said to the matchmaker. "But I am too poor to buy presents for the bride. What can I do?"

"You won't have to buy so much as a sheet of paper," replied the other. "Leave it all to me."

When the neighbour took Mo Ji's reply to Jin, an auspicious day was chosen for the wedding; and, instead of sending gifts to the bride, Mo Ji actually received new clothes for his marriage from his father-in-law. When he discovered that Yunu was both lovely and talented, he was overjoyed; for without spending a cent he had got a beautiful wife and a comfortable home. He felt as though he was in heaven! As for his friends, knowing his poverty they forgave him for marrying into such a family. None of them laughed at him.

When the young couple had been married for a month, Jin prepared a sumptuous banquet and bid his son-in-law invite all his scholar friends to honour them with their presence. But after they had been feasting for six or seven days in succession, Jin's clansman Scabby heard about it and was offended — with good reason too.

"He's a beggar chief, so am I," fumed Scabby. "The only difference between us is that his family had the job for

several generations and piled up a lot of money. As one of
his kin I should be invited to drink at my niece's wedding;
but he has invited outsiders to celebrate instead and they
have already been feasting for six or seven days, while I have
not even received an invitation card! His son-in-law is only a
scholar, not a minister or councillor of state. Am I not
Yunu's uncle? Am I not good enough to sit at the same
table? Why should he look down on me like this? I'll go and
cause trouble to spoil their feast!"

He called together some fifty or sixty beggars to go with
him to Jin's house. They arrived at the gate and made a great
commotion.

When Jin opened the gate to find out the reason for this
din, in rushed Scabby with all his beggars to raise pandemonium. Striding straight up to the feasters Scabby helped
himself to the good wine and food, shouting as he did so:

"Call the young couple to pay their respects to their
uncle!"

The scholars took to their heels in alarm, followed by Mo
Ji. Old Jin could do nothing but apologize profusely to
the beggars.

"Today my son-in-law was the host," he told Scabby. "I
had no say in this. I shall prepare a special feast some other
time to show how sorry I am."

He distributed largesse to all the beggars and asked them
to take two jars of his best wine as well as some chickens and
geese to Scabby's house for a feast there. The confusion
lasted till dark, when finally the trouble-makers dispersed.

Yunu, ashamed of belonging to such a low-class family,
Mo Ji stayed with a friend, returning only the next morning.
At the sight of his son-in-law Jin blushed for shame, for he
had lost face completely; and Mo Ji was considerably upset
too, but like his father-in-law he said nothing of his feelings.

Yunu, ashamed of beloning to such a low-class family,
determined to encourage her husband to make his way in the
world. She urged him to study hard, and spared no expense

Scabby and his beggars stir up a commotion

to buy all the books, ancient and modern, which he might need. Neither did she begrudge money to invite scholars to practise essay writing and study the classics with him. She also gave him a generous entertainment allowance so that he might enlarge his circle of acquaintances and thereby increase his reputation. In this way Mo Ji's scholarship improved daily and his fame spread, until at the age of twenty-three he passed the provincial examination and the highest examination in the capital and became a member of the Hanlin Academy.[1] After the feast to welcome the new academicians, he started riding home triumphantly in his new black gauze cap and palace robes; but as he drew near Jin's house, all the people on the street gathered round to stare and the children pointed their fingers at him.

"Look!" they cried. "The beggar chief's son-in-law has become an official!"

Mo Ji had to put up with such comments as he rode along, for he could not very well create a scene in the street. And when he arrived home and saw Jin, he still paid his father-in-law every outward respect, although he was thinking resentfully:

"If I'd know how successful I was going to be, I could have waited to marry into a noble family; but now I've got a beggar chief as my father-in-law. I shall never be able to live this down! Even when we have children, they will be descended from a beggar chief and people will point the finger of scorn at them. Well, what's done is done, and my wife's behaviour is examplary; she hasn't committed any of the seven sins for which I could divorce her. How true the saying is: Marry in haste, repent too late!"

He went about looking thoroughly depressed; and although Yunu asked several times why he was so sad, he would not tell her. The truth was that Mo Ji's good fortune had made him forget all his wife had done for him when he was poor. Indeed, his utter disregard for all her assistance shows that his heart was not in the right place.

Some days later, Mo Ji was appointed the Census Officer in the Wuwei Prefecture. His father-in-law prepared a farewell feast for him, and this time the beggars dared not come to make trouble. Since Wuwei was not far from the capital and could be reached by river, Mo Ji decided to take Yunu with him to his post; and after travelling for a few days by junk they reached Caishi Rock and moored by the north bank. That night a full moon made all as bright as day; so Mo Ji, unable to sleep, dressed and went out to enjoy the moonlight from th bow of the boat. There was no one in sight and, as he brooded bitterly over the disgrace of having a beggar chief for his father-in-law, a wicked thought flashed through his mind.

"If this woman were dead, I could marry another and rid myself of that everlasting shame."

Immediately he went to the cabin to call his wife up to watch the moon.

Yunu was fast asleep, but Mo Ji woke her and insisted on her getting up. Unwilling to refuse her husband, she threw some clothes over her shoulders and stepped to the cabin door to look up at the moon. Then Mo Ji, taking her by surprise, dragged her to the bow and threw her into the river. This done, he quietly woke the boatmen.

"Row on at once!" he ordered. "If you make good time, I shall reward you well."

Unaware of all that had passed, the boatmen hastily cast off and rowed rapidly away, not pausing until they had gone nearly four miles. After they had moored again, Mo Ji told them that while watching the moon his wife had fallen into the river, and he had been powerless to save her. Since he gave the men three taels of silver as a tip, they understood very well what had happened but dared say nothing. There were some foolish maids on board who believed that their mistress had really fallen into the river by accident, but after crying for some time they thought no more of the matter.

When Yunu was thrown into the river, she was utterly

terrified and feared her last moment had come. But she felt something support her feet beneath the water and carry her to the shore, where she struggled up the bank. Upon looking round, however, she could see nothing but a vast expanse of water. The boat had gone. Then she realized that her husband despised her now that he was great, and wanted to drown her so that he could marry into some respectable family; so, although she had escaped with her life she had nowhere to go, and the consciousness of her plight made her weep bitterly.

As chance would have it, soon after Mo Ji's boat cast off, the newly appointed Transport Commissioner of Huaixi, Xu Dehou, moored his boat just where Mo Ji had pushed Yunu into the water. Chatting and sipping wine before going to bed, Xu and his wife were looking at the moon through their cabin window when they heard a woman crying on the bank. She was weeping so pitifully that Xu immediately ordered his boatmen to investigate and they found a woman sitting alone on the shore. Invited abroad and asked whence she came, she told Xu that she was the wife of the Census Officer of the Wuwei Prefecture. At the commissioner's request she told him her whole story from beginning to end, weeping as she spoke. And Xu and his wife, moved to tears, comforted her.

"Don't cry now," they urged. "We will adopt you as our daughter and think of some way to help you."

Yunu bowed in thanks. Then Xu told his wife to give her dry clothes into which to change, and bade her rest in the back cabin. He made the servants address her as their young mistress, and forbade the boatmen to breathe a word of that night's happenings.

After some days Xu arrived at his post. And since the Wuwei Prefecture was within his jurisdiction and he was the census officer's superior, Mo Ji was among the many subordinate officials who came to pay their respects to the new transport commissioner.

"He is a handsome fellow," thought Xu, upon first seeing Mo Ji. "What a pity that he should stoop to such a dastardly deed!"

A few months later Xu told his subordinates: "I have a daughter who has her share of talent and beauty; and since she has reached the marriageable age, I would like to find a good husband for her who would be willing to live in our family. Can you suggest anyone suitable?"

All the officials had heard that young Mo Ji had lost his wife, so they recommended him, declaring that with his unusual talents he would make an ideal son-in-law for Commissioner Xu.

"I thought of him too," said Xu. "But a man who has won success so early in life may be ambitious. He probably won't want to live as part of our household."

"He comes from a poor family," rejoined Xu's subordinates. "With you as his father-in-law, sir, he will be as lucky as a reed protected by a fine tree. What objection could he have?"

"If you think it possible, will you suggest the match to Mo Ji?" asked Xu. "Propose it as your own idea to see what his reaction is. Don't say that I wish it, for fear of embarrassing him."

Accordingly, Mo Ji's colleagues spoke to the young man, offering to be his matchmakers. Mo Ji was only too eager to get on good terms with high-ranking officials, but an alliance by marriage with his superior had been beyond his wildest dreams.

"If you can arrange this," he answered joyfully, "I shall be eternally grateful."

"Just leave it to us," they assured him, and went back to report to the commissioner.

"It is very kind of Mo Ji to consent," said Xu. "We are so fond of this daughter that I fear we have spoiled her; that is why we don't want her to leave our house when she marries. Since Mo Ji is young and has a will of his own, we are afraid they may have occasional disagreements which would distress us very much. We must make this clear beforehand, and hope he will bear with her. Only on this understanding dare we invite him to our home."

When this was announced to Mo Ji, he agreed unconditionally. He was no longer a poor scholar now, so he sent gilt paper flowers and coloured silk to the bride's house. The auspicious day was fixed, and he was positively itching in his eagerness to become the commissioner's son-in-law.

Meanwhile Xu asked his wife to tell Yunu: "The commissioner does not think a girl of your age should remain single, so he wants you to marry a young scholar who has passed the palace examination. Please don't refuse!"

"Though I come from a low family," replied Yunu, "I know how I should act. As I married Mo Ji I should be true to him all my life. Even though he forsook me because we were too low for him, and acted so cruelly and wickedly, I must do what is right. It would be wrong to marry anyone else." After saying this she burst into tears.

Then Mrs. Xu, realizing that she was sincere, told her the truth.

"This young palace graduate is no other than Mo Ji. My husband is angry with him for his callousness, but wants to bring you together again; so he has pretended that you are his own daughter and asked his colleagues to arrange this match. Mo Ji has agreed readily, and tonight he is to become our son-in-law. You can have your revenge when he enters the bridal chamber."

Then Yunu dried her tears, powdered her face and adorned herself for the wedding. When evening came, Mo Ji dressed himself smartly with a gilt paper flower in his cap and a red sash over his shoulders, and rode to the commissioner's house on a fine horse with a decorated saddle and two groups of musicians in front. All the officials escorted the bridegroom to his new home, and the road was lined with cheering spectators.

That night carpets were spread and coloured silk hung in the transport commissioner's house, and trumpets and drums sounded to herald the bridegroom's arrival. Upon reaching the gate Mo Ji alighted from his horse, and Xu in robe and belt of state came out to welcome him. Then all the other officials took their leave, and Mo Ji entered the inner quarters. The bride, with a red silk veil over her face, was helped in by two maids; then the master of ceremonies outside the balustrade called upon the young couple to bow to heaven and earth, to the bride's father and mother, and finally to each other. After this, the newly-wed pair were escorted to the bridal chamber for their wedding feast.

By this time Mo Ji felt he was in heaven, and his happiness defied description. With his head in the air he swaggered to the bridal chamber. But no sooner had he entered it when from behind the doors on both sides darted seven or eight maidservants, some young, some old, armed with sticks and bamboos. Strokes rained down on his shoulders and back until even his gauze cap fell off; but though he cried out with pain he could not escape. At last, in desperation, he fell to the ground and shouted:

"Father-in-law! Mother-in-law! Save me!"

Then he heard a girl's voice order: "Don't beat the brute to death. Bring him to me."

At that the blows stopped. Tweaking his ears, tugging at his arms, and turning a deaf ear to all his protests, the maids lifted him almost off the ground to carry him to his bride.

"What have I done to deserve this?" Mo Ji cried.

But when he looked up, whom should he see seated calmly under the bright candlelight but his former wife, Yunu!

"Ghosts! Ghosts!" shrieked Mo Ji, frightened almost out of his wits.

The maids burst out laughing, and Xu came in.

"Don't worry," said the commissioner. "This is no ghost but the adopted daughter I found at Caishi Rock."

金玉奴棒打薄情郎

Jin Yunu has her heartless husband beaten

Then Mo Ji's heart stopped pounding so fast, and he made haste to kneel down and kowtow.

"I admit my guilt," he acknowledged. "Please pardon me!"

"This has nothing to do with me," replied Xu. "It is my daughter's forgiveness you should ask."

But Yunu spat in her husband's face and cursed him.

"You heartless brute!" she cried. "Don't you remember the ancient saying? A man should not forget the friends he made when he was poor; a prosperous man should never forsake the wife who shared his poverty! You came to my family empty-handed, and it was thanks to our help that you were able to study and win fame. That is how you gained your present success. I was looking forward to sharing your splendour, little knowing you would be so ungrateful as to think no more of all that had passed. But forgetting our love and repaying kindness with cruelty you threw me into the river! Luckily Heaven took pity on me and Commissioner Xu rescued me and made me his goddaughter; for otherwise I should certainly have been drowned and my body devoured by the fish. How could you be so heartless as to murder me in order to marry again? How can you even dare to look me in the face today?"

Then breaking down and sobbing bitterly, she heaped curses on him for his ingratitude and cruelty. Covered with shame, Mo Ji had nothing to say. He could only kowtow and beg to be forgiven. When Xu felt that Yunu had reviled her husband enough, he helped Mo Ji to his feet.

"Don't be angry now, daughter," he said to Yunu. "Your husband has repented, and I fancy he will always treat you respectfully in future. Though you were married before, you are making a fresh start today. Please spare him further reproaches for my sake."

To Mo Ji he said: "You brought this on yourself, son, and you can't blame anyone else for it. Tonight you must just accept your punishment. But I shall ask your mother-in-law to put in a word for you." So saying, he left the chamber.

After a short time the commissioner's wife arrived, and reasoned with Yunu until she persuaded her to forgive Mo Ji. The next day Xu prepared a feast for his son-in-law, and returned him all his wedding presents.

"A girl can accept wedding presents once only," he said. "You must have sent gifts to the Jin family, so I cannot accept any more."

When Mo Ji bowed his head and said nothing, Xu went on: "Your contempt for your father-in-law so poisoned your relationship with your wife that you nearly committed a fearful crime. Now I am only a transport commissioner, I fear my official status is too low for you."

Mo Ji blushed scarlet and bowed again and again to apologize.

From this time onwards Mo Ji and Yunu lived together more happily than before. Xu and his wife treated Yunu as their own daughter and Mo Ji as if he were indeed their son-in-law, while Yunu looked on the old couple as her own parents. Then Mo Ji, moved by their example, invited Jin to live with them for the remainder of his days. When eventually Xu and his wife died, Yunu mourned for them like a daughter to repay their kindness. And for generations after this the Mo family and the Xu family remained on intimate terms.

Notes:

1. Established in the Tang dynasty (618-907AD), the Hanlin Academy was, until the Mongol Yuan dynasty (1271-1368AD), in charge of astronomy-astrology, painting and calligraphy, cartography and medicine. At the time of the writing of this story in the Ming dynasty (1368-1644AD), the Hanlin Academy had become the official dynasty and imperial chronicler and biographer. Even from the time of its inception the Academy was the highest official centre of learning in the country.

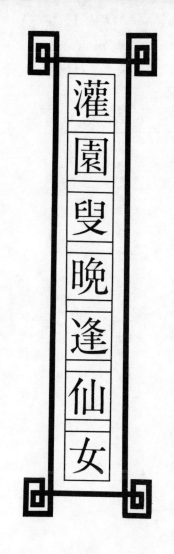

灌園叟晚逢仙女

The Old Gardener

from Stories to Awaken the World

During the reign of Emperor Ren Zong (1023-1063) of the Song Dynasty, outside the East Gate of Suzhou, there was a village called Changle. In this village, which lay only half a mile from the city, lived an old man named Qiu Xian. Coming from a line of farmers he owned a small plot of land and a thatched cottage. His wife had died and he had no children.

Since boyhood Qiu had loved growing flowers or cultivating fruit trees. He had, in fact, neglected farming to concentrate on gardening, and whenever he came upon some rare plant he was happier than if he had picked up a jewel. Even when out on urgent business, if he happened to see some flowering trees in a house he would slip in with a conciliatory smile, regardless of whether he was welcome or not. If he found only common plants or trees which were then blossoming in his own garden, he would leave quickly enough; but if he discovered some rare plant which he did not possess, or some plant which, even though he possessed, had ceased to bloom in his garden, then he would set aside his business and remain there all day unable to tear himself away. So he came to be called The Flower Maniac.

If Qiu met a flower-vendor with a good plant, he would insist on buying whether he had money with him or not — if he had no money he would pawn the clothes off his back. Some flower-vendors, knowing him, always raised their price when dealing with him, for he could never resist buying. Wastrels too, who had lost all their money, knowing his passion for flowers would break branches off rare plants they had discovered and stick them in mud as if they had roots, to deceive him. And he would always buy. The strange thing was, however, that when Qiu planted such shoots they always grew. And so, day by day and month by month he built up a fine garden.

Around this garden Qiu had raised a bamboo fence on which he trained rambling roses, briar roses, banksia, dog roses, hibiscus, cherry and broom; while at the foot of the fence he grew hollyhocks, balsam, cock's comb, mallow and poppies, as well as winter sweet, lilies, spring and autumn lychnis, cyclamen, anemones, rhododendron, wild ginger, white butterfly, elecampane, convolvulus and other flowers. They looked like a bright silk screen when in bloom. And a few paces from the fence he set other rare plants, so that before one flower had faded another was in blossom.

Inside the old gardener's double wicket gate, which faced south, was a path fringed by bamboos and shade-giving cypresses. This led to a three-roomed cottage which, although it had only a thatched roof, was high and spacious with large windows. In the hall hung a small painting by an unknown artist, and the plain wooden couch, table and chairs there were spotlessly clean; there was not a speck of dust on the floor either. Behind the hall were two fine rooms, one of which was the old man's bedroom. He had every kind of flower under the sun and they all grew well, so that each season there seemed like spring.

Qiu's wicker gate faced the great Chaotian Lake which joined Wusong River in the east, Zhenze Lake in the west, and Pangshan Lake in the south; so the view was delightful in all seasons, in bright or rainy weather alike. Here Qiu built an embankment which he planted with peach and willow trees, whose red blossoms and green leaves in spring rivalled the beauty of the famous West Lake in Hangzhou. He planted hibiscus along the bank and lotus of different colours in the water; and when these were in flower the whole lake seemed covered by a silk canopy and the air was filled with fragrance. Water chestnut gatherers sang as they paddled their small craft, and sailing boats raced each other when there was a wind, while under the willows fishermen who had moored their boats spread their nets to dry. Some fished, others mended their nets, lay drinking on the prow, or challenged each other to swimming contests. Their laughter could be heard all day.

On painted barges came pleasure-seekers, attended by musicians, to see the lotus, and when they turned home at dark, thousands of lanterns mingled with the light of glow-worms and the reflection of stars in the water till you could hardly distinguish one from the other. In late autumn, when cold winds blew and turned the maple leaves red or yellow, the withered willows and hibiscus on the bank contrasted with the white duckweed and red smartweed at the water's edge; and the mournful cries of the wild geese among the rushes pierced the sky. In the depth of winter, when snow clouds massed and snowflakes fell, all was white. The pageant of the four seasons defied description.

The old gardener's first care every day was to sweep away the fallen leaves from under his flowers, then water each plant in turn. And at night he would water them once more. Great was his joy whenever a tree was about to blossom. He would heat wine or brew a pot of tea, then bow low and pour a libation while he uttered three prayers for the tree's longevity. This done he would sit under the tree to sip his drink slowly, and once under the influence of wine he would sing. When he was tired, he would lie under the tree with a rock as his pillow, remaining there

from the time when the buds began to open until the tree
was in full blossom. If the sun was strong, he would sprinkle
the flowers with water from a whisk. If the moon was bright,
he would stay up all night. If a storm sprang up, in his straw
hat and fibre cape he would make a tour of inspection; and
wherever he found a branch battered by the wind he would
prop it up with bamboo. In bad weather he would get up
several times at night to inspect his charges.

When blossoms faded the old man would sigh or even
shed tears, but unwilling to part with the fallen petals he
always swept them up gently with his whisk and put them
in a dish so that he could enjoy them until they were withered,
when he would place them in a clean vase. As soon as the
vase was full, with a look of inexpressible sadness he would
offer libations again of tea or wine, then carry the vase to
bury it in the embankment. This he called 'Burying the
Flowers.' If any petals were spattered with mud during a
shower, he would carefully wash them clean and scatter them
in the lake. This he called 'Bathing the Flowers.'

The old gardener could not bear to see branches or flowers
plucked. He reasoned: "A plant blossoms only once a year,
and for a few days only during one of the four seasons. It
puts up with three seasons of neglect for the sake of these
few glorious days when it dances in the breeze and smiles
at all around like a true favourite of fortune. But then
all too often it is cut off in its prime. These few days are
hard to come by, but to destroy a plant is easy. If flowers
could speak, wouldn't they complain? Flowers first bud,
then bloom and quickly fade; thus their blossoming time is
very short. Then think of all the butterflies, bees, birds and
insects which attack a plant, and of the hot sun, bitter wind
and pelting rain. Men ought to protect flowers from all
this — how can they have the heart to pluck them instead?

"Think of the time it takes a seedling to put out roots,
branches and tender twigs before it can blossom for men's
delight. Isn't the tree lovely enough? Why must people

pluck the flowers? For plucked flowers and broken sprays can no more be restored to the branch than dead men can be restored to life or severed limbs rejoined to the body. If plants could speak, wouldn't they speak with tears?

"Some folk cut beautiful sprays for their vases just to divert guests for a moment while they feast, or pick rare flowers for their concubines to wear in their hair for a day. It never occurs to them that guests can be entertained in the garden itself and women can use artificial flowers for their hair. One twig broken means one twig less on the bough, and one branch cut this year means one branch less next year. But why not lengthen the life of a plant so that we can enjoy it year after year? There are unopened buds, too, which are plucked with the flowers and doomed to wither on the broken bough. Isn't that the same as when children die? Some people don't love flowers, but pluck them just for a whim, giving them to anyone who asks for them or tossing them carelessly away by the roadside. Isn't this the same as when men are unjustly done to death and have no one to avenge them? If flowers could speak, wouldn't they voice their hatred?"

With this philosophy, Qiu never broke a twig nor hurt a bud in his life. When he admired flowers in other gardens he would willingly linger there all day; but if the master of the house offered to pluck a spray or a blossom for him, he would utter a horrified refusal. If he saw men picking flowers he would beg them to stop, and if they paid no attention he would gladly go down on his knees to them to save a flower's life. Although people called him The Flower Maniac, they were often moved by his sincerity to desist, and then he would bow low to express his thanks.

Some boys who picked flowers in order to sell them were paid by Qiu to stop doing this. But if a flower was plucked in his absence, he would be most distressed when he discovered it, and seal the broken stem with mud. This he called 'Doctoring the Flowers.'

For the reasons already given, Qiu tried to keep people out of his garden. If relatives or friends wanted to come in and he could not very well refuse them, he would make this clear before admitting them. He also warned them that he did not like human breath to contaminate the flowers and that they must not go too close to the plants. And if some oaf picked a flower or bud behind his back, the old man would flush with anger and never admit him again, not even if the fellow cursed or struck him. So later on, when people learned what he was like, they dared not touch so much as a leaf of his.

Now wherever there are shrubberies or plantations birds will come to nest, especially if they find fruit or berries. If the birds would content themselves with feasting on the fruit, little harm would be done, but they invariably injure the buds too; so the old gardener scattered grain on the ground for the birds and prayed to them to be merciful. And the birds were sufficiently intelligent after eating their fill to fly low, warbling among the flowers, without injuring a single bud or swallowing a single seed. Hence Qiu's garden bore more fruit — larger and sweeter too — than any other. When the fruit ripened, he would gaze heavenward and sacrifice to the flower god before presuming to taste it, and offer some to all his neighbours before selling the rest. Yet every year he made enough money from his fruit to live on.

Since the old man found happiness among his flowers, he tended his garden for more than fifty years — from boyhood to old age — without wearying of it. In fact, he became healthier as the years went by, taking pleasure in his rough clothes and simple fare. When he had money to spare he would help the poor and destitute in his village; so all the villagers respected him and addressed him as Master Qiu, though he always called himself The Old Gardener.

We come now to the second part of our story. There was in Suzhou a cruel, crafty, mean young fellow named Zhang Wei who, coming from an official family, took advantage of his position to lord it over his neighbours and ruin innocent people. And woe betide anyone who offended him, for Zhang would not rest content until he had ruined the unfortunate man's family. His attendants were as savage as tigers or wolves, and some young vagabonds were always with him to help him in his evil deeds. They stirred up trouble wherever they went, and those injured by them were past counting. The time came, however, when Zhang crossed a man more powerful than himself who had him beaten within an inch of his life; and, when sued, this enemy pulled strings at court so that Zhang lost his case. Then, accompanied by four or five servants and his usual group of young ruffians, he went to the country to live down his humiliation; and his country house happened to be in Changle Village, not far from the old gardener's cottage.

One day, strolling half drunk in the village after his morning meal, Zhang passed the old gardener's gate and was struck by the fresh and pretty flowers on the fence and the cool groves of trees around.

"This seems a pleasant place," he remarked. "Whose is it?"

"This is the garden of old Qiu, The Flower Maniac," replied his servant.

"Ah, yes," said Zhang. "I did hear there was some old fool here called Qiu who grows very good flowers. So this is where he lives. Suppose we go in to have a look?"

"The old man is rather eccentric," answered his servant. "He won't let people look at his flowers."

"He may refuse others," retorted Zhang. "But he can't treat me like that. Go and knock. Don't keep me waiting."

At this time the peonies were in full bloom and the old gardener, who had just finished watering them, was enjoying himself beside the flowers with a pot of wine and two dishes of sweetmeats. He had not finished his third cup when he heard knocking and put down his drink to open the gate. When he discovered five or six men standing there smelling strongly of liquor, he feared that they must be wanting to see the flowers.

"What brings you here, gentlemen?" he asked, standing in the gateway.

"Don't you know me, old man?" demanded Zhang. "I am the celebrated Lord Zhang. That estate over there belongs to me. Hearing that you have many good flowers in your garden, we have come specially to have a look."

"Why, sir," replied Qiu, "I haven't any rare trees, only common varieties like peach and plum which have finished blossoming. There isn't much else."

"You old scoundrel!" roared Zhang with an angry glare. "How can it hurt you if we just have a look? How dare you say you haven't any? Are you afraid we'll eat your flowers?"

"It's the truth I'm telling," insisted Qiu. "There really isn't much."

Zhang paid no attention to him, however, but stepped forward and pushed the old man aside so roughly that he went staggering. Then they all rushed in. When Qiu saw how fierce they were, there was nothing he could do but closed his gate and followed them in. He cleared away his wine and sweetmeats, and then stood watching the intruders.

They saw that the garden was well stocked with plants, and the peonies were blooming in all their splendour. These were not just common varieties like 'Jade Pavilion in Spring,' but included the five famous species: 'Yellow Pavilion,' 'Green Butterfly,' 'The Melon,' 'Dark Beast,' and 'Red Lion.' The peony is the king of flowers, and the peonies of Luoyang are the best in the world,[1] one plant of 'Yao Yellow' or 'Wei Purple' from that city costing five thousand cash.

Do you ask why Luoyang has the best peonies? It is because Wu Zetian, the wanton Tang empress who had two favourite ministers named Zhang, thought she would like, one winter's day, to stroll in the palace grounds, and issued the following edict:

"Tomorrow I shall walk about my park;
Send word at once to let the Spring God know.
Bid all the flowers blossom in the night,
Before the morning wind has time to blow."

Since the empress was a sovereign ordained by Heaven, the plants dared not disobey her. They all began to bud and blossom that night; and on the following day, when she went to her pleasure grounds, she saw red and purple flowers blooming in all their fragrance. The peony alone, too proud to flatter the empress and her favourites, had not put forth so much as one leaf. Then Empress Wu in anger had the peony banished to Luoyang, since when the peonies of Luoyang have become the best in the world.

The peonies, planted opposite the old gardener's cottage, were surrounded by rocks from the lake; and around them he had erected a wooden frame with a cloth awning to keep off the sun. The plants ranged from six to over ten feet in height and the magnificent blooms, large as platters and of variegated colours, presented a dazzling sight. Zhang's party exclaimed in admiration and he himself stepped on to a rock the better to inhale the fragrance. But Qiu was very particular about this.

"Stand back, sir," he said. "Don't go up there."

Annoyed as he was with the old gardener for not admitting him more promptly, Zhang had been waiting to find fault.

"You live so near my house, don't you know who I am?" he cried. "With this gardenful of fine flowers, you coolly told me you had none. And now, instead of being thankful that I didn't take offence, here you are telling me what I can do! Does it spoil a flower to sniff at it? Just to show you who is master, I'll smell some more." Pulling the blossoms to him one by one, he started burying his nose in them.

Old Qiu was furious, but dared not say anything. He thought that Zhang would be leaving almost at once; but the scoundrel intentionally assumed the air of a connoisseur and said:

"Flowers like this call for a celebration. Let's have some wine and enjoy ourselves." He ordered his men to fetch wine quickly.

When the old gardener saw that Zhang meant to stay and drink there, he was even more alarmed.

"My cottage is too small," he said, stepping forward. "There is no place to sit. You had better just look at the flowers, sir, then drink your wine in your own house."

"We can sit here," retorted Zhang, pointing at the ground.

"The ground is dirty," protested Qiu. "How can you sit there?"

"Never mind," was Zhang's rejoinder. "I'll have a carpet spread over it."

Food and wine were brought in, a carpet was spread on the ground and they sat in a circle to play the finger-game and drink.[2] Long and merrily they caroused, while Qiu sat on one side fuming.

Then the loveliness of the flowers made Zhang conceive a wicked plan. He determined to make this garden his! Looking tipsily at Qiu, he said: "I never thought an old fool like you could grow flowers. That is to your credit. Here, drink a cup of wine with me."

The old gardener was in no mood to answer politely. "I never drink," he growled. "But don't let me stop *you*."

"Will you sell this garden?" demanded Zhang.

Qiu realized that this meant real trouble.

"This garden is my life," he answered fearfully. "How can I sell it?"

"Nonsense!" cried Zhang. "Just sell it to me. If you have nowhere to go, you can come to my house. I won't ask anything else of you but to grow flowers for me. What do you say?"

"You are in luck, old one!" chorused Zhang's followers. "His lordship is being very good to you. Hurry up and thank him!"

As they began to put pressure on him, the old gardener, numb with rage, turned his head away.

"What a surly old fool!" cried Zhang. "Why don't you answer?"

"I've told you I'm not selling. Why do you keep asking?"

"Curse you! If you still refuse to sell, I'll send you to the yamen with my card."

Old Qiu, who was furious, wanted to answer back. Then he thought: Zhang is a powerful man, and he is drunk. Why should I take him seriously? I had better give him a soft answer.

So swallowing his anger he replied: "You must give me a day in which to consider, sir. How can this be decided so quickly?"

"That's right," said the others. "You decide tomorrow."

By this time they were very drunk. Zhang and his roughs got up to go while the servants packed up the remains of the feast. Afraid that they might pluck the flowers, Qiu stood before the peonies to protect them; and when Zhang stepped forward to climb on the rocks, Qiu pulled at his sleeve and said:

"Though a flower is a trifle, a lot of work has to be put in every year to raise these few blossoms; so it is a pity to hurt them. And if you pluck them, they will wither in a couple of days. Why commit such a crime?"

"Crime? You are raving!" shouted Zhang. "Tomorrow the whole garden will be mine, so even if I pick all the flowers, it is none of your business!"

He tried to push the old gardener aside, but Qiu seized hold of him and would not let him go.

"Even if you kill me," he insisted, "I shan't let you pluck the flowers!"

"Curse you, you old fool!" cried the others. "What does it matter if his lordship takes a flower? Why make such an ado about nothing? Do you think you can frighten us out of picking?"

Then they began to pluck blossoms at random. Crying out in despair, the old man let go of Zhang and made a desperate attempt to stop the others; but when he barred the way on one side he could not protect the other, and soon many of his peonies had been plucked.

"You bandits!" cursed Qiu, whose heart was bleeding. "Swaggering in to play the tyrant here! I'll make you suffer for this!"

He charged so hard against Zhang, who was drunk, that the bully lost his balance and fell over backwards.

"Help!" cried the others. "His lordship is hurt!" And throwing down their flowers they rushed up to beat the gardener.

One of them was sober enough, however, to realize that since Qiu was an old man they might easily kill him, so he stopped the others and helped Zhang up. But angry and ashamed because of his fall, Zhang proceeded to tear up all the plants so that not a bud was left, strewing the ground with flowers which he trampled underfoot.

The old gardener rolled on the ground in his rage, calling on heaven and earth. Neighbours who heard the uproar rushed in and, shocked to see the garden being laid waste, they urged the cruel men to stop and asked what had happened. Some of the neighbours who were Zhang's tenants apologized to him on Qiu's behalf and bowed him obsequiously to the gate.

"Tell that old scoundrel," ordered Zhang, "if he hands over the garden quitely, I'll let him off! If he refuses again, let him beware!" Then he stalked furiously off.

Because Zhang was drunk the neighbours did not take his threats seriously, but came back and made Qiu, who was still weeping bitterly, sit up on the steps. Then after trying to comfort him, they left, closing the gate behind them. Some of them, who felt Qiu had been wrong in the past not to let people in to see his flowers, said:

"The old fellow is a bit queer in the head: that's why this

happened. It should be a lesson for him."

But others with a sense of justice protested: "How can you say such a thing? You know the proverb: Spend a year on growing a flower, enjoy it for ten days only. People who simply enjoy the sight of the blossoms don't know what trouble the gardener has had. Heaven knows to what pains he has been to raise these wonderful blossoms. How can you blame him for being fond of them?"

Meantime old Qiu, still grieving for his mangled plants, set to work to pick them up. But the sight of them, trampled, scattered and mud-stained as they were, made his tears fall anew.

"My poor flowers!" he groaned. "I loved you too much to injure one petal or leaf on any plant. Who could have thought that you would come to this?"

As he was weeping, he heard someone call: "Why are you crying so bitterly, Master Qiu?"

The old man turned to see a beautiful girl of about sixteen, simply but tastefully dressed. He had no idea who she could be and dried his tears to ask:

"Where are you from, young lady? What brings you here?"

"I live nearby," said the girl. "I came because I heard your peonies were in bloom. I did not expect to find them withered."

At the mention of peonies, Qiu broke down again.

"What is the matter?" asked the girl. "Why are you crying like that?"

Then the old gardener told her how Zhang had destroyed his flowers.

"So that is the reason," said the girl with a laugh. "Would you like the flowers to return to their boughs?"

"Don't make fun of me, young lady. How can fallen blossoms return to the boughs?"

"In our family we know how to restore blossoms to the bough. Our method always succeeds."

"Can you really do that?" Qiu's sorrow began to turn to joy.

"Of course," said the girl.

"If you will perform this miracle," said Qiu with a bow, "I have no other way of thanking you, but whenever my flowers blossom I shall invite you here to enjoy them."

"Stop bowing to me," replied the girl, "and fetch a bowl of water."

As Qiu hurried in for the water he was thinking: "How can she work such a miracle? Could she be making fun of me because she saw me weeping?" But then he reflected: "No. I have never seen this young lady before, so there is no reason why she should make fun of me. It must be true."

Returning to the garden after hastily filling a bowl with water, he discovered that the girl had disappeared. The flowers were back on their stems, however, not a single petal remaining on the ground. But whereas one plant bore one colour only before, red and purple were now mixed and pale and dark intermingled, with the result that the peonies looked more magnificent than ever.

Surprised and delighted, Qiu exclaimed: "I never thought the young lady could really do this wonderful thing." Thinking she was still among the flowers, he put down the water and stepped forward to thank her; but although he searched the whole garden she was nowhere to be found.

"Where can the young lady have gone?" he wondered. "She must be at the gate. I am going to beg her to teach me this art." He ran to the gate but found it closed, and when he opened it and looked out he saw two old men sitting there. These were his neighbours Yu and Shan, who were watching fishermen hang out their nets in the sun. They stood up to greet the old gardener.

"We hear Zhang Wei was here making trouble," they said. "But we were in our fields and so could not come to ask what was the matter."

"Yes," said Qiu. "I had a great deal of trouble with

those scoundrels. Luckily a young lady came who knew a good way to save the flowers; but she left before I could thank her. Did you see which way she went?"

"If flowers are spoilt, how can you save them?" asked the two old men in surprise. "How long ago did this girl come out?"

"Just now," replied Qiu.

"We have been sitting here for some time," said his neighbours, "but no one came out. There can't have been any girl."

Then Qiu realized the truth. "In that case, she must have been a fairy!" he cried.

"Tell us how the flowers were saved," requested the old men.

And when the old gardener described what had happened, they declared: "What an amazing thing! Let us go in and look."

They went in, and Qiu barred the gate behind them.

"This must be the work of a fairy!" exclaimed Yu and Shan after seeing the peonies. "No mortal could do such a thing!"

Then, while Qiu burnt his choicest incense and bowed to Heaven to express his thanks, the two old men said: "Your single-minded love for flowers must have moved the fairy to come down to earth. Tomorrow you should let Zhang's ruffians see this, to make them feel thoroughly ashamed."

"No, no," replied the old gardener. "Such men are like mad dogs. The best thing is to avoid them. Why should I ask them back?" And the two neighbours agreed that there was reason in this.

Since Qiu was very happy, he warmed up the wine he had been drinking and invited Yu and Shan to enjoy the flowers till it was dark. After they left they spread the news, so that by the next day all the villagers knew it and wanted to see the peonies but were afraid the old gardener might not let them. Qiu was, however, an intelligent man. The apparition of the goddess had filled him with a desire to leave the world and search for truth. He did not try to sleep that night but sat by his flowers, deep in thought, until it dawned on him that he had been to blame for the trouble with Zhang.

"I brought it on myself by selfishness," he decided. "If I were like the gods, who are kind to all, it would never have happened."

So the next morning he opened wide his garden gate to all who wished to come in. The few villagers who ventured in first found him sitting facing the flowers.

"You can come and see the plants whenever you like," Qiu told them, "so long as you don't pluck them."

And when this news spread, all the men and women in the village flocked to his garden.

The next morning Zhang Wei told his followers: "Yesterday that old ruffian knocked me down. Do you think I can let it go at that? Come on now to demand his garden. If he refuses, we'll get some more men to smash up the place completely."

"His garden is next to your house," said Zhang's friends. "You need not be afraid that he will refuse. But it was a mistake to spoil the flowers yesterday. We should have kept a few to enjoy ourselves later."

"Never mind that," said Zhang. "They will grow again next year. Let's go quickly before he has time to get up to any tricks."

They had not gone far when they heard that a fairy had appeared in Qiu's garden to restore all the broken flowers to the boughs, and that all his peonies had different colours now. But Zhang did not believe this.

"What good deeds has that old thief done to deserve a visit from a fairy?" he demanded. "And this fairy turned up just after we spoilt his flowers — as if she were his housekeeper! Depend upon it, the old man has made up this story and spread it because he is afraid we will go back. He wants to make out that he is protected by divine power, so that we will leave him alone."

Zhang's followers agreed with him. But when they reached the garden they found the double gates wide open and men and women streaming through, all of whom told the same story.

"It looks as if it really happened," said Zhang's men.

"Never mind!" retorted the bully. "I don't care if the fairy is sitting there — I'm going to ask for the garden!"

As they walked along the winding path to the thatched cottage, they saw that the news was true. And the flowers, strange to say, looked more splendid than ever now that so many people had come to see them, and seemed, indeed, to be smiling.

Though Zhang was very much taken aback, he did not abandon his scheme to obtain the garden; but after looking around for a short time he conceived another wicked plan.

"Let us leave now," he said to his men.

When they had gone out of the gate, his men asked: "Why didn't you demand the garden?"

"I have a good plan," said Zhang. "There is no need to argue with him: the garden will be mine tomorrow."

"What is your plan?"

"Wang Ze who practised black magic in Beizhou has recently revolted," replied Zhang, "so the Board of War has ordered all prefectures and districts to prohibit sorcery and arrest all magicians. Our district has offered three thousand strings of cash as a reward for information about sorcerers. Well, tomorrow I shall send Zhang Ba to the yamen to accuse Qiu of sorcery, on the grounds that he has restored these flowers to their stems. The old man will admit his guilt under torture and be thrown into gaol; then the garden will be publicly auctioned, but who will dare to buy it? It is sure to fall to me, and I shall pocket the three thousand strings reward as well."

"This is a fine plan," said his men. "We must lose no time in carrying it out."

They went straight into the city to write the charge, and the next morning Zhang Ba was sent to the prefectural ya-men to inform against the old gardener. Zhang Ba was Zhang Wei's ablest lackey and he knew the yamen officials well.

Since the city prefect was anxious to discover magicians, when he heard that the whole village had seen this miracle he naturally believed the charge and sent officers and con-stables with Zhang Ba to arrest Qiu. Zhang Wei, who had paid all the necessary bribes, told Zhang Ba and the con-stables to go ahead while he and his men followed. The con-stables marched straight into the garden, but the old gardener thought they had come to see his flowers and paid no atten-tion. Then they rushed forward with a shout and bound him.

"What have I done?" asked Qiu in terror. "Why have you arrested me?"

Cursing him as a magician and a rebel, they dragged him away without a word of explanation. And when the neighbours gathered round in consternation to ask what had happened, the constables said:

"Why do you ask? He is guilty of a great crime. How do we know you haven't had a part in it?"

At this the villagers were afraid and slipped away lest they become involved. Only Yu, Shan and a few other good friends followed the old gardener at a distance.

After Qiu's arrest, Zhang came with his men to lock up the garden. First they had a good look round to see if there were any people left inside, then they locked the gate and went back to the yamen. The constables had already ordered Qiu to kneel on the platform, and the old gardener noticed that there was another man kneeling beside him but did not recognize the informer. The runners, all of whom had been bribed by Zhang, had prepared the instruments of torture.

"Where do you come from?" shouted the prefect. "How dare you practise magic here to deceive the people? What followers have you? Tell the truth now!"

This was like a cannon shot in the dark — the old

gardener did not know who had attacked him.

"My family has lived for generations in Changle Village," he said. "I am not a magician from other parts. I know nothing about magic."

"The other day by means of black magic," declared the prefect, "you caused fallen blossoms to go back to the boughs. Can you deny that?"

Then Qiu realized that his accuser must be Zhang Wei. He told the prefect how the bully had demanded his garden and trampled the flowers, and how a fairy maid had appeared. The prefect, however, was too prejudiced to believe him.

"Many men practise religion all their lives in the hope of achieving godhead," he scoffed, "yet even then they cannot meet a fairy. Why should a fairy appear to you just because you weep? If a fairy did reveal herself to you she would leave her name so that people should know her, instead of disappearing without a word. Whom do you think you are fooling? No doubt about it, you are a magician! Put him to torture!"

With a shout of assent the runners rushed forward like tigers or wolves, threw Qiu to the ground, caught hold of his ankles and were just about to torture him when the prefect was seized by such dizziness that he nearly fell off his seat. Too faint to preside over the court, he ordered that Qiu be pilloried and imprisoned until the next day when the trial should continue.

As the gaolers led Qiu away weeping, he saw Zhang Wei.

"Lord Zhang," he said, "I have done you no wrong. Why should you do this cruel thing to destroy me?"

But Zhang turned away without a word and went off with his lackey Zhang Ba and the other young vagabonds.

By now old Yu and Shan had arrived and learned the charge.

"This is gross injustice!" they said. "But never mind.

Tomorrow we shall get all the villagers to bail you out."

"I hope so," responded Qiu tearfully.

"Curse you, you criminal!" shouted the gaolers. "Stop snivelling and get a move on!"

With tears in his eyes Qiu went to the gaol, where his neighbours sent wine and food for him. The gaolers did not give it to him, however, but consumed the gifts themselves. And at night they chained the old man to his pallet so that he became a living corpse, unable to move an inch.

"I wonder what fairy it was that saved my flowers but gave that bully a chance to slander me," he sighed. "Ah, fairy! if you will pity me and rescue me, I will give up my home and practise religion."

As he was musing, the fairy who had visited him the previous day appeared again.

"Mercy, fairy!" cried Qiu desperately. "Save me!"

The fairy smiled.

"Do you want me to end your agony?" she asked. And stepping forward she pointed a finger at him, whereupon his chains were loosed and fell to the ground. The old gardener knelt down and kowtowed.

"May I know your name, fairy?" he requested.

"I am The Keeper of Flowers and I serve the Heavenly Empress in the Western Paradise,"[3] she replied. "Because you loved your flowers so well, I made them whole again, little thinking this would give that bully a chance to slander you. Fate must have decreed that you should suffer this trial; but tomorrow you will be set free. As for Zhang Wei, the flower spirits informed the Heavenly Emperor how the wretch injured flowers and plotted to kill you, and he has died. The hangers-on who abetted him in his evil courses have been visited by calamities too. If you devote yourself in future to religion, in a few years I shall come to carry you to Heaven."

The old gardener kowtowed again.

"Please tell me, goddess, how to practise religion," he

begged.

"There are many ways," replied the fairy. "It depends upon a man's nature. Since you started by loving flowers, you will achieve holiness through flowers. If you feed yourself on blossoms, you will finally be able to fly."

After she had informed him how to draw nourishment from flowers, Qiu kowtowed again to thank her; but when he stood up she had vanished. Raising his head he saw that she was standing on top of the prison wall, whence she beckoned to him saying:

"Come up and leave with me."

But when the old man had climbed half way up he felt exhausted; and as he reached the top he heard the crash of gongs below and men shouting: "The magician has escaped!"

Terror made him lose his grip and fall headlong, to wake in a cold sweat on his pallet. Remembering clearly, however, what had passed in the dream, the conviction that all would be well gave him comfort.

Zhang Wei, meantime, who had seen that the prefect was convinced of Qiu's guilt, was exulting.

"The gardener is a cunning old rogue," he said, "but now let him spend a night on a prison pallet, leaving his garden for us to enjoy."

"The other day when the garden was still his we didn't have too good a time," said his men. "Now that it is yours, we can enjoy it to our hearts' content."

"That is right," said Zhang.

So they went out of the city together and ordered the servants to prepare wine and food. They marched to Qiu's garden, opened the gate and went in; and although the neighbours felt indignant, they were too afraid of Zhang to protest. But when Zhang and his men reached the thatched cottage, they found all the peonies scattered on the ground again — not a single flower remained on its stem!

They marvelled at this, and Zhang said: "It does look as if the old scoundrel is really a magician. Otherwise how could these peonies change back again so quickly? Could there really have been a fairy?"

"He knew that your lordship wanted to enjoy the flowers," suggested one young fellow, "so he has played this trick to make us feel foolish."

"Well," said Zhang, "since he has played this trick, we can enjoy the fallen blossoms."

With that they spread the carpet and sat on the ground as before. They drank heartily, and two extra bottles of wine were given to Zhang Ba as his reward. They caroused till the sun was sinking in the west and they were half drunk, when a great wind sprang up.

Caught up by this swirling wind, all the flowers on the ground were transformed in a twinkling into girls about a foot high. But before the men had finished crying out in amazement, the girls shook in the wind till they attained the size of human beings. They formed a bevy of beauties in magnificent clothes, and the men were dazzled by their loveliness. A girl in red began to speak.

"We have stayed here for many years," she declared, "and been well looked after by Master Qiu. We never thought to see the day when ruffians would pollute us with their foul breath and savage us with their cruel hands, nor that they would bring a false charge against Master Qiu and plot to seize this place. Now we have our enemies before us! Let us fall on them to requite the kindness of our friend and to avenge the cruel insult to ourselves!"

"You are right," replied the rest. "We must lose no time, otherwise they may run away."

Then, raising their arms, they swept forward; and their long sleeves, fluttering like pennons in the wind, sent cold shivers down the men's spines.

"Ghosts! Ghosts!" cried the men. And throwing down their cups they fled in confusion with no thought for each other. They stumbled over rocks, grazed their faces against the branches of trees, slipped, fell, and staggered to their feet only to fall again. When this confusion had lasted for some time they counted their number, and found that Zhang Wei and his lackey Zhang Ba had disappeared. By now the wind had dropped, and with lowered heads they ran home like rabbits through the gloaming, thankful to escape with their lives. After the servants had recovered from their alarm, they asked some bold young tenants to go back with torches to search for the missing men. Returning to the garden they heard groans issuing from under a great plum tree, and when they raised their torches to look they discovered Zhang Ba, lying with a broken crown against the trunk of the tree, unable to rise. Two of the tenants helped him home while the rest searched the garden; but they found everything quiet and still. The peonies under their awning were blooming as before — not a blossom was broken — but cups and plates littered the cottage, where wine had been spilt everywhere. Gaping in surprise, they gathered together the utensils and started searching again. The garden was by no means large, yet they went round it three or four times without finding any trace of Zhang Wei.

"Could he have been blown away by the wind or eaten by the fairies?" they wondered. "What can have become of him?"

After hanging around for some time, since there was nothing they could do, they decided to go home for the night and make a fresh search the next day. As they reached the gate, however, they met another group of men with lanterns coming in. These were old Yu, Shan and a few other neighbours who had come to see whether it was really true that Zhang Wei and his men had met ghosts, that he had disappeared and that a search party was looking for him. When the tenants declared that this was indeed the case, the old men were amazed.

"Don't go yet," they said. "We'll help you to look once more."

They made another careful search, only to be disappointed

again; and the tenants were making for the gate, sighing, when Yu and Shan said: "If you won't be coming back tonight, may we lock the gate? It is our duty to keep watch here."

By this time, having lost their leader, Zhang's men were like a snake without a head. All their swagger gone, they answered: "Of course! Of course!"

Just as they were leaving, however, a tenant called out from the east corner of the fence: "I've found the master!" And they all rushed over.

The worker pointed up.

"Isn't that the master's gauze cap with soft flaps hanging on the ash bough?" he asked.

"If the cap is here, its owner must be nearby!" cried the others.

But they had not groped more than a few paces along the fence when one of them exclaimed in horror.

From the cesspool at the east corner a man was projecting upside-down, and by the shoes and socks and lower garments they could tell that it was Zhang. In spite of the filth the tenants dragged his body out, while Yu and Shan, secretly thanking the gods, left with the other neighbours. Some of Zhang's men carried his corpse to the lake to wash, and others went home to inform his family, who wept and wailed as they prepared clothes for the funeral. That same night the fracture in Zhang Ba's skull proved fatal, and he died just before dawn. Thus retribution came to two evil-doers.

The next day the prefect felt well enough to preside over the court; and he was about to try the old gardener again when a constable reported how the informer, Zhang Ba, and his master, Zhang Wei, had both died the previous night. The prefect could not believe in this new miracle until more than a hundred of the local peasants and elders arrived with a joint petition which stated that Qiu was no magician but a flower-lover who did good deeds, and that Zhang Wei had been punished by Heaven for accusing the old gardener falsely. They explained and accounted for the whole affair.

The prefect's dizziness the previous day had made him suspect that injustice might have been done, and now he saw the truth. After ordering the immediate release of Qiu, who had fortunately not yet been tortured, he gave him a notice bearing the official seal to hang outside his garden gate, in order to prevent people from injuring his plants. The villagers expressed their gratitude to the prefect and left the court, and when Qiu had thanked all his neighbours, he went home with them. Yu and Shan unlocked the garden gate and went in with their friend; and when the old gardener saw his peonies blooming as before, he was very moved. Then there was merry-making for several days, for the neighbours gave feasts to celebrate Qiu's return, and he prepared feasts to thank all who had helped him.

After that the old gardener accustomed himself to feeding on flowers until he was able to do without cooked food; he also gave all the money from his fruit sales as alms. So in a few years' time, his hair, which had been white, turned black again and his cheeks became as ruddy as those of a young man.

On the fifteenth day of the eighth month one year, Qiu was practising yoga under his blossoms beneath a bright sun and cloudless sky when a holy breeze sprang up and coloured clouds rose like vapour. As clear music sounded in the air and rare incense was wafted from above, blue phoenixes and white storks alighted in his courtyard and The Keeper of Flowers appeared in the sky, surrounded by pennons, canopies and fairy maids making music. When the old gardener saw her, he prostrated himself on the ground.

"Qiu Xian, your time has come!" said the goddess. "I have requested the Heavenly Emperor to appoint you Protector of All the Flowers on Earth, and you are to go to Heaven now with your house. Your task will be to bless those who love and cherish flowers and to punish those who neglect and destroy them."

When Qiu had thanked her by kowtowing towards the sky, he ascended the clouds with the fairies, while his thatched cottage and garden rose slowly from the ground and floated southwards. Old Yu, Shan and all the villagers who witnessed this knelt down and saw the old gardener raise his hand in farewell to them from the clouds, where he remained in sight for a long time. After this the village was called Fairy Village or Flower Village.

Notes:

1. The peony (*mudan*) is often said to be China's national flower. It is, without doubt, the 'city flower' of Luoyang in Henan province.

2. The finger game or 'stone-paper-scissors' game is known among children in the West. The more complex and literary version of this game played by adults at banquets and other such gatherings is still popular in China.

3. The Western Paradise (*Xitian*) is the Buddhist paradise of Amida Buddha. Unlike the void (*kong* or *śunyā*) of ulimate liberation (*nirvāṇa*), the Western Paradise is a heaven where believers in Amida Buddha may enjoy eternal bliss.

杜十娘怒沉百寶箱

The Courtesan's Jewel Box

from Tales to Warn the World

Our story starts with the invasion of Korea by the Japanese general Hideyoshi in the twentieth year of Wan Li period (1592) of the Ming Dynasty. When the King of Korea appealed for help, the Son of Heaven sent troops across the sea to save him; and the Board of Treasury proposed that since the grain and silver allocated to the troops were insufficient for the expedition a special tax should be raised by the sale of places in the Imperial Colleges. To this the emperor agreed.

Now this system had many advantages for those with money. In addition to having better facilities for studying and passing the examinations, the students of these colleges were assured of small official posts. Accordingly, the sons of official or wealthy families who did not want to sit for the county examination took advantage of this scheme to purchase a place in one of the Imperial Colleges. So the number of students in both the colleges in Nanjing and Beijing rose to over one thousand each.

One of these students was called Li Jia. A native of Shaoxing in Zhejiang Province, he was the oldest of three sons of a provincial treasurer. Although a licentiate, he had failed to pass the prefectural examination, he had purchased a place in the Imperial College at Beijing under the new system; and during his residence in the capital he went with a fellow-provincial and fellow-student, Liu Yuchun, to the singsong girls' quarter. It was here that he met a celebrated courtesan called Du Wei, who, because she was the tenth girl in the quarter, was also known as Decima.

Since becoming a courtesan Decima had met countless young men of rich and noble families who had not hesitated to spend all they possessed for love of her.

Though Li was an experienced young fellow, he had never seen such a beautiful girl. At his first meeting with Decima he was absolutely charmed by her and fell head over heels in love. And since he was not only handsome and amiable but open-handed and untiring in his pursuit of her, the attraction soon proved mutual. Realizing that her mistress was grasping and heartless, Decima had long wanted to leave her; and now that she saw how kind and devoted Li was, she wished to throw in her lot with him. Although the young man was too afraid of his father to marry her, they fell more and more deeply in love, passing whole days and nights together in pleasure and remaining as inseparable as if they were already husband and wife. They vowed solemnly never to love anyone else.

After Li became Decima's lover, other wealthy men who had heard of her fame tried in vain to gain access to her. At first Li spent money lavishly on her, and the procuress, all smiles and blandishments, waited on him hand and foot. But when more than a year had sped past, Li's money was nearly exhausted. He could no longer be as generous as he would have liked, and the old woman began to treat him coldly. The provincial treasurer heard that his son was frequenting the courtesans' quarter, and sent letter after letter ordering him to come home; but the young man was so enamoured of Decima's beauty that he kept postponing his return. And later, when he heard how angry his father was with him, he dared not go back.

It is said that friendship based on money will end once the money is spent. Decima, however, loved Li so truly that the poorer he grew the more passionately attached to him she became. Her mistress told her repeatedly to send Li about his business and, seeing that the girl refused to do so, she began to insult him in the hope that he would leave in anger. But her insults had no effect on Li, who was naturally of a mild disposition, so she could do nothing but reproach Decima every day.

"In our profession we depend on our clients for food and clothing," she said. "As we speed one guest from the front door, another should be coming in by the back. The more clients we have, the more money and silk we shall heap up. But now that this dratted Li Jia has been hanging around for more than a year, it's no use talking about new clients— even the old ones have stopped coming. We seem to have got hold of a Zhong Kui[1] who keeps out devils, because not a soul will come near us. There'll soon be no smoke in our chimney. What's to become of us?"

Decima, however, would not quietly submit to this. "Mr. Li did not come here empty-handed," she retorted. "Look at all the money he has spent here!"

"That was before: it's *now* I'm talking about. You tell him to give me a little money today for fuel and rice for the two of you. In other houses the girls are a money-tree which needs only to be shaken to shower down riches: it's just my bad luck that I've got a girl who keeps the money away. Every day I have to worry how to make ends meet, because you insist on supporting this pauper. Where do you think our food and clothes are coming from? Go and tell that beggar of yours that, if he's any good at all, he must give me some silver; then you can go off with him and I'll buy another girl. Wouldn't that suit us both?"

"Do you really mean it?" demanded Decima.

"Have I ever told a lie?" replied the old woman, who,

knowing that Li had not a cent left and had pawned his clothes, thought it would be impossible for him to raise any money. "Of course I mean it."

"How much do you want from him?"

"If it were anyone else, I would ask for a thousand taels ; but I'll ask a poor devil like him for only three hundred. With that I could buy another girl to take your place. But there's one condition: he must pay me within three days, then I shall hand you over straight away. If he hasn't paid after three days, I'll give the wretch a good beating with my cane and drive him out, gentleman or no gentleman! Nobody will be able to blame me either."

"Although he is away from home and has run out of money," said Decima, "he should be able to raise three hundred taels. But three days is too little. Can't you make it ten?"

"The young fool has nothing but his bare hands," thought the procuress. "Even if I give him a hundred days, he won't be able to get the money. And when he fails to produce it, however thick-skinned he is he won't have the nerve to turn up again. Then I can get my establishment under proper control once more, and Decima will have nothing to say."

"Well, to humour you," she said, "I'll make it ten days. But if he doesn't have the money by then, don't blame me."

"If he can't find the money by then, I don't suppose he will have the face to come back," said Decima. "I am only afraid that if he does bring the three hundred taels, you may go back on your word."

"I am an old woman of fifty-one," protested the procuress. "I worship Buddha and fast ten days every month. How could I lie to you? If you don't trust me, I'll put my palm on yours to make a pledge. May I become a dog or swine in my next life if I go back on my word!"

That night in bed Decima discussed her future with Li.

"It's not that I don't want to marry you," said the young man. "But it'll cost at least a thousand taels to buy your freedom, and where can I get that now that all my money is spent?"

"I have already spoken to my mistress," replied Decima. "She wants only three hundred taels, but it must be paid within ten days. Although you have come to the end of your allowance, you must have relatives and friends in the capital from whom you can borrow. If you raise this sum, I shall be yours; and we shan't have to suffer the old woman's temper any more."

"My friends and relatives here have been cold-shouldering me because I have been spending too much time with you," said Li. "Tomorrow I'll tell them that I am packing up to leave and coming to say goodbye, then ask for money for my travelling expenses. I may be able to collect three hundred taels." So he got up, dressed and prepared to take his leave.

"Be as quick as you can!" urged Decima as he was going out. "I'll be waiting for good news." And Li promised to do his best.

On leaving the house, Li called on a number of relatives and friends, pretending that he had come to say goodbye. They were pleased to hear that he was going home, but when he mentioned that he was short of money for his journey they said nothing. As the proverb says: To speak of a loan is to put an end to friendship. They all, with good reason, considered Li as a young rake whose infatuation with a courtesan had kept him away from home for more than a year, and they knew that his father was furious with him.

"Who knows whether he is telling the truth?" they thought. "Suppose we lend him money for the journey and he spends it on girls again, when his father hears of it he will think the worst of us. Since we shall be blamed either way, why not refuse altogether?"

"I am so sorry!" said each in turn. "I happen to be short at the moment, so I can't help you." Li received exactly the same answer from each of them, not one of his acquaintances proving generous enough to lend him even ten or twenty taels.

He called at house after house for three days without succeeding in borrowing a single cent; but he dared not tell Decima this and put her off with evasive answers. On the fourth day, however, he was in such despair that he was ashamed to go back to her; but after living so long with Decima he had no other dwelling place and, having nowhere else to spend the night, he went to his fellow-provincial, Liu, and begged a bed of him. When Liu asked why he looked so worried, Li told him the whole story of how Decima wanted to marry him. Liu, however, shook his head.

"I don't believe it," he said. "Decima is the most famous courtesan in that quarter and her price must be at least ten pecks of pearls or a thousand taels of silver. Her mistress would never let her go for three hundred taels. The old woman must be annoyed because you have no money left and are monopolizing her girl without paying her; so she has thought of this trick to get rid of you. Since she has known you for a long time, she has to keep up appearances and can't drive you away outright; and, knowing that you are short of cash, she has asked for three hundred taels in order to appear generous, giving you ten days in which to raise that sum. They believe that if you can't get the money in time, you won't dare to go back; while if you do, they will jeer and insult you so that you won't be able to stay anyway. This is the kind of trick such people always play. Think it over for yourself and don't let them take you in. In my humble opinion, the sooner you sever relations with them the better."

When Li heard this he was filled with misgivings and remained silent for a long time.

"You mustn't make a wrong decision," went on Liu. "If you really want to go home and need money for the journey, your friends may be able to raise a few taels. But I doubt if you could get three hundred taels in ten months, let alone ten days, for people nowadays are simply not interested in their friends' troubles. Those women knew that you could never borrow such a sum: that's why they named this figure."

"I suppose you are right, my friend," said Li.

But, still unwilling to give up the girl, he continued to call on acquaintances to ask for a loan, no longer going back to Decima at night. He stayed with Liu for three days, until six of the ten days had passed, by which time Decima had become so anxious that she sent her little servant-boy out to look for him. The boy found Li on the main street.

"Mr. Li!" he called. "Our mistress is expecting you!"

Li, however, felt too ashamed to go back and said: " I am busy today. I will come tomorrow."

But the boy had his instructions from Decima and, taking hold of Li's coat, he would not let him go. "I was told to find you," he said. "You must come with me."

So Li, who was of course longing for his mistress, accompanied the boy to the courtesans' quarter. But when he saw Decima he was silent.

"What progress have you made?" asked Decima.

Li shed tears and said nothing.

"Are men's hearts so hard," she said, "that you cannot raise three hundred taels?"

With tears in his eyes, Li answered: "It is easier to catch a tiger in the mountain than to find a friend in need. I have been hurrying from house to house for six days, but I have not been able to borrow a cent; and it is because I was ashamed to come to you empty-handed that I have stayed away for the last few days. Today you sent for me, and I come feeling overwhelmed with shame. It is not that I haven't done my best, but people are heartless."

"Don't let the old woman hear you," said Decima. "Stay here tonight, and we'll talk it over." Then she prepared a meal and they enjoyed the food and wine together.

In the middle of the night Decima asked: "Couldn't you get any money at all? What will become of me then?"

But Li had no answer for her and could only shed tears.

Soon it was dawn and Decima said: "In my mattress I

have hidden one hundred and fifty taels of silver which I have saved up, and I want you to take that. Now that I have given you half the sum, it should be easier for you to find the other half. But there are only four days left: don't lose any time." Then getting out of bed she gave the mattress to Li, who was overcome with joy.

Ordering the servant-boy to carry the mattress for him, Li went straight to Liu's lodging, where he told his friend all that had happened that night. And when they unpicked the mattress they found in the cotton padding many silver pieces which, when weighed, totalled one hundred and fifty taels. Liu was very much impressed.

"The girl must really be in love with you," he said. "Since she is so much in earnest, you mustn't let her down. I will do what I can for you."

"If you help me now," replied Li, "I shall never forget it."

Then Liu kept Li in his house, while he went round himself to all his acquaintances. In two days he borrowed one hundred and fifty taels which he gave to Li, saying: "I have done this not so much for your sake as because I am touched by the girl's devotion to you."

It was a happy Li, beaming with smiles, who came to Decima with the three hundred taels on the ninth day — one day earlier than the appointed time.

"The other day you could not borrow a cent," said Decima. "How is it that today you have got one hundred and fifty taels?" And when Li told her about his fellow-student Liu, she pressed her hands to her forehead in token of gratitude. "We must thank Mr. Liu for helping us realize our wish!" she cried.

They passed the night in great joy together, and the next morning Decima rose early and said to Li: "Once you have paid the money, I shall be able to leave with you. You had better decide how we are going to travel. Yesterday I borrowed twenty taels from my friends which you can take for the journey."

Li had, in fact, been wondering where he was going to get the money for their journey, but had not liked to mention this difficulty. Now he was delighted to receive this twenty taels.

As they were talking, the mistress of the house knocked at the door.

"This is the tenth day, Decima!" she called.

When Li heard this, he opened the door to invite her in. "Thank you, aunty," he said. "I was just going to ask you over." And he placed the three hundred taels on the table.

The procuress had never thought that Li would produce the money. Her face fell and she was about to retract, when Decima said.

"I have worked here for eight years, and I must have earned several thousand taels for you in that time. This is the happy day on which I am to start a new life — you agreed to that yourself. The three hundred taels are here, not a cent less, and they have been paid on time. If you break your word, Mr. Li will take the money away and I shall immediately commit suicide. Then you will lose both the money and me, and you will be sorry."

The old woman had nothing to say to this. After some thought she finally went to fetch her balance to weigh the silver.

"Well, well," she said at last. "I suppose I can't keep you. But if you must go, go at once. And don't think you're going to take any clothes and trinkets with you." She pushed them out of the room, and called for a lock with which she padlocked the door.

It was already autumn. Decima, just risen from her bed and not yet dressed, was still wearing old clothes. She curtseyed to her mistress and Li bowed too. Then as husband and wife they left the old woman's house together.

"Wait while I call a sedan chair for you," said Li to Decima. "We can go to Mr. Liu's lodging before deciding on anything." But Decima demurred.

"My friends have always been very good to me," she said, "and I ought to say goodbye to them. Besides, they were kind enough to lend us the money for our travelling expenses the other day: we ought to thank them for that." So she took Li to say goodbye to the other courtesans.

Two of these girls, Yuelang and Susu, lived nearby and were Decima's closest friends. She called first on Yuelang, who, surprised to see her dressed in old clothes and with no ornaments in her hair, asked what had happened. Decima told her and introduced Li to her. Then, pointing to Yuelang, Decima told Li:

"This is the friend who lent us the money the other day. You should thank her." And Li bowed again and again.

Presently Yuelang helped Decima to wash and comb her hair, sending at the same time for Susu. And after Decima had made her toilet, her two friends brought out all their emerald trinkets, gold bracelets, jade hairpins and earrings, as well as a brocade tunic and skirt, a phoenix girdle and a pair of embroidered slippers, until soon they had arrayed Decima in finery from head to foot. Then they feasted together, and Yuelang lent the lovers her bedroom for the night.

The following day they gave another big feast to which all the courtesans were invited; and not one of Decima's friends stayed away. After toasting the happy couple, they played wind and stringed instruments, and sang and danced, each doing her best to give the company pleasure. And this feast lasted till midnight, when Decima thanked each of her friends in turn.

"You were the chief among us," said the courtesans. "But now that you are leaving with your husband, we may never meet again. When you have decided on which day to set out, we shall come to see you off."

"When the date is settled, I shall let you all know," said Yuelang. "But Decima will be travelling a long way with her husband, and their resources are rather limited. We must be responsible for seeing that she doesn't have to go short on the way." The other courtesans agreed to this, then left, while Li and Decima spent the night again in Yuelang's room.

When dawn came Decima asked Li: "Where are we going from here? Do you have a plan?"

"My father is already angry with me," replied Li, "and if he hears that I have married a singsong girl, not only will he make me suffer for it, but you will feel all the weight of his anger too. This has been worrying me for some time, but I have not yet thought of a way out."

"A father cannot help loving his son," said Decima, "so he won't be angry with you for ever. But perhaps, since going straight home would offend him, we had better go to some beauty spot like Suzhou or Hangzhou for the time being. You can then go home alone and ask some relatives or friends to persuade your father to forgive you. Once you have made your peace with him you can come to fetch me, and all will be well."

"That is a good idea," agreed Li.

The next morning they said goodbye to Yuelang and went to Liu's lodging to pack their baggage. When Decima saw Liu she kowtowed to him to thank him for his assistance, and promised to repay him in future.

Liu hastily bowed in return. "You must be a remarkable woman," he said, "to remain loyal to your lover even after he became poor. I merely blew upon the fire in the direction of the wind. Such a trifling service is not worth mentioning."

The three of them feasted all day, and the following morning chose an auspicious day for the journey and hired sedan chairs and beasts. Decima also sent her boy with a letter to Yuelang to thank her and bid her farewell. When they were leaving, several sedan chairs arrived bearing Yuelang, Susu and the other courtesans who had come to see them off.

"You are starting on a long journey with your husband

and you are short of money," said Yuelang. "So we have prepared a little gift to express our love. Please accept it. If you run short on your journey, you may find it useful." She told a servant to bring over a gilt box of the type used for carrying stationery; but since this was securely locked, its contents could not be seen. Decima neither declined the gift nor opened it, but thanked them all. By now the chairs and beasts were ready, and the chair bearers and grooms asked them to start. Liu offered the travellers three cups of wine in parting, and he and the courtesans saw them to Chongwen Gate where, wiping away tears, they all bid their friends farewell.

In due course Li and Decima reached Luhe River where they were to take a junk. They were lucky enough to find an official despatch boat returning to Guazhou and, having settled the amount of their fare, they booked places on this junk. Once aboard, however, Li discovered that he had not a cent left. Although Decima had given him twenty taels, it was all gone! The fact was that Li had stayed in the courtesans' quarter until he had nothing but old clothes to wear; so as soon as he had money he naturally went to redeem a few of his gowns at the pawnshop and to have new bedding made. What was left of the silver was enough only for the sedan chairs and beasts.

"Don't worry," said Decima, when she saw his anxiety. "The present that my friends gave us may prove useful." Thereupon she took a key and unlocked the box. Li, standing beside her, was too ashamed to look into the case as Decima took out a silk bag and placed it on the table.

"See what's in that," she said.

Li picked up the bag, which was quite heavy; and when he opened it he found it contained exactly fifty taels of silver. Decima meantime had locked the box again without saying what else it contained.

"How generous of the girls to give us this!" she exclaimed. "Now we have enough not only for the road but to help towards our expenses when we visit the beauty spots in Suzhou or Hangzhou."

Surprised and delighted, Li rejoined: "If not for your help, I should have died far from home without a burial place. I shall never forget how good you have been to me." After that, whenever they talked of the past Li would burst into tears of gratitude, but Decima would always comfort him tenderly.

After an uneventful journey of several days, they reached Guazhou Harbour where the junk moored. Li booked another passenger boat, had their luggage put aboard and arranged to set sail the next morning at dawn. It was midwinter and the full moon was as clear and bright as water.

"Since we left the capital," said Li to Decima as they sat together in the bow of the junk, "we have been shut up in the cabin with other passengers so that we couldn't talk freely. But today we have the whole boat to ourselves and can do as we please. Now that we are leaving North China and coming to the Yangzi Valley, don't you think we should drink a little wine to celebrate and to cheer ourselves up?"

"Yes," said Decima. "I haven't had a chance to chat or laugh for a long time. I feel just as you do."

Li got out the wine utensils and placed them on the deck, then spread a rug on which they sat down together to drink to each other. They drank until they were both under the spell of the wine.

"You had the loveliest voice in all your quarter," said Li, raising his cup to Decima. "The first time that I saw you and heard you sing so divinely, I lost my heart to you. But we have been upset for so long that I haven't heard your heavenly voice for many days. Now the bright moon is shining on the clear waves; it is midnight and there is no one about — won't you sing for me?"

Decima was in a happy mood, so, clearing her throat and tapping her fan on the deck to keep time, she sang. Her song was about a scholar who offered wine to a girl, and was taken from the opera *Moon Pavilion* by Shi Junmei of the Yuan Dynasty. It was set to the air known as 'The Little Red Peach Blossom.'

Now, as it happened, on another junk nearby there was a young man called Sun Fu, who was a native of Xinan in Huizhou. He had an estate worth millions of cash, for his family had dealt in salt in Yangzhou for generations; and now, at twenty years of age, he too had entered the Imperial College in Nanjing. This fellow Sun was a dissolute young man who frequented the courtesans' quarters in search of amusement or to buy a smile from the singsong girls: indeed, he was one of the foremost in the pursuit of pleasure.

Sun's boat was moored at Guazhou Harbour too on this particular evening, and he was drinking alone to drown his boredom when he heard a woman singing so clearly and exquisitely that not even the song of a phoenix could compare with her voice. He stood up in the bow and listened for some time until he realized that the singing came from the next boat; but just as he was going to make enquiries, the song ended. The servant whom he sent to put discreet questions to the boatman found out that the adjacent junk had been hired by a certain Mr. Li, but was unable to learn anything about the singer.

"She must be a professional, not a respectable girl," thought Sun. "How can I contrive to see her?" Preoccupation with this problem kept him awake all night.

At the fifth watch a high wind sprang up, and by dawn the sky was filled with dark clouds. Soon a snowstorm was raging.

Since this snowstorm made it impossible to cross the river, all boats had to remain in the harbour. Sun ordered his boatman to steer closer to Li's junk; and then, having put on his sable cap and fox fur coat, he opened the window on the pretext that he was watching the snow. Thus he succeeded in catching sight of Decima, for when she had finished dressing she raised the curtain of the cabin window with one slender white hand in order to empty her basin into the river. Her more than earthly beauty made Sun's head swim, and he fastened his eyes to the spot where she had appeared, hoping to gain another glimpse of her; but he was disappointed. After some reflection, he leaned against his cabin window and chanted aloud the lines by Gao Yin on the plum blossom:

As a hermit resting on a snow-clad hill;
Like a maiden come to a glade beneath the moon.

When Li heard someone chanting poetry in the next boat, he leaned out to look just as Sun had hoped he would. For Sun's plan was to attract Li's attention by this means in order to draw him into conversation. Now, hastily raising his hands in greeting, Sun asked:

"What is your honourable name, sir?"

After Li introduced himself he naturally asked to know Sun's name. And, when Sun had introduced himself, they chatted about the Imperial College until very soon they were on friendly terms.

"It must be Heaven's will," said Sun, "that this snowstorm should have held up our boats in order that we should meet. I am in luck. Travelling by junk is thoroughly boring, and I would like to go ashore with you to a wineshop where I can profit by your conversation while we drink. I hope you won't refuse."

"How can I impose on you like this?" Li replied.

"Oh, come," protested Sun. "Within the four seas all men are brothers."

Then he ordered his boatman to put down the gang plank, and told his boy to hold an umbrella for Mr. Li as he came across. He bowed to Li at the bow and followed him politely ashore.

A few paces brought them to a wineshop. They went upstairs, chose a clean table by the window and sat down. When the waiter had brought wine and food, Sun asked Li to drink; and as they drank they enjoyed the sight of the snow. After they had exchanged the usual platitudes about scholarship, Sun gradually steered the conversation around to courtesans; and now that they had found a common interest — since both young men had much experience in this field — they began to talk frankly and to exchange confidences.

Presently Sun sent his servant away, and asked in a low voice: "Who was the girl who sang on your junk last night?"

Li, only too ready to boast of his conquest, announced truthfully: "That was Du Wei, the well-known courtesan of Beijing."

"If she is a courtesan, how did you manage to get hold of her?"

Then Li told him the whole story: how they had fallen in love, how Decima had wanted to marry him, and how he had borrowed money to redeem her.

"It must, no doubt, be very pleasant," said Sun, "to be taking home a beauty. But will your honourable family approve?"

"I have no anxiety on the score of my first wife," replied Li. "The only difficulty is that my father is rather strict, and I may have trouble with him."

This gave Sun the opening he had been waiting for.

"Since your respected father may disapprove, where do you intend to lodge your beauty?" he asked. "Have you discussed it with her?"

"Yes, we have discussed it," replied Li with a frown.

"And does she have a good plan?" demanded Sun eagerly.

"She wants to stay for a time in Suzhou or Hangzhou," answered Li. "And when we have visited the beauty spots there, I will return home first to ask friends or relatives to talk my father round; then, when he is no longer angry, I shall fetch her back. What do you think of this plan?"

Sun looked thoughtful for a while, pretending to be very much concerned.

"We have only just met," he said at length, "and you may

take offence if a casual acquaintance advises you on such an intimate matter."

"I need your advice," protested Li. "Please don't hesitate to speak frankly."

"Well then," said Sun. "Since your father is a high provincial official, he must be very jealous of your family reputation. He has already expressed displeasure because you visited low haunts: do you think he will allow you to take a singsong girl as your wife? As for your relatives and friends, they will all take their cue from your respected father. It will be useless to ask their help: they are bound to refuse. And even if some of them are foolish enough to plead your cause to your father, once they realize that the old gentleman is against this marriage they will change their tune. So you will be causing discord in your family, and you will have no satisfactory answer to take to your mistress. Even if you enjoy the scenery in Suzhou and Hangzhou for a time, you cannot live like that indefinitely. Once your funds run low you will find yourself in a dilemma."

Only too conscious that all he possessed was fifty taels, the greater part of which was already spent, when Sun spoke of possible financial difficulties Li nodded and admitted that such, indeed, was the case.

"Now I sincerely want to give you some advice," went on Sun. "But you may not like to hear it."

"I am very much obliged to you," said Li. "Please speak frankly."

"I had better not," declared Sun. "Casual acquaintances shouldn't come between lovers."

"Never mind about that," protested Li.

"As the ancients said, women are fickle," argued Sun. "And singsong girls in particular are likely to prove untrue. Since your mistress is a well-known courtesan, she must have friends everywhere. There may be some former lover of hers in the south, and she may be making use of you for the journey here so that she can join another man."

"Oh, no, I don't think so," said Li.

"You may be right," replied Sun. "But those young southerners are notorious philanderers; and if you leave your mistress by herself, she may succumb to one of them. On the other hand, if you take her home you will make your father angrier than ever. In fact, there seems to be no way out for you.

"Now the relationship between father and son is sacred and inviolable. If you offend your father and abandon your home for the sake of a courtesan, you will be universally condemned as a dissolute wastrel. Your wife will not consider you worthy to be her husband, your younger brother will cease to respect you as his elder, and your friends will have no more to do with you. You will find yourself a complete outcast. So I advise you to think this thing out carefully right now."

This speech left Li at a complete loss. Moving his seat nearer to Sun, he demanded earnestly: "What do you think I should do?"

"I have a scheme which would be very much to your advantage," replied Sun. "But I fear you may be too fond of your concubine to consider it, and I will be wasting my breath even to tell you."

"If you have a good plan to restore me to the bosom of my family, I shall be tremendously grateful to you. Don't hesitate to speak."

"You have been away from home for more than a year, so that your father is angry and your wife displeased with you. If I were you, I would be unable to eat or sleep for remorse. But your worthy father is angry with you only because you have let yourself become infatuated with a courtesan and are spending money like water. You are showing yourself unfit to inherit his property, for if you go on in this way you are bound to bankrupt your family; so if you return home now empty-handed, the old gentleman will vent his anger on you. But if you are willing to part with your concubine and to make the best of a bad bargain, I don't mind offering you a thousand taels for her. With this sum, you can tell your father that you have been teaching in the capital instead of squandering money, and he will certainly believe you. Then peace will reign at home and you will have no more trouble. At a single stroke you will have turned calamity into good fortune. Please consider my offer carefully. It's not that I covet your courtesan's beauty: I just want to do what I can to help you out."

Li had always been a weak character who stood in great awe of his father; so Sun's argument convinced him completely and, rising from his seat, he bowed to express his thanks.

"Your excellent advice has opened my eyes," he said. "But since my concubine has come all these hundreds of miles with me, I can't sever relations with her too abruptly. I'll talk it over with her, and let you know as soon as I gain her consent."

"Break it to her gently," said Sun. "Since she is so fond of you, she can't want to estrange you from your father. I am sure she will help to restore you to your family." They went on drinking till dusk, when the wind dropped and the snow ceased. Then Sun told his servant to pay the bill, and walked hand in hand with Li back to the boat.

Meanwhile Decima had prepared wine and sweetmeats on the junk for Li, but he did not come back all day. At dusk she lighted the lamp to wait for him, and when he came aboard she rose to welcome him; but she noticed that he seemed flustered and upset. As she poured a cup of warm wine for him, he shook his head in refusal and went without a word to his bed. Decima was disturbed. Having put away the cups and plates and helped Li to undress, she asked:

"What has happened today to make you so sad?"

Li's only answer was a sigh. She repeated her question three or four times until he was asleep, and by then she was so uneasy that she sat on the edge of the bed unable to close her eyes. In the middle of the night the young man woke up and heaved another great sigh.

"What is preying so heavily on your mind?" asked Decima. "Why can't you tell me?"

Li sat up, drawing the quilt around him, and tried several times to speak; but he broke off short each time and tears poured down his cheeks.

Then taking Li in her arms Decima comforted him with kind words, saying: "We have been lovers for nearly two years and won through a thousand hardships and difficulties; and you have not looked depressed once during all this long journey. Why are you so upset now when we are about to cross the Yangzi and settle down to live happily ever after? There must be a reason. As husband and wife we shall live and die together, so we should discuss our troubles together too. Please don't keep it from me."

After she had begged him several times to speak, with tears in his eyes Li said: "When I was stranded far from home you were good to me and attached yourself to me in spite of every hardship, so that I am inexpressibly grateful to you. But I have been thinking things over. My father is a high provincial official who is a stickler for convention and a very stern man. If I anger him so that he drives us out of the family, we shall be forced to wander homeless, and what will become of us then? That would mean a complete break with my father, and we could not be sure of a happy married life either. Today my friend Sun from Xinan discussed this with me while we were drinking; and now I feel quite broken-hearted."

"What do you mean to do?" asked Decima, greatly alarmed.

"A man in trouble cannot see his way clearly," said Li. "But Mr. Sun has thought out an excellent plan for me. I am only afraid you may not agree to it."

"Who is this Mr. Sun? If his plan is good, why shouldn't

I agree to it?"

"His name is Sun Fu. He is a salt merchant from Xinan and a gallant young scholar. He heard you singing last night, so he asked about you; and when I told him our story and mentioned that we would not be able to go home, he offered a thousand taels for your hand. If I had a thousand taels, it would be easy for me to face my parents; and you would have a home too. But I can't bear to part with you: that's why I am sad." When he had said this, his tears fell like rain.

Taking her arms from his shoulders, Decima gave a strange laugh.

"He must be a fine gentleman to have thought out this plan," she said, "You will recover your thousand taels, and I shall no longer be an encumbrance to you if I can go to another man. What could be more reasonable and high-principled? This plan suits us both. Where is the silver?"

"Since I hadn't got your consent, my love," said Li, who had stopped crying, "the money is still with him. It hasn't yet changed hands."

"Make sure you accept his offer first thing tomorrow," urged Decima. "You mustn't miss this opportunity. But a thousand taels is a lot of money; be sure it is properly weighed and handed over before I cross to the other boat. Don't let this salt merchant cheat you."

It was now the fourth watch, and since dawn was approaching Decima got up and lighted the lamp to dress herself.

"Today I am dressing to usher out an old client and welcome in a new," she said. "This is an important occasion."

She applied her rouge, powder and scented oil with great care, then arrayed herself in her most splendid jewels and most magnificent embroidered gown. Her perfume scented the air and she was a dazzling sight.

By the time she had finished dressing it was already dawn and Sun had sent a servant to their junk for a reply. When

Decima stole a glance at Li and saw that he looked pleased, she urged him to give a reply at once and possess himself of the silver as soon as possible. Then Li went to Sun's boat to announce that Decima was willing.

"There is no difficulty about the money," said Sun. "But I must have the lady's jewel case as a pledge."

When Li told Decima this, she pointed to her gilt box. "Let them take that," she said.

Then Sun, in great exultation, promptly sent the thousand taels of silver to Li's boat. When Decima had looked through the packages and satisfied herself that the silver was of the finest and the amount was correct, she put one hand on the side of the boat and beckoned to Sun with the other, so that he was transported with joy.

"May I have that box back for a minute?" she asked, parting her red lips to reveal pearly teeth. "It contains Mr. Li's travel permit which I must return to him."

Satisfied that Decima could not escape him now, Sun ordered his servant to carry back her gilt box and set it down on the deck. Decima took her key and unlocked it, disclosing a series of drawers inside; and when she told Li to pull out the first drawer, he found it filled with trinkets, pearls, jade and precious stones, to the value of several hundred taels of silver. These jewels, to the consternation of Li, Sun and the others on the two boats, Decima suddenly tossed into the river.

Then she told Li to pull out a second drawer containing jade flutes and golden pipes, and a third drawer filled with curious old jade and gold ornaments worth several thousand taels. All these, too, Decima threw into the water.

By this time the bank was thronged with spectators. "What a pity!" they exclaimed.

As they were marvelling at her behaviour, she drew out the last drawer in which there was a casket. She opened the casket and they saw that it was packed with handfuls of bright pearls and other precious stones such as emeralds and

杜十娘怒沉百宝箱

Heart-broken Decima reproaches Sun and Li

cat's eyes, the like of which they had never seen before and the value of which they could not even guess at. The onlookers cried out loudly in admiration. When Decima made as if to toss all these jewels into the river too, a remorseful Li threw his arms around her and wept bitterly, while Sun came over to plead with her also. But Decima pushed Li away and turned angrily on Sun.

"Mr. Li and I suffered many hardships to come here!" she cried. "But, to gratify your lust, you lied cunningly to him in order to break up our marriage and destroy our love. I hate you! After my death, if I become a ghost, I shall accuse you before the gods. How dare you think of enjoying me yourself!"

Then Decima turned to Li.

"I led the unhappy life of a courtesan for many years," she said, "and during that time I saved up enough to support myself in my old age. But after I met you, we swore to love each other for the rest of our lives. When we left the capital I pretended that this box was a present from my friends, whereas actually it contained jewels worth over ten thousand taels of silver with which I intended to fit you out splendidly, so that when you returned to your parents they might feel well disposed towards me and accept me as one of the family. Then I could have remained happily with you ever after. But you did not trust me and were easily swayed by lies; and now you have abandoned me midway, caring nothing for my true love. I have opened this box in front of all these people to show you that a paltry thousand taels is nothing to me. I had jewels in my casket, but you, alas, had no eyes. Fate must be against me. I escaped from the bitter lot of a courtesan only to be cast aside by you. All of you here today can be my witnesses! I have not been unfaithful to him, but he has proved untrue to me!"

Then all who were present were moved to tears. They cursed and spat at Li, accusing him of ingratitude and disloyalty; while shame, unhappiness and remorse made the young man weep bitterly. He was turning to beg Decima's forgiveness when, clasping the casket in her arms, she leapt into the river. They shouted for help, but there was a thick mist over the river and the current was strong, so she could not be found. How sad that such a beautiful and famous courtesan should fall a victim to the hungry waves!

Gnashing their teeth in rage, the onlookers wanted to fall upon Li and Sun; and the two young men were so alarmed that they shouted to the boatmen to cast off, escaping in opposite directions. As he stared at the thousand taels of silver, Li longed for Decima; and he sat brooding all day in shame and sorrow until he lost his reason. He remained insane all his life.

As for Sun, he fell ill with fright and kept to his bed for over a month. But he was haunted day and night by Decima's ghost, who cursed him until he died a slow and lingering death; and all men said this was a just retribution for the crime he committed on the river.

When Liu Yuchun completed his studies in the capital and packed up to return home, his boat also moored at Guazhou; and while he was washing his face by the side of the junk, his brass basin fell into the river. He asked a fisherman to cast his net for it, but the man drew up a small casket; and when Liu opened this he found it full of priceless jewels, pearls and other treasures. Liu rewarded the fisherman well and put the casket at the head of his bed. That night he dreamed that he saw a girl coming over the waves of the river, whom he recognized as Decima. She came up to him and curtseyed, then told him how faithless Li had proved.

"You were kind enough to help me with one hundred and fifty taels," she said. "I meant to repay you after we reached our destination, and although I was unable to do so I have never forgotten your great kindness. So this morning I sent you this casket through the fisherman to express my thanks. We shall never meet again." Suddenly awaking, Liu realized that Decima was dead, and he sighed for her for several days.

Later generations, commenting on this, condemned Sun for his wickedness in plotting to obtain a beautiful girl by a thousand taels of silver. Li they considered beneath contempt because, like a fool, he failed to understand Decima's worth. As for Decima, she was a pearl among women; the pity was that instead of finding a husband worthy of her, she wasted her affection on Li. This was like casting bright pearls or rare jade before a blind man, and resulted in her great love changing to hate and all her tenderness vanishing with the flowing stream.

Notes:

1. According to Chinese mythology, Zhong Kui was a chaser of ghosts.

轉運漢巧遇洞庭紅

波斯胡指破鼉龍殼

The Tangerines
and
the Tortoise Shell

from Astonishing and Miraculous Tales I

During the Cheng Hua period (1465-1487) of the Ming Dynasty outside the West Gate of Suzhou there lived a man named Wen Shi, who was so clever that he could turn his hand to anything. He learned chess, calligraphy and painting, could dance and sing after a fashion and play most musical instruments tolerably well. While he was a child, a fortune-teller predicted that he would become very wealthy; and, confident of his own gifts, instead of applying himself to any business he lived in idleness until he had run through most of his patrimony. When he realized that he had not much left, and saw that other men often succeeded in doubling or trebling their capital by trading, he decided to go into business too. But, whatever he tried, he lost money.

One day, hearing that fans sold well in Beijing, Wen found a partner and laid in a stock of fans. He bought some fans of the best quality, skilfully made and covered with gold paper, and sent these with gifts to well-known scholars, requesting them to write a few lines or paint a picture on the paper of these fans, for then they would fetch about a tael of silver apiece. He also bought slightly inferior fans which could be painted in the style of the masters and sold as the genuine article to unsuspecting purchasers, this counterfeiting, indeed, Wen could do himself. Last of all, he bought some of the cheapest white paper fans, bare of any calligraphy or painting, which cost only a few dozen cash; but even these Wen was certain he could sell at twice their original price. Then, choosing an auspicious day, he packed his fans in a box and set off for Beijing.

How could he guess that it would rain almost every day that summer in Beijing? It remained so cool that the sale of fans started late, and autumn set in early. Then at length the weather cleared, and some dandies started looking for Suzhou fans to tuck in their sleeves or flourish as they walked. When they came to buy, however, and Wen opened his box, he exclaimed in horror. For in Beijing things grow mouldy in the summer, and the unusual humidity this year had made the ink and glue on the fans stick tightly together. When he opened them by force, he tore the paper. All the fans which were worth money because of their calligraphy and painting were ruined; only the inferior white ones were unspoiled. But how much were they worth? By the time he had sold them at a loss to raise money for his journey home, all his capital had gone.

All Wen's ventures ended in a similar way. He not only lost money himself, but usually ruined his partners into the bargain. So his friends nicknamed him Unlucky Wen.

In a few years his whole estate was gone, and he had not even succeeded in getting a wife. He eked out a miserable existence by occasional copying work and odd commissions. But because he was a witty fellow, who knew plenty of jokes and anecdotes, he made an entertaining companion and no party was complete without him. So although he could never acquire property, he never went hungry.

Having once lived in style, Wen did not mix very well with the common run of spongers. Some friends who were sorry for him recommended him as a private tutor, but respectable families considered him too much of a dilettante.

Thus he could please no one: the rich and their hangers-on alike jeered at him for his bad fortune. But so much for this.

One day Wen heard that over forty merchants in the neighbourhood — the usual Zhangs, Lis, Zhaos and Qians — were about to set off on a trading trip overseas.

"I have no roots here," he thought, "and no means of livelihood. I might as well go with them to see the slights abroad; then I shan't have lived in vain. They will surely not refuse me; and I shall have a pleasant trip instead of worrying about food and fuel at home."

As he was turning the matter over in his mind, up came Zhang Chengyun, a merchant who specialized in overseas trade. Because he could recognize rare jewels, was generous and ready to help the unfortunate, his companions called him Canny Zhang. Wen now told this merchant what he was thinking.

"Nothing could be better," said Zhang. "We often find these voyages dull; but if you come, with your jokes and stories the days will pass quickly. I'm sure everybody in our party will be glad to have you. But we are all taking goods and you have nothing. It would be a pity to make the trip empty-handed. I'll see if we can't raise enough for you to buy a little merchandise to take along."

"It is very kind of you to suggest it," replied Wen. "But I am afraid no one else will be as generous as you."

"Well, I can but try," said Zhang as he left.

Just then a blind fortune-teller passed by, sounding his gong; and Wen, finding a coin in his pocket, stopped the man and asked to know his fortune.

"Your luck is amazing," declared the blind man. "No ordinary wealth is coming to you, but a fortune!"

"I am only going on this trip for pleasure," thought Wen, "to pass the time. What business can I do abroad? Even if they do raise some money for me, it won't amount to much. So how can I possibly make a fortune? This fellow must be lying."

Just then Zhang came back, fuming.

"Mention money and friendship is finished!" he said. "Those merchants are a strange lot. When I told them you were coming, they were all pleased; but when I asked them to help, not one of them would. So two of my best friends and I have raised one tael of silver for you. It's not enough for any goods, but you can buy some fruit to eat on board. We shall look after your food."

Wen thanked him warmly as he accepted the silver.

"Hurry up and pack," said Zhang, starting off. "We're going to leave at once."

"I have nothing to pack," replied Wen. "I shall be with you immediately."

Weighing the silver in his hand, he looked at it with a smile.

"What can I get with this?" he wondered.

But as he walked on he saw vendors with baskets lining the streets.

On the two Dongting islands in Lake Taihu the sun is as warm and the soil as fertile as in Fujian or Guangdong, where the world famous tangerines of Shantou and Fuzhou grow; and the Dongtine tangerines have the same colour and fragrance as these. When first ripe they taste a little sour, but they soon sweeten; and their price is only one-tenth that of the Fuzhou fruit. These tangerines are called Dongting Reds.

"With one tael of silver I can buy over a hundred catties of these tangerines," thought Wen. "They will quench my thirst on the junk, and I can share them with my friends to show my appreciation of their kindness."

So he bought the tangerines, had them packed in a bamboo crate, and hired a man to carry them with his luggage to the boat. The merchants clapped their hands and laughed when they saw what he had brought.

"Here come Mr. Wen's precious wares!" they cried.

Though made to look a fool, Wen swallowed his resentment and boarded the ship; but he dared not mention the tangerines after this. Soon the junk set sail and reached the open sea, where all that could be seen were rolling silvery waves tossing up snowy foam, and floating reflections of the sun, the moon and the stars.

They sailed before the wind for several days — how far exactly they could not tell. Then they sighted land and saw from the junk a populous city with towering walls, which they knew must be the capital of some country. Having moored in a harbour where they would be safe from storms, the seamen pegged down the mooring rope, cast anchor and made everything fast. Then most of the crew and passengers went ashore, and discovered that this was the land of Killah,[1] where some of them had been before.

In this country Chinese goods could fetch three times their original cost, and the same was true of goods carried from here to China. By taking merchandise from one to the other you might gain a profit eight or nine times your original outlay; so merchants risked their lives to make this trip. All Wen's friends had traded here before and knew where to find agents, lodgings and interpreters: so they went ashore to dispose of their wares, leaving Wen behind to keep an eye on the boat. Indeed, as he was a stranger to the place he had nowhere to go. While sitting there idly, he suddenly remembered his tangerines.

"I have never opened that crate," he thought. "The fruit may be spoiling. Now that the others are out of the way, I may as well have a look."

He asked a sailor to hoist the crate up from the hold. When he opened it, the fruit on top looked all right; but to make quite certain he took all the tangerines out and spread them on the deck. And this was the beginning of the change in his luck.

The tangerines gleamed like fire all along the deck, looking from a distance like thousands of points of fire or the sky on a starry night. And when the native on the shore saw this, they drew near.

"What are these fine things?" they asked.

Wen did not answer. He had noticed a few white spots on one or two of his tangerines, which he now picked out, peeled and ate. Meantime more people had gathered on the shore.

"Oh, they're to eat, are they?" they exclaimed, laughing.

Then one more enterprising than the rest asked: "How much does one cost?"

Wen did not understand their language; but a sailor who did raised one finger in fun, and said: "One coin each!"

Then the man who had asked the price undid his gown, revealing a red cotton waist-band from which he took a silver coin.

"Let me try one," he said.

Wen weighed the coin in his hand, and reckoned that it was worth about a tael.

"How many does he expect for this?" he wondered. "There doesn't seem to be a balance here. I'll give him one first to see."

He picked out a big tangerine which was a lovely red, and handed it over. The other man took it and fingered it curiously.

"What a beauty!" he said.

As soon as he split it open he was struck by its fragrance, and all near him cried out in admiration because it smelt so sweet.

This foreigner did not know how to eat a tangerine, but he peeled the skin as he had seen Wen do. Instead of dividing it into quarters, though, he stuffed the whole thing into his mouth, let the sweet juice pour down his throat, then swallowed the fruit pips and all.

"Marvellous!" he exclaimed, laughing heartily, then produced another ten silver coins from his waist-band. "I'll buy another ten to present to the chief."

Killah people rush to buy Wen's tangerines

Delighted with this unexpected luck, Wen picked out ten more tangerines for him; and when the onlookers saw this they came forward to buy too. Some bought one tangerine, others two or three; but all paid with silver coins, and all went away delighted.

Now the people of this country used silver coins with different designs on them. Those with dragons and phoenixes on them were considered the most valuable, then those with human figures, animal figures, and trees, and lastly those with water-weeds. All were of pure silver, however, and weighed the same. The first man to buy the tangerines had used the coins designed with water-weed, happy to think that he was buying such excellent wares at so reasonable a price; for they were just as fond of driving a good bargain as the Chinese.

Before long, two-thirds of the tangerines were sold. Those of the crowd who had not brought money bitterly regretted their lack of foresight and hurried home to fetch some. And Wen, seeing that he had not much fruit left, decided to put the price up.

"I am keeping the rest for myself," he announced. "These are not for sale."

Then someone offered to pay double.

"Just my bad luck, coming so late," he grumbled, as he bought two tangerines for four coins.

When the others saw this they complained: "We still want to buy. Why do you let him raise the price?"

"Didn't you hear?" demanded the last customer. "He said he wouldn't sell."

As they were arguing together, who should arrive but the man who had bought the first ten tangerines. He galloped up on a grey horse, dismounted and pushed his way through the crowd.

"Don't sell them one by one!" he shouted. "Don't sell them one by one! I want to buy the lot. Our chief wants them to send to the khan."

When the others heard that, they stepped back to watch from a respectful distance. Wen had all his wits about him, and he realized at once that here was a good customer. Hastily taking out all the tangerines from his crate, he counted them and discovered there were little more than fifty left.

"Just now I said I meant to keep these for my own use," he declared. "I don't want to sell them. But if you'll add something to the price, I'll let you have a few more. I am already selling at two coins each."

Then the other picked up a big saddle bag from the horse's back and took out some coins bearing the tree design.

"How about one of these for each?"

"No," replied Wen. "I want the same as before."

The other smiled and took out another coin with the draggon and phoenix design.

"How about one of these?"

But again Wen replied: "No, I want the same as before."

The man laughed.

"One of these is worth a hundred of the others," he said. "I wouldn't have given you these in any case: I was only joking. If you prefer the water-weed coins to these you must be a fool. But if you will sell all your fruit to me, I am quite willing to add another small coin to the price."

Wen counted his tangerines and found there were fifty-two left, and for these he received no less than one hundred and fifty-six of the water-weed coins. His customer wanted the bamboo crate too, and tossed him another silver piece for it; then fastened the crate to his horse, cracked his whip and rode joyfully off. At that the rest of the crowd scattered, seeing that there was nothing more for sale.

When they had gone, Wen went to the cabin and weighed one of the coins. It was nearly nine-tenths of a tael, and others which he weighed were the same. He had about a thousand coins in all, and having given two to the sailors as a tip he wrapped up the rest.

"That blind fortune-teller was right," he chuckled.

He waited cheerfully for the merchants' return to tell them this joke.

"Why, story-teller, you must be wrong!" I seem to hear someone say. "If silver there was so cheap and they did business like that, why didn't those merchants who regularly carried silk and brocade overseas sell for silver coins? Then they could have made a hundred times as much profit!"

No, reader, you don't understand. The people of that country liked to barter goods for silk and brocade. And only by taking goods could our merchants make a profit; for if they sold their wares for money the people of Killah always used the coins stamped with dragons and phoenixes or human figures, so that even if the price was good the silver did not weigh much. Therefore such transactions were not profitable. When Wen sold his tangerines he was paid in their inferior coins; but since these weighed the same as the coins of higher value, he made money.

"No, story-teller, that doesn't make sense either," you may protest. "For in that case why didn't all the merchants just sell fruit for the water-weed coins, and make a bigger profit? Why should they lay out so much capital on other merchandise?"

That is not the way to look at it, reader. Wen's success was a pure chance. If he had taken fruit a second time and not been so lucky, in three or four days his tangerines might have gone bad. Before his luck changed his fans were spoilt, although fans are much less perishable than fruit. One cannot argue like that. Enough, however, of this.

After the merchants had found their agents and purchasers and come back to the junk to dispose of their goods, Wen told them what had happened.

"What luck!" they exclaimed, surprised and delighted. "So the one without capital has been the first to make a profit."

"Everybody calls him Unlucky Wen," said Zhang, clapping

his hands. "Now his luck has evidently turned." Then he addressed himself to Wen. "These coins will not buy you many goods here," he warned him. "Your best course would be to purchase a few hundred taels' worth of Chinese goods from your friends to exchange for some rare local products which will sell at a great profit once we get home. That would be better than keeping this silver without using it."

"I never have any luck," answered Wen. "Each time I tried to do business I invariably lost all I had invested. Now thanks to your kindness I have been able to come here and make a profit without capital. I have never known such luck in my life! How dare I tempt providence by trying to make more money? If I were to fail again as usual, I couldn't hope for another piece of luck like this with my Dongting Reds."

"We can do with more silver," said the merchants. "And we have plenty of goods with us. Can't we do a deal which will be to the advantage of both sides?"

But Wen was adamant.

"A man who has been bitten by a snake shudders at the sight of a straw rope three years later," he said. "The mere mention of goods makes me break into a cold sweat. I'll just take this silver back with me."

The others clapped their hands together in astonishment.

"What a pity not to make several times the profit," they said, "when it's yours for the taking."

Then they went ashore again to barter their goods in the warehouses for native products.

During the next fifteen days Wen saw many fine sights and was well content, for he did not desire anything more. Then, the merchants' business at an end, they boarded their junk and after sacrificing to the gods and drinking to the success of their voyage set sail again.

Some days later, the weather changed.

When this gale sprang up, the seamen shortened sail and steered no definite course, but scudded before the wind until they sighted an island. They reefed sail and stood in for the land, but on drawing nearer saw that it was uninhabited.

The sailors dropped their iron anchor at the stern of the boat, then landed with their mooring pegs to make the vessel fast.

"You can rest here," they told the merchants, "till the storm has blown over."

Wen with his silver had wished he could grow wings to fly home instead of sailing, so he felt doubly impatient now that they were waiting for the wind to drop.

"I'm going ashore to have a look at this island," he told the others.

"What is there to see on a desert island?" they demanded.

"Well, there's nothing to do on board, anyway," he retorted.

Still dizzy after their tossing in the storm, his friends could not stop yawning and would not go with him. But summoning up his resolution he leapt ashore.

If I had been there then, reader, and able to foretell the future, even if I were lame I would have tottered after him with a stick. It would have been worth it! But nobody else had such luck: all his friends were too lazy. Since no one would go with him, Wen tried to impress his friends by clambering straight up to the summit of the island, using creepers to haul himself up. The hill was not high, so it was not too strenuous a climb, though there was no path through the wild grass. When he reached the top and gazed at the vast ocean all around him, he felt as forlorn as a floating leaf, and shed sad tears.

"For all my cleverness, bad luck has dogged me the whole of my life," he thought. "All my property has melted away, so that I had to come empty-handed on this trip. And although by a stroke of good fortune I have made over a thousand silver coins, Heaven alone knows whether I am destined to enjoy them or not. I am on a desert island, not on firm ground, and my safety still depends on the dragon king of the ocean."

In the midst of these melancholy reflections his eye fell on a strange object projecting from the wild grass in the distance, and going nearer he discovered an empty tortoise shell as large as a bed.

"I never knew there were tortoises as big as this," he marvelled. "I swear no living soul has ever seen such a thing, and no one would believe me if I told them of it. I haven't bought a single thing since coming abroad; but if I take this home with me as a curiosity and people see it, they won't be able to say all Suzhou men are liars. Besides, if I were to saw the top from the bottom and put four legs on each half, they would make two beds."

Taking off his cloth leggings, he knotted them together and tied them to the shell to pull it along. When he neared the shore and his friends saw him dragging something after him, they hailed him with laughter.

"Is that another boat you've got there, Mr. Wen?" they demanded.

"This is my foreign merchandise, I'd have you know," replied Wen.

When they looked up and saw an object resembling a two-layered bed without legs, they were amazed.

"What an enormous tortoise shell!" they exclaimed. "But what have you lugged it here for?"

"It's such a curiosity," replied Wen, "I thought I'd take it along."

"You wouldn't buy anything good," they chuckled. "Now what do you intend to do with this?"

"I know what he can do with it," said one. "If anyone has a really serious problem to settle, he can use this shell for divination. The only trouble is there aren't herbs big enough to heat it with!"

"When the physicians need tortoise shell for their ointment, they can break this up," proposed someone else. "It's as big as several hundred small ones put together."

"Never mind whether it's useful or not," said Wen. "It's a rarity, and it hasn't cost me anything; so I'm going to take it back with me."

He called a sailor, and between them they hoisted the shell on board. If it had looked big out in the open, here on deck it seemed enormous; and had this not been a sea-faring vessel, there would have been no room for such a huge object. The merchants laughed loud and long.

"When we get home and are questioned about our cargo," said one, "we'll tell them Mr. Wen has been dealing in oversized tortoises."

"Don't you laugh!" retorted Wen. "I shall be able to turn it to account. It's bound to come in useful."

Paying no attention to their laughter, he cheerfully fetched some water, washed the shell inside and out and wiped it dry, then put his purse and luggage inside and roped the two ends of the shell together so that it became a trunk.

"Look!" he said, beaming. "Here is a use for it right away."

"Well done! Well done!" They roared with laughter. "We always said Mr. Wen was a clever fellow!"

The next morning the wind dropped and they set sail again, and in a few days reached the coast of Fujian Province. No sooner had they moored when a group of agents and brokers whose business it was to watch out for overseas traders came aboard. They laid hold of the merchants, crying: "Deal with Mr. Zhang!" "Come to Mr. Li!" And only when the merchants set off to see their habitual dealer did these agents leave.

Wen and his friends went to a big shop belonging to a Persian dealer, where they sat down and waited. When the dealer heard that traders from abroad had arrived, he hastily gave his cooks money and ordered them to prepare a feast for several dozen men. Having given his instructions, he walked over to the shop.

This Persian's surname was Ma, and his personal name

Baoha.[2] He dealt only with sea-faring merchants, bartering Chinese goods for their rare merchandise, and his capital ran into hundreds of thousands of silver taels. All traders who sailed the seas knew him well; Wen alone of his party had never met the man before. This Persian had been in China for many years, and in dress and behaviour was not very different from the Chinese; but he kept his eyebrows shaved and his beard clipped, while his deep-set eyes and high nose gave him an odd look. He came out now to greet the merchants, and they sat down together. Then, after two rounds of tea, he stood up and invited them into a great hall where a splendid banquet was spread.

It was a time-honoured custom that when traders arrived from abroad their dealers should entertain them before talking business and disposing of their goods. Now, holding a cloisonne tray with a chrysanthemum design, their host bowed.

"May I see the invoice of your goods, gentlemen?" he asked. "Then we can decide how to sit."

Do you know the reason for this, reader? The fact is that this Persian valued money above everything else. When he saw an invoice for goods worth tens of thousands of taels, he would ask the owner of this precious merchandise to take the seat of honour and place the others according to the value of their wares, without any consideration for age or family status. So each merchant from the junk, knowing the amount and value of his friends' goods, took his wine cup and sat down, leaving Wen standing alone.

"I have never met this gentleman before," said the Persian. "I take it he is new to the trade and has not bought much merchandise."

"This is a good friend of ours, who accompanied us for the sake of the trip," they replied. "He has money but didn't invest in any goods, so we shall have to ask him to take the lowest seat today."

Blushing for shame, Wen sat down, while the Persian

took the place for the host, and the feast began. One merchant boasted how much cat's eye he had purchased, another how many emeralds. While they boasted and bragged, Wen had not a word to say, and he began to regret that he had not taken their advice and bought some goods; for now, though he had several hundred taels of silver in his wallet, he could take no part in their conversation.

"Still," he thought with a sigh, "I had no capital at all to start with. I've had more than my share of luck, so I should be content."

Occupied with these reflections, he had no heart to drink, but looked on while his friends played drinking games and feasted merrily. Their host was an experienced man. He saw that Wen looked unhappy, but could not draw attention to it and simply invited him to drink a cup or two of wine. Then the merchants rose from the table.

"We have had enough wine and it is late," they said. "We had better go back to the boat. We shall bring you our goods tomorrow."

Thereupon they took their leave; and their host, having seen that the table was cleared, went to bed.

Early the next morning the Persian went to the harbour to call on the merchants. And the first thing he set eyes on when he boarded the junk was the huge object cluttering its deck. He started with astonishment.

"To which of you does this precious thing belong?" he asked. "You didn't mention it yesterday at dinner. Is it not for sale?"

The merchants laughed and pointed at Wen.

"This treasure belongs to our friend here," they said.

"And he seems likely to have it on his hands for some time," added one.

The Persian glanced at Wen, and flushed red with consternation and anger.

"After all these years we have done business together how could you play such a trick on me?" he reproached the merchants. "Why did you make me offend a new client by giving him the lowest seat?"

Then, taking Wen by the arm, he said to the others: "Let us leave your goods for the time being. I must first go ashore to apologize to Mr. Wen."

The merchants were nonplussed. About a dozen of them who knew Wen well or were naturally inquisitive followed the Persian back to his shop to see what would happen. The dealer led Wen in, set the central chair straight in the place of honour and, ignoring all the others, urged Wen to be seated.

"I have been very remiss," he said, "very remiss. Please sit down."

Wen was consumed with curiosity.

"Can the old tortoise shell really be valuable?" he wondered. "Can I possibly be so lucky?"

The Persian left them, to return presently and invite them into the hall where they had feasted the previous day. Again they found several tables laid, but the chief table was even more sumptuous than the last time. The dealer toasted Wen.

"This gentleman ought to take the seat of honour," he told the rest. "For all the other goods on your boat are nothing compared with what he has. I have been very remiss, very remiss."

Amused and curious, not knowing what to make of this, the merchants sat down. And after three cups of wine the Persian came to the point.

"May I ask, sir," he inquired of Wen, "whether this treasure of yours is for sale?"

Wen was no fool. "If I'm offered a good price for it, why not?" he answered promptly.

On hearing these words the dealer was nearly overcome with joy. Beaming with smiles he rose from his seat.

"Name your own price," he said. "You will not find me niggardly."

Wen, of course, did not know how much the shell was worth, and was afraid of exposing his ignorance if he asked for too little, or of being laughed at if he asked for too much. He thought so hard that his cheeks flamed and his ears burned, but he could not name a price. Then Zhang winked at him and, putting his hand behind his chair where their host could not see it, raised three fingers and made a dash with his second finger.

"Ask that," he whispered, meaning three thousand taels.

But Wen shook his head and raised one finger.

"Even this seems too much," he replied softly.

"How much do you mean?" asked the Persian, who had observed this interchange.

"Judging by the sign he just made," said Zhang jokingly, "I assume Mr. Wen means ten thousand taels."

The Persian laughed heartily. "You must mean that he doesn't want to sell and is merely joking with me," he said. "How could such a precious object be worth so little?"

When the merchants heard this they were flabbergasted. Rising from their seats they pulled Wen outside.

"What luck!" they exclaimed. "It must be worth a fortune! But we have no idea what price to ask. You had better name an exorbitant figure and let him bargain it down."

Still Wen hesitated, ashamed to speak.

"Go on. Go on," his friends prompted him.

"You can speak frankly," said the Persian.

Then Wen asked for fifty thousand taels. The dealer, however, still shook his head.

"Too little! Too little!" he protested. "I can't allow that."

He took Zhang aside and talked to him privately.

"You have made many trips abroad, sir," he said, "and everybody calls you Canny Zhang. Is it possible you don't know what this shell is? You can't be in earnest about selling, but just want to make a fool of me."

"I will be frank with you," replied Zhang. "Wen is a good friend of mine, who accompanied us on this trip for his own pleasure, but didn't make any purchases. He came across this shell by accident when we put in to an island during a storm; and not having paid for it he has no idea of its price. If you will give him fifty thousand taels for it, he can live in luxury for the rest of his life and will be perfectly satisfied."

"In that case," said the Persian, "I want you to be guarantor. I will make it well worth your while. But you must promise not to go back on our bargain."

He bade his assistant bring brushes and ink, folded up a piece of strong paper specially designed for contracts, and handed a brush to Zhang.

"I will trouble you to take charge and to draw up an agreement so that we can settle this business," he said.

Zhang pointed to a fellow merchant.

"This gentleman, Zhu Zhongying writes a good hand," he said, passing the paper and brush to him.

Zhu ground the ink on the ink-stone, spread out the paper, and taking up his brush wrote as follows:

MEMORANDUM OF AGREEMENT
WITH ZHANG CHENGYUN AND PARTY

The Suzhou merchant, Wen Shi, having brought, carried and transported from abroad one large tortoise shell, and Ma Baoha, the Persian, having agreed and covenanted to buy the said tortoise shell for fifty thousand taels of silver, both parties hereby agree that after the signing of this contract one party shall hand over the goods and the other party the money. And if either party attempt to retract, he shall forfeit one-tenth as much again as the sum herein before agreed upon.

This was written out in duplicate, then the date was put down and all present signed as witnesses. Zhang's name headed the list, and Zhu as clerk signed last. After this the two documents were put together and the date and the word "contract" written over the junction of the two sheets, so that half of the characters appeared on each. This done, Wen and the Persian, as the two principals sealed the agreements, followed by all the rest.

"Our middlemen's fee should not be too low," said Zhang when it came to his turn. "Not if you want this business to go smoothly."

"You need not worry about that," replied the Persian with a smile.

When the signing was completed, the dealer fetched a casket of silver from an inner room. "Let me first pay the middle-men's fee," he said, "before I go on to what I have to say."

The merchants gathered round as he opened the casket to show the packets of silver inside. There were twenty packets, each containing fifty taels of silver, making a thousand taels in all. The Persian presented this casket with both hands to Zhang.

"You might distribute this while you are all here," he suggested.

The feast and contract had taken the merchants so much by surprise that they had been rather dubious about the genuineness of the transaction; but now that the Persian brought out this glittering white silver as middlemen's fee they realized that he was in earnest. Wen felt as if he were drunk or dreaming, and could not utter a word. He looked on dumbfounded until Zhang pulled at his sleeve.

"How are we to distribute this?" asked his friend. "It's for you to decide."

"Let us finish the chief business first," replied Wen.

"I want to discuss that with you," said the Persian, smiling all over his face. "The silver is in an inner chamber. It has been weighed and not a cent is missing. If one or two of you will step inside and weigh a packet, you won't have to weigh all the rest. Fifty thousand taels is a lot of money, though, and you can't move it all at once. Besides, Mr. Wen, you have no family here, and you can't take all that silver abroad. If you take so much home that will be very inconvenient."

"You are right," agreed Wen after a moment's thought. "But what do you suggest?"

"In my humble opinion," said the Persian, "you had better not go home yet. I have a silk shop here in which I have invested three thousand taels of silver. It is quite a large establishment consisting of over a hundred rooms, and the premises are worth another two thousand taels. This shop is only a few hundred yards from here; and my proposal is to reckon this shop with the land it stands on as worth five thousand taels and turn it over to Mr. Wen. Then he can stay here to carry on the business, and transfer the silver in several lots to his shop without attracting attention. Later, if Mr. Wen wants to go back to Suzhou, he can entrust the shop to some reliable assistant and travel with an easy mind. Otherwise, though it will be easy for me to hand over the silver, it will be hard for Mr. Wen to dispose of it. This is just my suggestion."

"An excellent proposal!" exclaimed Zhang and Wen, stamping their feet to express approval. "It has everything to recommend it."

"I have no wife or family at home," Wen was thinking, "and nothing left of my patrimony. If I were to take all that silver back, I should have no place to keep it in. Why shouldn't I take his advice and settle down here? Such good luck is ordained by Heaven in any case, so I had better fall in with all that is proposed. Even if the shop and the goods aren't worth five thousand taels, I shall be getting them for nothing."

"Your advice is very sound," he said to the Persian, "I agree completely."

Then the Persian asked Wen, Zhang and Zhu to accompany him to an inner chamber. "There is no need to trouble the rest of you," he said to the others. "Please be seated."

When the four men had gone inside, the merchants left behind burst out in exclamations of amazement and envy.

"What an extraordinary thing!"

"What a stroke of luck!"

"If we had known," said one, "we would have gone ashore too when we moored by that island. Maybe we should have found some other treasures."

"No, such luck is Heaven-sent," said another. "You can't make such things happen."

Presently Wen, Zhang and Zhu came back.

"What is in there?" asked the merchants.

"A high pavilion where silver is stored in barrels," replied Zhang. "Just now we saw ten barrels, each containing four thousand taels; and five caskets, each containing one thousand taels. That makes forty-five thousand taels altogether. They have been sealed with paper bearing Mr. Wen's name, and after his tortoise shell is delivered they will be his."

Then the Persian came in.

"I have the deeds of the property and the accounts of the silk shop here," he said. "You will see they are worth a good fifty thousand taels. Let us go to your junk now to fetch the goods."

As they walked together to the boat, Wen warned the others: "There are too many people on the junk. I shall pay you well if you keep quiet about this."

The others also feared that if all the merchants on board knew what had happened, they would demand part of the fee; so they agreed to say nothing. Upon reaching the junk, Wen removed his luggage and bags from inside the shell, stroking it as he congratulated himself on his luck.

Then the Persian ordered two young men from his shop to carry the shell away.

"Take it straight inside," he cautioned them. "Don't leave it outside the house."

When the other men on the junk saw this shell being

carried away, they remarked: "So even this rubbish has been sold. I wonder how much he got for it?"

Wen, however, kept silent as he carried his luggage ashore. Those who had accompanied him the first time also hurried ashore to examine the shell carefully, peering inside and feeling it all over. Then they exchanged mystified glances.

"What's so wonderful about this?" they demanded.

After inviting them back to his shop, the Persian proposed that they visit Mr. Wen's new property. They all went to the middle of the business quarter, where they saw a fine large building. In front was the shop, and at the side was an alley which led to a massive stone gate. Inside were a big courtyard and a great hall on which there hung a placard bearing the inscription: Hall of the Advent of Jewels. This hall was flanked by rooms lined with cupboards and shelves containing all manner of silks and brocades; and behind the main building were many other rooms and pavilions.

"A house like this is as good as a prince's mansion!" thought Wen. "And with this silk shop there should be no end to the profits I make. I may as well settle down here. Why should I want to go home?"

"This is very good," he said to the Persian. "But I am all by myself. I shall have to find some servants and assistants before I can move in."

"That should present no difficulties," said the Persian. "I can provide you with all the staff you need."

Overjoyed, Wen walked back with the others to the Persian's shop, where the dealer offered them tea.

"There is no need for you to go back to the junk tonight, Mr. Wen," said the Persian. "You may as well move straight into your new quarters. There are assistants and servants in your shop already, whose number you can gradually increase."

"Now the deal has been completed," said one of the merchants, "there is really no more to be said. But there is one thing we would like to know —— what makes the shell so valuable? May we ask you to enlighten us?"

Wen joined in this request too.

"It is strange that you gentlemen have crossed the seas so many times and yet don't know this," chuckled the Persian. "Haven't you heard that the dragon has nine sons, one of whom is the Tuo Dragon?[3] If you use its skin to make a drum, the sound can be heard dozens of miles away; and it is called a Tuo Drum. After ten thousand years a Tuo Dragon discards its shell and becomes a dragon proper. Its shell has twenty-four ribs to match the twenty-four festivals of the year, and in the joint of each rib there is a big pearl. It cannot shed its shell or become a dragon before the ribs are fully formed; and if it is caught before then, its skin alone is of any use —— there is nothing inside the ribs. But when the twenty-four ribs are complete with a pearl in each one, it becomes a dragon and flies off, leaving the shell behind. This shell of Mr. Wen's was discarded in the right season and the ribs are complete, so it is much bigger than the shells of Tuo Dragons caught before their metamorphosis. Though we know that such a thing exists, who can tell when or where the dragon will discard its shell? The shell itself is worthless, but the pearls, which shine at night, are priceless. It is sheer luck that this has come into my possession today."

When the merchants heard this they were still rather incredulous; but the Persian went into an inner room for a short time, to reappear smiling.

"Gentlemen," he said, taking a wrapper of foreign cloth from his sleeve. "Look at this!"

When he undid the wrapper, in a nest of threads they saw a pearl of dazzling brightness, about one inch in diameter. The Persian put the pearl on a black lacquer tray which he set in a dark place; whereupon the pearl started rolling from side to side without stopping, and emitted rays of light a foot long. Then their host turned to the merchants, who

波斯胡指破
鼉籠殼

The Persian tells the story of the tortoise shell

were gaping in astonishment.

"I am very much indebted to you all for your help," he said. "In my country this single pearl will fetch what I paid for the shell just now. That means the other twenty-three are presents you have been kind enough to give me!"

They were all thunderstruck. Yet they had signed an agreement, and could not go back on their word. When the Persian saw their dismay, hastily putting the pearl away he left the room again to order his servants to fetch a box of brocades. To all but Wen he gave two lengths of brocade each.

"I have put you to a great deal of trouble," he explained. "I would like to show my appreciation by giving you this to make a couple of gowns."

Then he took from his sleeve over a dozen strings of small pearls, and gave them a string apiece.

"This is a small present for light refreshments," he said.

To Wen the Persian gave four strings of larger pearls and eight lengths of brocade; and Wen and the merchants were pleased and thanked him. Then the Persian and the others escorted Wen to his silk shop, where all the assistants and apprentices were called out to be introduced to their new master. After this the Persian took his leave and returned to his own shop; and presently several dozen porters arrived carrying the ten barrels and five caskets of silver marked with Wen's seal. Having seen these stowed in a safe place in his bedroom, Wen rejoined the merchants.

"I am deeply indebted to you all for taking me on this trip," he told them. "Without your help I could never have met with this unexpected fortune."

Then going into an inner room he fetched from his baggage the silver he had received for the sale of his tangerines, and gave the merchants ten coins each, presenting an extra ten coins to Zhang and the two others who had helped him with money at the beginning of the trip. By now these silver coins meant very little to Wen, but the merchants were delighted to have them and thanked him again and again. Then Wen took out a few dozen more coins.

"I'll trouble you to divide these among our fellow travellers on the junk," he said. "Give them one each from me. After I have settled down a little, I mean to come home. But since I shan't be going with you now, I will say goodbye for the time being."

"There are still those thousand taels for the middlemen which are not yet divided," Zhang reminded him. "You will have to distribute those, so that there will be no argument."

Wen admitted that he had forgotten this matter. After discussion with the others he allotted one hundred taels to the other men on the junk, dividing the remaining nine hundred among those present, but giving one extra share to Zhang who had taken the lead in this affair, and to Zhu, who had drawn up the contract. Then, fully satisfied, they all thanked him heartily.

"But we let that Mohammedan off too lightly," said one. "Mr. Wen should have put up the price and demanded more."

"One mustn't be too grasping," replied Wen. "I had a long run of bad luck, when, whatever I tried, I lost my capital. Now fortune has smiled on me and showered this wealth on me out of the blue. It shows that everything is ordained by fate and it is useless to strive for more than is allotted to you by Heaven. If the Persian had not recognized the shell as a treasure, it would have been of no value to us. We are indebted to him for pointing it out. How could I be so ungrateful as to wrangle over the price with him?"

"Mr. Wen is right," agreed the others. "In fact, this fortune he has received is a reward for his virtue."

Then with profuse thanks they went back with their various gifts to the junk, to go about their business.

Thus Wen became a wealthy merchant in Fujian, where he married and settled down; and not for some years did he return to Suzhou on a visit to see his old friends. Many sons and grandsons were born to him, and his family remains wealthy to this day.

> *Fine gold will lose its sheen when fortune frowns,*
> *Rough iron will shine like gold when fortune smiles;*
> *But let not fools who hear a tale like this*
> *Go seeking dragons' shells in distant isles!*

Notes:

1. According to Chinese and Arab accounts, Killah or Kalah (Chinese 'Jiling') was an important trading post in the Middle Ages; but whether it lay in southern India or the Malay Archipelago we do not know.

2. Ma, the Chinese shortening of Mohammed, was the surname given to most people from Islamic countries. Baoha may be the transliteration of some name like Abu Hassan or Abu Hamid.

3. The 'Tuo Dragon' is a type of alligator peculiar to China. The skin of the 'alligator sinensis,' or 'Yangzi alligator,' as the Tuo Dragon is also known, was often used to make drums, the sound of which would benefit greatly by the special qualities of the Tuo Dragon skin.

神偷寄興一枝梅

俠盜慣行三昧戲

Lazy Dragon

from Astonishing and Miraculous Tales II

During the Jia Jing period of our own dynasty (1522-1566) there lived in Suzhou a marvellous thief called Lazy Dragon, about whom many tales are told. Although a thief, he was loyal to his friends and fond of joking, so, many of his adventures make amusing stories.

Up the first lane before Xuanmiao Temple in the east quarter of Suzhou lived this man whose real name we do not know, but who called himself Lazy Dragon and was generally known by this nickname. From his childhood, Lazy Dragon was small but brave, cunning yet open-handed.

In addition to his great skill Lazy Dragon had some remarkable abilities and habits. From childhood he could walk up a wall in his boots and imitate the accents of thirteen provinces. He could go for several nights without rest or sleep, for days at a stretch without food or drink. Sometimes he would consume several pecks of rice and several gallons of wine at a sitting, yet not feel satisfied. At other times he would go for days without food, yet not feel hungry. With straw ashes in the soles of his shoes, he walked without a sound. And when he fought, he moved as swiftly as the wind. Birds of a feather flock together, and since Lazy

Dragon could not hide his talents he naturally mixed with other young loafers and took to stealing. In those days there were several clever thieves, but as soon as they saw Lazy Dragon's dexterity they knew that they were outclassed.

Lazy Dragon had never owned much property, and after he became a thief he left his home to drift from place to place, so that none knew where to find him. When he wandered about by broad daylight in public or slipped into some house, only his shadow could be seen flitting past — never the man himself. He would often pass the night in a rich man's house, curling up to sleep like a hedgehog among the rafters, under the raised floor of a pavilion, behind the screen or in the painted hall, as the fancy took him. And, whenever opportunity offered, he would steal.

Lazy Dragon's constant transformations and his habit of sleeping all day won him his nickname. He was also known as Plum Blossom, however, because after stealing anything he would invariably sketch a plum blossom on the wall — in white chalk if it was a dark wall and in charcoal if the wall was white.

There was a great storm at the beginning of the Jia Jing period, when sea serpents raged among the hills near Dongting Lake and a cliff by Taihu Lake crumbled to reveal an ancient tomb and a red lacquered coffin containing many jewels, all of which were promptly stolen. When news of this reached Suzhou, Lazy Dragon happened to be sailing with some friends on the lake, so he made his way to the spot. The vines binding the coffin had been severed and nothing remained inside but a skeleton, while beside the tomb lay a broken stone tablet bearing an old, blurred inscription. Lazy Dragon realized that this must be the coffin of some ancient nobleman, and out of compassion for the dead he sealed it up again, hired some local labourers to pile up earth, and poured a libation of wine over the new grave mound. This done, he was preparing to leave when his foot touched something in the grass, and stooping down he discovered an

Lazy Dragon leaves a mark of plum blossom

old mirror which, unknown to all, he hastily hid in his stocking. On his return to the city, his first act was to go to a quiet spot and clean the mirror. Its glittering surface was only four or five inches across, and the knob on its back was surrounded by monsters, sea-fish, dragons and waves. The whole was encrusted with a green patina stained by cinnabar and quicksilver and gave, when tapped, a clear tinkling sound. Knowing that this was a rarity, Lazy Dragon kept the mirror on him; and when night fell he discovered that it emitted light which made all around as bright as day. After that he carried it with him wherever he went and found it a great boon, for now he no longer needed a light at night. While others dreaded the dark, he could walk about as if it were day; and this made it even easier for him to steal.

Though a thief by profession, Lazy Dragon had a number of virtues: he never ravished women, never robbed good people or those in distress, and never broke his word. In fact, he was just and generous and would give away all he stole to the poor. All his dislike was for wealthy misers and moneyed men who had got rich by unjust means, whom he loved to mock by his pranks. Thus wherever he went people flocked to him, and his fame spread.

"I have neither parents nor family to support," he would say with a laugh. "So I borrow from those with a superfluity of wealth to help the poor. It is Heaven's will that the haves should help the have-nots — this is not simply my idea of justice."

One day Lazy Dragon heard that a great merchant had deposited a thousand taels with a weaver named Zhou, and determined to lay hands on that silver; but being slightly tipsy that day he missed the place and landed by mistake in a poor man's house where almost the only furniture was a large table. Having made an entrance, however, Lazy Dragon did not want to leave at once, so he hid himself under the table. Presently the master of the house sat down to a meal with his wife; but their fare was poor, and the husband wore a worried expression on his face.

"That debt has fallen due," he told his wife, "but I have no means of paying it. I see no way out but suicide."

"You mustn't take your own life!" protested his wife. "You had better sell me, and with the money you get start a small business."

Their tears were falling like rain when they were startled to see Lazy Dragon leap out from under the table.

"Don't be afraid," said he. "I am Lazy Dragon. I am here by mistake — I was really looking for a merchant I had heard of. You seem to be in a bad way, so I shall give you two hundred taels with which to do business. Take heart, and don't do anything desperate."

The unhappy couple, who knew him by reputation, bowed.

"If you will be so kind, we shall owe our lives to you," they said.

Then Lazy Dragon went out. Two hours later there was a thud within their closed door, and when they looked they found a cloth bag containing two hundred taels of silver — money Lazy Dragon had taken from the merchant. They nearly danced for joy. And later they set up a tablet bearing Lazy Dragon's name before which they did reverence as long as they lived.

A man who had played with Lazy Dragon as a lad lost all his money when he grew up, and was in rags when he met his former friend on the street. He hid his face with his fan for shame and would have gone past, but Lazy Dragon laid hold of him.

"Don't I know you?" asked the thief.

The other admitted in embarrassment who he was.

"Have you come to this!" exclaimed Lazy Dragon. "To-morrow I shall take you to a rich man's house to get some money. But don't say a word to anyone about it."

The other knew Lazy Dragon's ability and knew, too, that he always kept his word; so the next evening he sought him out and accompanied him to the mansion of an official.

Bidding his friend wait outside, Lazy Dragon leapt on to a tree and vaulted over the wall. He was away for a long time. Crouching with bated breath outside the wall, the poor man waited until dogs started barking and rushed towards him with bared fangs. As he ran around the wall to escape, he heard a faint splash on the other side of the wall; then something like a water bird alighted from a tree, and he saw Lazy Dragon — wet through and thoroughly crestfallen!

"I nearly lost my life for you!" panted Lazy Dragon. "There are piles of gold in there — bushels of it! But no sooner did I get the gold than dogs outside started barking and woke the people inside, who came after me. So I had to throw away the gold and take to my heels. It's too bad for you."

"You usually get whatever you want," said his friend. "If things have turned out like this today, it must be owing to my bad luck." He sighed and was very sorry for himself.

"Don't worry," said Lazy Dragon. "I'll do something for you another day."

So his friend left disconsolately.

More than a month had passed when Lazy Dragon met the fellow again on the road.

"I really can't carry on any longer," lamented the poor man. "Today I had my fortune told, and received a very lucky omen. The fortune-teller said I should come into sudden wealth thanks to a friend. I think that friend must be you — who else could it be?"

"Yes," said Lazy Dragon with a laugh. "I had nearly forgotten. I filched a box of gold and silver for you that day; but I was afraid that if I gave it to you then and the official's family raised a hue and cry, you might not be able to hide it. So to be on the safe side I left the box in the pool inside his courtyard. Now over a month has passed without any trouble; he must have given up hope of recovering it, and it should be safe to collect it. Let's go back there tonight."

As soon as it was dark the poor man called for Lazy Dragon, and before long they reached the place.

In a flash Lazy Dragon came back with a box on his back. Hastily repairing to a quiet spot, they opened the box, illumined it with the mirror, and saw that it was crammed with gold and silver. But Lazy Dragon took nothing. Without even troubling to find out how much there was, he gave the whole box to his poor friend.

"These treasures should last you a lifetime," he said. "Make good use of them, and don't be like foolish Lazy Dragon who has never been able to keep any property."

The poor man thanked him and took his advice. He used the money to set himself up in business, and later became a wealthy man. Such generosity was typical of Lazy Dragon.

You may say: No doubt Lazy Dragon was very skilful, but did he never run into trouble?

Well, readers, it is true that sometimes luck went against him and he found himself in a tight corner; but with his ready wit he could usually extricate himself. One day, for example, when he entered a house and found a wardrobe open, he slipped inside, meaning to steal some clothes. But before the inmates of the house went to bed they locked the wardrobe with a padlock so that he was a prisoner! As soon as he found he could not get out he hit upon a plan. Wrapping some clothes tightly round himself and making a big bundle of some more garments which he set against the door, he imitated the noise of a rat gnawing clothing.

When the master of the house heard this, he called for the maid.

"Why have you shut a rat in the wardrobe?" he shouted. "Do you want to ruin all our clothes? Hurry up and open the wardrobe to drive it out!"

The maid brought a torch and unlocked the wardrobe. But the moment she opened the door the bundle of clothes fell to the ground, and swift as thought Lazy Dragon rolled out after it, knocking the torch out of the maid's hand so that she gave a shriek. Afraid that more people would gather and make it difficult for him to escape, he seized the bundle, tripped the maid up, and was off. When the master got up and stepped on the maid, thinking she was the thief he started kicking and beating her; and she screamed at the top of her voice until the rest of the household heard the noise and rushed in. But when they lighted a torch, they found the master struggling with his own servant; and by the time peace was restored Lazy Dragon was far away.

Another time there was a weaver who received advance payment for a large order of silk. He kept the silver in a box on the inner side of the bed where he and his wife slept, so that they could guard it at night; but when Lazy Dragon heard of this money he determined to get it. Entering their chamber, he set one foot on the outer edge of the bed and reached over for the box on the other side. Just then the weaver's wife woke up and realized that there was something on the edge of the bed. Groping about in the dark, she caught hold of the robber's leg and held it fast.

"Quick!" she called to her husband. "Get up! I've got a thief here by the leg!"

That same instant Lazy Dragon took hold of the weaver's leg and gave it a hard pinch.

"It's my leg! It's my leg!" The weaver shouted with pain.

Thinking she had seized her husband's leg by mistake, the woman immediately let go. And while husband and wife were arguing the matter, Lazy Dragon grabbed the box and dashed from the room.

"It *was* a thief's leg," said she. "But you made me let go."

"My leg still aches from that pinch you gave it," declared her husband. "Thief's leg? Nonsense!"

"Your leg is inside," insisted his wife, "and the one I caught was on the outside. Besides, I wasn't pinching it."

"Well then," retorted her husband, "it was the thief who pinched my leg. But in that case you shouldn't have let go."

"You confused me by shouting," she countered. "So naturally I thought I'd made a mistake and let go. That's how he got away. Well, he's tricked us properly. He must have stolen our money."

When they felt for the box on the inner side of the bed and found it gone, they fell to accusing each other again and kept at it hammer and tongs for hours.

On another occasion Lazy Dragon broke into the storeroom of a second-hand clothes shop, and since it was dark he took out his mirror in order to pick the best clothes.

There was an amorous couple awake upstairs in the house next door, and when they saw through their window a bright flicker of light in the storeroom, their suspicions were aroused. They knocked on the window and called to the clothier:

"Watch out, neighbour! There seem to be thieves in your house!"

Then the shop people sprang up in alarm, shouting: "Thief! Thief!"

Lazy Dragon had noticed in the front courtyard a huge pickle jar covered with matting, so now he raised this cover and crept inside, pulling the matting back into place after him. When the shop people had lighted lanterns and searched the whole premises without finding him, they went to the backyard.

"This jar is the only thing they missed just now," thought Lazy Dragon. "When they don't find me in the back, they are bound to look here. I had better hide in some place which they have already searched."

Realizing that his clothes were soaked with pickles and would leave a trail wherever he went, he stripped himself and climbed out of the vat naked to make pickle stains with his feet all the way to the gate. Then, leaving the gate ajar he came back and hid himself in the storeroom.

After the shop people had searched the backyard, they returned with their lanterns to the front; and this time, to be sure, they uncovered the jar and found a suit of clothes inside which was none of theirs.

"These must belong to the thief!" they cried.

But then they saw the footprints from the jar to the gate which was wide open.

"The thief must have taken fright and hidden in the jar," they said. "When we went to the back, he took off his clothes and fled. It's too bad we let him slip through our fingers."

"Well, we're rid of him now," said the clothier. "Let's shut the gate and go to sleep."

Confident that the theif had gone, after setting things to rights they went back to bed and fell sound asleep.

All this time, however, Lazy Dragon was reclining comfortably on the bales of fine clothes in the storeroom. Now he chose the best, wrapped them tightly round himself and slipped an old, dark coat on top. He then did up some more finery in a cloth coverlet and, as dawn approached — having spent most of the night at this work — he picked up his swag, vaulted to the roof without rousing a soul in the shop, and jumped into the street. The sun had not yet risen, and as he was walking along he met three or four men, whose suspicions were aroused at the sight of this solitary figure carrying a heavy bundle at such an early hour.

"Who are you?" they demanded, barring his way. "Where have you come from? You must account for yourself before we let you pass."

Without saying a word Lazy Dragon reached behind his back for a round package which he tossed to the ground; and while the other men were snatching at it he proceeded on his way. The bundle was so tightly wrapped that they were sure it must contain something precious; so they gathered round to undo it. As if peeling bamboo shoots, they unfastened layer after layer, only to reveal further layers underneath, each tightly bound to the next. Even after they had undone quantities of wadding one foot thick, there still remained an object as large as a fist.

"What can it be?" they demanded, snatching at it to unwrap it, and scattering the rags and cotton they had already removed on the ground. Just then another group of men came up.

"So you stole our clothes and are dividing the loot here!" cried the newcomers.

Without waiting for an explanation, they brandished their sticks and rushed forward. The accused men tried in vain to stop them, then fled — all but one old man who was seized. It was still too dark to see his face; but they belaboured him all the way back to the clothier's shop, ignoring his protests in their rage. Soon it grew bright, however, and the shop-keeper saw that the old man was none other than his son's father-in-law, who lived in the country. Though he ordered his assistants to stay their hands at once, the old fellow had already been beaten black and blue, and all the clothier could do was apologize and offer him wine to express his regret. He told him, too, about the theft.

"I was walking with two or three friends from our village before dawn," said the old man, "when we saw a fellow with a big bag on his back come towards us. We stopped him to ask him his business; but he dropped a bundle, and while we were snatching at it he slipped away. Who could have guessed that it was nothing but layer after layer of rags and cotton! After he tricked us into letting him go your men came up and, without a word of enquiry, started beating us and frightened my friends into running off. By now — luckily for him — the theif must be miles away."

When the shop people heard this they reproached them-selves bitterly; and when the neighbours knew that instead of catching the thief the clothier had beaten his relative, they thought it a great joke. As for the bundle, Lazy Dragon must have made it while waiting to get out of the storeroom, so that if ever he were chased he could use it to delay his pursuers. These stories show his cunning in emergencies and his skill in getting himself out of tight corners.

The fame of Lazy Dragon, the marvellous thief, spread far and wide until Commander Zhang of the garrison headquarters in Suzhou heard of him and ordered his sergeants to bring this man to him.

"Are you the chief of the thieves?" he demanded.

"I am no thief, much less their chief," replied Lazy Dragon. "I have never been convicted in court or involved in a single case of robbery. I happen to know a few tricks and sometimes play pranks on my relatives and friends; but if I have done anything wrong, I beg Your Honour to overlook it. If ever you have need of me, you may be sure I shall gladly go through fire or water to oblige you."

The commander was impressed by his nimble appearance and frank speech; he considered that with no evidence it would be difficult to convict this thief; and now Lazy Dragon had promised to work for him and might prove useful. Accordingly he decided not to arrest him. As they were talking, a man named Lu who lived near the West Gate presented a cockatoo with a red beak and green plumage to Commander Zhang, who bade him fasten the bird's chain to the eaves.

"I have heard that you are wonderfully light-fingered," said the commander to Lazy Dragon with a smile. "Though you claim merely to have played pranks but never stolen, you must have robbed a good many people in your time. And though I mean to pardon you, I would like to see your skill. If you can take this cockatoo of mine tonight and return it to me tomorrow, I promise to let you off."

"That should not be difficult," rejoined Lazy Dragon. "Allow me to take my leave now. I shall return you your bird tomorrow morning." He then bowed and left.

The commander ordered two night watchmen to guard the cockatoo carefully, threatening them with severe punishment if anything should happen to the bird; so the two guards stayed glued to the spot. Although their eyelids were heavy they tried hard not to sleep, dozing off to waken again at the slightest sound as the hours dragged painfully by.

At the fifth watch, just before dawn, Lazy Dragon made an opening in the roof and let himself down into the commander's study. On a clothes-hanger he saw a dark brown silk cloak, on the table a cap, and on the wall a small lantern inscribed with the title: Garrison Commander of Suzhou. At once an idea came to him. Donning the cape and cap, he took out the smouldering spill he carried, blew up the flame and lit the lantern. Then holding the lantern so that its light would not fall on his face and imitating the old commander's voice, walk and manner perfectly, he opened the door of the hall and walked out under the eaves. Since there was little moonlight then it was quite dark, and the two exhausted guards were nodding at their post.

"It is growing light," said Lazy Dragon, patting them on the shoulder. "You need not watch any longer. Off with you!"

As he spoke, he raised his arm to take the cockatoo by its chain, then swaggered back into the hall. The two watchmen had been having a hard time of it trying to keep their eyes open, and this sudden dismissal was as welcome as an imperial amnesty to a condemned man. Not suspecting for a moment that anything was wrong, they were off like a streak of smoke.

Soon day dawned and the commander came out. When he saw that the cockatoo had gone, he shouted for the guards; but they were nowhere to be seen. He ordered them to be summoned, and they arrived still half asleep.

"I told you to watch that cockatoo!" bellowed the commander. "Where is it now? Why did you leave your post?"

"At the fifth watch you came out yourself, sir," protested the guards. "You took the bird inside and told us to be off. Why do you ask *us* where it is?"

"Nonsense!" roared the commander. "When did I come

out? You must have seen a ghost!"

"It really was you, sir. We were both here. How could we both see something that wasn't there?"

The commander began to be suspicious. On going back to the study he happened to look up, so he saw the hole in the roof and knew how the thief had entered; and while he was puzzling over the matter he was told that Lazy Dragon had come to return the cockatoo. Commander Zhang went out smiling to ask how he had done it, and was surprised and pleased when Lazy Dragon explained how he had masqueraded in the garrison commander's cloak and cap and taken the cockatoo to the study. The commander treated Lazy Dragon well thereafter; and the thief for his part took him various presents in exchange for Commander Zhang's trust and protection. It is, alas! all too common for police officers to protect thieves.

Lazy Dragon was always up to tricks. One day a gambler who had won a thousand cash in the gaming house was on his way home when he met the thief.

"Tonight I shall put this under my pillow," he told Lazy Dragon, pointing to his money. "If you can get it, I'll treat you to wine tomorrow. If you fail, you treat me."

"Done!" replied Lazy Dragon with a laugh.

When the gambler returned home he told his wife: "I did pretty well today. I'll put the money under my pillow."

His wife was so pleased that she killed a chicken and heated some wine for a little feast. They did not finish the chicken, however, and the good woman put away what was left in the kitchen. As they went to bed her husband told her of his wager with Lazy Dragon, and each urged the other to keep awake, little knowing that Lazy Dragon was already outside the window and could hear all they said. When he realized that they would be lying awake, so that taking the money would prove difficult, he hit on a plan. Going to the kitchen, he picked up a hemp stalk and chewed it to make a noise like a cat eating chicken. The woman sat up with a start.

"There is still half a chicken left — enough for a meal tomorrow!" she said. "I'm not going to let that dratted cat run off with it!"

Jumping out of bed she ran to the kitchen. Lazy Dragon immediately bounded to the courtyard where he dropped a large stone into the well. The big splash it made startled the gambler.

"Surely she hasn't fallen into the well just for half a fowl!" he exclaimed. "That would be no joke."

As he rushed out to look, Lazy Dragon slipped into the room and took the money from under the pillow. When husband and wife had called to each other in the dark and satisfied themselves that all was well, they walked back hand in hand to their bedroom. But finding the pillow moved and the money gone, they cursed their stupidity.

"The two of us were awake and on our guard, yet we let him fool us like that! Disgraceful!"

At dawn Lazy Dragon came to return the money and to demand that the loser pay his forfeit. With a laugh the gambler put a few hundred cash of his winnings into his sleeve and invited Lazy Dragon to a nearby tavern.

While drinking they discussed the theft, clapping their hands and roaring with laughter; and when the tavern-keeper asked what the joke was, they told him.

"I have always heard of your great skill," said the tavern-keeper to Lazy Dragon, "but I never could believe it before." Then he pointed at the pewter winepot on the table. "If you can take this pot tonight I'll treat you tomorrow," he said.

"Done!" answered Lazy Dragon with a laugh. "That's easy."

"I won't have you spoiling my door and windows, mind!" said the tavern-keeper. "I shall leave it on this table, and we'll see how you get it!"

"All right, all right!" replied Lazy Dragon, then left.

That night the tavern-keeper had the door well bolted,

and searched the premises with a lamp to make sure that there was no way for Lazy Dragon to enter.

'I'll put the lamp on the table and sit here watching the pot," he decided. "I'd like to see what he can do then!"

He sat there till midnight, but nothing happened; and between boredom and exhaustion he found himself dozing off. At first he struggled to keep awake, but soon he could resist no longer and leaning his head on the table he started to snore.

When Lazy Dragon heard this snoring outside, he noiselessly climbed the roof and removed a few tiles. Then he fastened a pig's bladder on to a thin, hollow bamboo, and lowered it slowly into the winepot. The winepots in these taverns are broad at the base but narrow at the neck, so when he blew through the bamboo the bladder swelled up to fill the pot; and when he stopped the end of the bamboo he was able to pull the winepot up, after which he replaced the tiles exactly as before. When the tavern-keeper awoke, the lamp on the table was still burning but the winepot had gone. And when he looked around and saw that none of the windows had been forced, he could not imagine by what magic it had been spirited away.

Another time Lazy Dragon was standing with a few cronies by a tavern at the North Gate, when a young gentleman from Fujian whose boat had moored by the river bank ordered his attendants to air his clothes and bedding on deck. The bright silks and satins dazzled all who saw them, but they marvelled most at one coverlet of a rare and seldom seen material from the West. When Lazy Dragon's friends saw how the gentleman flaunted his wealth, they said:

"If we could filch that foreign coverlet from him, it would be rather a joke. Here's a chance for you to show your skill, Lazy Dragon. What are you waiting for?"

"I don't mind getting it for you tonight," chuckled Lazy Dragon. "Tomorrow you can return it to him and ask him for money for a few drinks."

After visiting a bath-house and washing himself clean, he returned to the riverside to watch for his opportunity. He waited till ten o'clock when the gentleman from Fujian and his friends, drowsy and half drunk, spread their bedding together on the cabin floor, blew out the lamp and lay down. Then swift as lightning Lazy Dragon leapt aboard, burrowed under the quilts and, chatting in the Fujian dialect, rolled this way and that so that the others complained they could not sleep. Still mumbling sleepily in Fujian dialect, Lazy Dragon jostled his bedfellows and created such a disturbance that he was able to take the foreign coverlet. Rolling it up he opened the cabin door, walked out and jumped ashore without any of the passengers realizing what had happened.

When dawn came and the loss of this valuable coverlet was discovered, a hubbub broke out aboard; and the gentleman, very much upset, discussed the matter with his friends. Although it was not worth going to court over a coverlet, he did not like to do nothing; so he offered a reward of a thousand cash to anyone who would recover it for him.

Then Lazy Dragon and his friends went to the boat.

"We have found the coverlet," they said. "If you give us the reward to buy wine, we guarantee to return you your bedding."

The gentleman ordered a thousand cash to be brought immediately and promised that this should be theirs as soon as his property was brought back.

"You might send a servant with us to fetch it," suggested Lazy Dragon.

The gentleman bade his steward accompany them, and they repaired to a Huizhou pawnshop where they found the coverlet.

"This comes from our boat," said the steward. "How did it get here?"

"Someone brought it in this morning," replied the pawn-broker. "When we saw that it wasn't a local product, we smelt a rat and wouldn't give him the money. 'If you don't trust me,' he said, 'I'll find a friend to be my guarantor. You can be weighing out the silver for me while I fetch him.' When we agreed he left, and that was the last we saw of him; so we knew it must be stolen property. Since it belongs to your boat, take it. And if that fellow comes back, we shall catch him and send him over too."

They took the bedding back to the man from Fujian and told him what the pawnbroker had said.

"We are strangers here," said the young gentleman. "I am quite satisfied to have recovered my property — why should we look for the thief?"

He gave the thousand cash to Lazy Dragon and his friends, who spent it in the tavern. The man who went to pawn the coverlet had, of course, received instructions from Lazy Dragon to leave it there while they went to claim the reward. This was just one more of his many tricks.

A practical joker like Lazy Dragon knew how to make things hot for anyone who annoyed him. Once a party of thieves invited him to go with them by boat to the Huqiu Hill to drink and enjoy the scenery. At Shantang they moored behind a rice shop and passed through the shop to buy fuel and wine; but the rice merchant, who objected to having this boat moored at his back door and these pleasure-seekers passing in and out, swore at them and tried to drive them away. The thieves were protesting indignantly when Lazy Dragon winked at them.

"Since he doesn't want us to pass through his shop, let's move further downstream and find another landing place," he said. "Why lose your tempers?"

He bade the boatmen cast off, but the thieves were still angry.

"It's not worth arguing with such people," said Lazy Dragon. "Tonight I'll get even with them."

They asked what he proposed to do.

"Find me a boat this evening," said Lazy Dragon. "And

leave me a keg of wine, a hamper of food, and a stove and fuel to heat the wine. I mean to row back to enjoy the moon all night. You'll understand my scheme tomorrow — there is no need to disclose it now."

That night after feasting at Huqiu they went their different ways, having agreed to meet Lazy Dragon early the next morning. He kept only a good drinker as his companion and an able punter, who returned with him on the small boat to the rice shop. The shop was already closed, and since there were many boats on the river that evening with passengers aboard fluting, singing and enjoying the moon, the men in the rice shop went to sleep suspecting nothing. Lazy Dragon moored his craft close by the rice shop's back door.

He had observed during the day that there was a rice bin in one corner of the shop over the water next to the back door; so now he took from his sleeve a small knife, cut out a knot in the wooden door, took from his pocket a bamboo tube, thrust the tube through the hole into the bin, and gave it a gentle shake. Immediately rice from the bin started cascading down the tube like water; but the noise Lazy Dragon made by toasting the moon and shouting and laughing as if he were tipsy drowned the swish of the rice. Passing boats had no inkling of what was happening, much less the shop people sleeping inside.

In the early hours of the morning when rice stopped flowing from the tube, Lazy Dragon knew that the bin was empty; and by then their cabin was full too, so he bade the boatman cast off and they punted slowly away. Presently they reached a quiet spot where all the thieves had gathered as arranged, and Lazy Dragon explained what he had done. They clapped and roared with laughter as he bowed.

"Divide this between you," he said, "as a token of my thanks for last night's party." He himself took nothing.

Not till the rice shop assistants opened that bin did they discover that it was empty; but they could not conceive when or how the rice had disappeared.

There was a time in Suzhou when hundred-pillar caps were all the rage, and every young man of fashion swaggered about in one. The Daoist priests of White Cloud Monastery near Nanyuan also bought such caps in secret, to wear when they went out to enjoy themselves disguised as laymen. One summer day they decided to set off for the Huqiu Hills the following morning, so they booked a boat and ordered a feast. The third son of Weaver Wang was friendly with these Daoists and often joined them on their jaunts in which each paid his own way; but since he always expected others to treat him and was rowdy after drink, the priests decided not to ask him this time. Young Wang got wind of their scheme, however, and was annoyed at being left out, so he asked Lazy Dragon to help him spoil their fun. Lazy Dragon agreed, slipped into White Cloud Monastery and stole the priests' Daoist caps.

"Why didn't you take their new caps?" asked Wang. "What use are these priestly caps?"

"If they lost their new caps, they wouldn't go to the Huqiu Hills tomorrow," replied Lazy Dragon. "What fun would that be? Don't you worry. Just see what trick I play on them tomorrow."

Mystified as he was, Wang had to let Lazy Dragon have his way.

The next day the priests disguised themselves as young gentlemen in light gowns and caps, and set off by boat on their pleasure trip. Dressed in black, Lazy Dragon followed them aboard and squatted at the helm, so that the Daoists took him for one of the crew, while the boatmen thought he was the gentlemen's attendant. When the boat started the priests unbuttoned their clothes and took off their caps to drink and make merry; and Lazy Dragon seized this opportunity to pick up the new caps and stow them in his sleeves, substituting for them the priestly caps which he had stolen the previous day and kept in his pocket. When they reached the bridge and moored, Lazy Dragon jumped to the bank and made off. The priests were about to put on their gowns and caps to stroll ashore when they discovered that their hundred-pillar caps had gone, while neatly folded and piled in their place were the priestly caps of gauze which they usually wore.

"How extraordinary!" they exclaimed. "Where are our caps?"

"Don't ask us," said the boatmen. "You put them there yourselves. There's no hole in the boat: they can't be lost."

The Daoists looked round once more, but still found no trace of their caps.

"There was a small fellow in black aboard, who has gone ashore now," they said to the boatmen. "Call him back, will you? He may have seen our caps."

"He isn't one of us," said the boatmen. "He came with you."

"He wasn't with us!" the priests shouted. "You must have worked in league with a thief to steal our caps. Those caps cost several taels apiece. Don't think you can get away with this!"

They seized the boatmen and would not let them go; and when the men protested indignantly and loudly a crowd gathered on the bank to watch, and a young man stepped forward and leapt aboard.

"What is all the trouble about?" he asked.

The priests and the boatmen told their different versions of the story; and since the priests knew this man they thought he would help them. But with a stern look he started reproaching them.

"You are all Daoist priests," he said. "Naturally you would come aboard in Daoist caps. Your own caps are here. What hundred-pillar caps could you have? You are obviously blackmailing these boatmen."

When the onlookers heard that these were Daoist priests who had their caps there but were accusing the boatmen of taking some other caps, they raised an indignant outcry.

Some local idlers and busybodies even stepped forward shaking their fists.

"Curse these thieving priests!" they cried. "Let's beat them up and send them to the magistrate!"

"Don't beat them!" cried the young man, waving his hand to stop the bullies. "Let them go!" Then he leapt ashore.

Fearing trouble if they delayed, the priests urged the boatmen to cast off at once. Their fine caps gone and their disguise seen through, they could not roam the hills in any case; so they started glumly back, their money wasted and their pleasure spoilt.

Now who was the man that jumped aboard? It was young Wang. Lazy Dragon let him know after he changed the caps; so while the priests were raising a hubbub, Wang came forward to show them up and spoil their fun. Having reached their destination, the Daoist were still refusing to let the boatmen go when Wang sent a man to return their caps and tell them: "Next time you decide to have a feast and show off these caps, be sure to let Master Wang know."

When the priests received this message, they realized that young Wang had made fools of them and guessed that this was Lazy Dragon's work, because they had heard of his fame and knew he was Wang's friend.

At that time, in the neighbouring county of Wuxi, there lived a magistrate who was notorious for his rapacity.

"The magistrate of Wuxi has piles of gold and jewels in his yamen," someone told Lazy Dragon. "And all his treasures are ill-gotten gains. Why don't you relieve him of some of them to distribute among the poor?"

Lazy Dragon thought this was a good idea. He went to Wuxi and crept stealthily one night into the magistrate's mansion, where he was struck by the luxury that met his eyes.

There was more wealth here than Lazy Dragon could count.

"The gates are locked," he reflected, "and watchmen keep sounding their clappers and bells outside. It will be difficult to take much."

Then he saw a small cask which was so heavy that it must contain gold or silver; and he was taking this when it occurred to him: "Since this is the yamen, I had better make sure that the magistrate doesn't punish innocent people to-morrow. Taking out his brush he painted a plum blossom on the wall by the shelf, then quietly left by way of the eaves.

Two or three days later the magistrate, looking through his treasures, discovered the loss of a small cask containing more than two hundred taels of gold, which was worth over a thousand taels of silver. Then his eye fell on the plum blossom drawn near by, which looked recently sketched. He was dumbfounded.

"This is obviously not the work of any of my men," he thought. "But who could enter my chamber and coolly draw this plum blossom as his sign? This is no common thief. I must catch this fellow."

He summoned some sharp-witted police officers to look at the mark left by the thief, and the constables were amazed when they saw it.

"We know who it is, Your Honour," they announced. "But he can't be caught. This is the work of Lazy Dragon, the wonder thief of Suzhou. Wherever he goes he draws a plum blossom as his mark. His is no ordinary skill, for he can come and go in the most miraculous manner; and he is so loyal to his friends that he has many devoted followers. To try to catch him would stir up worse trouble than the loss of some gold or silver. You had better let him go, Your Honour. It is not safe to offend him."

"You scoundrels!" declared the magistrate angrily. "If you know who it is, why can't you catch him? You people are in league with thieves and try to protect them. I've a good mind to have you all beaten; but I'll let you off for the time being so that you can go out and arrest him. And I warn you: if you fail to bring him to me within ten days, you will pay with your lives!"

When the police dared not answer, the magistrate ordered his secretary to draw up a warrant for two of the constables to take, and to inform the magistrates of Suzhou and Changzhou that he wanted this criminal apprehended.

Much against their will, the two constables travelled to Suzhou, and no sooner had they entered the West Gate than they saw Lazy Dragon standing there. They patted him on the shoulder.

"Friend!" they said. "We don't mind your robbing our magistrate; but why did you have to show off by drawing the plum blossom? Now he has ordered us to arrest you by a certain time. What do you say to that?"

"Don't worry, friends," replied Lazy Dragon coolly. "If you'll step into a tavern with me, we can sit down and talk."

He took them to a tavern where they chose a table and started drinking.

"This is my proposal," said Lazy Dragon. "Since your magistrate is so keen to arrest me, I certainly won't make things difficult for you. But if you will give me one day's grace, I shall send a message to him which will make him cancel the warrant and countermand his order for my arrest. How about it?"

"It's all very well to say that," rejoined the constables. "But you took rather a lot from him — all gold he said it was — so how can he just let the matter drop? If we go back without you, we'll get into trouble."

"Even if you insist that I go with you," reasoned Lazy Dragon, "I haven't got the gold any more."

"Where is it then?"

"I shared it with you as soon as I got it."

"Stop joking, old fellow!" they protested. "You'll find this no laughing matter in court."

"I've never lied in my life," retorted Lazy Dragon, "and I'm not joking. You've only to go home to see." He lowered his voice to whisper: "You'll find the gold in your gutters."

The officers knew his skill. "If he makes a statement like this in court," they reflected, "and if it's true that there are stolen goods in our homes, we shall be considered his accomplices."

"Very well," they agreed. "We dare not ask you to come with us. What do you propose to do?"

"If you go back first," said Lazy Dragon, "I'll follow immediately; and I guarantee that the magistrate won't dare press the matter. I would never do anything to land you in trouble." Then he took from his belt about two taels of gold and gave it to them. "This is for your travelling expenses," he said.

As flies to blood, so officials are drawn to money. The constables' eyes sparkled at the sight of that ruddy, glittering gold, and they pocketed it with broad grins. The suspicion that this gold probably came from the magistrate's cask made them more reluctant than ever to arrest Lazy Dragon.

When they had left, Lazy Dragon travelled by night to Wuxi. He got there the following morning and entered the magistrate's house after dark. This magistrate had a wife and a concubine, and since he was sleeping this night with his wife, his concubine was alone in her bed. Lifting her bed curtain Lazy Dragon groped about till he found her glossy hair coiled in the shape of a dragon, and gently clipped most of it off. Then he found the magistrate's seal box, prized it open, put the coil of hair inside and closed the box again. This done, he drew another plum blossom on the wall, and slipped away without touching a single other thing.

The next morning, upon waking, the concubine was surprised to feel her hair tumbling about her neck; and when she put up her hand and found her long tresses gone, she gave a shriek which roused the whole household. Everybody came rushing to find out what had happened.

"Who played this cruel trick and cut off my hair?" sobbed the concubine.

This was reported at once to the magistrate, who hurried over. When he found her shorn like a nun in her bed, he could not imagine what had happened; but he was grieved and horrified at the loss of her lovely hair which had floated down like dark clouds.

"Last time gold was stolen, and the thief has not yet been caught," he mused. "Now another bad man has been here. Nothing else matters very much; but what if he has taken my official seal!"

He called quickly for his seal box which was brought to him, sealed and locked as usual. Upon opening it, he was relieved to find the seal still in the top compartment; but then he noticed some hair, and the removal of the top shelf revealed a thick coil of hair underneath. He examined his other treasures, but nothing was missing. Then he saw another plum blossom on the wall, making a pair with the first.

"What, again!" uttered the magistrate in consternation. "Finding me after him in earnest, he has played this trick as a warning. By cutting off my concubine's hair, he means to show that he can cut off my head! By putting the hair in the seal box, he means that he can take my seal. This man is a thoroughly dangerous character! The constables were right the other day to advise me not to offend him. If I don't stop, I shall get into great trouble! The gold is a trifle; I can make it up by squeezing a few rich men. I had better let this matter drop."

He hastily ordered the two officers sent to Suzhou to be recalled, and cancelled the warrant.

Upon leaving Lazy Dragon, the two constables had gone straight home to search their gutters as the thief had directed; and, sure enough, each found a sealed packet of gold bearing the date of the theft in the magistrate's yamen. Not knowing when Lazy Dragon had planted this money there, they could only suck their fingers in amazement.

"It's a good thing we didn't arrest him," they said. "If

he confessed and they found the stolen goods here, we should never have been able to clear ourselves — not if we had a hundred tongues. But what answer are we to give the magistrate?"

They were worrying over this with their assistants when a messenger arrived from the yamen and, thinking he had brought a warrant for their arrest because they had failed to catch the theif by the time appointed, they were even more alarmed. It turned out, however, that he had brought a countermand. And when the constables asked the reason, the messenger told them what had happened in the yamen.

"This magistrate has had the fright of his life!" he said. "How dare he arrest Lazy Dragon?"

Then the two officers realized that Lazy Dragon had kept his promise by going back to the yamen to play this remarkable trick.

Towards the end of the Jia Jing period the magistrate of Wujiang was a crafty, cruel officer whose greed and corruption were notorious. One day he sent a trusted runner with presents to Suzhou to request Lazy Dragon to call on him in Wujiang County. Lazy Dragon accepted the gifts and went.

"In what way may I be of service to Your Honour?" he asked.

"I have long heard of your fame," replied the magistrate. "And I want to entrust a secret mission to you."

"I am nothing but a vagrant," replied Lazy Dragon. "Since you show such regard for me, I will go through fire and water to carry out your wishes."

Then the magistrate dismissed his attendants in order to speak freely.

"The imperial inspector has reached my county and means to find fault with me," he said. "I want you to go to his yamen and steal his official seal,[1] for then I can make him lose his job. That would please me, I can tell you! If you succeed, I shall reward you with a hundred taels of silver."

"I shall bring you the seal without fail," promised Lazy Dragon.

He was away for half the night, coming back with the inspector's seal which he courteously presented with both hands to the magistrate.

"How clever you are!" exclaimed the magistrate, over-joyed.

Hastily rewarding Lazy Dragon with a hundred taels, he bade him leave quickly for another county.

"Thank you, Your Honour, for you gift," said Lazy Dragon. "But may I ask what you intend to do with the seal?"

"With this seal in my hands," chuckled the magistrate, "I shall stop him from taking any action against me."

"I am so grateful for your kindness," said Lazy Dragon, "that I would like to offer you some advice."

"What is it?"

"I hid myself for half a night above the rafters in the inspector's office, and I saw him going through the official reports by lamplight, writing swiftly and endorsing documents. This shows that he is a quick-witted, capable man, and no trick can fool him. I would advise Your Honour to send the seal back to him tomorrow, saying that it was found during the night by a watchman but that the thief has escaped. Even if he has his suspicions, he will be grateful to you and a little awed, and will certainly not find fault with you."

"How can I stop him from having his way if I return his seal?" demanded the magistrate. "No, no, that doesn't make sense. Be off with you now, and don't worry about me."

Then Lazy Dragon dared say no more but left quietly.

The next day when the inspector opened his seal box, he found it empty. He ordered all his household attendants to make a thorough search, but they could find nothing.

"The magistrate knows that I have a low opinion of him," he thought. "Since this is his territory, he must have his spies everywhere; so he has sent someone to take my seal.

Well, I know how to deal with him."

Ordering his attendants to say nothing of his loss, he sealed the box as before; then on pretext of illness he stopped attending office, ordering all official documents to be sent to the chief of police for the time being. The magistrate knew that this was not a real illness and laughed up his sleeve; but after several days etiquette demanded that he call on his superior officer to inquire after his health. When the inspector heard that the magistrate was at the gate, he ordered his attendants to open the side door and invite his guest into the inner chamber where he lay in bed. There he chatted pleasantly about local customs, questions of administration, taxes and duties, speaking frankly and cordially and offering his visitor one cup of tea after another. Puzzled by these signs of cordiality, the magistrate was beginning to feel rather embarrassed. But as they were chatting, word was suddenly brought that the kitchen had caught fire; and attendants, runners and cooks rushed in.

"The fire is coming this way!" they shouted. "Run, Your Honour!"

The inspector's face fell. Hastily rising, he picked up his seal box, which was locked and sealed, and gave it to the magistrate.

"May I trouble you to keep this safely for me in your office for the time being?" he requested. "And will you send men to put out the fire immediately?"

The magistrate was panic-stricken, but dared not refuse: he had to leave with the empty box. By then all the local firemen had gathered, and they put out the fire. Only the two kitchens were burned; all the offices were uninjured; and the inspector ordered the gates to be closed. Everything had happened in accordance with the instructions he had given after his seal was lost.

When the magistrate reached home he thought: "The inspector has put this empty box in my hands. If I return it like this, when he opens it and finds the seal missing he will hold me responsible."

In vain he racked his brains: he could not think of a way out. Finally he had to moisten and remove the sealing paper, put the stolen seal back into the box and seal it up again. The next morning when the inspector had taken his seat in court the magistrate returned the box, and the inspector asked him to stay while he opened it and put his seal on all the documents he had left unsigned. That same day the inspector announced his departure and left Wujiang. He told the provincial governor about this theft, and together they reported the magistrate's evil deeds to the government and had him dismissed.

After Lazy Dragon became so well-known, he was occasionally suspected of thefts committed by others. When a dozen silver ingots disappeared from the treasury of the Suzhou prefectural government, the officers said: "The thief has left no trace. He may be Lazy Dragon."

Lazy Dragon had, in fact, had nothing to do with this theft; but when he saw that he was considered responsible, he decided to get to the bottom of the business. Suspecting the warden of the treasury, he hid himself one night in a dark corner of the yamen, then went to eavesdrop outside the man's room.

"Since I took that silver," he heard the warden say to his wife, "everybody has started suspecting Lazy Dragon. That's a stroke of luck. But Lazy Dragon will never plead guilty; so tomorrow I'm going to write out a detailed account of his thefts and send it to the prefect. Then, you may be sure, he will be arrested and have to shoulder the blame."

"This looks bad!" thought Lazy Dragon. "I had nothing to do with this, but now the warden who stole the silver in his charge wants to clear himself by pinning the theft on me. And since all officials stick together, and my record isn't exactly spotless, I shall never be able to prove my innocence. It would be better to disappear. I don't want to be tortured for something I didn't do."

He left the same night for Nanjing, where he roamed the streets as a blind fortune-teller. But some time later a man called Zhang from Suzhou Prefecture, who was very good at spotting thieves, happened to visit Nanjing and knocked into Lazy Dragon on the street.

"This blind man looks odd," thought Zhang.

A closer look satisfied him that this was Lazy Dragon in disguise. He took him aside to a quiet spot.

"There is a warrant out for your arrest," said Zhang, "because of that silver you stole from the treasury. That's why you've fled here and disguised yourself like this. But you can't deceive me."

Lazy Dragon took Zhang's hand.

"You know me," he said. "You should be able to clear this matter up for me, instead of taking the same line as the rest. That silver was stolen by the warden of the treasury himself — I heard him admit as much to his wife when they were in bed. I swear this is the truth. But he was plotting to put the blame on me and I was afraid the prefect might believe him, so I fled here. If you will go to the yamen to report the matter, you will receive the government reward and clear me at the same time; then I shall make you a present too. Don't spoil my trade here now."

Since Zhang had been commissioned by the prefectural government to investigate this theft, now that he had a reliable clue he left Lazy Dragon and went back to Suzhou to make a report. And when the warden of the treasury was examined and the silver found in his house, Lazy Dragon's innocence was established. After receiving a government reward for solving this case, Zhang went back to Nanjing where he found Lazy Dragon still walking the streets as a blind man. Zhang went up to him and nudged him.

"Your Suzhou trouble has been cleared up," he said. "How is it you've forgotten your promise to me the other day?"

"I didn't forget it," replied Lazy Dragon. "Look in

your rubbish heap at home and you will find a little token of my gratitude."

Zhang was very pleased, for he knew that Lazy Dragon never lied. He took his leave of the thief and went straight home where he found a package of gold and silver buried in the ashes of his rubbish heap next to a glittering dagger. Then Zhang stuck his tongue out in dismay.

"This man's really dangerous!" he muttered. "He's put this dagger here with his gift so that I won't dare to interfere with him another time. Heaven knows when he hid these here — his skill is amazing! I certainly won't risk offending him again."

When Lazy Dragon learned from Zhang that he had been cleared in Suzhou, he knew that he was in no immediate danger; but he feared that if he remained a thief he would be arrested in the end, so he decided to give up stealing and make an honest living as a fortune-teller. He stayed for a few years in Changgan Temple where he died eventually of old age. Although so celebrated a thief, he was never bastinadoed and never had his arm tattooed in punishment,[2] while even today the citizens of Suzhou like to relate his endless pranks and tricks. Such a prince of thieves is infinitely superior to those men in official robes who say one thing but mean another, and will commit any injustice in their greedy search for personal gain. With his wonderful skill, if Lazy Dragon had been able to spy behind the enemy's lines or to lead a surprise attack at night, he could have achieved great deeds. Unfortunately he lived in a time of peace when literary attainments alone were highly regarded, and his escapades could merely furnish material for the gossips.

Notes:

1. The seal (*yinxin*) of a government official was the symbol of his authority and power. Without an official seal an official would be unable to carry out any governmental business. When leaving an office the official would have to pass his

seal on. Even in modern China seals are used by companies, government bodies and individuals rather than a hand written signature.

2. A tattoo on the arm was a sign of previous convictions. Marking or disfiguring criminals was a widely used form of punishment that also served as a permanent visible record of a person's past convictions.

Bibliography

Baoweng Laoren（抱甕老人）, ed. *Strange Stories of the Past and Present* (*Jingu qiguan,* 今古奇觀). Hongkong: Guangzhi shuju (廣智書局).

Feng Menglong （馮夢龍）, ed. *Tales to Illuminate the World* (*Yushi mingyan,* 喻世明言), 2 vols. Hongkong: Zhonghua shuju（中華書局）, 1978.

——. *Tales to Warn the World (Jingshi tongyan,* 警世通言), 2 vols. Hongkong: Zhonghua shuju, 1978.

——. *Tales to Awaken the World*（*Xingshi hengyan,* 醒世恒言), 2 vols. Hongkong: Zhonghua shuju, 1978.

Ling Mengchu（凌濛初）, ed. *Astonishing and Miraculous Tales I & II* (*Chuke pai'an jingqi,* 初刻拍案驚奇 and *Erke pai'an jingqi,* 二刻拍案驚奇). Shanghai: Gudian wenxue chubanshe (古典文學出版社), 1957.

Liu Kairong （劉開榮）. *Researches on the Tang Short Stories* (*Tangdai xiaoshuo yanjiu,* 唐代小説研究). Beijing: Shangwu yinshuguan （商務印書館）, 1950.

Lu Xun（魯迅）. *A Short History of Chinese Fiction* (*Zhongguo xiaoshuo shilüe*, 中國小説史略). Beijing: Remin wenxue chubanshe （人民文學出版社）1973 .

Miao Yonghe（繆詠禾）. *Feng Menglong and The Three Tales* (*Feng Menglong he Sanyan,* 馮夢龍和三言), *Zhongguo gudian wenxue jiben zhishi congshu* （古國古典文學基本知識叢書). Shanghai: Shanghai guji chubanshe （上海古籍出版社）, 1979.

Yang Xianyi （楊憲益） and Yang, Gladys（戴乃迭）, trans. *The Courtesan's Jewel Box: Chinese Stories of the Xth– XVIIth Centuries.* Beijing: Foreign Languages Press, 1957.

Beijing daxue zhongwenxi （北京大學中文系）. *A History of Chinese Fiction* (*Zhongguo xiaoshuoshi,* 中國小説史). Beijing: Remin wenxue chubanshe, 1978.